☆HI!!! HI!!! HI!!!☆ Roaring☆Hot☆Vermillion.

◇Who are you talking to?◇ Clear◇White◇Whistle.

☆It's the big floating rock! It's talking now! I think it wants to play!☆

The red cloud changed its body ripples from the slow, wave-leaning gait that it had been sharing with Clear◇White◇Whistle and slithered off toward the distant pinging ahead.

Jill's sonar system saw the distant blobs separate. One came directly at it at high speed. Jill increased its interrogation rate and switched to a modified chirp in an attempt to pick up shape information. The blob was about three meters wide, ten meters long, and one meter thick, but it had almost the same density as the ocean and no discernible internal structure.

◇Careful!◇ came the call from the distant white cloud. ◇It might be a new type of Gray⊗Boom! It might explode and catch you.◇

The thought slowed the advance of Roaring☆Hot☆Vermillion, but didn't decrease the volume of its voice, which raised to a shout.

☆HI!! WANT TO SURF!?!☆

ROBERT L. FORWARD

BAEN BOOKS

ROCHEWORLD

Copyright © 1990 by Robert L. Forward

A Baen Books Original

Baen Publishing Enterprises
260 Fifth Avenue
New York, N.Y. 10001

ISBN: 0-671-69869-9

Cover art by David Mattingly

First printing, April 1990

Distributed by
SIMON & SCHUSTER
1230 Avenue of the Americas
New York, N.Y. 10020

Printed in the United States of America

For Eve

Who thought it would be fun to ride on a flouwen.

ACKNOWLEDGMENTS

Thanks to:
   Edouard Albert Roche (1820–1883)
   —who showed that the world isn't
        always round,

      Charles Sheffield
—who also thought this system was fun,

Paul L. Blass, Carl Richard Feynman, David K. Lynch, Patrick L. McGuire, Daryl Mallett, Hans P. Moravec, A. Jay Palmer, Zane D. Parzen, Jef Poskanzer, Daniel G. Shapiro, Jacqueline Stafsudd, and Mark Zimmermann, who helped me in several technical areas. My love and special thanks to Martha for her encouragement and literary assistance.

The "Christmas Bush" motile was jointly conceived by Hans P. Moravec and Robert L. Forward, and drawn by Jef Poskanzer using a CAD system.

All final art was expertly prepared by Sam Takata and the rest of the group at Multi-Graphics.

CAVEATS

This book is based on the original 150,000 word manuscript I wrote in 1981. A condensed version of 60,000 words was serialized under the title "Rocheworld" in *Analog Science Fiction/Science Fact* in 1982. A longer version of about 100,000 words was published in hardcover by Timescape under the title *The Flight of the Dragonfly* in 1984. A slightly longer version of about 110,000 words was published in paperback by Baen Books under the title *The Flight of the Dragonfly* in 1985. This version of 155,000 words prepared in 1989 combines the best features of all the prior versions—I hope you enjoy it.

For those readers who care, Robert L. Forward, who writes hard science fiction novels, is not to be confused with his son, Robert D. Forward, who writes hard-hitting detective novels, animation scripts for television, and live action scripts for motion pictures.

BEGINNING

The torn shred of aluminum lightsail rippled lightly down through the thin atmosphere and settled onto the calm ocean. The robot probe the sail had once carried continued on its way back into the interstellar blackness, its flyby study of the Barnard planetary system completed. The messages of its discoveries would reach Earth six years later. The microthin film of aluminum sail material was no match for the ammonia-water ocean covering this egg of a planet. It dissolved into a bitter taste of aluminum hydroxide.

Clear ◊ White ◊ Whistle was warming on top of the ocean in the red glare from Hot. Hot suddenly became less. The darkness was not like that from a storm shadow, but much sharper. It was almost as if Sky⊗Rock had suddenly moved in front of Hot. The darkness came closer, then there was a sharp thin taste of bitterness in the ocean.

Clear ◊ White ◊ Whistle dove under the ocean to escape the bitterness, then came to the surface. The taste was still there. Another dive—it was there, too. A sounding dive a long distance away, it was still there, but the taste was weaker and the sheet of darkness was being eaten by the ocean. Hot peered through the holes.

For a long time Clear ◊ White ◊ Whistle tasted the bitterness and thought about the strange thing that came from nothing but was something. Thoughts came too about exploring the nothing above, but that was impossible . . .

◊ But only carefully contrived mathematical propositions are truly impossible, ◊ mused Clear ◊ White ◊ Whistle. ◊ After all, the bitter darkness came from nothing, and I can look into nothing, although poorly. I know from looking that Hot and Warm are sources of light and heat, but though I have tried hard, I cannot see them. If only my looking portions could be focused like my seeing portions . . . ◊

A thought came to the alien, and the large amorphous body of white jelly started to condense. Clear ◊ White ◊ Whistle squeezed the water out of its body, turned into a dense white rock, and sank to the bottom of the ocean. The concentrated whiteness of the fluids that constituted its "brain" now thought at a higher rate.

Equations for a focusing detector based on time differences went through a sophisticated mathematical transformation into the equations for a focusing detector using distance differences. This detector would "look" using light instead of "seeing" using sound. The mathematical solution now obvious, Clear ◊ White ◊ Whistle, the toolless engineer, dissolved and swam up again to the surface as an undulating white cloud.

The thinking had taken a long time. Hot was gone. It had moved behind Sky⊗Rock, a large object that hovered motionless in the sky above this region of the ocean. Sky⊗Rock was dark, and no longer gave off its rocklike, reddish-gray light. The sky was not completely dark, however, for Warm had risen and was now a weak flare overhead.

Using the mathematical equations as a guide, Clear ◊ White ◊ Whistle formed a portion of its body into a sphere and concentrated. The white thought substance in the sphere flowed out into the rest of its body to leave the sphere a clear gel. Further concentration, and water dripped from the surface of the sphere until it was a dense clear ball. Through the now crystalline sphere streamed the rays of light from the heavens to come to a crude focus in the opposite side of the sphere. The white flesh next to the clear sphere looked at the tiny spots of light focused on its surface. The light patterns showed Warm as a small disk of mottled red. Around Warm were smaller bright lights with sharp cusps and fuzzy edges.

A slight adjustment of the gelatine sphere into a crude lens, and the distorted spots turned into smaller disks. As the lens focused on the moons of the giant red planet, Gargantua, the blackness of the night sky all around the planet blossomed with hundreds of tiny pinpoints of light.

Clear ◊ White ◊ Whistle stared with its newly invented "eye" at the multicolored stars in the sky and wondered.

PICKING

Boredom is a Space Marine's worst enemy, but *these* Marines were not bored.

"Close in! You squinty-eyed offspring of a BASIC program. So what if you've lost your outside video! You've still got radar and ground plots! Close in!"

The words came from deep inside a short, chunky, round-faced woman with dark-black skin, a close-cropped head of curly black hair, and a crisp Marine officer's uniform seemingly tattooed on her muscular body.

General Virginia Jones punched her supervisory keyboard as her parade-ground voice echoed off the naked beams and taut pressurized walls of the crowded cubicle. Crammed into the compact control room of a Space Marine Lightsail Interceptor, the programmers were short-circuiting the software in the ship's computer to optimize an "unwilling capture" trajectory between their low-acceleration twenty-five-kilometer diameter sailcraft and the radar image of a lumbering cargo hauler. The huge heavy-lift vehicle was rising slowly from its launch pad deep in Soviet Russia on its way to resupply one of the Soviet bases in geosynchronous orbit.

"Boarding party!" General Jones roared to the deck below. "You've got ten minutes to do the fifteen-minute suiting drill! Move it!"

There was a bustle as hammocks were stowed to give a

little more room in the tiny communal barracks. Suits were lifted from lockers and donned—rapidly, but carefully. General Jones looked sternly around at the organized pandemonium and took a bite of her energy stick. She looked at it in distaste, thought blissfully of the excellent mess back at the Space Marine Orbital Base, then stoically took another bite of the energy bar. If it was good enough for her Marines, it was good enough for her.

Like the PT boats in World War II almost a century ago, the Interceptors had to be fast. With only the light pressure from the Sun to push them, that meant keeping weight down. It was battle rations every meal when the Space Marines were on Interceptor duty.

General Jones carefully watched the captain of the Interceptor as he swung his ungainly craft smoothly around. Captain Anthony Roma was short and handsome, with dark flashing eyes and a youthful wave of hair over his forehead that had Jinjur's mind wandering slightly. Captain Roma was the best lightsail pilot in space (with the possible exception of Jinjur herself).

The lightsail scooped, dumping its cross-orbit excess speed in the upper atmosphere by using its huge expanse of sail like a sea anchor. It tilted to maximize the solar photon pressure and rose again in a pursuit trajectory of the bogey. Ten minutes later General Jones called a halt to the hunt of the phantom fox.

"Freeze program," she said, then turned and tapped a code word into her command console. The computer memory of the practice pursuit was locked until she released it. The primary purpose of this exercise had been to test the reconfiguration skills of the human element of her computer-operated spaceship—the programmers. By reconfiguring the software in the computer to take into account its loss of components and capabilities, the programmers could hopefully tune the program to obtain its optimum response time. She wished the Interceptors could have the latest in self-reprogramming computers, or at least the touch-screen input terminals, but that was many fiscal-budget cycles away.

The study of the programmer responses could take place

later. General Jones lifted herself up in the weak acceleration, coiled her short, powerful legs under her compact
body, hooked the toes of her corridor boots under the
command console, and launched herself toward the "sortie"
port. There was more to a Space Marine Interceptor than
sail, computer, and programmers, and she was the pre-
ventive maintenance technician for that fourth component.

The Space Marines were still frozen at attention in the
sortie port, their 'stiction boots firmly attached to the deck.
Their commander swam in free-fall among them, the lieutenant of the boarding party close behind her.

She approached the first Marine, punched a code into
his chest-pack and read the result.

"Fine, Pete," she said. "Shuck the suit and take a break."
She moved to the next one.

"Hi, Amalita." She punched the Marine's chest-pack
and read out the performance index.

"Good timing!" she said. Her eyes grinned up at the
proud Marine. "Seven minutes, thirteen seconds, and no
suit flags! I'm proud of you!"

She moved on to the next. The readout had no flags, but
her instincts knew something was wrong. She stared at the
face of the Marine through the visor. His bewildered eyes
indicated something unknown was bothering him. She
grabbed him by both arms, planted herself on the deck,
lifted him bodily, and turned him around. He felt oddly
out of balance. She examined the tell-tales on his support
pack. They were fine—both tanks full of air. She stopped
and raised a sharp pale-brown knuckle and gave the rounded
ends of the two air tanks a rap. One tinked like a fiber-
wound titanium balloon stretched to its utmost. The other
tonked.

In her rage, she smashed the offending tell-tale with her
fist and jerked the poor Marine around until he was facing
her. Tears welled from her dark brown eyes.

"Everlasting elephants, Mike!! If it doesn't feel right,
don't put it on!!! Even if the blazzflaggin' thing says it's
OK! I want you alive!!"

She jammed the stricken Marine back down to the floor
where his 'stiction boots took hold again. Then pushing

against him, she rose up and grabbed a handhold in the ceiling of the crowded port.

"I want you *ALL* alive!" she roared, looking around at the ranks of cowed killers. "The next time one of you blue-nosed monkeys puts on a bad suit, I'll personally kick you from here to PLUTO!"

She turned and, sucking the back of her hand, swam out the lock, leaving a thoughtful lieutenant to finish the inspection. General Jones had not yet mentioned his responsibilities in this infraction, but he expected to hear about it as soon as they were where the troops couldn't overhear. He wasn't looking forward to it, for General "Jinjur" had not gotten her nickname by being lenient with officers who allowed her troops to get into danger.

General Jones was halfway through the analysis of the interception exercise when a message came through from the Space Marine Orbital Base. The Russians had announced a launch to resupply one of their geosynchronous-orbit manned space stations. The Interceptor that Jinjur was inspecting was in the best position, and was assigned the job of monitoring the launch. She carefully watched the Captain of the Interceptor as he swung his ungainly craft smoothly around. The sunlight hit the sail, the acceleration built up to a few percent of Earth's gravity, and the floating objects in the room drifted downward. The Captain called on one of the orbiting space forts above him for more power, and there was a blinding flash in the video monitor as a powerful laser beam struck the sail with light five times brighter than the Sun. The acceleration rose to one-tenth gee and they skimmed rapidly above the Earth's atmosphere, gaining speed by the minute.

Soon the sailcraft's trackers had the Russian booster on their screens. Jinjur watched as the massive payload pushed its way slowly up out of the sea of air, rising vertically to over two thousand kilometers. As it reached the peak of its trajectory, the tiny image began to grow wings. The wings became larger and larger until they dwarfed the twenty-five-kilometer diameter sail of the Interceptor. Jinjur admired the deployment speed of the lightsail. The pilot must be Ledenov or Petrov with a new deployment program.

The huge sailship caught the Sun's rays and started its climbing spiral outward to the distant space station thirty-six thousand kilometers overhead. Unlike the Interceptor, which was built for speed, this was a tug. It would take almost a month to haul its heavy load into the heavens.

The Interceptor Captain glanced at Jinjur and she nodded approval. He reached for a microphone and made a call to the UN Space Peacekeeping Authority. UNSPA had no forces. They used those of the spacefaring nations instead. The United States had put Jinjur's sailcraft in a position where it could carry out an interception to check and make sure that no unauthorized weapons were in the enemy cargo. But not all ships were searched, only a random sample. The keeper of the random number generator was UNSPA.

"This is Captain Anthony Roma of the Greater United States Space Marine Interceptor *Iwo Jima* calling United Nations Space Peacekeeping Authority. I have intercepted a cargo light-tug of the Union of Soviet Socialist Republics. Request permission to board for Space Peacekeeping inspection," he asked.

There was a pause as the UNSPA operator consulted a UN official. The official pushed a button on a carefully guarded machine.

"Permission granted," came the reply.

"GONG!" shouted Jinjur. "We've hit the jackpot!"

"Attention all hands!" said Captain Roma. "Prepare for an authorized inspection of a foreign spacecraft." There was a bustle as the control room filled up, while down below, spacesuits recently stored away in lockers were removed again, checked over carefully, then just as carefully donned.

Jinjur watched through the next hour as Captain Roma closed in on the Russian sail. They zoomed in with their video camera and explored the outside of the payload section. It was nearly lost in the immense sea of shining aluminum film.

"Looks like a perfectly ordinary cargo hauler to me,"

said Jinjur to the Captain. "But the way to keep those Russkies honest is to give them a good shakedown whenever we get permission. I want one of the crew to take a remote flyer over every square centimeter of that sail, and I want computer backup, so that no little package stuck out in some rigging tens of kilometers from here is missed."

"The communications operator has established contact with the Russian ship, General," the Captain said. "Do you wish to talk to them yourself?"

"If you don't mind," said Jinjur. "I think I know the Captain."

The call was transferred to her console, and the face of a handsome middle-aged Russian filled the screen.

"I thought it was you, Petrov," she said. "I compliment you on your sail deployment. You're going to be a formidable opponent at the next Space Olympics in the light-sail races."

"Just practice, Jinjur," said Captain Petrov. "I hear from our UN friends that you will be paying us a visit."

"Yes. I apologize for having to bother you, but it's part of the job."

"I understand," he said. "But with you coming it will be a pleasure instead of a bother. I look forward to seeing you again. It has been almost three years since we worked on the Space Weapons panel for the last disarmament talks."

"See you soon," said Jinjur, turning off the console and heading for the locker that held her personal space-suit.

Within an hour, the small boarding crew was floating on tethers outside the Interceptor. Captain Roma kept his sail trimmed to match the speed of his lightweight Interceptor with the larger tug. Both ships were still accelerating in the sunlight, however, so they all held on to keep from drifting away. A small jet scooter was unlashed from the rigging. It had a number of handholds along the side, and soon, looking like a cluster of white grapes, the scooter and boarding party jetted the few kilometers that separated the two tiny payload capsules.

Jinjur, being just a visiting general, kept out of the way as the boarding party searched the outside of the cargo ship. There were a few unusual cylinders found, but a flash X-ray and a scan with a Forward Mass Detector showed that they only contained the usual emergency gear in a new package shape. They boarded, and while the crew proceeded with their hours-long methodical inspection, Jinjur met with Petrov in his cabin.

"This is certainly a lot nicer than an Interceptor," said Jinjur as she admired the view of her distant ship out the large glass port.

"Running a cargo ship does have its amenities," replied Petrov. "By the way, while you were removing your suit, we received a call from your ship requesting to speak with you."

Jinjur looked puzzled, then asked, "May I use your console?"

Petrov padded over to the console, pushed a few buttons, then backed off to let her use it. Captain Roma was on the screen.

"You have a message from the Marine Commandant," he said. "It's encoded and marked 'Personal.' "

"It'll have to wait till I get back," she said. "We can't be discussing codes over the air."

She signed off and turned to Petrov. He was holding a small sheet of paper.

"Permit me to be of service," Petrov said. "Here is your message. Congratulations! I only wish I were going in your place."

Jinjur frowned as she took the piece of paper. A concerned look grew on her face as she realized that the Russians had intercepted her message and broken the code in the time it took for her to get out of her suit. She began to wonder if she would be allowed to get back to report the fact.

"Relax," said Petrov with a smile. "From the latest intelligence briefing I received about you when I learned you were on the Interceptor, I was pretty sure what was in the message, so I asked one of our people to feed it to our computer. With the hints I gave it on content, it only took five minutes of computer time to unscramble it. Too bad you change your codes randomly for every message; it might have proved useful."

Relieved that there was no permanent breach in communications security, Jinjur allowed herself to read the message.

"I'm Commander of the Barnard expedition!!" she cried.

"As I said: Congratulations!" said Petrov. "Could you use a good deckhand?"

"I'm already stuck with somebody for my second-in-command, a Lieutenant Colonel George G. Gudunov. Sounds Russian. Do you know him?"

"Lieutenant Colonel Gudunov is the one who pioneered the idea of laser-driven sailcraft for interstellar travel," said Petrov.

"I was in high school when the first interstellar probes went out," said Jinjur. "I remember thinking how I wished that I were riding on them. Now it looks as though I'm going to get my wish." She paused and shook her head in puzzlement. "But this *can't* be the same Gudunov; if he were still in the service he would be a general by now. I guess this George is his son, or one of his relatives. The last thing I need on this trip is a political appointee."

"I have been thoroughly briefed," said Petrov, his massive iron-gray brows furling. "Your George Gudunov is not a general, and will probably never see his star. He *is* the one that sent out the probes twenty-five years ago."

"But that would mean that he was in his early twenties at the time, and at most a captain," said Jinjur. "He wouldn't have been able to order such a major undertaking. There must be some mistake."

"I'm sure of my sources," said Petrov.

"Well, that can wait until I get back to my ship," said Jinjur. "Meanwhile, we have a more serious problem. The lieutenant in charge of the inspection party reported to me that you have a secret compartment in your cabin."

"Secret compartment?" exclaimed Petrov. He was indignant, yet worried.

"Yes," said Jinjur, moving over to a wall filled with equipment. "This section here," she said, "is hollow."

"Hokay! You win," he said. "But not even the KGB

knows about that one." He moved over next to her, then pushed quickly on the side next to the bulkhead. The panel swung open to show a small refrigerator and an eight-inch Questar telescope. He opened the cooler to display a rack of bottles.

"My private vices," he admitted. "California champagne and an American telescope." He pushed back to the cabin door, locked it, barked a few commands in Russian to his crew over the intercom and closed it down.

"I have turned over the ship to my second-in-command," he said. "But first I had them rotate the ship to give us a different view." He took out the telescope and mounted it on the frame of the port. They watched as the stars twirled slowly by the window, then stopped as the ship came to rest again. He lined up the telescope, then pushed back.

"Have a look," he said. Jinjur put her eye to the eye-piece and looked for a long time.

"It's just a small red star," she said. "Nothing unusual about that."

"Except for its speed and its name," he said. "That is Barnard, the fastest moving star in the heavens."

She heard a pop, then turned around. Petrov was an expert at drinking champagne in free-fall. Keeping the cork almost in the neck, he let the bubbling liquid ooze out a little at a time to form small grape-sized balls in the air. The trick was to catch them in your mouth before they settled to the carpet in the low acceleration of the light-tug. Jinjur had to dive within centimeters of the floor to get one of them.

Barnard set behind the limb of the Earth, followed by the Sun. Night fell. The champagne flowed till dawn—forty-five minutes later.

A large, slightly overweight, middle-aged man in a well-worn Air Force officer's uniform walked slowly into the cavernous Pentagon anteroom of the Air Force Chief of Staff. His round, smiling, ruddy-complexioned face was topped by a thick mane of white hair. George wasn't surprised that he'd been summoned, for the pressure had been building up for the past three years since the data started coming in from the Barnard system. His only concern now was his age. At forty-nine he was getting awfully old. It had been decades since he had been in the Pentagon. Being stuck as a flight instructor in the hottest corner of Texas for the past twenty-five years sort of kept you out of things.

George checked in with the secretary in the front office. A civilian, she was gowned like a dressmaker's mannequin and made up as carefully as a *Vogue* model. He wondered if the Chief of Staff had chosen her for looks or intelligence. He knew the answer as soon as she glanced up and batted her lashes at him.

"You must be Col-o-nel Gud-o-nov!" she exclaimed, her bright eyes glowing behind the fluttering fan of her eyelids. "Weren't you on the Jimmy Collins show? Such excitement! A whole new universe to explore, and you were the one that shot us there with lasers!"

George started to explain that Barnard wasn't a new universe, just another star system. But another look at her depthless eyes, with the shining excitement tingling on their surface, made him hesitate. She, in her own feather-brained way, had learned as much as she was ever going to learn about the Barnard planetary system. Any attempt now to explain the difference between a universe and a planetary system would only destroy whatever appreciation she had of the topic.

"Yes," he admitted, "Jimmy is certainly an interesting person."

"Oh!" she exclaimed. "General Winthrop said to send you right in as soon as you came." She glanced up and down his uniform. Her eyes hesitated at his shoes. He took the implied hint and looked down to find, sticking in the narrow seam between the stiff leather soles and the mirror-buffed top of his regulation Air Force shoes, a tiny ball of fluff picked up in his traverse across the deep acres of Air Force blue pile. He grinned thankfully at her, brushed the offending blue clump away on the back of his trouser leg, and headed for the ornately carved door as she pushed an intercom button and announced his arrival.

George walked smartly into the room. He skirted the

huge oak conference table, carefully avoided the seal of the Air Force Chief of Staff woven into the blue rug, and headed for the large desk flanked by two flags. One flag had a field of blue carrying the Air Force emblem. The other was the Stars and Stripes of the Greater United States with its fifty-nine stars in four rows of eight alternating with three rows of nine. Next year there would be sixty stars as the Northwest Territories finally became populous enough to become a state. That only left the Yukon to go (and, of course, Quebec, if they ever came to their senses). He came to attention in front of the desk and saluted, his eyes straight ahead.

General Winthrop glanced up from the papers in front of him, the glitter of four silver stars broadening his shoulders. There was a momentary flicker of raw hatred in his eyes, which faded into a formal politeness.

"Good afternoon, George," he said. "Sit down."

Colonel Gudunov perched on a nearby straight chair and listened.

"Saw you and Senator Maxwell on the Jimmy Collins show last night," Winthrop started. "Quite some company you keep there."

"They wanted someone that could explain what there was in the Barnard system that justified the interstellar expedition, and Senator Maxwell suggested me."

"I've got to admit you did an excellent job of explaining the laser drive in terms even my secretary could understand. She talked about nothing else for the entire coffee break this morning." He shuffled some papers, then drew one out.

"Your friends in Congress have been good to you again, Gudunov." His tone chilled a little. "By all rights, no forty-nine-year-old should be allowed on the Barnard expedition, especially since you're not a regular, but ROT-C." Winthrop didn't even have the courtesy to spell out the initials of the Reserve Officer Training Corps, but gave it the slang pronunciation he had learned at the Academy.

He must've been pushing one of his people for the position, thought George.

Winthrop straightened and became more formal. "Lieutenant Colonel Gudunov: You have been selected to participate in the Barnard expedition to take place in two years. You are hereby promoted to Colonel and will be second-in-command, reporting to Major General Virginia Jones, Space Marine Corps."

George winced and grinned internally at the same time. He had never met "Jinjur," but had heard a great deal about her. He had wistfully hoped that he would be chosen to lead the expedition, but that was politically impossible. His many friends in Congress could protect him from the vengeful types in the military, but they didn't have enough clout to go over their heads, especially at his age. He didn't care, he'd got what he wanted—a chance to go to the stars. He only half-listened as General Winthrop dropped his formal tone and verbally lashed out at him.

". . . and I'm goddamned glad you're going. You've been a goddamn thorn in the flesh of every goddamned Air Force Chief of Staff since you were twenty-three, starting with my father, General Beauregard Darlington Winthrop the Second. I don't know why you stayed in the goddamned Air Force anyway after that stupid goddamned trick you pulled in 1998 when you were a goddamned Captain.

" 'Why don't we test out the laser forts by using them to push a sail-probe to the nearest stars?' you said. Unfortunately, my father agreed with you and approved the test. You made a fool out of him when ten percent of the nation's defense capability failed in the first goddamned minute . . ."

". . . As it would have if it'd been a real attack instead of a test," George reminded him, uncowed.

"ALL RIGHT!!!" shouted the General. "Since then you've been protected by your goddamn friends in the goddamn Congress. I can't touch you, but I don't have to promote you any GODDAMN faster than necessary."

He subsided and sat back in his chair. He smiled grimly. "You realize that if you accept this appointment, Colonel Gudunov, you'll be going on an expedition from which you'll never return. There will be life-extending drugs

available, but at your age there is no chance of you ever
coming back."

George looked at General Winthrop with a slight air of
bewilderment. He then realized that even though the
General had been well briefed on the interstellar mission,
he apparently had not allowed himself to recognize the full
truth about the expedition.

"Sir . . ." said George, hesitantly, "As planned, the
mission will take over sixty years. Forty years to get there
and twenty years of exploration. Even with life-extending
drugs, most of the crew will be old and well into retire-
ment age before the work there is done. Besides, there is
no provision for a return flight. This first expedition is a
one-way mission."

Hearing, but refusing to hear at the same time, General
Winthrop brushed off George's statement and launched
into the final sentences that he had been saving.

"Well, I'm glad to hear that you realize you're too old to
return from this mission. I hope you recognize, however,
after this latest assignment, that you can't transfer to a
command position that rates a general's rank."

He paused to savor his next words.

"You may have used your influence to bribe your way
onto this mission and into a promotion, Colonel Gudunov
. . ."—he paused on the word "Colonel," letting it sneer
out the side of his mouth like it was the name of a
particularly loathsome disease—". . . but you'll *never* get
your star!"

George rose, saluted, and turned to walk back across
the carpet. The glitter of hate flared back in General
Winthrop's eyes as he stared at George's departing back.

"Within one month after he was fired as Air Force Chief
of Staff, my daddy died," muttered Winthrop. ". . . And
you killed him! I don't care how long it takes or what it
costs or who else gets hurt—but, one way or the other,
I'm going to see you *suffer*, Gudunov. You're not going to
escape me by going to the stars."

Colonel Gudunov was waiting in the VIP lounge when
the flight from Cape Kennedy landed at National Airport.

He fished a thirteen-sided two-dollar coin from his pocket, bought a plastican of Coke, pulled up the sip-tab, and wandered over to the window to inhale his morning dose of caffeine and phosphoric acid. It was a windy fall day. The leaves were beautiful, but the dust was terrible. He heard the clamor of an approaching group of press reporters and photographers outside the door of the lounge. Underneath the yapping of reporters and the whirr and snap of cameras there was a firm tenor voice.

"No comment."

"Excuse me, please."

"No comment."

The door to the suite opened. A pair of huge Marine guards seemed to fill the opening; then they were gone, herding the press away in front of them. George lowered his eyes to see a slightly disheveled female Marine officer slapping the dust off her uniform with her overseas cap. She suddenly noticed him and stopped.

"Are you Gudunov . . . ?" she asked.

"I hope so," said George, with a broad smile, taking the unfair advantage that his name sometimes gave him against the fair sex.

"I'm glad to meet you," said Virginia, extending a pudgy black hand to cancel the sexual overtones of the previous exchange. "I've heard a lot about you in my briefings. I'm glad you got to go on the mission. After all, if it hadn't been for you, there wouldn't be a mission. What's next?"

"Choosing the rest of the crew," said George. "You and I were picked by the President and Congress. The choice of the rest is up to us. Actually, the Space Agency doctors and evaluators have prepared a list of those qualified for each specialty needed. Mostly it will be a matter of following their guidelines."

"Good," said Jinjur. She walked to the door of the VIP suite and looked through the peephole.

"The reporters are gone," she said. "Let's take the Metro to the Space Administration headquarters. It'll be faster than waiting for a VIP limo."

*   *   *

George tossed the thick stack of folders onto the table. "They're all good," he said.

"I'm going to take the one that the evaluators gave the highest grade," said Jinjur. "He not only is an excellent general practitioner and surgeon, but he has a Ph.D. in leviponics."

"That could come in handy in the hydroponics gardens. What's his name?"

"Dr. William Wang," she said. "It's spelled W-A-N-G, but as he said in his application—'You'll always get it right if you remember to pronounce it Wong.'"

Dr. Susan Wang climbed slowly up the short flight of steps to her large home in rural Virginia, opened the front door, and closed it tiredly behind her. She looked over the letters left on the hall table for her. There was a message from the maid—little Freddie had been in trouble at school again, and she was supposed to see the teacher. She glanced through the mail and picked up an electro-mail message in its distinctive blue and white envelope. Her tired face fell even further when she saw it was from GNASA. This was the letter she had been dreading, although she knew in her heart that its arrival had been inevitable.

The letter was addressed to her husband William. No— not her husband. He wasn't her husband any longer, for she had insisted on getting a divorce to improve his chances of being selected for the Barnard expedition. With a heavy heart, she went through the rest of the mail, took out the letters for William and put them in on his study desk. She went off into the kitchen to see how the maid was coming with dinner.

"Good evening, Dr. Wang," said the maid. "Did you see my note about Freddie?"

"Yes, I suppose I'll have to take time off from work tomorrow and go in and see his teacher," Susan said. "I'm sure it's just because he's worried about his Dad leaving him. Well, he's just going to have to get used to it."

They both heard the door open in the front hall. A cheery voice rang out. "Hi there! This is your friendly neighborhood sneak thief. Anybody home?"

A thin oriental man with big ears and a smiling face came bouncing into the kitchen, his youthful-looking features belying his forty years and his triple doctorate in organic chemistry, leviponics, and medicine.

He came over, put his arm around his wife's shoulder and asked, "How'd it go at the labs today? From the way you look, I would think that one of your ten-day syntheses had blown up on the heater or gotten poisoned by a side-reaction."

"No, William," she replied, forcing a smile. "Actually things worked out fairly well at the lab today. There was a little trouble with Freddie at school, though."

"Oh, he's just a mischievous thirteen-year-old," William said. "He'll grow out of it."

"I hope so," she replied. She paused, then continued, "There was also a letter from the Space Agency."

His face took on a wide-eyed expression, then he looked at her thoughtfully. "What'd it say?"

She said, "I haven't opened it yet, but I'm sure I know what's in it." She gave a weak smile. "Come on, let's go read it."

They walked into his study together. He picked up the envelope and quickly slit it open. As he pulled out the letter he glanced at her and felt a combination of exhilaration, fear, and sorrow. He read the letter aloud. "Dear Dr. Wang: You have been chosen to go on the first interstellar expedition to the Barnard planetary system . . ."

This was the culmination of his life's ambition—yet it was going to tear them apart. Still holding the letter in his hand, he put his arms around the woman who used to be his wife. He held her close.

"How much time do they give you?" she asked.

"Not very long," he said. "I'm going to be ship's doctor for the entire crew. I have to go to GNASA headquarters tomorrow morning to help choose them. Then after a break to close out my affairs, I'll spend more time learning their entire medical histories, as well as brushing up on my leviponics and organic chemistry."

"I can help with the organic chemistry," she said.

"So you could!" he said, glad to have something else to talk about. "What's the latest?"

Susan started to give him a history of the advances that had been made in the field of organic chemistry since he had stopped working as a research chemist to study for his M.D. They walked out of the room into the immense yard of their rural Virginia home.

With two incomes well in the upper brackets, the Wangs could afford a big home. Their backyard was not only huge, it was built along the lines of a zoo, for William Wang loved animals, the more exotic the better.

"It's going to be hard leaving you and Fred," he said.

She smiled. "It's going to be even harder for you to leave this menagerie of yours. As you well know, I really don't want to keep them."

"I know. I know," he said. "I'll just have to find good homes for them."

"You've only got a few months," she reminded him. "How many people want pygmy elephants and Bengal tigers, other than zoos?"

"Well, it's a matched pair of pygmy elephants," he replied. "Surely somebody will want them."

William, still holding the letter, walked over to the cages. He patted the Bengal tiger, while the furry beast brushed its huge catlike face against the thin yellow hand reaching through the bars and lowered its head to have its ears scratched.

"I'm going to miss you, Ben," said William. He turned and looked around the yard at the other animals in his private zoo.

"I'm going to miss all of you," he said. "But I've got to go to the stars . . ." He paused. ". . . and I'm never coming back."

CHOOSING

The next morning the three of them gathered together to resume the choosing of the crew for *Prometheus*.

"Who's recommended for Communications Officer?" asked Jinjur. "Technically, whoever is in that position is third officer."

"The person recommended is Colonel Alan Armstrong," said Dr. Wang. "But there's a portion of his file that's classified."

"*That* hunk of pseudo-Adonis?" shouted Jinjur. "I'd love to have him in bed, but not in my command. Who else?"

"There are others, General Jones," said George. "But methinks thou doth protest too much. What saith you, chirurgeon?"

"George is right, Jinjur," said Dr. Wang. "Alan is the best choice."

"OK," said Jinjur. "But I still don't trust Greek faces bearing cleft chins."

Colonel Alan Armstrong walked briskly through the familiar corridors of the Pentagon and made his way to the office of General Beauregard Darlington Winthrop III, Chief of Staff of the Air Force. The General's secretary had her back to the desk, putting something in the filing cabinets along the wall. Alan looked her over before he spoke and noticed a slight bulge of plumpness that was not there two years ago. She must have let herself go once he'd stopped seeing her.

"Hello, Maybelline," he said in a deep voice.

The secretary jumped—then turned with a wide-eyed, hopeful smile on her face.

"Why, hel-lo, Col-o-nel A-rm-strong," she said, batting her eyelids nervously at him. Her face developed a longing expression.

Alan's automatic protective mechanisms turned on his charm. His blue eyes sparkled, his cheeks dimpled, and the radiant smile above his cleft chin so dazzled the poor girl that she forgot her heartache at being jilted, and just wanted to do anything to please this wonderful man.

"Could I see General Winthrop now?" he asked her.

"Su-re-ly," she said, and without taking her eyes off him, she reached for the intercom lever.

"Col-o-nel A-rm-strong to see you, sir," she announced. She turned to watch him as he walked past her through the ornate wooden doors. His smile shifted rapidly as it switched from emitting one type of charm to another more suitable for friendly superiors instead of idolizing inferiors.

Alan walked across the acres of blue carpet with little concern, for he had scuffed his feet across the Seal of the Air Force Chief of Staff many times in his career. He thought back to his first time. He had been scared then, when as a young first lieutenant he had risked his career by demanding a private meeting with the Air Force Chief of Staff. It had been General Youngblood at that time. Alan, fresh from studying mathematics and astrophysics at Cambridge on a Rhodes scholarship after a brilliant career at the Air Force Academy, had found a military use for the new digital astronomy technique that he had invented, and he refused to tell anyone about it but the Chief of Staff. Fortunately for his neck, he had been able to convince General Youngblood that he knew what he was talking about.

The Russians had always wondered why the space astronomy budget for the Greater National Aeronautics and Space Agency suddenly grew almost as big as GNASA's

budget for manned space flight. They also noticed the
meteoric rise in rank of a young Air Force officer named
Armstrong, but fortunately they never connected the two,
and Armstrong's invention was still one of the best-kept
secrets of the Greater United States.

Alan marched briskly up to General Winthrop's desk,
gave a snappy salute and a "Colonel Armstrong reporting,
sir," and without waiting for permission, turned and sat in
the straight chair sitting at the side of the desk.

Winthrop looked up and beamed at the bright young
man. His face then took on a worried look as he paused to
figure out how to break the bad news. Colonel Armstrong
had asked to be commander of the Barnard interstellar
mission. It was beyond Winthrop's understanding why
anyone would want to set off in a cramped spacecraft for a
forty-year one-way trip to nowhere. But what Alan wanted,
Alan usually got. Not this time, however. Alan's lack of
flight experience had made it impossible for Winthrop and
the rest of the Air Force to convince the President to
make Colonel Armstrong the mission commander. Major
General Jones, the Marine Lightsail Interceptor Fleet Commander, had been chosen for that position. Winthrop had
been sure that he could get the second spot for Armstrong, and had promised Alan the position and a promotion to brigadier general.

Winthrop had forgotten about Colonel Gudunov's friends
in Congress. When the dust had settled, Gudunov was
second in command and Alan was third. As far as Winthrop knew, this was the first time Alan had come in third
at anything—sports, school grades, and womanizing included. He coughed nervously and looked off to one side,
refusing to meet Alan's eyes. Armstrong's famous smile
faded during the long pause. There was now a furrow of
concern on his brow. Suddenly, they were interrupted by
a buzzer on a pink telephone. Winthrop grabbed it.

"Winthrop here," he said. "We're secure." He listened
for a moment, then spoke.

"I'll be right down. I'm bringing Armstrong with me.
Alert the guard."

He turned to look at Alan, who had risen to his feet at the words.

"They have your 'Pink-Eye' locked on General Molotov, Head of the Russian Strategic Forces, and he's receiving his classified dispatch case."

Winthrop led the way through a door to his private suite at the rear of the office. A small bedroom, bathroom, parlor, and kitchen/bar made it possible for him to stay within reach of his command desk and their all-important colored telephones twenty-four hours a day.

They didn't go into the suite, but stopped at one of the three multicolored elevators at the end of the small hallway. Winthrop entered the pink one, waited for Armstrong to board, then pushed the single button inside. A pink door hissed shut and they dropped rapidly downward into the bombproof bunkers deep below the Pentagon.

The door hissed open and they stared at the barrel of a machine gun sticking through a swivel-port under a thick pane of bulletproof glass embedded in a tiny triangular room lined with armor plate. The guard recognized them, and a tinny voice echoed in the cramped metallic box.

"You first, General Winthrop."

Winthrop went to the featureless door on the right side, palmed a panel, and walked into a man-lock. A moment's pause, another hiss, and the voice spoke again.

"The lock is clear, Colonel Armstrong."

Armstrong palmed the door open and stepped in as the door closed automatically behind him. Having been here many times before, he knew the procedure. Both palms on the slanted glass plates and both eyes in the rubber cups of the iris scanner. There was another hiss and the exit door opened. He stepped out and hurried after Winthrop, who was halfway down the corridor. They met another guard, who opened a pink door. They entered the room that only a small handful of people knew existed, the Pink Room, run by the Air Force Space Intelligence Office, an organization that never appeared on organization charts.

Across the front of the room were a number of status boards. The first showed a picture of the globe and the present position of the large GNASA Interstellar Telescope. It was an unusual telescope and its basic design had been invented by Alan when he had been studying at Cambridge. It was a spiderweb mesh of glass fibers carrying optical signals back and forth from the complex optical computer at the center to millions of coherent optical detectors sitting at the intersection of each node in the hundred-kilometer-diameter net. Each optical detector peered outward into the blackness of the deep sky through a holographic tissue-lens that captured as many of the weak interstellar light photons as it could. Each lens was a meter across, and was only capable of resolving moderately spaced binary-star pairs.

Alan's design for the telescope as a whole, however, had a phase-locked reference laser signal sent to each detector to mix with the incoming light photons. The result was an amplified copy of the incoming photons, with a frequency and phase tag that told the central computer just exactly where in space and time that particular photon packet had been captured. The computer took all these quadrillions of pieces of information and used them to electronically synthesize a perfect telescope lens a hundred kilometers across. The GNASA astronomers (sometimes they were Russian astronomers on exchange visits) were not only able to resolve close binary-star systems throughout the galaxy, but were also able to resolve continent-sized objects on the planets around the nearest stars. They were currently mapping Gargantua and its many moons in the Barnard system.

The Russian intelligence experts had originally been suspicious of such a large eye-in-the-sky. But the design was in the open literature, and as long as the array of lenses was pointed outward toward the stars, they stopped being concerned about it.

What they didn't know, and what Armstrong had suggested to General Youngblood many years ago, was that one hologram lens looks just like any other, a colorless sheet of plastic film. It is trivial to design the rings of varying index of refraction in the hologram lens so that the sheet acts like two lenses at one time. It can be an outward-going lens at one frequency, and a retro-reflecting lens at another frequency. It had been simplicity itself to set up a covert holographic lens manufacturing facility and under-bid the competition for the production of the lenses for the GNASA construction contract. As a result, GNASA got more than they paid for—two lenses in each holo-tissue instead of just one. The only other modification was a separate laser tuned to the frequency of the retro-lens and a covert optical demultiplexer that extracted the retro-beam information before it got to the GNASA computer.

There were three optical computers on board the Inter-stellar Telescope for redundancy. They were all kept pow-ered up so that the backup computers would be instantly ready in case the prime computer failed. They were good designs, and it was seldom that the Air Force had to turn off its covert connection to the third backup computer to allow the GNASA astronomers to use it. Right now, every-one was happy. Some visiting Russian astronomers at the GNASA Space Astronomy Center at Goddard were pulling high-resolution images of planets in the Barnard solar sys-tem from one side of the telescope, while the Air Force intelligence officers in the Pink Room at the Pentagon were pulling high resolution images of General Molotov's office from the other side.

On the other screens in the room were pictures of various scenes inside Russia, such as submarine pens, railroad cars, and truck convoys, while on the central screen was a picture of an office taken through French doors that opened onto a small garden on the roof of a windowless fourteen-story office building. The desk in the room was large and ornate. It reminded Winthrop of his, with its many different telephones. There was a flag to one side, and the sharp point of a sickle could be seen in the folds in the upper corner. There were three men in the room. The burly one with his back to the window stood up to sign a piece of paper, which he handed back to the smaller man. In return he received a locked dispatch case. The messenger saluted and left and the third man ap-proached the desk holding a key. He unlocked the case and left, taking the key with him. The bulky man sat down and Alan could see the four stars on his shoulders. It was Molotov, all right.

"Now just lean back a little," said Winthrop under his breath, and obediently the image leaned back comfortably in his swivel chair and started reading the highly secret document, little realizing that someone was reading over his shoulder from ten thousand kilometers out in space.

The intelligence officer zoomed in until the sheet of paper filled the screen. A tell-tale blink indicated that an image had been permanently recorded.

"Noviye Strategicheskiye Obyekti . . ." said Armstrong softly.

"You can read those goddamn hashmarks!?!" asked Winthrop in amazement. "What does it say?"

"Russian is one of the three languages I picked up at Cambridge in addition to Etonese," said Armstrong. "The heading of the letter is 'New Strategic Targeting Assignments,' and it seems to be a list of the principal strategic targets in the Greater United States, Europe, and China. The interesting thing is that a number of missiles that used to be targeted for us have been switched to China."

"That's consistent with the heating-up of tensions on the Mongolian border," said the head of the Pink Room staff, who was standing on the other side of Winthrop. As General Molotov reached the end of the first page and turned it over, he sat up in his chair and leaned forward to rest his elbows on his desk.

"Lean back, you goddamn Commie!" hollered Winthrop. But the head of the Pink Room, having seen the blink, reassured him.

"We got it before he moved, General," he said. "Let me show you." He went over to a nearby console, and soon one of the side screens showed a still picture of General Molotov reading the first page. He flicked through a series of stills, then froze on one showing General Molotov's hand flipping the first page. Except for a small portion near the bottom where the General's shoulder had gotten in the way, they could read every word on the second page.

"We'll keep watching him until the satellite position

gets so bad we can't maintain a beam," he said. "I just thought you'd like to see your old buddy in person."

"He's no buddy of mine," said Winthrop. "I could kick his goddamn ass for all the goddamn hassle he gave me on the Strategic Missiles subpanel at the last disarmament talks."

Winthrop turned to Armstrong. "Too bad you couldn't put some kickback into that spy system of yours, Armstrong," he said. "We seem close enough so I could kick that goddamn fat rump of his."

Winthrop turned and marched out the door. "C'mon Alan," he said. "Let's go back to my office."

"So that's the way it turned out, Alan," said General Winthrop. "General Jones got the top post and that goddamn Gudunov was made second in command. I did my goddamnedest, but the best I could get for you was third post."

"I don't understand it," said Alan. "I outrank George. He's only a lieutenant colonel and I'm a bird colonel."

"He isn't anymore," said Winthrop. "The President gave him a promotion along with the position."

"Well, then, why don't you promote me? That way I'll outrank him, and he and I would have to switch posts. Besides, you promised me a promotion."

"I know I did," said Winthrop with a frown. "And I thought it would be easy, especially if you were picked for the second spot. But that would make you the youngest general in the Air Force at only thirty-one years of age. You may be good, but I couldn't get the rest of the Joint Chiefs of Staff to go along with me, especially considering the problems it would cause by having that goddamn Gudunov over you. Even though it is technically a non-military mission, it just wouldn't do to have a colonel bossing a general around."

"You promised me a star, sir," said Alan petulantly. "I want my star."

"OK! OK!! I'll work on it."

Suddenly Winthrop grew pensive. "Hmm," he said. "That may be the way to pay that goddamn Gudunov back for all the goddamn trouble he's caused. Once the mission is underway, General Jones will be in complete charge. Even the President won't butt in to tell her what to do. Jinjur is a strict do-things-by-the-rules military commander, and even though this is technically a civilian mission, she wouldn't allow a General to be subordinate to a Colonel.

"You just take this third-rank slot, Alan, and once the mission is underway, and there is no way anyone can do anything about it, I'll get you promoted to general. Then, unless you goof up, like not giving the General what she wants"—he paused at this point, an evil-minded sneer on his face—"you'll soon find yourself second-in-command, and that goddamn Gudunov will get the kick in his goddamn ass that he deserves.

"Now. What we need is some way for you and me to communicate without anyone else knowing, especially Jinjur and that goddamn Gudunov. Since you're going to be in charge of communications, that should be easy. But how?"

Alan looked upward at the ceiling for a moment. "There are a number of ways," he said. "Let's see . . ."

"Now the rockhounds," said Jinjur. "I really feel at a loss here. These types love to muck around in the mud, while the last thing I want to do is pound dirt again. Whom do the GNASA people recommend?"

"We have a real dilemma here, Virginia," said George. "The one most qualified has a number of significant problems. He doesn't have an advanced degree, he's too tall for the beds on *Prometheus,* and worst of all, he's forty-three years old."

"You should talk, graybeard," said Jinjur. "Who is he?"

"The head of the Galilean satellite mapping expedition, Sam Houston."

"He's too tall?" said Jinjur, in genuine bewilderment. "I've escorted a number of his expeditions and met him many times. Are you sure he's tall?"

William looked at George questioningly. George figured it out and told him in a loud stage whisper.

"When the only time you meet someone is at a station in free-fall, everyone comes to the same level. It's a comment on Jinjur's ego that she always thought she was taller than Sam. I've met him twice, and there was never any question in *my* mind."

Jinjur ignored them. "Sam it is, then," said Jinjur. "But we need two of them. Who has the next best recommendation?"

"It's a brave young man," said William, with a flash of his mischievous smile. "He has a generally good background, but there's a reservation in it."

"I'm beginning to catch on to your twings, Sail-Ears," said Jinjur. "It must be Richard the Red."

Richard Redwing leaned his not inconsiderable hundred-plus kilograms on the ice drill and lifted himself up on tiptoe. He could feel the motor whining through the gloves of his space-suit, but there was no downward motion. He wished he had some purchase so he could use his muscles to drive the drill-bit through the rounded pebble that was blocking its path, but on Callisto there was never any purchase, no topography whatsoever . . .

". . . And no gravity to speak of," complained the planetary geophysicist, who finally gave up and pulled the incomplete core from the hole, breaking it into segments as he did so, and throwing the striated columns of ice to the crust in disgust. He moved over a meter and started in again, cursing under his breath in resignation. He was three meters down when his suit speaker relayed a message.

"Sam requests your presence at the Main Dome as soon as convenient," the whispered sonorance announced.

Richard was bewildered by the message. He stopped the drill and asked, "What in Sam Hill does Sam Houston want?" There was a long pause from the speaker, and Richard finally realized that the commsat had gone over the horizon. He leaned on his drill again.

"GOOD NEWS!!!" boomed the speaker in an imitation of Sam's voice. "Sorry that I didn't check the 'sat positions before I called. Can you come in?" Richard didn't physically flinch at the booming voice, but emotionally he had almost jumped out of his skin.

As subtle as a tomahawk in the ear, he murmured to

himself. "I'll be there as soon as I finish this core, Sam," he replied. "Can the good news wait?"

"Sure," said Sam. "See you soon."

Richard loped into the office of the head geophysicist on the Outer Planets. He was relieved that he didn't have to duck as he came through the door. Sam was not only big enough in status to obtain special treatment for his living and working quarters, he was big enough physically to need them. At a full two meters, Sam Houston's spare frame had to bend to get through any doors but his own specially constructed ones. Richard's hairline, nearly five centimeters less, went through without ruffling the invisible feather that he subconsciously wore on his head like some people wear a chip on their shoulder.

"Good news!" Sam boomed again, this time in person. He didn't waste time. "You've been chosen to be one of the crew of *Prometheus*!" he said.

Richard was elated.

"Wow!" he said, his normal reserve dissolving into a smiling, exuberant caricature of himself that was more appropriate for a college freshman than a professional. He had stoically resigned himself to the fact that there were hundreds of applicants for each position on the crew. When he had lost two toes during a mountain rescue in his twenties, he had figured that the minor physical handicap would be enough to keep him out. It wasn't much of a handicap, but when you have a dozen young, intelligent, fully qualified applicants, why pick one that was stupid enough to lose two toes?

"That *is* good news," Richard said. "When do I go?"

"The ferryboat coming to pick you up will be arriving in three days," Sam replied. "You'd better get ready."

"Gee, Sam," Richard said, "I hate leaving you in the lurch like this, with us five ice-cores behind schedule."

"Found another round-rock layer, have you?" Sam grinned, his smile getting broader as he talked. "But that is neither your problem nor mine," he said. "You aren't leaving me in the lurch."

"But all those cores . . ." protested Richard.

"All those cores are the next director's problem," Sam said. "You weren't the only one chosen for the expedition! "We're *both* going to the stars!!!"

"We need two heavy-lift pilots," said Jinjur. "This handsome young one with the stuttering name, Thomas St. Thomas, is an obvious first choice. What bothers me is the rich bitch, Elizabeth Vengeance," said Jinjur. "Why did the evaluators pick her over hundreds of other candidates for lift pilot? And why would she want to give up all her billions to spend the rest of her life cooped up in tin cans? I think she's on a publicity kick."

"Red was the first of the asteroid belt miners and has more experience landing on small rotating moons than anyone else," said George. "As for her billions, it all came in a lucky find of a ten-kilometer asteroid of nearly pure nickel-iron. I think she is getting tired of being a rich ground-pounder."

"Did you read *all* the way through her file?" said Dr. Wang.

"No, Doc. I didn't," said Jinjur. "I know her type only too well."

"Read it again," said William. "Especially the handwritten part after the signature."

General Jones pawed her way through the voluminous file, ignoring the numbers in the financial section that seemed to exceed those found in the Space Marine budget. She finally came to a hand-printed line below the scrawly signature. It looked like the printed grade-school scratchings of a twelve-year-old.

"I want to go to the stars."

A tall aristocratic woman with a lean, high-boned, freckled face walked across the exoplush carpet toward the wall communicator. She touched a tiny circle on the control plate and stared at the face that appeared in full color on the screen. She frowned slightly, her green eyes flitting over the image. In a smooth motion, her right hand reached down to pick up a hair brush on a table in front of the viewer as her left index finger touched another circle on the control plate. The image on the screen reversed as if she were looking in a mirror. A few quick brushes of her short, close cap of red hair and she was satisfied. She blanked the screen and set up a call to her financial advisor. It didn't take long—calls from Miss Vengeance had priority at Holmes and Baker, Pty.

The face of a young business executive flashed into view.

"Good afternoon, Mycroft," she greeted him.

"The same to you, Miss Vengeance," he replied. "Although it is still early morning here. What can I do for you?"

"What's my net worth today?" she asked.

"Hmmm . . ." he replied. "That will take a few seconds." As he talked, his hands flickered over the control plate in front of him and numbers appeared at the top of both their screens.

"Well, your stocks are worth about 22,475 million, and you have about fifty million in your various checking and credit accounts, but that is offset some by about thirty million in short-term debts . . ."

"No—not just my accounts," she protested, "I mean my total net worth—businesses, asteroid mining leases, real estate, homes, cars, everything. Right down to the clothes on my back."

The image on the screen took on a puzzled expression, and Red smiled secretly at his discomfiture. If he thought this request was unusual, wait till he heard her next one!

"Everything?" he said after a pause.

"Everything," she insisted. His hands continued to flicker across the control plate hidden below the view screen. "It'll take a bit of time," he apologized. "The computer can only make guesses at what we can sell some of your personal possessions for."

"That's OK," she said. They both watched a figure at the top of the screen grow in size, then finally stabilize, fluctuating slightly in the last five or six places as the stock and commodity markets around the world continued with their buy and sell transactions.

"It looks like 61,824 million dollars, plus or minus a few hundred million," he said.

"Damn!" she exclaimed, "I thought I'd be over a hundred billion by now. But it's still pretty good for a slum-kid grade-school dropout from Phoenix." Her eyes dropped from the numbers and stared straight into his eyes.

"Liquidate it," she ordered. "You have six weeks."

"Yes, Miss Vengeance," he said with a noticeable gulp. Then, with an avid curiosity, he asked, "What are your re-investment plans? Mining on the moons of Jupiter?"

Her face took on a pixie-like grin as she replied, "No. I am not going to reinvest it. I want you to turn it into cash."

His face broke into a frown, and he forgot his formal business manner as he protested, "But, Elizabeth, you won't get anywhere near a decent return on your investment if you put your money into a savings account . . ."

Her smile grew broader, "You don't understand, Mycroft," she replied, "I want you to turn it all into *cash*."

"Cash!?!" he exclaimed.

"Yes," she replied calmly, "I want about ten million in gold coins, and the rest in bills."

"But . . ." he protested, "There isn't that much cash in the banking system, and if you piled it all up in one place it would fill a football stadium!"

"You may not find that amount of cash in the banks, but I'm sure you can find it in Las Vegas or Atlantic City. Why, I'll bet even Las Lunas has that much floating around. And don't worry, Mycroft, I'm not going crazy. I'm just indulging in a whim, and since it's my money, I don't see why I can't do with it what I want."

"Yes, Miss Vengeance," he replied, his past dealings with Red Vengeance having taught him that it was no use to argue with her when she was in this mood. "I'll arrange for the warehouse and let you know its location, then start the liquidation."

"Fine," she said, "Oh . . . and make sure the warehouse is heated," she added, reaching for her control panel to make another call.

"Heated?" Mycroft said as he stared at the blank screen.

"She wants to convert everything to cold cash, and then she wants to warm it up. I wonder what she's up to?" His fingers played over his control plate as he got busy. Meanwhile, Red Vengeance's next call was wending its way through the system-wide comm nets.

"Hello. Fred? This is Red Vengeance. Do you remember that conversation we had last year at the Ford Foundation banquet? You mentioned that with the new IRS rules on disbursement of assets the Foundation was going to run out of money soon. I think I've got the solution for you, but it's going to cost you. I want your Blake & Company twenty-dollar gold piece . . .

"I know there are only two in the world, and with one in the Smithsonian the other is worth millions, but . . .

"Are you sure it's not for sale? Ask the Board of Directors if they will take sixty billion for it . . .

"That's right, billion, not million. Ask them and let me know by next week."

Thirty days later Mycroft was standing by a cinderblock warehouse in the secured section of the Los Angeles Air Freight yards as truck after truck pulled in to discharge its cargo of green paper. The first fifty trucks had been able to enter the doors to drop their cargos, but the rest pushed their loads into a blower that expelled a green and black blizzard into the interior of the large building.

The Brinks guards near Mycroft half-consciously reached for their hips as a humming sound that had been hovering on the horizon of their consciousness burst into a burbling roar. A high-powered car appeared, weaving its way around the armored trucks. Mycroft motioned to the security guards, who relaxed as the fiery-red Liberian Sword came to an expertly controlled stop in a parking space beside the building. A tall, red-headed woman dressed in a green satin jumpsuit unfolded herself from the front seat and strode over to Mycroft.

"How's it going, Mycroft?" Red asked.

"About three more loads, Miss Vengeance," he replied, "The total keeps fluctuating because of the gold prices and the extra costs that Brinks keeps adding when I ask for something else, but the last calculation was $61,834,745,901.34."

". . . and 34 cents," echoed Red with a wry smile. "Mycroft, your devotion to detail amazes me, but that's why I wouldn't have anyone else for my personal accountant." She smiled and walked through the small entry door into the guard room, Mycroft following close behind. One of the Brinks guards was watching the four electrocameras that were monitoring the interior of the warehouse from the four corners. There was a blizzard of paper blowing in from one side, and the floor of the huge warehouse was piled deep with paper bills. Mycroft watched Elizabeth's face looking at the cloud of greenish gray and spoke up.

"I had quite a bit of problem with the banking system when I asked that your accounts be paid in cash and not checks. Most of them were willing to go along, but I had to read the Banking Act to a few of them before they admitted that their checks were not an adequate substitute for the cash money that they had implicitly promised when they took your account."

She turned to look at him, then lifted an arched red brow in a silent query at his concerned gaze.

"You aren't going to keep all this cash out of circulation, are you?" he asked. "It could cause a serious financial disruption until the Treasury gets around to replacing it. Besides," he went on, "these assets are drawing no interest while they're in cash."

"And that is anathema to your accountant's soul," laughed Red. "No. These bills will all be back working for their keep in one or two days, but it won't be for me."

Mycroft looked at her quizzically, but had found out long ago that the best way to handle the legendary Red was to keep quiet and listen, for she had her own puckish brand of humor.

Red Vengeance turned back to the screens, and looked at one of them intensely. "I see that you took that bit about the bathtub seriously," she remarked.

"Of course, Miss Vengeance," he replied, "and all the gold coins in the buckets next to it are either proof or uncirculated."

As they were talking, the snowstorm of cash had stopped, and they gazed into a room stacked with drifts of bills.

"How many more loads to go?" Red asked.

"That was the last one," said the guard, looking up with awe at the legendary billionaire. Red looked at the guard, and smiled inwardly. It seemed to be a characteristic of the personality that would work for Brinks. The guard was not as tall or as Irish as she was, but her makeup and hairstyle were as close to a copy of Red's as the beauticians could get.

"OK. Everybody out!" ordered Red. Mycroft and the Brinks guards went outside and the door slammed shut on one of the largest fortunes in the world.

It was nearly an hour later when a call came from one of the perimeter gate guards.

"There's a guy here who says his name is Fred Fortune from the Ford Foundation. It sounded phony to me, so I alerted the local police, who are on their way. I'm reporting in case he's a diversion and some other trick is being tried somewhere else."

A voice spoke from the door to the warehouse. It was Red Vengeance. "Believe it or not, that's his real name. I asked him to come here tonight. Please tell the guards to let him in."

Fred Fortune was escorted to the Brinks command post.

"Do you have it, Fred?" Red asked.

Fred hesitated, looking at the strangers. Fortunately, two of them seemed to be in police uniforms. "Yes," he finally replied. "Do you have the check?"

Fred's question was the culmination of a tense evening for Red Vengeance. She started to laugh, and the sight of Fred's discomfiture at her undignified behavior just sent her into further hysterical fits of laughter. The guards and Mycroft had initially joined Fred in their bewilderment over Red's behavior, but after a few seconds Mycroft suddenly broke into a fit of giggles himself. ". . . a CHECK!" he finally exploded, and with that the billionaire and the account executive fell helplessly to the floor in a paroxysm of laughter and tears.

*   *   *

"I'm very sorry for my rude behavior, Fred," Red finally apologized. "I've been under quite a strain lately."

"Has this been a joke?" asked Fred quizzically. "If so, I don't think it's very funny."

"No!" said Red seriously. "I really *am* going to give the Ford Foundation sixty billion dollars. Do you have the Blake?"

"Yes," said Fred, taking a small leather case out of his coat pocket. He opened it up to show a small round gold coin. Red reached for the case, and as she took it she spoke to the lieutenant.

"Open the door to the warehouse," she said. As the door opened, Fred Fortune looked in and his eyes widened.

"Now you can see why your request for a check brought on my fits of laughter. There is your sixty billion—in CASH! Is it a deal?"

Fred nodded, too numb from the sight of the money to reply.

Red started to leave, then turned at the door. "Watch out for the newly-printed bills, Fred, they can cause paper cuts when you roll in them."

Red opened the small leather case that she still held, stuck a green-lacquered fingernail under the small gold coin, and levered it out of its niche in the case. She looked at both sides closely, threw the leather case away, then buttoned the coin into one of her breast pockets. Fred looked askance at the cavalier treatment of a mint-quality numismatic gem.

"What are you going to do with it?" he asked. "You certainly can't sell it for what you paid for it."

"I'm not going to sell it," said Red. "I'm going to keep it—as a good luck charm. I'm going to need all the good luck I can get where I'm going." She walked outside, Fred and Mycroft following in her footsteps.

". . . going?" echoed Fred.

"Haven't you heard?" said Red. "I'm taking a tour, Mycroft."

"A tour?"

"The grandest tour the human race can devise!" she

said. "I'm going to the stars! And this gold coin is going along with me to keep me company. Soon there will be one of them shining by sunlight, and one shining by starlight."

She thought about that for a moment, then reached back into her amply-filled pocket and took out the flat disk of gold. A green-enameled thumb flicked the disk upward toward the stars, where it crossed the beam of a laser perimeter fence. There was a momentary flash of red-gold light, echoed by an alarm from some distant guard post. Red chuckled throatily as she caught the coin. She folded herself into her Sword and drove away—free forever from her avaricious drives.

"The next batch is really a rubberstamp choice as far as I am concerned," said Dr. Wang. "We need at least two computer types that understand the systems built into *Prometheus*, the planetary landers, and the atmospheric aircraft. GNASA's top choice for the hardware side is the astronaut and aerospace engineer, Shirley Everett. She was chief engineer for the design and test of the airplane we will use and was also involved in the building of our lander. For the software side of things, the GNASA experts's first choice is David Greystoke. He wrote most of the programs for the computers on the various craft."

"Haven't heard of him," said Jinjur. "A typical computer-nerd, I suppose. Yet the name sounds familiar."

" 'Visions Through Space,' " said George, trying to help.

"*That* David Greystoke?" said Jinjur. "But he's a sonovideo composer."

"Just one of his many talents," said Dr. Wang. "And we'll be privileged to have him illuminating our humble abode with delicate sights and sounds on our long voyage together."

The computer console screen was alive with writhing brightly-colored abstract forms that roiled and curled in deep blues and lavenders, while scintillating sparks of orange and white marched over and under the billowing waves of color. The display stopped suddenly, then started over again with the lavender shades just a bit less red in color.

Watching the screen critically was a tiny, thin, quiet young man with orange-red hair—a computer leprechaun. The long fingers on his neat hands played over a specialized input panel as they controlled the computer-generated images on the screen. He finished the sequence, saved it in a computer file, then combined it with several others. He pushed his glasses up on his long thin nose, sat back in his console chair, and watched the performance as the computer played the whole sequence back from its memory.

As the artistic computer-animated show was reaching its conclusion, some white letters appeared in the upper part of the screen.

MAIL FOR DAVID GREYSTOKE

David noticed the words, but waited for the end of the file before saying, "Read mail."

The screen blanked and a short letter scrolled its way rapidly down the screen and hung there. David's eyes widened as he read the message. He gave a quiet smile of satisfaction and reached for his sonovideo panel. As the realization of the meaning of the message sank into his body, his soul was reaching out through his fingers to create a new optical masterpiece, a moving view of the splendor of the heavens as seen from the bridge of a starship leaving the solar system and stretching for the stars.

As the starship approached a distant deep-red point of light, the ship grew wings—long, thin gossamer wings. The winged spaceship-turned-dragonfly circled the star, then swooped in to land on a small planet with a tenuous breath of atmosphere. It was all imagination, but the magic of the motion through the imaginary air gave a reality to the dragonfly as it settled slowly to the surface of the indigo planet.

"At least three of the planets in the Barnard system have an atmosphere," said George. "Including the strange double-one. We're going to need some good pilots."

"I've got one," said Jinjur. "You. Unless you've lost your flight instructor's rating."

"But I'll have to sleep sometime," said George.

"There's no question about the other pilot," said Jinjur. "Arielle Trudeau wins it hands down. Y'know, after that exploit where she singlehandedly landed a crippled shuttle with two dead pilots, I always thought she was the best aerospace pilot in the world. As for the rest of the crew, I don't see why we don't just go along with the choices of the Space Administration experts. Let's call a meeting."

"We'll be missing a few people," said George. "Sam Houston and Richard Redwing are both busy on Callisto. Rather than coming all the way back in, they'll meet us at our training base on Titan. The hydroponics expert, Nels Larson, and the computer expert, David Greystoke, are already on *Prometheus* checking out the systems they designed. The solar astrophysicist, Linda Regan, is stationed on Mercury. We'll pick her up there when we visit the Mercury laser transmitter base. The rest should make it to the meeting. The three astronauts should be on their way back now if they aren't already on Earth."

Two women sat side by side in the Super-Shuttle cockpit. The one in the pilot seat was small and fair, almost delicate in appearance. She sat quietly, her hands folded in her lap. The flickering dark-brown eyes under the short, curly light-brown hair scanned the board and flight display, missing nothing in their vigilant watch over the nerve center of the multiton spacecraft.

The woman in the copilot seat was working the controls, her strong capable hands making tiny adjustments as her eyes alternated views of the flight display and the curved arc of the horizon outside the windshield. She was a very tall, superbly-built young woman with blue eyes and a blonde mane of long hair—a California palomino. While she nervously handled the controls, the other woman's calm test-pilot voice quietly guided her through the reentry procedure.

". . . Keep nose at right attitude, Shirley. Also watch those nose and wing thermometers. If nose go down, we dive in too fast. If nose go up, we skip out, miss landing field, and have to dump our nice Super-Shuttle in the ocean. Hold steady now . . . that is good. That is very good."

The vacuum outside the windshield started to have some substance. They could look out at the wings and see the dull red glow of the protection blanket. Bits of dust and frost were swept from between the expansion cracks in the frothy protective skin as the thin supersonic wind flew by.

There was a dull thud. The view outside the windshield started to roll.

"What's happened, Arielle?" said Shirley, her voice tight with panic. "There's no roll response!"

Arielle didn't move, but her eyes were studying a distant corner of the status board where a red light had come on.

"Attitude control propellant tank is busted," she said. "Shut him down and bring up auxiliary system."

Shirley searched over the board, found the proper switches and flicked one down, then the other up. The new propellant tank pressure dropped as Shirley used the jets to reverse the roll and bring the heavy spacecraft around.

"You let nose get low," Arielle remarked calmly. Shirley looked out the window at the wings. The white-hot incandescence left green-yellow streaks in her vision as she glanced back and looked at the temperature indicators. They were all high, with the right wing indicator well above the danger line.

"Take over!" pleaded Shirley, "I'm going to lose it."

"You doing just fine," Arielle replied in a soothing tone. "You already have nose up. Besides, we may have computer glitch if consoles be switched now."

The air was getting thicker. The temperature indicators were dangerously high, but as the massive craft shed its orbital energy to the air outside, the temperatures started to drop. They were nearly through the critical reentry phase.

"You start switch to aerodynamic controls?" Arielle re-

minded and was pleased to see that Shirley had anticipated her.

There was another warning klaxon and the spacecraft
started to roll again. A red message light flashed, indicating that the main hydraulic system was failing. Shirley
reached to switch on the backup system. Arielle started to
warn her that she should turn off the malfunctioning system first, but just then the high pressure oil hit the
inactive actuators and jerked them wildly about. The nose
dipped, and the view outside started to whirl violently.
The windshield turned red, glaring white, then black . . .

A cool Arielle popped the top of the Super-Shuttle
trainer and stood up. She stared over the head of the
shaken Shirley at a grinning black face peering over the
top of the simulator console.

"Thomas St. Thomas!" she said severely. "She's third
time on a reentry and you dump two breakdowns at her.
You be shamed! Look at her!"

Shirley quickly recovered, gave them both a weak grin
and extracted her long frame from the copilot seat.

"The trouble with that landing wasn't Thomas's fault, it
was the simulator. It's so realistic I was fooled into thinking
it was the real thing and panicked. Shall we try it again?"

Arielle was about to protest when the door to the simulator room opened and the Chief Administrator of the
Johnson Space Center strode in, followed by a few
newstapers.

"Don't you three ever take a break from training?" he
said as he approached. He stopped, looked at the names
on the front of three envelopes that he held in his hand
and reading them off, passed them one at a time to the
three astronauts.

"Captain Thomas St. Thomas, Arielle Trudeau, and Shirley Everett."

Thomas got his open first.

"YAHOO!" he hollered. "I'm going to Barnard."

He looked at the expressions on the faces of the two
women as they looked at their letters, then he hollered
again, "YAHOOO! We're ALL going to Barnard!!"

He leaped over the console, picked up Arielle, whirled her around once, and deposited her on the top of the simulator. He started to pick up Shirley, but she just stared him down with her two-centimeter height advantage. He passed her by and proceeded to pump the hand of the Chief Administrator vigorously as the newstapers got it all on tape.

The Houston TV stations that night ended their news program with a shot of the three astronauts—Thomas with one arm around Shirley's shoulder and talking, while Arielle stood in front of the other two. She looked out of place. One would have thought she was a beauty queen, with her pretty face and short curly hair, rather than what she was—one of the best aerospace pilots in the world. As usual, it was Thomas that had the last word as their pictures faded for the commercials.

"We're going to the STARS!!!"

It was another drizzly winter day in Washington, D.C., so George stood in the narrow portico at the front of the Space Administration Headquarters building and waited for the crew to arrive while Jinjur and Dr. Wang were upstairs checking out the meeting room with the Space Administration staff. The first to arrive were Caroline Tanaka, fiber-optics engineer and astronomer; John Kennedy, mechanical engineer and nurse, who bore a striking resemblance to his distant relative; Captain Anthony Roma, lightsail pilot from the Space Marines; and Katrina Kauffmann, former nurse and now a biochemist with a specialty of levibotany. She would help Nels Larson and Dr. Wang keep the hydroponics tanks and tissue cultures healthy. They had all flown into town yesterday and had spent the morning across the street at the National Air and Space Museum. During a lull in the rain they ran down the short block on Sixth Street to where George was waiting. He greeted them and sent them upstairs to the briefing room.

It was five minutes later when he saw a tall uniformed figure come up from underground on the Metro escalator on Maryland Avenue. It was Colonel Alan Armstrong. He had taken the Metro over from the Pentagon. He shook hands with George perfunctorily.

"I look forward to being in your command," said Alan coolly. "I think I'll go see if General Jones needs any help."

Just then a Space Administration station wagon pulled up with the three astronauts. They had flown in that morning in their trainer aircraft. Alan, seeing that two of them were women, paused to wait. The first one up the steps was a good-looking young black man. He headed for George and stuck out his hand.

"Hi, Colonel Gudunov. Remember me? I was one of your students in flight school."

"I never forget a one, Thomas," said George, smiling and shaking his hand. He turned to Alan.

"Alan," said George, "I'd like you to meet three of your crewmates, Captain Thomas St. Thomas, Shirley Everett, and Arielle Trudeau. This is Colonel Alan Armstrong."

They shook hands around. At the end, Alan kept hold of Arielle's hand and looked quizzically at her face.

"Such a gorgeous creature you are," he said in a flattering tone. "I'm sure I've seen you before. Say . . . weren't you Miss Quebec in ought five, just before Quebec separated from Canada?"

Arielle blushed. "Yes," she admitted, "but the Quebecois always want to live in past. I want to live in future, so like rest of Canada, I leave Quebec and become citizen of Greater U.S."

Alan took her by the arm. "Let me take you to the meeting room," he said. "I know the way." Ignoring the others, he took her off.

A humming sound in the distance became louder. A high-powered sports car appeared, working its way down Independence Avenue through the Washington traffic. They turned to watch as the fiery-red Liberian Sword pulled into the reserved parking area in front of the building. A security guard compared the license plate with the numbers on a list and went down to put a special card under the windshield-wiper blades. A tall, redheaded woman dressed in a green satin jumpsuit that matched her green eyes unfolded herself from the front seat and strode up the short flight of steps toward them. Her long thin legs glistened in their shiny-green high-heeled alligator boots.

George stared in fascination at the legs. *Probably the new mutation-green stock from the hide farms,* he thought. He started forward to greet her, but Thomas beat him to it.

"I bet you're the famous Red Vengeance," said Thomas, sticking out his hand. "Few people can afford a Sword, much less drive it so well. Y'know, you're the dream girl of the heavy-lift pilots. We'd all like to take a prospecting trip with you."

Red raised her eyebrows and shook his hand politely. "Not all at one time, I hope," she said, with a faint smile on her face. "I'm Elizabeth, and you . . . ?"

"Thomas," he said. "Thomas St. Thomas, and this is Shirley Everett, and over there is Colonel Gudunov."

Red stared for a long moment at George as she slowly extracted her hand from Thomas's grip. George tried to return the look but finally had to glance away from the deep green eyes. He coughed nervously.

"We're all here," he said. "Let's go up to the briefing room."

Jinjur was waiting at the podium in the front of the briefing room when they entered.

"Get yourself a hot cup of coffee to ward off the chill and have a seat," said Jinjur. "Thomas? You'll be talking right after me, so get your viewgraphs out."

After introductions around, Jinjur returned to the podium. "Welcome, ladies and gentlemen. I don't know all of you well now, but since I am going to be spending the rest of my life with you, I hope that soon you'll all be my friends." She paused, and took a sip out of a coffee cup that had the laser and lightsail emblem of the Space Marines on one side and black letters spelling "THE BOSS" on the other.

"This is not a military mission, but we will be light-years away from Earth authority, so like the old-time sea captains, I will have final authority on everything. I will allow discussion and even straw votes, but this mission will not be run by popular vote. I know you all understood that when you volunteered, but if you don't agree, then now is the time to say so. There are plenty of others willing to take your place." She waited for a few seconds, then relaxed.

"Enough of that," she said. "We're off on an adventure to visit some exciting worlds. We only got a long-distance look at them as the robotic interstellar probe flew through at one-third light speed, but Thomas, Alan, and Caroline have put together a picture of the Barnard system. Thomas?" She stepped down and Thomas took her place.

"First, let me give some details about the star," said Thomas. "Here is a dull table that summarizes what we know about it." He put a viewgraph on the machine. "Barnard is a small, red dwarf star about six light-years away. The only star system closer is the Alpha Centauri system with three stars. As you know, exploring that three-star system will require a larger and more complex operation than ours. They will launch later than we will, but will get to their target first.

"Barnard was called 'plus four degrees thirty-five sixty-one' until an astronomer named Barnard measured its proper motion and found it was tearing through the sky at the terrific clip of ten seconds of arc per year. It is an M-five red dwarf with a temperature of thirty-three hundred degrees Kelvin compared to the G-zero yellow-white fifty-eight hundred degrees of the Sun. Probably the thing we will find hardest to get used to is the dull red illumination. It will be sort of like living by the light of a charcoal fire. Not only is the temperature low, but the diameter of the star is only twelve percent of the Sun's diameter. It is going to be cold there—except very close to Barnard.

"Now comes the interesting part," said Thomas. "The planetary system around Barnard. The robotic probe only got a glimpse as it went through the system, but it looks as though there are only two planets. However, one of the planets is so large and has so many moons, that it is practically a planetary system by itself." He replaced the Barnard data table with an orbital diagram, then walked up to the screen with a pointer.

"The main planet is a gigantic one, called Gargantua. It is a huge gas giant like Jupiter, but four times more massive. If Gargantua had been slightly more massive, it would have turned into a star and the Barnard system would be a binary star system. Gargantua seems to have swept up all the material for making planets, since there are no other large planets in the system. Gargantua has four satellites that would be planets in our solar system, plus a multitude of smaller moons. We plan on visiting as many of them as possible after we have taken a look at the most interesting planet—Rocheworld." He switched to a viewgraph drawing showing a double planet.

"Rocheworld is a corotating double planet whose two halves are so close to each other that the planets are not spherical, but are drawn into egg shapes. This shape was first calculated by an ancient French mathematician called Roche, hence the name for the system. Rocheworld is in a highly elliptical orbit about Barnard. Caroline, using Alan's hundred-meter optical multiferometer, was able to resolve the planets and track the orbits for the last two years. According to her, Rocheworld has a period that seems to be exactly one-third the period of Gargantua. We know that such orbital 'reasonances' are usually unstable. Whether this nearly three-to-one ratio is real or a coincidence is one of the things we hope to figure out when we get there."

"What are the sizes of the orbits?" asked Anthony.

"Small," said Caroline, turning around to look at him. "The radius of Gargantua's orbit is thirty-eight gigameters, while the semimajor axis of Rocheworld's elliptical orbit is a little over eighteen gigameters. The whole thing would fit inside the orbit of Mercury."

"What are the conditions on Rocheworld and the moons around Gargantua?" asked John. "Can we land on them?"

"We know that Rocheworld and the larger moons have atmospheres," said Thomas. "And that one of the two parts of Rocheworld seems to have a liquid on its surface. But the probe couldn't get very much detail during the flyby. That's one of the other things we're going to have to study when we get there."

Next came other briefings for the crew. Some by Space Administration experts and some by members of the crew.

"Now we come to one of the more sobering aspects of our journey," said Jinjur. "Dr. Wang, could you please give us a short medical briefing."

"Certainly," said Dr. Wang, smiling as he rose and took Jinjur's place at the podium. "This expedition is a long one. Longer than the normal lifespan of the human body, even with all the medical advances we have made. Therefore, after the initial launch phases of the mission, we will all be treated with the life-extending drug, No-Die. When it has thoroughly saturated our tissues, it will slow our aging process to one-fourth of normal rate. Thus the forty years that it will take for us to travel to Barnard will only produce ten years of aging in our bodies.

"Unfortunately, our intelligence will also be lowered by roughly the same factor. That is why No-Die is not used more on Earth. Fortunately, you all have been picked as persons with higher than normal intelligence, so that the No-Die will merely reduce your functional level to that of a small child. We will have a semi-intelligent computer on board to keep us out of trouble during the trip out. It will stop administering the No-Die as we approach Barnard so that we will be back to normal intelligence when we arrive.

"As for sexual matters. The engineers cannot make *Prometheus* go any faster. So even if they designed the system for a round-trip journey, No-Die couldn't stave off death long enough to bring us back alive. Thus, this trip is a one-way journey for all of us. The planets there are not habitable without using highly technical life-support systems to protect us against the poisonous atmospheres, so this cannot be a colonization mission. There must be no children born during the mission, and since we cannot count on your intelligent cooperation during the No-Die phase, all of you will have to undergo surgical operations to ensure that your reproductive organs are blocked."

George leaned over and whispered into Jinjur's ear. "I'm already fixed so I only shoot blanks."

Jinjur didn't blink an eye. "Bang, bang," she muttered.

Dr. Wang continued. "Although this procedure should have no physical side effects, there are occasionally psychological reactions to the loss of your reproductive capability that produce physical effects, including loss of sexual appetite and impotence. If this happens to you, please don't hesitate to consult me." A twinkle came to his eye. "If the normal medical procedures are ineffective, I have a book describing some ancient Oriental procedures that are guaranteed to produce spectacular results." He sat down amidst whispered conversations.

"Thanks, William," said Jinjur. "Well, that's enough today. I assume you are all taking care of your personal affairs. After your final physicals, we'll head down to Mercury to visit the laser propulsion center, then go out to Titan for some practice sessions using the planetary landing rockets and the aerospace planes, then board *Prometheus* for the trip out. Good day."

TRAINING

The training of the first true astronauts took them through-out the solar system to learn about the disparate portions of the solar-system-wide machine that would toss them to the stars on a beam of light. First they dropped inward to the orbit of Mercury to see the "engine room" of their star-spanning spacecraft, for the lasers that propelled their starcraft would stay in the solar system where they could be maintained, repaired, and replaced by the Sunlubbers that remained behind.

They approached Mercury from shadowside, heading for the thin bright manmade halo behind the planet that could be seen in telescopes over interplanetary distances. This was the sunhook, a ring-shaped structure of gossamer that hovered halfway down Mercury's shadow cone. The intense light from the Sun bouncing off the reflective surface was enough to keep the sunhook levitated against the pull of the planet below. As Mercury rotated about the Sun, the play of the solar photons on the ring kept it centered about the shadow cone. Hanging below the sunhook, at the point of a cone of tethers, was MERLAP–4C, the Mercury Laser Propulsion Construction, Command, and Control Center, safely suspended in the deep shadow of the planet. As they came closer to Mercury Center, they could see a steady stream of robot vehicles hauling material out from the Center toward the sun-edged rim of the planet.

51

As they docked, they could see through the portholes the bright dress uniforms of the small contingent of the Space Marines at Mercury Center waiting to welcome their General Jinjur. The interconnection hatch opened, and there was a piercing whistle.

"Air leak!" shouted Shirley as she jumped for the hatch controls.

Fortunately Jinjur was in her path and deflected Shirley's flying body before someone's fingers were caught in an emergency closing of the hatch. Shirley turned with bewilderment at Jinjur's interference. Then she heard the piercing whistle change pitch while a voice gave some commands. There was a slap of hands on stungun butts.

"They're just piping me aboard," said Jinjur. "But you're right, that bosun's whistle does sound like an air leak."

Jinjur led the way through the airlock. There were portholes in the short metal docking tube, and they could look up through them to see the brilliantly glowing ring hanging above them in the sky. Portions of the sail were tilting, turning from a dull gray to brilliant white as the ring control computer added sail to compensate for the weight of the docked transport craft.

They were greeted by Linda Regan, a short, bouncy young woman with long brown curls and sparkly green eyes. Shirley looked down in envy at the naturally curly hair, then her expression changed to that of puzzlement.

"Haven't I seen you somewhere before?" she asked.

"I wondered if you would remember me," said Linda. "I was a sophomore cheerleader at USC when you were a second-string forward on the men's basketball team."

Linda led them to a large central room used as a combination dining room and meeting hall. As they made their way through the corridors, Red felt uncomfortable. There was something wrong and she couldn't quite figure it out. She frowned and swam after the rest of the group.

In the meeting room they were met by the Chief Administrator of the Center.

"I want to welcome our distinguished group of astronauts to the Mercury Laser Propulsion Construction, Command, and Control Center," he said. "It is here that we will generate the propulsion energy to send you off to Barnard. When the mission starts next year, we want you to know that we will be behind you, pushing all the way."

There were a few chuckles. He smiled and continued. "There is one very important fact you must always remember while you are here on Mercury Center; especially when you're off looking around on your own after the planned tours." He paused and continued, "You're NOT in free-fall."

With those words he pulled himself over to a table fixed in the center of the dining hall. Using it for purchase, he crouched, and jumped expertly upward to the center of the domed ceiling, where he held onto a light fixture. He damped out his motion and hung there some ten meters overhead.

"Mercury Center is not in orbit about Mercury, but is floating at a point some eighty thousand kilometers above the surface of the planet. The pull of Mercury is counteracted by the large ring-sail that you all saw as you arrived. The ring-sail stays outside the shadow cone of the planet, while we are hanging in the comparative coolness of the shadow. This arrangement is not completely stable, so it is necessary to have active control of the sail area to keep us at constant altitude and in the center of the shadow cone as Mercury orbits about the Sun.

"The gravity pull from Mercury at this distance is weak, only one part in three thousand of Earth's gravity, but it's enough to kill you." He paused to let the last words echo off the walls of the large room. His voice took on a stern tone as he continued. "And the more free-fall time you've had, the more likely you are to forget, so I want you space veterans to pay close attention.

"Suppose you're outside being shown something, and you let go of your handhold for a second," he said. He let go of the light fixture for a few seconds. As far as the group could tell, he just hung there as if he were in free-fall. He regained his hold on the light fixture and said, "For the first few seconds, you will only fall a few millimeters, and you can easily regain a handhold. However, let yourself get distracted for ten or twenty seconds . . ." He released his handhold and started counting. After ten seconds he had dropped noticeably. When he reached the count of twenty he desperately attempted to regain his handhold on the light fixture, but he had dropped over half a meter and it was out of reach. He stopped trying, then turned to look down at them.

"You will continue to accelerate," he said very solemnly as he slowly fell toward them. "If we don't see you within two or three minutes and launch a rescue vehicle, you are *dead*." His feet punctuated the last words as they hit the table-top with a dull thud.

"That's what's wrong!" Red said out loud. The others looked at her. "When I was coming through the corridors, something bothered me. Now I know what it was. The air was too clean and the floors were too dirty. In free-fall you're always bothered by specks of dust and pieces of loose equipment. Here everything collects on the floor after a minute or so."

"You're right," said the Administrator. "Please keep it in mind all the time you are here. Now, let me turn you over to my Chief Engineer, who will explain the things you will be seeing during your visit here."

Their first tour took them out to one of the laser generator stations. There were a thousand of them, spaced in a sun-synchronous orbit about Mercury—a sparkling diadem for the innermost planet. Each consisted of a large light reflector thirty kilometers across, which collected the sunlight and concentrated it on a light-pumped laser at its focus. The astronauts visited the sites in groups of five in small flitters. They did all their observing from behind the heavily tinted portholes of the flitter, for it was too hot outside for ordinary space-suits.

Red, who had gazed down at many a planetoid from orbit, suddenly broke her contemplative silence.

"How come the terminator is curved?" she asked. "I thought the lasers were supposed to be in a sun-facing orbit. In that case, we should be right over the terminator and Mercury should be cut in half by its shadow."

"For the same reason that the lasers and their collectors

are here flying around Mercury instead of in their own orbits about the Sun," said the engineer conducting the tour. "Light pressure may not be much, but the solar photons would blow those lightweight collectors away if they were not anchored by gravity to the mass of the planet. In fact, the light pressure is so strong that the sail and laser are not even orbiting the center of Mercury. The light pressure actually pushes the orbit a few hundred kilometers toward the dark side. That pressure also keeps the orbit precessing so that it stays facing the Sun."

"Things have sure progressed since the early laser space-fort days," said George as he gazed at the huge expanse of light collector that seemed to go on and on to some distant horizon like the surface of a small sea. He paused, then queried in a perplexed voice, "The collector has a funny color to it."

"That's the special reflective coatings on the plastic," said the engineer. "The solar flux here at the orbit of Mercury is almost ten kilowatts per square meter, but not all of it can be used by the laser. The coating on the collector only reflects those portions of the sunlight that are at the right frequency to be converted into laser power."

"*Prometheus* needs thirteen hundred terawatts of power for propulsion, and there are one thousand lasers, so each one has to produce thirteen hundred gigawatts," said George. "That's a lot of power. What's the efficiency?"

"The overall efficiency of solar power to laser power is only twenty percent, but the important thing is to get rid of the eighty percent that you don't use," said the engineer. "The total solar flux incident on the thirty-kilometer-diameter collector is sixty-five hundred gigawatts, but only about fifteen hundred gigawatts is reflected to the laser itself; the rest just passes on into space."

"So, since the laser puts out thirteen hundred gigawatts, the efficiency of the laser itself is quite high," said George. "Still, even two hundred gigawatts is a lot of heat to get rid of."

"Not if you have a high enough temperature and a big enough surface area," said the engineer. The flitter moved closer to the laser itself. "They're about to do a test," he said.

Control jets flashed on the side of a one-hundred-meter-diameter mirror. The mirror turned and deflected the focused sunlight from the collector sail into the end of a block-long, office-building-sized laser with four jet-black wings spread out into the blackness of space. After a few minutes the central portion of the laser started to glow a deep red, then it turned yellow as the base of the radiating fins took up the deep red color.

"Is the laser on?" asked George. "You can't tell, I guess; nothing to scatter light from the beam."

"The laser radiation is in the short infrared, so you couldn't see it anyhow," said the engineer. "But you can tell it's on by looking at the color of the beam-deflector mirror."

They looked at the deflector mirror at the output end of the laser and saw a deep red glow near the center, where the fraction of a percent of the thirteen-hundred-gigawatt laser beam had been absorbed by the material in the mirror instead of being deflected off to the distant laser-beam combiner.

"The tests are coming along fine," said the engineer. "All the lasers should be operational long before launch time. Let's go look at the beam combiner."

A few hours later the small group had moved from the orbiting ring of lasers to the combiner at the Lagrange point L–2 that was close to Mercury on the side away from the Sun, just beyond the tip of Mercury's shadow cone.

As they approached the site of the laser-beam combiner, they saw a lot of robot transporter traffic.

"It looks only half-finished!" Alan exclaimed with a perturbed note in his voice.

"Actually, it is only about one-third complete," said the engineer, "but we'll have it done in another three or four years."

George, noticing the concerned look on Alan's face, chided him. "You're going to have to get used to thinking in interstellar terms, Alan. For the first few years of our trip, we're going to be so close to the solar system that the laser-beam combiner won't be needed. In fact, if it were used, it would burn a hole in our sail. We need the power of all the lasers, but each one of them can easily send a beam to the sail by itself. Since the combiner won't be needed until long after launch, they saved its construction until last."

The collector lens of the beam combiner system looked like a fine lace doily sprinkled with dew. It was sitting in space a number of kilometers away from a long cylinder that was the main portion of the combiner. The lens was an open net structure that faced Mercury and its sparkling crown of laser generators. In the openings were transparent sheets of plastic a hundred meters across. They flashed the colors of the rainbow as the flitter moved across it.

"Those are hologram lenses impressed in thin plastic," the engineer explained. "When the collector is complete, there will be one thousand of them in a close-packed array some three-and-a-half kilometers in diameter. The light from each orbiting laser is captured by one of these lenses, which concentrate the beam and send it on to the smaller lenses in the combining cylinder. There, the one thousand separate beams are combined into a single coherent beam of thirteen hundred terawatts of power, and sent on to the final transmitter lens.

"Since the orbital plane of the lasers is almost exactly at right angles to the collector at all times, there is very little shift in laser frequency due to the doppler effect," said the engineer. "The little frequency shift there is, is easily predicted and compensated for at the laser. The main adjustment of the phases, however, is taken care of by sampling each of the one thousand beams as it enters the combiner cylinder and then adjusting the internal lens positions to correct any phase errors."

They flew behind the cylinder and stared back at the Gatling-gun appearance of the output of the beam combiner. They could see right through.

"It seems to be empty," remarked Tony. "Are you sure you'll get all the lenses in on time?"

The engineer laughed. "Actually, all the internal lenses

are already installed in the combiner. The reason that you can't see them is that they are made of ultrapure plastic so they don't absorb the laser light. Also, note that the output mirror is tilted slightly compared to the input mirror. That's because the combiner not only combines the various laser beams into one beam, but also transfers from solar system coordinates to Barnard coordinates. Barnard is four degrees above the ecliptic, so the top mirror has to be tilted slightly. Also, as Mercury orbits around the Sun, the output mirror rotates to keep the beam pointed at Barnard."

It was a long journey out to the transmitter lens. This was the other major portion of their spacecraft that would remain in the solar system while the rest of the ship made the journey to Barnard. The transmitter lens was situated halfway between the orbits of Saturn and Uranus, where the Sun was weak and space seemed cold. The lens was under construction and was already a few kilometers in diameter. The gossamer structure of threads and plastic sheet was invisible until they went around to the far side and looked back at the Sun. The light scattering from the threads lit up the spiderweb structure and they could see the evidence of the alternating rings of plastic and emptiness. The construction was progressing slowly, since only a small crew of robots was assigned to the repetitive task of adding threads and thin sheeting. There was plenty of time to work on the lens, however, for the first one hundred kilometers would suffice for initial test and for propulsion of the interstellar craft for the first five years of thrust. More diameter would be added, as needed, during the forty-year duration of the mission, until it reached its maximum diameter of one thousand kilometers.

The best parts of the training program were the practice sessions on *Firefly*—a one-third scale model of the payload section of *Prometheus*, the interstellar spacecraft. *Firefly* had a sail diameter of one hundred kilometers, and carried a single lander-airplane combination. Here the crew learned to work with James, the spacecraft computer program.

James was gaining experience on *Firefly* that it would use to modify its pre-programmed procedures before it was transferred to the *Prometheus* computer. It was on *Firefly* that they were first introduced to the computer motiles that James used to communicate with each crew member and carry out necessary repairs and maintenance.

The first four aboard *Firefly* were David Greystoke, General Jones, Colonel Gudunov, and Shirley Everett. They were crowded together in the airlock waiting for the pressure cycle to finish. David was expounding on the characteristics of the super-computer that he had helped design and program for the mission.

"The computer on *Firefly* is as nearly complete as we can make it and still fit it into this scaled-down version of *Prometheus*," he said. "The central processing unit is the same size as the one on *Prometheus*, so that the computer and its program will be as 'intelligent' as it will be on *Prometheus*, but it does have some limitations in input and output circuitry. It can't handle as many sensors at one time as it will be able to do on *Prometheus*, and it can't control as many devices, but other than that it'll be a good simulation." The airlock cycled through and the inner door opened. David climbed out, followed by the others, and they helped each other remove their suits. Shirley looked around, found the suit locker, and after fussing over each suit, hung them neatly in their racks.

George noticed a fuzzy-looking metallic object in the corner. It was about forty centimeters tall and looked like a six-armed chimney-sweep brush. From the tips of each of the fibers in the brush there flickered bursts of pure-color laser light. George noticed that the blue beams scanned over the bodies of the crew as they moved around, while the red and yellow beams monitored the rest of the room. The green beams, however, seemed to be for illuminating various portions of the brush itself, giving the brightly reflecting metallic surface of the multibranched structure a deep green internal glow.

"That must be the 'Christmas Bush,'" said George to David, pointing to the small green cluster of twigs with its multicolored blinking lights.

"Not quite," said David. "James doesn't have enough brain power here on *Firefly* to control a bush-sized motile. This is only a small branch, a 'Christmas Branch' if you will. The Christmas Bush James will have on *Prometheus* will be as big as we are and can do anything a human can do. The Christmas Branch here is pretty capable, however, just not as big." David was still holding his suit helmet. He tossed it at the Christmas Branch in the corner. "Put this away for me, James," he said.

The helmet sailed at the Christmas Branch in a nearly straight trajectory in the low gravity. Crouching like a miniature stick figure with three "legs," the Christmas Branch jumped into the air. The smaller twigs on the bottom side of the trifurcated structure whirled in the air, propelling the Christmas Branch through the air. The top portion of the Christmas Branch opened up into three furry paws that grasped the helmet gently with fuzzy fingers. The Christmas Branch shifted position, swam over to the suit locker, and put the helmet in its proper place in David Greystoke's suit rack. As it performed, it uttered a series of happy barks and came bounding back to pause in midair in front of David, one of its rear twigs wagging in the air and the tiny cilia near its front portion emitting a series of breathy pants.

Jinjur listened in amazement, then broke into laughter at the performance. "Maybe 'Fido' would be a better name than James," she said, still laughing.

David smiled. "No, that's not its normal response pattern. I deliberately programmed that 'eager dog' response into James's repertoire as a method of chiding a crew member whenever they got lazy and misused one of James's motiles. That's one of the reasons that the program has the name James."

"It sounds like an English butler," said George.

"Exactly. James is here to serve us just as a good butler would, but the computer will also be responsible for running the ship and taking care of the legitimate needs of twenty crew members. Note that James did what I asked it to do, but at the same time it gently reminded me that I should have taken care of that particular job myself. Now, let me show you some of its other tricks." He reached into his shirt pocket and pulled out a pressurized ballpoint pen. He then unbuttoned his shirt front and used the pen to push out a bit of lint from behind a buttonhole. He kicked over to a nearby wall and deliberately made an ink mark on the wall. As he kicked back, he let loose the bit of lint into the air. As he came to a halt back with the group, they watched as two tiny segments of the Christmas Branch detached from one of the arms. The smaller one, a minuscule cluster of cilia not much bigger than the bit of lint, flew rapidly through the air with a humming sound like that of a mosquito, captured the floating ball, and flew out the door to another part of the ship, zig-zagging as it went.

"It's picking up other bits of dust on its way to the dustbin," explained David. "They're too small for us to see, but its little laser radars picked them up from their backscatter."

The larger sub-motile jumped from the Christmas Branch to the wall, and like a spider, used its fine cilia to cling to the wall and walk over to the ink smudge. The cilia scraped the ink out of the wall pores and formed it into a drying ball. The wall now clean, a sub-section of the spider detached and swam off through the low gravity, while the remainder of the spider jumped back to the Christmas Branch where it resumed its normal place.

"The Christmas Branch here on *Firefly* and the larger Christmas Bush on *Prometheus* will normally stay in their assembled shape," said David. "They're easier for James to control that way, since each portion has a significant amount of computer power built into them. Each segment, down to the tiniest hexad of cilia, is practically identical in shape. There is a hexagonal central body that is the point of attachment to the next larger level of the structure. From six 'shoulder joints' on the central body radiate six 'arms,' each with an 'elbow' joint. The next smaller hexad is attached to the ends of the arms. Its central body acts as the 'wrist' and its six 'fingers' form a 'hand.' But unlike a human hand, each 'finger' has a smaller 'hand' and so forth for ten levels. The smallest 'fingers' are cilia only twenty microns long. Each subset has its own tiny rechargeable permabattery in the central section, 'muscle' portions near the ends, and logic and control circuitry. Each also has diodes that can both receive and emit laser light at many different frequencies. The various levels of structure are only connected mechanically, not electrically. The logic and power connections are through the laser diodes."

"Because it's laser light, the efficiency of power transfer is nearly ninety-five percent," said Shirley. "James feeds power from lasers in the corners of the room to the main trunk of the Christmas Branch to keep that battery charged, and the Christmas Branch trickles the energy down to the various sticks, twigs, and cilia with the green lasers that you see. The power beams are modulated to send information back and forth between the logic circuits in each twig until you have a fairly sophisticated computer. All James has to do is tell the Christmas Branch where to go, and the Christmas Branch generates all of the subcommands needed to trifurcate its 'feet' and walk or swim there. If a smaller portion is detached, however, then James has to use some of its own brain-power to run it, so that's why the motiles are usually kept in clumps. Yet housekeeping is a continual chore, so don't be surprised if you see a mosquito flying through the air or a spider walking across the ceiling. They will just be collecting all the dirt and dust you've made that day."

"I'm not so sure I'm going to like living with mosquitoes and spiders," said Jinjur. "That's one of the things I really liked least about being a ground-pounder."

"Once you've gotten used to your imp, Jinjur," said David, "I'm sure you'll get used to James's other minimotiles."

"Hummm. The 'imps.' I guess they're necessary, but when Shirley was talking about them in the briefings, I really didn't look forward to the experience."

"They're not so bad once you get used to them," said David. "And there's no time like now."

He turned to face the Christmas Branch. "Could I please have two personal imps, James? One for me and one for Jinjur?" He held out his hand and two portions of the

Christmas Branch detached and flew through the air to David's finger, where they perched like two skinny sparrows.

"These personal imps are to stay nearby at all times so James has a way of communicating with you. It doesn't really matter much where you keep them, but I like to have mine riding my shoulder." David put one of the imps on his shoulder. It scrambled for a second and soon was perched on his collar, looking like a tarantula with six hairy legs. Jinjur noticed that one leg was resting gently on the side of David's neck.

"They not only serve as a means of communication," said David. "They also allow James to keep track of the state of each crew-member's health." He turned his head slightly and talked to the imp out of the side of his mouth.

"How'm I feeling today, James?" he asked.

The cilia on the legs of the tarantula vibrated into a blur. "Pulse seventy-five, temperature thirty-seven celsius, blood pressure one-forty over eighty, blood constituents all fine except your triglycerides are a little high. Probably need to get that weight down. Calcium levels are slightly up and bone density is down, but that is normal for free-fall."

David continued his briefing, "The personal imps have special illuminators and sensors that can monitor the small blood vessels in the skin and practically carry out a complete blood analysis. James doesn't know my weight yet, but after a few days of monitoring the frequency response of the various portions of my body as I push myself around the ship, it'll be able to tell from the changes in frequency whether I've gained or lost weight, and even which portion of the body contains the new fat."

"Pretty nosy," said Jinjur. "But I guess it's better than being wired with thermocouples and pressure sensors. I don't particularly care to have a spider sitting on my shoulder. Can I put it somewhere else, like in my pocket?"

"You could," said Shirley. "But James would sound kind of muffled unless you left your pocket unbuttoned. Here, let me show you how I wear mine." She turned to look at the Christmas Branch. "James?"

Another imp-sized motile detached from the Christmas

Branch and flew over to Shirley where it landed in her hair. The imp flattened into a crescent moon on the side of her head. Shirley turned her head to show them the shiny barrette in her hair with its twinkling multicolored lights. "Pretty, isn't it?"

Jinjur grudgingly admitted that it was, and reached to take the other imp from David's finger. She held it in her hand, looking at it closely. She jumped when it spoke.

"Hello, General Jones," said the imp. "May I be of service?"

Jinjur scowled, a little annoyed with herself for being startled, then forced a determined grin.

"Well, to start with," she said, "you can cut the General Jones business and call me Jinjur like everyone else. I may be boss of this outfit, but it's not a military mission, and titles often get in the way."

"Certainly, Jinjur," replied the imp. "Have you decided where you would like to have me?" Jinjur looked at the imp, bemused at herself for talking seriously to such a tiny, fragile bundle of fibers and twigs.

"Do you know what a hair comb looks like?" she asked. Quickly the six-legged star reconfigured itself into a six-pronged comb with most of its mass and lights clustered into an ornate comb-back. Tiny cilia clutching gently at her skin kept the comb balanced in the light gravity.

"Like this?" the comb-imp asked.

"Yes," said Jinjur, her face expanding into a pleased smile at the sight of the bejeweled comb. "I used to wear them when I was a teenager in high school, so I guess I could get used to you in that form."

She picked up the comb in her other hand and started to place it into her mop of thick black curly hair. She hesitated, then brought the comb down to talk to it.

"You look pretty fragile, are you strong enough for me to use you as a comb?"

"My motiles are quite strong. They are made of the hardest durasteel. You will find them as hard to bend or break as a needle." There was a pause, then James continued as Jinjur lifted the comb to her head and stuck it in. "You must also learn to realize that the imps are only sensors and transducers. You must not think of them as individuals. You might someday be tempted to try to save them in an emergency situation."

Jinjur wasn't really listening. She had turned to face the glass port that looked into the darkened airlock. She noticed a flat space where her short afro had been squashed by the helmet in her space suit. She reached for the imp-comb to fluff it out.

"Allow me," said the imp in James's most butlerish voice. Jinjur's hand hesitated, and the imp splayed out into its normal star shape, moved rapidly through Jinjur's hairdo, and within one second every hair on her head was in its proper place. Jinjur's eyes widened. Then, as the star reconfigured into a comb shape and resettled into its place behind Jinjur's ear, Shirley laughed.

"Isn't it nice having your own personal hairdresser at your beck and call?" she said.

"I thought we weren't supposed to have James do personal things for us," said Jinjur.

"The personal imps are with you all the time. Their job is keeping you healthy, happy, and informed. You can have them help you in any way that they can," said David. "Misusing the main motile is discouraged, however, since it is essential to the proper operation of the entire spacecraft."

"Let's see the rest of the ship," said Shirley. "Lead the way, James." She followed the Christmas Branch out the door with David, Jinjur, and George following. George noticed that the Christmas Branch had left a motile behind. It buzzed up to hover in front of him.

"Colonel Gudunov?" it queried.

"Hop aboard, James," he said. "And please call me George."

"Certainly, George," said the imp as it settled on his shoulder. Within five minutes George's peripheral vision had stopped seeing the softly blinking cluster of lights that flickered in the lower right hand corner of his eye. The imp and its lights would be there for the rest of his life.

* * *

Using the light pressure from the Sun and an occasional long-distance laser assist from Mercury Center, the rookie crew and computer flew *Firefly* to a rendezvous with Titan. The crew made one of the runs without James's help under simulated emergency conditions. Thomas and Red each got to take the surface lander down onto the one moon in the solar system that was the nearest match to the moons in the Barnard system.

The lander was an ungainly, purely functional machine for getting them down to the surface of a planet and off again. The GNASA engineers called it the Surface Lander and Ascent Module, which resulted in an acronym that did not conjure up visions of safety. Except for its height and the amount of cargo it carried, the SLAM was not much different than the Lunar Excursion Module used in the first landing on the Earth's Moon. Its main body was a cylinder eight meters in diameter and forty meters high with a long groove down one side. Nestled in the groove was the fuselage of the aerospace plane, its chopped-off wing stubs with their capped VTOL fans sticking out to the sides. The tall tail of the aerospace plane fit neatly into a slot in the lower body of the lander that ran between the four rocket engines in the base. The lander had three landing pads, with the struts for one of the pads doubling as the lowering rail for the body of the aerospace plane. The upper third of the lander contained the three crew decks and the ascent engine needed to take them back off the planet. The computer in the lander was a copy of James, but it had the name Jack and was given a different voice to aid in communication.

Landing the SLAM on Titan was valuable experience, but it didn't seem like the real thing to Red, since she was used to landing on the unprepared surface of an asteroid, while these landings were made on the flat landing pads at Titan base. After the second landing, the aerospace plane was lowered from the side of the lander using a winch attached to the nose of the plane. After the plane had traveled down the lowering rail and had been rotated to a horizontal orientation, the winch was used to remove the nested sections of wing from inside the lander. The wing sections were attached to the wing stubs to turn the aerospace plane from a stubby-winged missile into a graceful glider.

The main body of the aerospace plane was built more like a submarine than an airplane. The atmospheres on the planets and moons they would be visiting would either be nonexistent or dangerous, so the hull had to be airtight. Entry and exit were made through an airlock under the left wing. On both sides of the plane, right behind the cockpit windows, were hemispherical blister windows that allowed the science scan instruments almost a 180–degree field of view horizontally and vertically. The bubble windows looked like insect eyes, which led the crew to name the aerospace plane *Dragonfly*. The name was more imaginative than its official designation of "Surface Excursion Module" or "SEM."

The main power supply for the *Dragonfly* was a nuclear reactor with a thermoelectric blanket. The reactor always ran at low level to provide the heat and electricity needed to keep the humans alive and operate the plane. The electricity was also used to power the electrically-driven VTOL fans in the wings that allowed the *Dragonfly* to hover and move in all directions, just like its namesake. For high-speed travel, the fans were used to get *Dragonfly* up to speed, then the reactor power was increased and used to heat air that was scooped from the atmosphere and blown out a jet in the tail. In front of the reactor shield were tanks of monopropellant that was used for reaction mass and attitude control when the plane was rocketing through vacuum.

At the back of the crew section was the work area for the Christmas Branch. The "work wall" was crammed from floor to ceiling with hundreds of tiny synthesizing and analytical instruments ranging from miniature chemical laboratories to microscopes to X-ray machines, all scaled for operation by the tiny detachable hands of the motile, although they could also be operated and viewed from the science console up front. In front of the work wall was the air conditioning and renewal system, the laundry, the airlock and suit storage lockers, then a toilet and shower, and finally the crew quarters and work area, all as far from the reactor as possible.

The radiation level in the forward part of the aerospace plane was significantly higher than would have been allowed back on Earth, but since the crew would be having no children and would be experiencing the radiation quite late in their lives, the radiation levels were of no real concern. Since the aerospace plane would be under gravity most of the time, the crew had horizontal bunks with Sound-Bar doors that lowered and latched, for exploration was a twenty-four-hour-a-day shift operation. The galley was tiny, since only one or two would be eating at any one time. Between the galley and the science scan section was the operational center of the *Dragonfly*. One side of the aisle held the ship's computer, with a console for the computer operator, while the other side had two consoles for control of the science and engineering activities. The computer program for the aerospace plane was a miniature version of the computer program on *Firefly* or *Prometheus*. To keep confusion down during communications with James back on *Firefly* and Jack in the lander, this computer was given a female voice and christened "Jill."

Arielle, George, and Jill took the plane through its paces and Arielle tried it a few times as a pure glider. It was a little heavier than the powerless planes Arielle had flown as a child, but because of its enormous wingspan it performed well despite the weight of its heavy nuclear power plant.

The final test of the aerospace plane was a high-speed leap into space. Arielle and George practiced gaining speed with a shallow dive, then heading for altitude until the controls got mushy and had to be replaced with attitude control jets. Their last jump took them halfway around Titan. At the peak of the forty-five-minute hop, they rendezvoused with *Firefly* as it sailed by in a closely-timed maneuver, and an alternate means of getting off a distant world was verified and stored in James's memory.

The training drew to a close. From all over the solar system the crew came in small groups to board their interstellar spacecraft, hanging below a silvery sail as big as a small moon. *Prometheus* was a cylinder some sixty-six meters long and twenty meters in diameter, an insignificant seed hanging by shrouds from a one-thousand-kilometer-diameter lightsail. They flew in from the backside of the sail, where they could see the hexagonal trusswork that held the large ultrathin triangular sheets of perforated aluminum sail, and docked at the airlock coming out of the top deck. The top two decks would take the brunt of the cosmic radiation during their long journey, so they contained the storage areas and the work area for the Christmas Bush.

Running completely through the length of *Prometheus* was the lift shaft. It was four meters in diameter and ran from the starside science dome on the back side of the sail to the Earthside science dome in the center of the bottom control deck. A lift elevator was available for heavy cargo, but the crew mostly ottered their way up and down the shaft using the handholds built into the walls.

After the top two decks, the next forty-four meters were taken up by four Surface Lander and Ascent Modules arranged in a circle around the lift shaft. They were upside down, with their landing rockets pointing upwards and their docking ports attached to four access ports in the hydroponics deck. Below the hydroponics deck, which supplied another layer of protection from cosmic rays, came the two crew decks. Each crew member had a luxurious hotel suite with a private bathroom, sitting area, work area, and a separate bedroom. The wall that separated the bedroom from the sitting area was a floor-to-ceiling view-wall that could be seen from either side. In addition, there was another view screen in the ceiling above the bed.

Below the crew decks was the Living Area deck, with a dining area, lounge, exercise room, and two small video theaters. Separating the lounge from the dining area was a large sofa facing a three-by-four-meter oval view window that was the focal point of social life on the ship.

The Control deck at the bottom of the checker-stack was all business. Here was another airlock, all the electronics, and the consoles to operate the sail and the science instruments in the two science domes. In the center of the Control deck was the Earthside science dome—a three-meter-diameter hemisphere in the floor surrounded by a thick circular waist-high wall containing racks of scientific instruments that took turns looking out the dome or directly into the vacuum through holes in the deck.

Prometheus was already on its way out of the solar system, flying slowly on the rapidly diminishing photons from the Sun. It was skippered by a busy GNASA checkout crew, and an updated and trained James copied from the memory of the *Firefly* computer. As each load of astronauts boarded, their ship was taken back by some members of the checkout team, until one day the twenty crew members were all gathered on the ship that would be their home together for the rest of their lives. They then started the shakedown phase that tested out the crew, computer, ship, and distant lasers as they moved around the solar system driven by a combination of solar light and laser light.

The shakedown had been going well for three months. Jinjur had just run them through an emergency drill where one of the hydroponics tanks on the upper deck was hypothetically punctured by a large meteor. There were supposedly tons of water loose on the upper deck, compounded by a rapid loss of air pressure. The crew, James, and the Christmas Bush had gotten the simulated emergency under control. Jinjur now had them all in the lounge for a critique, most of it supplied by James's perfect memory.

George, feeling his age after the strenuous activity, had stopped by the galley to grab an energy stick. He sank slowly into a chair, nibbling bites as he fell. The room was silent except for heavy breathing coming from a tired crew. George took a deep breath himself and started to cough. He struggled, coughed some more, grew a little red in the face, and just as Dr. Wang was coming over to pound him on the back he finally coughed up the little crumb that was the cause of the commotion.

"Excuse me," he said.

"Say!" said Sam, his eager intellect again picking something unusual out of what everyone else took for granted. "That is the first cough, or sneeze, or wheezle I've heard in nearly a month!"

It was quickly realized that not one of the entire crew of twenty had the slightest cold. They asked James about it.

"This phenomena often occurs when small groups are isolated for long periods from the rest of the world. The scientific teams in Antarctica that stay over the winter often are free from colds until the first supply plane comes in with its new strains of virus."

The crew, feeling better than they had for most of their lives on the bug-infested habitats of human space, turned their attention to Jinjur as she started the critique of their emergency drill.

A general doesn't stay on the Joint Chiefs of Staff forever, and for General Winthrop there was a good reason to leave. One of the two Senatorial seats in South Carolina was up for grabs. The present incumbent was an upstart Republican who had used his photogenic face and a highly successful career as a video actor to win the seat six years ago on the strength of his name alone. He had proved incompetent in the job and had begun to wonder whether the glamour of being a Senator made up for all the money he was losing.

General Winthrop announced he was retiring from the Air Force and running for the Senate at the same press conference. A lifelong Democrat, with roots in the South Carolina aristocracy that went back before the Civil War, and carrying the impressive name of Beauregard Darlington Winthrop III, he had no trouble wresting the Senate seat from an apathetic Rip Thorn.

Once elected, Senator Winthrop had no intention of allowing his "junior member" status in the Senate to moderate his actions. He had been in Washington long enough to know that the acres of empty space in newspapers and video screens had to be refilled each day with print, pictures, and words. He who supplies that voracious appetite gets attention, and through that, action. He had always thought that the whole interstellar exploration business was a great waste of time, especially since it was that goddamned Gudunov who had started it by sending out the first probes. He would get this goddamned nonsense stopped and send that goddamned Gudunov back to oblivion in Texas.

The interstellar mission was a popular project, however, and had developed a terrific amount of momentum. It would be hard to stop, but Winthrop would give it his best try. He first tried financial arguments, but the economic health of a Greater United States, still realizing the potential of the great northern wastes of Canada it had acquired, was so great that the country could not only have guns and butter, but art and exploration, too.

He tried national security arguments, but the recent passage of the latest disarmament treaty and the amazing event of a Sino-Soviet Peace Treaty that seemed to be more than just a piece of paper made that approach untenable, too.

He finally hit upon the key. It made no logical sense, but it appealed to the emotions of the public in such a way that there was an instinctive gut reaction that this mission was wrong and ought to be stopped. The Senator harped on the subject every chance he got.

"Ah have nothing but respect for the people in GNASA who are planning this mission," he said on a Meet-the-Press interview. "And Ah have even greater respect for the brave crew of boys and girls who have volunteered to throw away their lives in a grand spectacle that we will not even *hear* about for almost half a century. But Ah think there is a moral issue here.

"Are we not sinning against our God by allowing this ship to leave on a one-way suicide mission with *no* chance of returning? The sinners are not the crew—they are the ones who are sinned against. The sinners are not the planners at GNASA—they are just doing their duty as we have instructed them." He looked directly into the camera. The thick Senatorial mane of white hair that had replaced his Air Force crew-cut gave an almost Sistine-Chapel aura to his image.

"You are the sinners," he said, pointing his finger straight at the camera. "You are *murderers*—for sending your children to certain death!"

He dropped his eyes, and the video camera pulled back to show him bowed in prayer, his hands reverently clasped in front of him. The reporters were quiet as he murmured— almost too low to hear,

"Forgive these poor sinners, Lord. For they know not what they do."

For the next month, Senator Winthrop harped on the suicide-mission aspect of the flight. He never relented in his insistence that if the public allowed the expedition to proceed, that each and every one of them was a murderer. One after another, church officials joined in the clamor. The American Civil Liberties Union filed a suit against GNASA, asking for an injunction to prevent the lasers from being turned on because the GNASA officials were violating the civil rights of the crew. The protests of the crew that they did not want to be associated with the suit only led to accusations of brainwashing.

The planned launch date was only two months away, and Jinjur was getting worried. Senator Winthrop had used his considerable influence to persuade the Senate Majority Leader to schedule a week-long debate on the subject, with full media coverage allowed. GNASA staffers began a headcount. There were a lot of previous supporters for the program that were now undecided. It was going to be close.

"We need to do something to turn this around," said the GNASA Administrator. "How about you or the crew giving a press conference?"

"That's the last thing in the world I want to do," said Jinjur, "but I guess I'll have to. It would be a complete flop if we tried to do it at long distance. Waiting a half-hour between the reporter's question and my answer is ridiculous on the face of it. I'll just have to come in on one of the ion ships that have been monitoring us. See you in about a week."

Soon Jinjur was under one gee again as the laser-beam-powered ion rocket accelerated to cover the millions of kilometers back to the Earth. Having gotten used to the low-gee environment of *Prometheus*, Jinjur spent most of her time in a soft chair, and was in nasty humor when she reached the Space Marine Orbital Base. The original plan was to have her come back down to Earth and give her press conference in the lion's den—Washington, D.C.— with the President and the GNASA Administrator backing her up. She vetoed that.

"I've been in space so long that I can't stand Earth— either its gravity or its crowds or its smells," she said. "Let me fall once on camera or lose my temper at some reporter, and the mission is dead. I'm a creature of space, and I'll hold the press conference in space. Let the Press come to Mohammed."

Most of the major reporters had been in space before as privileged guests of the GNASA establishment. This was to be the first major press conference held *in* space, however, and every little paper that could get a reporter to either Vandenberg or Kennedy was welcome. It took three crowded shuttle launches with bays full of double-decker passenger capsules to get everyone to Jinjur's press conference. Jinjur had wanted the conference to be at the Space Marine Orbital Base, but as the press list grew, the number of reporters soon exceeded the capacity of any of the rooms on the station. The press conference was shifted to the Sheraton-Polar. Although the hotel was still under construction, the wing containing the large low-gee ballroom had been completed. Placed in a Sun-synchronous nearly-polar orbit around Earth, the Sheraton-Polar would have perpetual sunlight and a permanent view of a half-crescent Earth turning below, the cities blinking their lights on and off as they slipped into and out of the darkness.

Jinjur walked into the ballroom. It had a quarter-gee gravity supplied by the slow rotation of the partially completed torus. She bounced a little as she walked. The quarter-gee would be just right for dancing. Enough to give you traction on the floor, but weak enough to make the leadest-footed dancers light on their feet. The ballroom was big enough so that she could see some curvature to the floor. That took a little getting used to, but cover the floor with a crowd and social dancing could have a new renaissance.

Jinjur had decided against wearing her uniform. A soldier, especially a Marine, is expected to risk her life for her country. She came here as a civilian, a human, a woman—who was about to be denied one of the greatest things that could ever happen to her: a chance to have her name immortalized in history as one of the first of the human race to leave the warm womb of the solar system and become one with the cold crystal stars.

The press conference went well. Jinjur fielded the questions adroitly, whether they were meaningful or stupid. She made it clear that the crew was under no compulsion. A question about them being bribed was easily proved to be nonsense when Jinjur patiently reminded them that one of the crew had left behind a sixty-billion-dollar fortune. The press conference was drawing to an end when a reporter from the *Charleston Gazette* rose and repeated Senator Winthrop's charge against the mission.

"I read from your résumé that you are a member of the Abyssinian Baptist Church, General," he said. "I presume you are a religious woman."

Jinjur stared at him levelly. "Since they face the threat of death daily, most soldiers are more religious than most civilians," she said.

"Then since you are a religious woman," he persisted, "don't you agree that the people of this country are murderers if they allow this mission to send you and your brave crew to certain death?"

There was a silence as the reporter sat down with a smug smile. Jinjur spoke. Her low tenor voice was quiet, but the fervor that rang through it carried her words to the farthest reaches of the ballroom.

"The good Lord has nothing against death, for death is just a rebirth of the spirit from a tired, worn-out body. The people of this country are not murderers, and I resent anyone, reporter or Senator, trying to lay nonexistent guilt on them. This expedition to Barnard *is* a one-way mission. We will not return alive. But . . . it is *not* a suicide mission.

"Think about it. Every one of us has been launched by God onto a *one-way* mission through life. We are born, grow up, work at a job, retire, and die. If you are one of the lucky ones, you find a job that is interesting and fun. So much fun that you don't *want* to retire. You find these lucky people staying in the harness until they drop in their tracks, doing what they enjoy and getting paid for it.

"We—I and the rest of the crew—are like those lucky people. We were born, raised, and for most of our lives have yearned to travel to the planets and the stars. We finally have been given the chance. It will take the rest of our lives to make the long journey to Barnard, and thoroughly study the star and the many planets and moons in the system. There is enough work there to keep us busy and happy until we, too, die in our harnesses—of *old age*. And when we die, we'll have a tomb floating between the worlds that is larger and more splendid than any Pharaoh's."

Her voice rose to parade-ground level, "You're not sending us to our deaths . . . you're sending us to *GLORY!*"

Her triumphant words echoed through the silent ballroom. There were no more questions. Jinjur turned her back on the awed group of reporters and walked out of the room.

Senator Winthrop still insisted on having his debate. Jinjur watched the proceedings on video as the ion ship carried her back out to *Prometheus*. Winthrop talked, pleaded, prayed, and talked some more. But in the end it was an overwhelming eighty-nine to thirty, with the senior Senator from Manitoba abstaining. The mission was on!

Winthrop didn't give up, however. He immediately started hatching a scheme that would strike one last smashing blow at "that goddamned Gudunov" before he got too far away.

Jinjur, despite her elation, didn't feel well as she neared the end of her journey back to the outer solar system. She thought it was due to the one-gee thrust of the ion ship. She was glad she would never in her life feel that again. She didn't know how the ground-pounders survived the constant drag on their bodies. While she was getting out of her suit back on *Prometheus* she broke into a sweat.

"Must be getting out of condition," she said to the small welcoming-home committee. A victory dinner had been planned, with veal from "Ferdinand," one of Nels Larson's famous tissue cultures, and strawberries from the hydroponics tank. They didn't have meals like that very often and it was a welcome break from the various strains of algae mush. The party had already started and Jinjur was welcomed warmly as she entered the lounge.

In the center of the lounge was a porcupine of fresh strawberries. For a second Jinjur didn't recognize the fixture, then realized it was a small section of the Christmas Bush, holding each strawberry tenderly until human fingers removed it from the grasp of a robot twig. She took one and popped it in her mouth, then grimaced in pain, tears coming to her eyes as she swallowed. Dr. Wang looked across the room at her, tucked a finger-slice of veal back into his food tray, and came over.

"I knew we should've never let you out of our sight," he said. "I bet you've picked up a bug from those disease-laden reporters."

"It's just a sore throat, Bill," she protested.

"Open up!" he commanded, pulling a tiny permalite from his pocket.

He took a quick look down her throat, then reached out to touch her neck. One side gave no response, the other side brought a gasp of protest from Jinjur.

"And what a bug!" said Dr. Wang. "You couldn't be satisfied with bringing back some cold bugs or flu bugs, could you? You get into your room and stay there, General. You have the mumps and are quarantined until you get over them. We boys may all have our shots and are fixed to boot, but if we catch those mumps from you in the wrong place, it could louse up our hormone balance for the rest of our lives, *if* we are lucky enough to survive."

"Flazz-bazz," she replied tiredly, and turned to George.

"Take command of the ship," she said. "I'm tired and I think I'll go to sleep for a week or so." She tumbled up the lift shaft and headed for bed.

"Is it really that serious?" asked George, concerned.

"The probability is low," said Dr. Wang. "But just because you had mumps as a child, doesn't mean you can't catch them again if your antibody level is down. And if they get into your other glands as well as the lymph nodes in the neck, they can kill you or damage you severely."

"Hmm," said George. "I'm not sure, but I don't think I've ever had mumps."

"Your medical records show no mention of it," said the imp in his ear. He noticed that Dr. Wang's imp was also whispering to him.

"George, Shirley, Alan, and Katrina are all prospects," said Dr. Wang. "The rest of us are pretty safe. I want each one of you to report to me the minute you feel ill or have a sore throat."

Shirley picked a strawberry from the holder and ate it.

"Feeling fine so far," she said, then took another strawberry, and another, eating them with obvious relish.

"Just a minute," said Richard, his huge bulk flying across the room. "I saw that one first!" There was a tussle as the two behemoths wrestled in mid-air over the bruised morsel of fresh fruit.

George took the strawberries off into a corner and stayed to make sure nobody interrupted them.

LEAVING

The day finally came. Deep down in the gravity well of the Sun, concentrated sunlight from square kilometers of collector were injected into a block-long laser in orbit about the innermost planet. Glowing warmly, the laser flickered into life, followed by another and another until a thousand lamps were lit. The invisible beams flashed outward and two hours later their presence was felt by the thin reflecting sail on *Prometheus* waiting patiently in space. The sail tugged at its rigging, dragging its precious cargo out into the darkness of space.

The human race was going to the stars!

Two days after launch, Jinjur heard the door to her room slide open, then shut quickly again. She turned off the scan-book on the view-screen in her bedroom ceiling and listened. It wasn't anywhere near time for dinner, and usually the Christmas Bush left her alone except when it was bringing her meals.

"Hello?" said a voice tentatively.

She rolled off her bed, the sticky patch on the back of her coveralls coming loose with a rip.

"Alan?" she said. She went to the door of her bedroom and looked out. Alan Armstrong was standing in the middle of her room, looking elated.

"What are you doing in here?" Jinjur said. "Although

I'm nearly over the mumps, I'm technically still under quarantine."

"I had to see you," Alan said, quite intent on his own business. "It's important."

"What is it?" she asked impatiently.

"I just got a private message from Senator Winthrop," he said. "You'll be hearing about it tomorrow in the coded official mail, but I wanted to talk to you about it now, before the rest of the crew finds out."

"Is something wrong?" she asked.

"No! Something is right!" he exclaimed. "Senator Winthrop just informed me that a special board has promoted me to brigadier general. I've got my star!"

Jinjur took a deep breath, then muttered to herself, "That conniving skunk. He must have demanded that in exchange for giving up gracefully instead of filibustering. Well, I'd better make the best of it."

"Congratulations," she said, coming out of her bedroom. She extended her hand in order to shake his, then quickly withdrew it. "I'd better not shake. Might give you the mumps. Say . . ." she added. "With no base exchange, you're going to have a hard time finding a star for your collar. I could give you one of mine and you could have the Christmas Bush cut it in two and make fasteners for it."

"Thanks, anyway," said Alan. "I brought a set with me."

Jinjur raised her eyebrows as she thought about what a cocksure cock Alan was. Then she said, "Now! Out of here before we have two generals in quarantine."

"No!" Alan protested. "I've got to talk with you. Since I'm now a Brigadier General, and George is still a Colonel, I outrank him, and it is obvious that I should be second-in-command."

Jinjur stared at Alan quizzically, as if she had never looked beyond his pretty face before. At first she thought he was kidding, and was just in her room to use his new rank to garner a special "favor." Then she finally realized that all he was interested in was that title—"second-in-command".

"You realize, Alan, that George was named for this mission by the President himself," she said.

"But that was when we were both colonels," said Alan. "I'm a general now, and he should be third-in-command."

"Alan . . ." She paused as she tried to figure out how to explain it to him. "The second-in-command is supposed to be in charge of the landing crews, while the Commander stays aboard the sailship. George has a flight instructor's certificate, and has been checked out in heavy landers. Your hottest license is for a motorcycle."

"I can still be landing commander. The pilots can fly the ships; they don't need me for that," he protested. "Besides, with my star I outrank George."

"Alan. George is the one that made this mission possible. If it hadn't been for his foresight and courage decades ago, there would be no mission now. Are you going to take that away from him?"

"I'm not taking anything away from him. He's on the mission, isn't he? It's just that he should recognize his place. You don't mean to tell me that you are going to allow a colonel to order a brigadier general around, are you?"

Jinjur looked at the emotion-flushed face of the darling of the Pentagon. *He thinks he's so right*, she thought to herself. *Yet he's so wrong, so very wrong.*

"No, Alan," she said quietly. "I'm not going to let a colonel order a brigadier general around."

"Good!" said Alan. "I'll see you tomorrow when my promotion is announced in the official mail." He started to leave.

"Alan!" Jinjur called to him firmly. He turned to look at her. "You have broken Dr. Wang's quarantine. As Major General Virginia Jones, I order you, Brigadier General Alan Armstrong, to go to your quarters immediately. I know this will be a hardship on you, general, since you will want to receive personal congratulations from your crewmates, but I am sure that you, as a general officer, realize the need for strictest health measures on a mission such as this."

"Oh! Yes! You're right, Jinjur. I guess I did break the quarantine, but it was important I see you, you know."

"Yes, I agree," said Jinjur. "It was very important that you came to see me when you did."

"You won't forget about colonels ordering generals around, will you?"

"No," said Jinjur. "I won't forget. Now will you get to your quarters?"

"Sure," said Alan, greatly relieved. He started to salute, then stopped and grinned. "Us generals don't have to salute each other, do we?"

"No," said Jinjur. "Except in special cases, like when we are saying good-bye for a long time."

Alan turned and awkwardly made his way out her door.

"Go right to your room now!" she reminded him.

"Right!" said Alan with a glance back at her. He neglected to palm her door shut, and she heard him as he started to whistle. The tune continued as he jumped up to the next crew deck, made his way around the railing circling the lift shaft, and palmed open his door with a loud splat. The whistle was cut off in mid-note by the swish of his door as it closed. Jinjur was sure she knew the tune, but her brain seemed to resist finding the name. She had to ask James.

"It is from an ancient Disney movie," James informed her. "The title is: 'When You Wish Upon a Star.'"

"I've got to get him off this ship!" Jinjur said as she palmed her door shut and flicked her fingers furiously over the screen of her console. "There's something wrong with the way that guy thinks. I've *got* to get him off my ship!"

Two days later General Jones spoke to her imp.

"Set up a direct link to General Armstrong, and turn up the volume," she commanded.

She heard a rapid breathing and the sound of a brush running briskly through short hair.

"General Alan Armstrong," she barked, and a flash of satisfaction flickered over her face as she heard a sharp gasp before the spoken response. James must have set the volume at maximum and its imp was shouting her voice into his ear.

"Yes, General Jones?" came the hesitant reply.

"I want you in my room in five minutes!" she commanded.

"Yes'm," came the prompt reply. She could hear him sliding back the door to his storage closet. She moved her fingers up near her imp, twisted them in the air like they were turning down an invisible volume control knob, and the imp, interpreting the signal, turned off the link.

Jinjur padded her way into her bedroom area, changed the view-wall into a mirror with a flick of her fingertip, and looked her image over critically. Many a dressing-down had lost its impact when the inflictor had neglected dressing-up for the occasion. She was in a freshly-pressed Space Marine uniform, designed and tailored to look impressive even in the wishy-washy environment of free-fall. It looked like the regulation summer dress shirt and tie in Gyrene green, but there were subtle patches of elastic and velcro that kept everything properly tucked away on its proper position on the body even after strenuous exercise in zero gee. Two stars glistened on each collar and across her left chest was a thin metal board containing the full panoply of ribbons she had become entitled to during her many years in the Ground and Space Marines.

The one she was most proud of was the special Presidential Citation she had received when she was just a lieutenant. Seemingly stuck forever in an assignment at the Women's Section of the Marine Corps Training Camp in San Diego, she had despaired of ever seeing any action when the action came to her. One weekend every fuel distributor in Southern California went on strike over a special transportation tax. After two days, all air, car, bus, train, and small ship traffic in or out of San Diego had stopped. Within hours, hungry bands of frustrated tourists had formed into riotous mobs. The President foolishly flew into this mess to "investigate." Shortly after landing at Lindbergh Field in San Diego, Air Force One was surrounded by angry mobs of affluent voters. They got uglier and uglier as they absorbed booze stolen from ransacked liquor stores. The Secret Service and Lindbergh Field Security were still arguing about what to do when Jinjur took over. At her order, holes were cut in the fence between the Marine Base and Lindbergh Field. Her parade-ground voice reverberating from barracks wall to barracks wall, she soon had every female recruit out in formation in tee shirts, shorts, and sneakers. She handed out pugil sticks and wooden drill rifles, formed her command into a narrow flying wedge, herself at the point, and with the strange chant of "Excuse me, please. Excuse me, please," the troop of nubile young women easily penetrated the mostly male mob, formed a protective circle five women deep about Air Force One, and led the President off to safety in their nearby barracks. It had meant a ribbon, an instant promotion to captain, and the start of the meteoric rise of one of the best line commanders in all the services.

There is one thing a good commanding officer never does, and that is to let misfits get away with insurrection and insubordination. Jinjur strode out into her lounge and palmed the bedroom door shut. She set the view-wall to show a static background consisting of the Official Seals of GNASA and the Secretary of Defense. Below the seals was her official major general's flag with its two stars. She stood in front of the view-wall at parade rest and waited. Court was in session and the judge was impatiently waiting for the defendant to arrive so she could sentence him up the river.

There was a firm knock on the door.

General Jones called out, "Come in."

General Armstrong palmed open the door and entered. The door slid shut again, closing off the view of two inquisitive faces peering into the room as they drifted upward past the door. Armstrong was in an Air Force blue version of the uniform that General Jones wore, although with fewer ribbons and a single bright new star on his collar points. His handsome face broke into his most charming smile as he tiptoed in on his velcro corridor boots and gave a formal salute and a perfunctory "General Armstrong reporting, Ma'am." Looking behind him, he started to sit down on the lounge seat.

"At attention, General!" she barked. His smile dropped

as he stumbled, lost contact with the carpet, then scrambled around in midair until he had planted both feet together onto the floor and stood at attention, his body swaying lightly as his rigid muscles attempted to maintain verticality in a room that almost had no vertical.

She stared up at him for a minute, her cold glance peering over his whitened cheeks that seemed to have lost their famed dimples. His eyes were properly staring straight ahead, right over her head and straight into the two-starred flag on the view-wall. She broke her parade rest position to stride two steps to the right, turned carefully around without losing her firm footgrip on the carpet, then paced back again. For the first five steps she didn't say anything, then she spoke.

"General Armstrong, I called you in here today to tell you that I have made a decision that is going to affect you and your career. The decision has been made, approved all the way up to the President, and the actions to initiate it began many hours ago. The decision is irrevocable, and nothing you say or do can prevent it. I felt the least I could do is to explain in detail why I have taken this decision, so that's why I called you here.

"Now it may not have occurred to your pinquito-bean-sized brain that we are on a dangerous scientific voyage, not some nerdling Pentagon paperchase where pusillanimous wit and a few judicious backstabbings can ensure a rapid advance up the ladder.

"For too long you have survived on those watery blue eyes with their waddy-wiping eyelashes, that baby-bottom face, and the hunk of musclebound meat you call a body. You've survived so long on your looks that you have lost your brain and your soul." She stopped pacing and turned to yell at the frigid figure.

"What do think we're living in!?! A pot-boiler science fiction novel . . . with good guys and bad guys, personal feuds, treachery, and insubordination?

"That kind of nonsense may be necessary in stories where the scenery is so dull the characters must struggle with each other to get some action going. In the real world of space missions, it's the deadly scenery of space that

produces the action, and the characters must work together as a team to overcome it. If the characters start
fighting each other, that almost inevitably leads to danger
and death. There may be room for troublemakers in the
movies, but there's no room for one in this mission."

There was a pause as they both felt the small amount of
acceleration from the laser-driven sail stop. Armstrong
broke his rigid position slightly to glance down at General
Jones's face.

"The laser drive was stopped four hours ago," she reported solemnly. "I've aborted the mission and there's an
ion ship coming out with your replacement."

"But . . ." started Armstrong.

"SILENCE!!!" roared Jinjur, and Armstrong resumed
his rigid stance, eyes straight ahead.

"In case those elfin ears of yours didn't hear, or in case
that midget brain of yours is so small that your ears can't
find it in that vacuum-filled swollen skull of yours, I told
you at the start that this decision was irrevocable. No
amount of flattering words from those pouty lips and no
pleading glances from that imitation-Adonis face is going
to change it. It's going to cost GNASA over two hundred
million dollars to replace you, but it's going to be worth
every cent. We found someone qualified on Titan, only
ten AU away, but even at one gee it will take them nearly
a week to get here."

Jinjur stopped her tirade, and her voice changed from
that of an annoyed commander to that of an administrator
patiently explaining a dull plan to a dull subordinate.

"The official story for the record is that the mumps that
you picked up from me had such a permanent debilitating
effect on your body that it is now doubtful that you would
survive the flight phase of the mission without extensive
medical care. For your own benefit we will be transferring
you back to Earth where you can receive the medical care
that you will need. With a medical discharge from the
mission, you should be able to reestablish contacts with
your Pentagon pals.

"You are to stay in quarantine. You will have contact
with the rest of the crew only through James. I would

suggest you not try anything funny. James is programed to 'interrupt' anything blatantly subversive, and I'll be monitoring everything you say. I'm letting you off with this medical excuse since you were put up to it by Winthrop, but try anything funny before your replacement comes and everyone will know that you were kicked off the mission and why. That would be the end of you and probably Winthrop. Do you understand me, Armstrong?"

"Yes, General Jones."

There was a rustle at the door, and the Christmas Bush trotted in holding a plastic decontamination suit. Jinjur took it and handed it to Armstrong.

"Put this on, General. The Christmas Bush will lead you to your room. You're to stay there until your replacement arrives, and you're to wear the suit when you leave.

"I feel sorry for you, Alan. For the sake of some points in a game of interoffice politics, you blew a chance to be one of the legendary heroes of the human race." She watched Alan don the suit. Then silently, the Christmas Bush leading, he floated out the door.

She saluted the departing back. *Small minds have small goals,* she thought sadly. She turned and pushed herself back to the view-wall controls where she arranged a waterfall scene to replace the forbidding courtroom wall. She then asked James to call a crew meeting in the lounge to explain why the light drive had stopped.

"That's right, Operator. Carmen Cortez calling Señora Cortez, Mexico City, Area Code 905–876–1432.

"Hello, Mom. This is Carmen . . . I'm calling from the Space Station on Titan, Mom . . . It will take ninety minutes before I can hear what you say, so just listen for a while. Now, Mom, don't panic. It doesn't cost anything. The Space Agency is paying for the call.

"Mom, do you remember the story in the newspapers about the plans to send a human crew to the star called Barnard? One of the crew has gotten sick or something, and I was backup. I never thought I would get a chance to be on this mission, but now I'm going. Yes, Mom, I'm taking another trip into space with a bunch of people.

There will be twenty of us—including some men. I know you don't approve, since there will be no chaperons, but it will be all right. Mom, I *will* be good. Don't worry." Carmen pushed the off button and went to the lounge for a drink. Even the kaleidoscopic evening sky of Titan didn't attract her attention while she thought through what she would say next. Three hours later she was back at the communications console. She waited through the interminable crackling and thunder. Finally her mother was on the phone, asking questions.

"When will I be back? Mom, I'm going to be all right, but the trip is going to take a long time. No, I'm afraid I won't be back for Rose's birthday. Mom, you've got to understand that a trip to the stars takes a long, long time . . . many years. Mom . . . I won't be coming back . . . ever. It just takes so long, that I will be too old to come back." She didn't know what else to say. Tears welling in her eyes, she viciously jabbed the comm-off button. Three hours later she was back again, eyes still red.

"Mom . . . Please don't cry . . . Mom . . . I do *too* love you . . . Mom! I've *got* to go to the stars!"

A week later, James reported that it had the ion ship in sight on radar. A few hours later the ship had rendezvoused with *Prometheus* and two space-suited figures interchanged places. As the new crew member came through the hatch, it was obvious that the new suit was much smaller than the one that had exited.

Jinjur watched as the excited crew of *Prometheus* gathered around the hatch.

"There is one thing that I will never forgive that petty-minded brain of yours, Alan. It took away from us women one beautiful hunk of man—and gave us this . . ."

A curvaceous brunette wiggled out of her spacesuit. Her tailored jumpsuit tightly covered an ample bust and rounded hips connected by a wasp-waist that Jinjur had long since lost. The new member of the crew was very young, only 28 years old. She had been in training for the second mission that was leaving for Alpha Centauri in about three years.

"Hi, everybody!" she said cheerfully, her coquettish eyelashes batting unconsciously at all the males. "I'm Carmen."

"May a perpetual plague of pimples prey on your pubescent proboscis, Alan!" murmured Jinjur under her breath. "I could forgive you the troubles you caused. I could forgive you the two hundred million dollars it cost. But I'll never forgive you for lousing up the sex ratio. It's now eleven females to nine males." She went forward to greet the new crew member as Carmen gave a little sneeze.

"Excuse me!" said Carmen, "I seemed to have picked up a little cold from one of the crew on the ion ship." She looked around, bewildered at the chorus of groans.

TRAVELING

For almost a year the lightship accelerated outward, slowly gaining speed under the constant thrust of the thousand beams of laser light. They were at three hundred astronomical units, ten times farther out than the most distant of the solar system planets. The lightship was now moving at one percent of the speed of light, but it would have to accelerate for nineteen more years before it got up to its coast velocity of twenty percent of the speed of light. They were now far enough away to start using the full potential of their solar-system-sized flashlight.

The lasers in orbit around Mercury flickered off one by one. Their pointing mirrors, which had been tracking a moon-sized speck of sail beyond the solar system, now reconfigured their surfaces to focus on a nearby object— the laser beam combiner out at the L-2 point of Mercury. Once again the sunlight reflected from the thousand large light collectors was injected into the thousand block-long lasers in orbit about the innermost planet. Glowing warmly, the lasers burst into bloom. Their beams of invisible radiance converged on a glistening spiderweb that sent the beams on to where they met side-by-side in a crystal-clear cavern of index of refraction, to later emerge as a single coherent beam of pulsating light. Bouncing off a mirror, the light sped outward away from the Sun, channeling the terawatts of Sun-power out into the cold of deep space. It

traveled for two hours before it reached the first of its
targets—the transmitter lens, drifting out in space between Saturn and Uranus.

A thermal sensor on the top side of a mechanical spider
noticed an increase in the temperature of the sun-facing
portion of the mechanism it was monitoring. The change
in temperature was duly noted and passed on to the control center at the next engineering check period. Although
the temperature increase was significant, it was still well
within the design limits for the mechanism. The spider
continued laying down the thin layer of plastic sheeting
between the spoke threads that stretched out ahead of it
for hundreds of kilometers. The huge spiderweb was only
partially completed, but the finished central portion was
adequate for the purpose, and its alternating rings of plastic and nothing sufficed to capture all of the powerful laser
beam and send it out of the solar system toward a distant
speck of aluminum reflectance.

Two days later most of the crew were down on the
control deck, watching the screens showing the output of
an infrared telescope focused on the inner solar system.
Slowly the bright glare from a point near the Sun faded
away as the lasers were turned off one by one, leaving only
the Sun on the screen. As the blinding searchlight glare
faded away, the crew could feel a lightening under their
corridor boots.

The crew waited for the hour it took to reconfigure the
laser mirror systems, then they drifted back to the floor as
the laser beam relit and the sail billowed again under the
light pressure. The light beam was now coming from the
transmitter lens, a point far from the Sun in the outer solar
system.

"We're finally on our way," said Jinjur. "I guess it's
time."

Everyone looked uncomfortable.

"I wonder if we'll notice it?" asked George.

"According to most clinical studies of No-Die," said
Doctor Wang. "The effects come on so gradually that most
users have no idea they are mentally impaired, unless they

are asked to do some difficult task. But even then, there is a tendency to believe it is only because they are 'tired' or 'sick,' not because the No-Die has slowed their mental processes."

"I'll be just as happy to be fooled," said Jinjur. "I don't think I could stand knowing I was a drooling idiot."

"It won't be that bad," said Dr. Wang. "We all have high IQ's to begin with. Even when we are reduced to twenty-five percent of normal, we'll still be high-grade imbeciles and can probably even button our own clothing."

David noticed some disgusted expressions and tried to cheer them up.

"Besides, even if we forget how to tell our right shoe from our left, we still have 'Mother' James and the Christmas Bush to take care of us. It can button our shirts, tie our shoes, and wipe our noses."

Jinjur spoke to her imp. "Start putting the No-Die in the water, James."

"It is done," replied a low whisper.

"All of a sudden I don't feel very thirsty anymore," said Sam. "I think I'll go up to my room and open my last bottle of Scotch. Anyone for a drink—straight?" He ambled over under the lift shaft hole in the ceiling, and crouching his two-meter-high body low, leaped upwards. He was followed by five others.

Meanwhile Jinjur made her way to the galley. George was there, filling his monogrammed drink flask from the water spout. Beneath George's name on the flask was a picture of a T–33 trainer. He glanced up at Jinjur's approach.

"I thought I'd get a head start," said George. "At fifty-two I need to slow down fast if I'm going to make it to Barnard. Suddenly I feel old. I'm afraid that I'll die on the way out there and miss out on all the fun of exploring."

"You're not so old, George," Jinjur said softly. "At least you still have all your hair, and it's beautiful." She brushed her stubby black fingers through the gray waves on George's head and grabbing a handful, gave his head a friendly shake. She turned, lifted her drink-ball, with its two stars and the monogram "THE BOSS," from its place in the rack and filled it from the coffee spout.

"I don't think I could stomach drinking just water, knowing what's in it. At least this way I can blame the taste on the ersatz coffee flavor." She took a deep draught, held the hot liquid in her mouth for a moment, hesitating, then deliberately swallowed. She looked up at George slowly sipping away at his flask of water.

"I hear that this stuff slows everything down. Even your sex drive."

"That's right," said George. "It's one of the first things to go."

"Rowrbazzle!" Jinjur said softly.

"What?" asked George.

"Just swearing," said Jinjur. "Like a good general I've been keeping myself under control, since it doesn't do to have the boss sleeping around with the troops. Now that we're underway and there's nothing to do but coast, I'll soon forget that there's any difference between boys and girls."

"I can still tell the difference," said George. He reached over to her well-stuffed shirt and grabbed the button under the most strain. "Girls button their shirts the wrong way." His fingers slowly and deliberately undid the button to release the tension.

She grinned at him and reaching up to her chest took his hand in hers. "I'm sure there are other differences," she said. "Let's go up to my room and see if we can find them."

"Let's do a scientific experiment," said David. "Why don't we have a chess tournament. That way we can monitor our mental level. James can keep track. It has the Chess 9.6 program stored in it. It's got a grandmaster rating."

"Count me out," said Richard. "I played in college a little but I'm not at that level."

"James can adjust the program to different levels of skill," said David.

"OK," acquiesced Richard. "Not much else to do anyway."

"It might even be scientifically valuable," said Dr. Wang. "This is the first time such a large group of people under similar environmental conditions have been taking No-Die at the same time. I'll have James keep track and save it for later analysis. I may even get a paper out of this one for the *Journal of Psychology*."

"You forget, Dr. Wang," said George. "By the time James collects a significant amount of data, you won't be in any condition to analyze it."

Dr. Wang put on a serious expression, as if he were finally realizing for the first time what he was facing. He shrugged and sighed. "I guess I'll have James transmit the results of the experiment back. Someone else will have to write the paper."

"We can't be playing chess all the time," said Shirley. "We *do* have some things we're supposed to do, even if most of them are makework."

"One game a day with James should be enough," said. Dr. Wang. "Just plan a 'chess hour' right after you've had your sleep-shift. You should be at your best then. But the exact time is not important, just that it be consistent."

"I think I'll start right now," said David. He pulled himself up to a console. As he was wiggling in the seat to firmly attach the sticky patch on the back of his jumpsuit to the console chair, the screen flashed and there was a full-color display of a chess set in perspective.

"White or black?" asked James. "And what level of play?"

"I'm brave enough to take you at full grandmaster level, James," said David. "But I'll take white just to be on the safe side."

The board rotated in space and David reached out a finger to a pawn on the screen and gave it a push. It was immediately countered by another pawn. A few more pushes, a move of a knight and a bishop, and the game was underway.

"I wonder why I ever had us play these silly games every day," said Dr. Wang. "I'm bored with this board game." He gave a delighted chuckle at his joke. "Get it, James? As a board game it's boring."

"Yes. A real pun, William," said James. "Your last move,

however, has a slight problem. When you castle on the queen's side, you are supposed to move the rook three spaces and the king two spaces, not three spaces for the king."

Dr. Wang looked at the board on the screen and frowned. The king and rook were blinking, indicating an erroneous move. He shook his head and said in an annoyed voice, "Well—fix them!" The pieces were put into their proper place and James made his move. Still angry with himself, Dr. Wang jabbed a finger at a piece on the screen and moved it forward.

James muttered a polite machine cough. "Are you sure you want to make that move?"

Dr. Wang looked carefully at the screen, bewildered. He couldn't see anything wrong. The piece he moved was certainly not in any danger. "Yes. I'm sure," he said, and was relieved to see James move his queen somewhere else on the board, leaving his piece untouched. He moved again. Then it was James's turn. A rook slid across the screen into his back row.

"Checkmate," said James.

David Greystoke slid into the console chair and wiggled his back onto the sticky patch. It had been two weeks since the chess "tournament" had started and he had done well. Six games out of fourteen, although he suspected that James had lowered his level of playing from the grandmaster level. He had never asked how low. Didn't want to know, really.

"Ready, James," he said. "But just to make it interesting, let's you take blue and I take pink. Pink moves first."

Instantly, the black and white pieces on the screen changed to blue and pink.

"Hmmm," thought David to himself. "I think I'll try a defensive opening." He pushed the rook's pawn on the queen's side forward two spaces. James countered with a move of its king's pawn. Wanting to build up a triangle of pawns as a wall, David pushed the knight's pawn forward on the same side. James moved its queen out to sit in front of the pawn row.

"Now to beef up the triangle," said David under his breath. He hopped the knight up into the upper corner. James moved his bishop up as if to threaten the rapidly building defense formation. It stopped short of the wall by a square. It could have taken the knight, but the rook was protecting it. David grinned internally at his cleverness in making sure his knight was protected. He reached out to touch the pink-colored bishop next to his pink queen and slid it diagonally forward to fill up the inner wall of the defensive triangle.

"Are you sure you want to make that move?" asked James.

David looked carefully at the board. The right-hand side of his line of pieces had been untouched, and they were still as impregnable as they had been at the beginning of the game. His left bishop was uncovered, but there was no piece within striking distance, and besides, after James made its next move, he would move the queen over to form the third line of defense. Then, after a castle, his defensive fort would be completed.

"Sure," he replied. "You're in for a long hard game, James."

The blue queen slid slowly forward through the empty battleground on David's right and entered his front line, taking the pawn in front of the king's bishop.

"Fool's mate," said James.

"James is no fun to play chess with," complained Jinjur. "That old game is too stuffy. I wanna play a tough game with lots of hard things." She and George were sitting on either side of a table in the lounge and she was moving the pieces around on the board. She put all the pawns to one side.

"Those are dumb pieces. Can't do anything except stumble forward." She took the other pieces and put them on the black squares of the first two rows.

"I'll call this Super-Chess," she said. "It'll be a hunnerd times harder than chess. All the pieces are bishops and can only move diagonally, and when they meet an enemy they jump over them and take them. Then if they get to the back row they get made into queens, and can jump backward and forward."

George followed her example and soon the two of them were having the time of their lives.

"Double jump!" hollered George. "Got you that time Jinjur. Now you have to give me a kiss!"

"No! That wasn't part of the game. I made up the rules and that wasn't part of the game."

"It is now!" said George. "C'mon, you gotta give me a kiss."

Jinjur squealed as George reached clumsily for her. She swept the pieces off the table in her scramble to get away from the pest. The pieces tumbled through the air, to settle slowly to the floor, where a busy Christmas Bush found them and put them back in the toy chest.

"What'cha doin', Jinny?" asked William. He gazed vacantly at the black smudges that Jinjur was marking on the floor, wall, and ceiling of the exercise room with a black crayon. They were big squares—big enough to stand in.

"Making a chess game," said Jinjur, marking up another square, and staying inside the lines most of the time.

"On the ceiling?" asked Dr. Wang.

"Sure, Billy," she said. "This is going to be the neatest chess game ever. Three-dibenshenal."

"Three dibensinal?" asked Dr. Wang.

"You know. Three-D. Up and down and sideways," she replied. "See. I'll show you." She stood in one of the crayoned squares. "Each one of us will be a chess piece, and we can jump any way we want." She jumped to the mat hanging on one wall. Her feet, clad in corridor boots with sticky bottoms, slammed into the wall and she stuck there. She then slowly pulled herself to the wall by bending her knees, then jumped to the ceiling, where she stuck again. She hung downward in the light gravity.

"Tell the rest of the gang to come here," she said. "Then we can all play."

"OK, Jinny," he said, and started out the door.

"And tell them they'd better come," she hollered after

him. "Or I'll tell James to turn off their cartoons. After all, I'm the boss."

Soon fifteen of the crew were bouncing around the exercise room, playing 3-D "chess."

"I jumped you, Richie," screamed Jinjur. "I'm the boss and I say I jumped you first."

"No, you didn't!" hollered Richard. "I jumped you first. Didn't I, Georgie?"

"I'm jumping you *both* now," said George. "So you're both out and I win."

"No, you didn't! You cheater!" screamed Jinjur, so mad that she was jumping back and forth from the ceiling to the floor, making a half-somersault each time.

"I am not a cheater," replied George, getting angry. "You're the cheater."

"Cheater! Cheater! Georgie is a cheater!" sang Jinjur as she backed away and pushed herself out the door.

"I'll get you, Jinny," said George, moving after her as fast as he could go in the low gravity. "I'll get you yet."

The game broke up with everyone following along as George, his face livid with anger at the insult, chased after Jinjur. The chase took them all the way up the lift shaft, around the hydroponics tanks and back down the shaft again. By the time everyone had reached the living area deck again, they were all tired. Their imps buzzed in their ears.

"Time for a rest, everyone," said James. "I've got a nice movie for you to watch. It's an old Road Runner cartoon that you haven't seen before."

"Oh! Boy! A Road Runner cartoon!" exclaimed Shirley. She led the way to the theater. The crew settled down in a heap on the long bench seats as the music started and the video wall flickered into life. George was exhausted and lay back to rest. He was probably going to go to sleep before the cartoon was over, and he fought to keep his eyes open. Somebody lying half on him moved to a new position and his view was blocked. It was Jinjur. Her shirt had come unbuttoned while she was racing through the ship and James had not made sure that she had put on all her underclothing before letting her out of her room.

George stared at the large black mound blocking his vision. Grunting, he pulled it down with one hand and rested his cheek on it. He could see the cartoon now, and the soft part of Jinjur made a good pillow. He soon fell asleep.

Senator Beauregard Darlington Winthrop III was in his third term of office, and as Chairman of the Senate Appropriations Committee he wielded an influence only slightly less potent than the Senate Majority Leader. GNASA officials winced when they heard that budget-hearing time was coming around again.

"Now. Ah'm sure you honorable gentlemen realize that this nation, as rich and as glorious as it is, cannot afford every space boondoggle there is. Ah trust that you've come up with a budget that realizes that there are people here on the ground that desperately need money to keep their family businesses alive . . ."

"He probably means subsidies for the tobacco farmers," thought the Honorable Leroy Fresh, as he prepared to defend GNASA's budget before the committee.

"There is one item that the Chairman noticed in the preliminary reports that he would like to question the Honorable Dr. Fresh about, if he may." Without waiting for a reply, Winthrop continued. "I notice this line-item number one hundred eight, for four hundred million dollars to expand the transmitter lens for the Barnard laser propulsion system. I didn't notice that in the previous year's budget, and since the mission is not slated to reach Barnard for another twenty years or so, surely this item could be deferred a year or two to release a few funds to succor the poor people of this nation?"

Leroy was ready for this one. "May I remind the Chairman, the reason the item was not in last year's budget was that it was removed by the Senate Appropriations Committee, as the committee has done each year for nearly the past decade. The transmitter lens doesn't have to be full size at the start of the mission, and can be built slowly as time passes and the Barnard expedition moves farther away, but the lens must be made ready for the deceleration phase, which requires it to be at maximum diameter. The amount of money in the budget is that needed to bring us back on schedule."

"But the lasers are turned off, and the Barnard lightsail is merely coasting on its way to its destination. Surely we can defer work on the lens expansion since it's not being used. Especially since I notice in line-item one hundred ten the fifty million dollars for the construction of the Tau Ceti lens. The increase in diameter planned for each lens is fifty kilometers. Surely that indicates that they should have equal budgets. Perhaps we should just make those two lens-construction items both equal in size at fifty million?" Senator Winthrop looked around at his committee and smiled.

"Is that agreeable, gentlemen? . . . Oh, yes. Excuse me, Madam Ledbetter. Is that agreeable, gentlemen and lady?" He raised a blue pencil and scratched away at his copy of the budget.

"But Senator Winthrop, sir," Leroy protested. "The Ceti lens is going from a diameter of twenty kilometers to seventy kilometers, while the Barnard lens is going from three hundred and twenty to three hundred and seventy kilometers. Even though both have the same increase in diameter, the increase in area of the Barnard lens is eight times larger than that of the Ceti lens. The cost goes as the square of the diameter."

"Well, Ah must admit Ah'm a little 'square' when it comes to that scientific math, Dr. Fresh, but Ah'm pretty good at figures when they have a dollar sign in front of them." There was a polite laugh at the Chairman's joke from the committee and staff. Fresh was silent, knowing that he had lost another skirmish. "After all," said Senator Winthrop with a smile that seemed entirely sincere over the TV cameras. "That's what we have you scientific types at GNASA for, to take care of all that 'square root' and 'cube root' type math stuff. And Ah must say," he said, with only a trace of sarcasm, "you've been doing an excellent job on an austere budget—like the true Greater American patriots that you are. Now, let's go on to line-item one hundred thirty-three, the million-channel receiver to search for signals from aliens. Surely a single channel is all that you need. It's obvious. One receiving antenna, one receiving channel . . ."

"Carmen's got the mumps! Carmen's got the mumps!" teased Billy. He bounced after her and attempted to jab his sharp skinny fingers into the plump jowls of his curvaceous playmate. James admonished him to stop through his imp, but it took the Christmas Bush to separate them. The Bush paused to allow its sensors to look carefully at the thin young man with the brain of a child. There was something bothering him.

"But she's got the mumps," Billy protested. "And she should stand still while I poke them, since I'm the doctor."

"I will take care of Carmen," replied James, then noticing the disturbed look on Billy's face, it softened the rest of its response.

"But if you promise not to tease Carmen any more, I'll let you play Dr. Wang and help me," said James.

Billy contorted his face at the seldom-used title. He seemed to go into a trance as he tried to marshal his weakened brain to place on the tip of his tongue what many months of nagging thought had been trying to bring to the surface.

"Not mumps . . . Ho-Ha-Hansen . . ." His normally clear yellow cheeks grew flush with the effort to find the word.

"Hansen's disease? No, Billy, that's leprosy. Carmen does not have leprosy," James said firmly.

"Ha-Ho-Hodge . . ." said Billy determinedly.

"Hodgkin's disease," intoned James. "Cancer of the lymph glands."

"Yeah!" said Billy, beaming at having been relieved of the responsibility of trying to think anymore. Good ol' James would take care of things now. He returned to his normal self and bounced out the door, alternating between floor, wall, and ceiling in the zero gravity, leaving a stationary Christmas Bush in the playroom. The incessant play of lights from its many strands was strangely subdued, as though its master computer was busy analyzing years of accumulated medical data and trying to fit them into a pattern.

James had been programmed to look for changes in the health of the crew. It had measured and reported every tiny detail of response of each of the twenty human bodies entrusted to its care under the unusual combination of weightlessness and the still experimental drug No-Die. Even now, the latest strange behavior of Billy—Dr. Wang— had been recorded and duly transmitted. It would reach the medical monitors on Earth in a little over two years. Any recommendation they might make on that unusual outburst would be received by James back at *Prometheus* another three years later, for the lightship was moving away from the solar system at one-fifth of a light-year per year and the distance from *Prometheus* to Earth was widening rapidly.

After thinking for two hours, James completed its evaluation. Billy, trying to act as Dr. Wang would have, had come to a tentative diagnosis that Carmen Cortez had Hodgkin's disease, a usually fatal glandular cancer. Hodgkin's disease usually starts in the neck glands, but then spreads to the other glands and the spleen. Carmen certainly showed the initial signs of the disease—a swollen neck gland. Yet according to the medical documentation in James's files, the disease only struck one out of one hundred thousand in any population, while nineteen out of the twenty people onboard *Prometheus* had swollen neck glands, including Billy. It was obvious from the high statistical correlation that the swollen glands were due to the strange combination of years in free-fall and years on the body-disrupting drug No-Die. There was no need for James to be concerned.

By his fifth term in the Senate, Winthrop had developed a very effective and loyal cadre of "monitors." They were not "informers" in the usual sense, since they only did their duty as they saw it. Just because Senator Winthrop would often hear of their concerns before they told their immediate supervisors in the federal bureaucracy did not seem important. After all, Senator Winthrop was a senator. Besides, he always took good care of those who assisted him in monitoring the slackers and hoodlums who would disrupt the smooth flow of government.

One day Winthrop heard a buzzer attached to the gray telephone that reposed in the bottom drawer of his desk. As he pulled the drawer open and lifted the receiver, he carefully listened to the conversation taking place between the caller and Ernest Masterson, one of his personal aides. Ernest was quizzing the caller, knowing that the senator was probably listening while at the same time looking at a "Reagan-raster" display Ernest had prepared for him. The three-line liquid-crystal display gave the name of the caller, his present position in the federal bureaucracy, and a short summary of why he had called.

JAMES MALLOY (Son of Billy Roy Malloy, Myrtle Beach.)
GNASA Deep Space Network, Barnard Mission
Medical problem with crew.

It took only a second for Senator Winthrop to remember that he had recommended young Jimmy Malloy for a job many years ago. The young man had been deeply grateful at the time, especially since he was black and he and his dad had never expected to receive anything from a honky, especially a multi-descended white aristocrat like Winthrop. But Winthrop was neither altruistic nor dumb. Jimmy's daddy, Billy Roy, had pasted together a black-Jewish political combine that had run Myrtle Beach for nearly two decades, and in the process had kept that city clean of street, clean of beach, clean of violence, and clean of debt. Winthrop admired a man like that, even if he was a Negro. Billy Roy's boy, Jimmy, had all the smarts of his old man, but wanted to go into space instead. Winthrop had used his influence to help, and had already collected from Jimmy's dad in his last election, when only the late votes from Myrtle Beach had saved him from an ignominious defeat for his fourth term. Jimmy didn't need to know that, for Winthrop had visited him personally nearly a decade ago and had used his massive presence, Sistine mane of hair, and commanding manner to recruit young Jimmy into his network of monitors.

"As a 'monitor,' you are not expected to do anything that would be in conflict with your normal job. However, if you hear or see something that would be of concern to the *Senate of the Greater United States* (Winthrop always dropped into his declaiming voice at that point), you should call and let my office know so that we can be prepared to take the appropriate action."

Jimmy Malloy was quite impressed with his important mission and with the personal attention that the senior senator from South Carolina had lavished on him. He never forgot it and even turned down two promotions to stay in a position where he would be able to intercept the information that the senator needed.

Winthrop heard the voices coming from his desk drawer and listened carefully. Ernest was doing his job. Not admitting that Winthrop was there and trying to make sure that the call was worth bothering the senator with, even if it had come in over one of his confidential lines.

"Could I please have you repeat that again, Mr. Malloy," said Ernest.

"The Barnard crew is dying of cancer," came the strained voice, a mixture of cool, calm space-controller combined with the frantic worry of someone who has tied his whole life up into monitoring the future of twenty brave people, and now those people had no future.

"I'm here, Masterson," said Winthrop. He waited for a click that indicated that Ernest had cut off his connection while continuing to record the input side of the conversation. (Winthrop had learned from Nixon. There were no records of Winthrop's voice. Let them learn what they may from the caller's side of the conversation.)

"This is SENATOR WINTHROP, Jimmy. How's your father? And what can I do for you today?"

"Just fine, sir," said Jimmy. "I just wanted to tell you that there is something wrong on the Barnard starship *Prometheus.*"

"WHAT?!" demanded Winthrop, putting on his senator voice.

"I . . . I think it's cancer, sir," came the hesitant reply.

Winthrop thought for a moment. In a crew of twenty over a period of twenty years, it was not surprising to have one of the crew members come down with cancer. It was worth knowing, but not really something to tie up his grey-line network with. Still, Jimmy had been helpful, and he didn't want to lose his carefully cultivated sources.

"Ah want to thank you for your report, Jimmy. Ah appreciate it. Please let me know if anything else happens, but as for this crew member, Ah guess it would be just as good if we let any further reports on his progress trickle in through regular channels."

"Oh! But it isn't a him, sir. It's a her. Actually, it's nearly all of them."

"All of them?" echoed Winthrop.

"Yessir, Senator Winthrop, that's what the report says, nearly all of them have a fatal cancer. Hoskin's disease, or something like that."

Winthrop looked at the sender end of the gray telephone handpiece. "All of them?" Winthrop said again.

"All but one," admitted Jimmy Malloy.

"Who is the one?" said Winthrop, braced to hear that one name that he despised the most. It would be just like that goddamned Gudunov to be the one to escape the plague.

"Don't know, sir," said Jimmy, trying to be as helpful as he could. "But I'll look into it and let you know."

"Thanks, Jimmy," said Winthrop. "You've been a real help, and Ah'll let your daddy know." He hung up and leaned back in his swivel chair to stare up at the ceiling. The fluorescent fixture had a bunch of dead flies lying on its diffuser. He counted them. There were nineteen, with a single live one buzzing erratically among the drying corpses of its comrades.

Senator Winthrop asked for video time from the networks. With his political stature he could have gotten a half-hour on prime time except during Monday Night Football. As it was, he only asked for fifteen minutes of Sunday morning Bible-Belt time. It was readily granted despite the protests of some airways' ministers who had been counting on the "free-will" offerings that they would have generated during that time.

The publicity that Winthrop organized before his speech was effective. Priests and ministers preached to empty pews, and golf links heard the chirp of birds instead of the plop of birdies. Everyone got up on that Sunday morning and turned on their video.

Winthrop was quiet as the camera picked him up, standing in front of an ordinary wood podium. He stood majestic and solemn as the announcer's voice intoned. "Senator Beauregard Darlington Winthrop the Third."

The senator looked out from the screen with a stern visage. A low backlight on his mane of pure-white hair gave his head a halo of light. His voice started low and slow.

"A score and two years ago this nation sent forth its sons and daughters into the black void of chaos—deliberately casting the lives of their children away in a grandiose suicide mission. Ah struggled, Ah fought, Ah pleaded, Ah prayed—to get that mission halted so that the lives of those dear people could be spared.

"It was all for naught . . . Smiling happily the twenty went cheerfully to their deaths."

His voice grew louder and sterner as his accusations rang from the echoing walls of the empty studio. "Not since the barbarous days of the Children's Crusades, when tiny tots were shipped off in boats to slavery and death, have the leaders of a people so betrayed those who trusted them. It was not the engineers who turned on the lasers that are to blame, it was not the planners in GNASA who authorized the mission that are to blame, it was not the leaders of this country that are to blame, it was you!" His stern finger rose abruptly and jabbed at the screen.

"You! The people of this country who allowed this to happen. You are the sinners and you are being punished. Yes, Ah said, 'You are being punished.' Right now. This very instant. And for an eternity of instants in the future. You say you don't feel any different? You aren't hurting? You aren't being punished? But Ah say you are, and Ah have proof of it right here." Winthrop grabbed a handful of papers off the podium and crumpling them into a splayed sheaf, he shook them at the screen.

"Personal pain and torment is too good for murderers such as you are. Instead, the pain and endless torture that should rightfully be yours are being visited right now on your innocent victims. Every single one of the crew on *Prometheus* has developed a hideous form of cancer called Hodgkin's disease. The cancer first attacks the glands. They swell painfully. It's like having mumps, but worse, for you never get better. The swelling spreads to all the glands in your body, then the rest of your organs. Then finally comes the slow and painful death."

There was a long pause as Winthrop slowly bent his head, shook it a few times in sorrow, then slowly lifted it up. The expression on his face had changed to that of firm determination.

"The doctors don't understand how so many people can catch the same kind of cancer at the same time. Ah say to those doctors that Ah can understand it only too well. That is a sign that God is displeased with us. God has spoken and we must respond. We must stop this defilement of his heavens with the murder of innocent children. We must stop these insane, sinful launchings of suicide missions to the stars. We must turn off the lasers. We must destroy the lenses. We must bring back those that we can, and must abandon those that we cannot. The crews that are too far away to rescue, such as those on *Prometheus* and the others going to Alpha Centauri, Lelande, and Sirius, are fortunately under the influence of the drug No-Die. Their minds are as those of innocent children. They are happy, though sinned against. It is better that they never be allowed to return to full mental capacity, for as intelligent adults they will experience the double torture of mental as well as physical anguish. For they will know that they have thrown their lives away in a vain attempt to satisfy the grandiose dreams of a foolish world of sinners."

Winthrop paused, then his already large body seemed to grow in stature as he grasped the corners of the lectern, squared his shoulders, and raised his chin determinedly into the air.

"I, Senator Beauregard Darlington Winthrop the Third, do hereby now, and in front of these witnesses, swear a mighty oath that Ah shall do everything in my power to halt this abomination in the heavens of God. Ah will not rest until the lasers are turned off, the lenses dismantled, and this whole sinful project is stopped. Ah do so swear, in the name of GOD! May-God-give-me-the-strength-to-carry-out-his-call." His thumb pressed a button on the podium, and the screen flickered to black.

Dr. Susan Wang flicked off the video as an announcer tried to pick up the slack. Winthrop had given a short speech, but an effective one. Susan sat pensively as she thought about the speech. She finally stirred into action.

Long ago, Susan had met the President of the Greater United States during one of the publicity functions that had preceded the launch of *Prometheus*. Susan and the President had developed an instant rapport since they were both career women with husbands and families. Susan had never misused that instant friendship by bothering Margaret Weaver with requests for favors. Margaret had been out of office for sixteen years, but she was still the Grand Dame of the Democratic Party and had a good deal of influence on the present President. After all, he was her son. Susan flicked on the videophone and called up information. She finally got through.

"President Weaver," said Susan, "This is Dr. Susan Wang. Ex-wife of Dr. William Wang, the medical doctor on the interstellar starship, *Prometheus*."

"Hello there, Susan," said the warm wrinkled face on the screen. "But only 'ex-wife' on paper, I'm sure. What can I do for you, dearie? I'm sure Beauregard's speech has something to do with it. I only wish that old bastard would spend as much energy managing Timmy's bills on the senate floor as he does fighting the space program."

"I'm not a medical doctor, but I picked up a lot when Bill was going through medical school," started Susan. "From what I have been able to learn from people at GNASA, there are nineteen of the crew with the preliminary symptoms of Hodgkin's disease, although the other one is certainly suspect until he has been cleared by a thorough examination. Hodgkin's disease is one of the few forms of cancer that have definitely been shown to be associated with a virus infection. The close quarters of *Prometheus* probably made sure that everyone was thoroughly infected with the virus, although why it turned into cancer in nearly all of them is unknown. The problem that the GNASA doctors have is that although the computer on *Prometheus* is smart enough to act as a nurse, it doesn't have the memory or training to be a surgeon, except for preprogrammed operations like an appendectomy. They are now light-years away, and the round trip communication time is about five years and growing, so instructions from Earth are practically useless. Fortunately, the viral infection is being slowed by the No-Die to the same rate as the rest of the reactions in the body, so the disease will take some time to spread. It's difficult to do, but the disease can be cured with a combination of surgery, chemotherapy, and radiation treatment. It's doubtful, however, that the single computer motile on the ship can take care of nineteen or twenty very sick mentally-retarded people at the same time, when physically it is barely a match for one of them."

"It sounds pretty desperate, doesn't it?" said Margaret with a frown on her wrinkled brow.

"William wanted so much for this mission to succeed," pleaded Susan. "In his present mental state he is incapable of making any decision, but I know that *if* he could be asked, he would insist on being taken off the drug long enough to help the computer save the crew. Could you please get President Weaver to give the orders to wake him up?" she pleaded. "Please?"

"I'll mention it to Timmy," said the kindly grandmotherly face over the screen. "And if the experts agree that it would be a wise thing to do, then I'm sure it will be done. You do realize, however, that if your husband is taken off the drug, his cancer will be, too, and it will start to spread at its normal rate."

"I KNOW!!!" screamed Susan, her control breaking. She burst into tears.

"There, there, dearie," said the soothing voice, trying to break through the sobs. Margaret had always wished that these videophones had hands. "There, there. I'll talk to Timmy as soon as I can. There, there . . ."

HEALING

Thirty-three months later a message came wandering back over the interstellar blackness to the laser receiver on *Prometheus*, now over two-and-three-quarters light-years away from the solar system and still not quite halfway to the Barnard star system. James read the message, and after a short period of self-analysis to ensure that the conditions that the senders had assumed still applied, decided to act. It sent the Christmas Bush up to the workshop on the starside deck where it fashioned a special container with a drinking spout. Dodging the curious kids, especially Shirley, who was always getting into its tools, the Christmas Bush floated slowly down the lift shaft, stopped at the upper crew quarters deck, and entered one of the rooms. As the door hissed open, Billy woke from his nap. His imp spoke to him softly.

"It's just the Christmas Bush, Billy," it said. "Bringing something special just for you."

Billy, puzzled and excited, slipped out from under the tension sheet and peered around his bedroom door. The Christmas Bush was setting something up in one corner of his room.

"What is it?" he asked. The Christmas Bush didn't reply, but went quickly off to take care of some business elsewhere on the ship.

"It's your own private drinking fountain," said James

through the imp, with an overtone of delight in its voice.

"Big deal," said Billy. "I thought I was going to get my own doctor kit."

"Well, Billy," said the imp in its most conspiratorial tone, "if you promise to drink water only from this dispenser, then I might be able to find a doctor's kit for you."

"You mean it!" said Billy, his dark brown eyes dancing above his yellow high-boned cheeks. "How many days!"

"It will be more than days, Billy," said the imp. "It will be many weeks. I know that seems like a long time to you, but I promise it will get easier as the time passes."

"I'll make it come even faster," said Billy. He floated over to the dispenser and pushed the button down hard. A ball of clear water grew on the end of the dispenser and Billy gulped it down as soon as it became the size of an egg. He gulped one egg after another until his belly ached.

"I don't feel so good," he said.

"You'll be all right," said the imp. "But just in case, why don't I have the Christmas Bush bring you your dinner tonight. I will have it fix a special one, just for you . . ."

After a month, most of the No-Die had been leached from William Wang's body tissues. James now found it easy to keep William from drinking some of the drugged water that was still the diet of the rest of the crew. William was annoyed with the childish behavior of the rest of the crew. "The Babies," he called them. As a sophisticated young man, he preferred to stay in his room and read. James often led him to medical texts and William attempted to read them, since they sounded interesting and familiar, but there were too many words that he didn't know, and he found them hard going. He preferred science fiction, especially the genre where some brave and intelligent but otherwise ordinary hero is able to save the day with his foresight and intelligence, after the more muscular types of heroes have failed. It took three months before James finally got the question that it had been waiting for. It came after William had been reading a story where one of the characters used the longevity drug, No-Die.

William lay on the couch in his lounge, his sticky patches holding him firm. His eyes were staring right through the video wall that was still on page 112 of "Heroes Die But Once." The page had been there for over five minutes. William was not reading it anymore, he was thinking instead.

"How far are we from Barnard, James?" he asked in a soft voice.

"Three light-years," James answered. William thought about that for another minute. His face contorted as he worried the answer through his mind.

"We're only halfway there," said William finally. It was not a question, so James didn't answer. Finally it came.

"Why'd you take me off No-Die early, James?"

"There's something wrong with the crew and I need your help, Dr. Wang," said James.

"What?!?" said William, galvanized by the words and the weeks of reading heroic science fiction.

"I need you as a doctor, William. And unfortunately, you are still affected by the traces of No-Die left in your system. You will need many more weeks before you have returned to your full mental capacity and can be allowed to treat the rest of the crew."

"I feel fine, James," William protested. "All you have to do is tell me those things that I can't yet remember, and you and I together can save the ship!"

"I am pleased to hear that you are so eager to help," said James through the imp on William's shoulder. "But it is not as simple as that."

"But what can I do to help?" said William. "I'll do anything you tell me."

"Fine," said James, as the viewscreen on the wall flickered. Page 112 of "Heroes Die But Once" flashed off, and the title page of a new book flashed on the screen. The title was as deadly as the problem that they faced.

"MANUAL AND PROCEDURES FOR TREATMENT OF HODGKIN'S DISEASE IN THE CREW OF PROMETHEUS," it said. It was written by President Timothy Weaver's Special Medical Commission for the Prometheus Problem, and was dated July 2048. It was now August 2051. "Start reading this," said

James's voice through the imp. "Let me know if you want help with any of the words."

William set his jaw and started reading. He was only on the fourth page when he began to realize that being an intellectual hero might involve as much work as being a muscular hero. It reminded him of his days back in medical school. Night after night of staring at screens, trying to force all the necessary knowledge into a limited number of brain cells. It hadn't been easy. He had been older than most of the med-school students and had had a wife to pay attention to. Of course, she was a help at times. Especially the fun times when she was a willing partner while he played "doctor" with her naked body. Some part of him that he'd almost forgotten stirred below his belt. He grinned at the sign that the No-Die concentration level was dropping.

"There's life in the old boy yet," he said, flicking the viewscreen to the next page and forcing himself to concentrate.

"Hasn't it been long enough, James," complained William. He had just finished reading again through the entire section in the library on lymphomas plus the Manual prepared by the President's Commission. "The sooner we get a firm diagnosis and start treatment, the better their chances are. I'll go slow with the first few and you can watch over my shoulder and see if I make any mistakes."

"I think you've been off the drug long enough, William, but this is the first time a healthy person has been on the drug for this long, and we don't really know how long it will take for the drug to be leached out of your system. You should be back to normal, but just to make sure, I have a test for you."

The screen blinked, and a fearfully familiar title page flashed into view carrying the deadly initials "MSAT."

"I thought I was through with that forever," William groaned. He shifted wearily in his chair and paged the screen to the first question on the test.

Eight hours later, a bleary-eyed William answered the last question.

"How'd I do?" he asked his imp.

"Not as good as the last time you took it, but good enough to prove you are an M.D. again, Dr. Wang," said James. "If you would now please get a good eight hours sleep, we will start work when you wake. We will examine George and Sam first."

"Very good," said Dr. Wang. "Being older, they are more likely to be moving into the Hodgkin's sarcoma phase. If they've gotten that far, it isn't likely we can do much for them, even if the cancer is running slow under No-Die." He ripped himself from his chair in front of his console, where he had been rooted for the last eight hours, floated over to the door to his bathroom, marked humorously with a copy of an ancient World War I poster flaunting the symbols "Chinese Relief," and went in.

Georgie was playing hard with the rest of the gang. The game they were playing was, "Around the World and Don't Fall In." It had originally been called just, "Around the World." You started playing by running around the inner wall facing the Lift Shaft on the Crew Quarters deck. With all the ten room-doors shut, you could build up enough speed running, that the centrifugal force from your circular path across walls and doors would produce enough outward acceleration that your feet would stick to the wall and help you to keep running. Then somebody got the bright idea of hiding in one of the rooms and randomly opening the door and shutting it again to see if they could trip up one of the runners. Since the most acceleration a runner could generate was about one-third gee, the tumbles weren't dangerous. Besides, the sliding doors had safety features that prevented anyone from getting pinched. James originally was concerned about this potentially dangerous game, but soon realized that the exercise was good for the crew. Besides, while they were playing, the kids would be out of the cilia of the Christmas Bush and it would have time to pick up the playroom. Today, however, James insisted that the crew play the game on the lower crew quarters deck only, since Dr. Wang was getting some well-deserved rest up above. The last thing he needed was the patter of idiot feet pounding on the door of his room.

Georgie had just been tripped up and had "fallen in." He was thirsty. He dropped out of the game, drifted down the lift shaft and went over to the water dispenser on the wall next to the galley to get a few balls of cold water. He was intercepted by the Christmas Bush. The hairy hand of the Bush was holding Georgie's personal drink squeezer. The squeezer flask had some funny squiggles that Georgie knew was his name, since the imp had told him that was what they were, but he couldn't tell "his" squiggles from the squiggles on the rest of the squeezers. Instead, he always looked for the airplane picture.

"You've been running hard, Georgie," said the Christmas Bush solicitously. "James made up some grape soda for you."

"Oh, boy! Grape soda!" said Georgie, reaching eagerly for the odoriferous purple globe. He squeezed the container and inhaled ball after ball of fuzzy deliciousness. The grape balls took him back to dimly remembered years swigging grape soda with the rest of the gang that he played baseball with. Their team had been sponsored by the local soft-drink distributor, and they got to drink all the grape soda they wanted.

It took him five minutes to squeeze out the last of the drink, and by that time he was feeling sleepy.

"I think I'll take a nap," he said.

"The rest of the gang is still playing 'Around the World' on your deck," said James through the imp on his shoulder. "But there is a bed right around the corner you can use."

"Where?" said George, floating sleepily along the wall and turning the corner. He faced a white door that was always closed. He and the rest of the gang had sort of stayed away from it. Some of the guys had said that a ghost lived in there, but George didn't believe that.

"Right in here," said the imp, as the door opened to show a shiny steel bed made up with clean white sheets and a woolly tension blanket. The crisp pillow looked inviting, and soon George was tucked away peacefully by the tender paws of the Christmas Bush. The door to the sick bay hissed silently shut on the graying child.

Dr. Wang took out his permalite and, delicately lifting the eyelid of the sleeping man-child, flashed the light across the unseeing irises.

"Good," he said. "The sedative is still working. Hand me the local."

The Christmas Bush passed over what looked like a small pistol. Dr. Wang pressed it to each side of George's neck. There was a slight spit of noise as the high-velocity spray of local anesthetic was injected through the skin. Dr. Wang waited for a few minutes, then said, "Scalpel." There was a precise slice, then the rapid response of a multi-fingered automaton that clamped off all blood vessels smaller than sixty microns. Another slice, another perfect clamp . . .

Five minutes later, biopsy samples from the two cervical lymph nodes were on slides and stained, and the Christmas Bush's nimble fingers were gluing up the tiny incisions on each side of George's neck. The Christmas Bush detached its fingers, leaving them to hold the incisions while the glue solidified, and moved over to assist Dr. Wang at the opto-electronic microscope.

"Reed-Sternberg cells," said Dr. Wang with finality as the giant cells with their owl-like mirror-image double-nuclei swam into focus. "It's Hodgkin's disease, all right. But has it passed the paragranuloma stage?

"Take X-rays," Dr. Wang said to the Christmas Bush. "Especially the lymph nodes and spleen." He watched silently while the Christmas Bush picked up a massive X-ray generator, spread itself out until it formed a rigid network attached to the wall and bed, and proceeded to take shot after shot of George's body, some of its appendages rotating the floating body this way and that while others oriented a flat electrofilm plate in back of the body. Dr. Wang watched on the screen as the digitized images flashed past. From what he could tell, there didn't seem to be any abnormalities, and the spleen looked about the right size. He was beginning to feel relieved, for if the disease had spread to the spleen or bones, the outcome was nearly always fatal. Yet his eye was no match for

James's digital image-processing capability. He would await the analyses before allowing himself some hope.

It took only two minutes for James to compare the recent images with those taken of George before they left the solar system.

"All organs are within normal tolerances, except the cervical lymph gland, which is abnormally swollen," said James.

"We've got a chance, then," said Dr. Wang with relief. "It's still in the paragranuloma stage, and has not yet progressed to granuloma."

"Shall we start treatment?" asked James.

"No," said Dr. Wang. "George can wait a few days while we get the rest of the crew diagnosed. Take him up to his room and let him sleep it off, then bring someone else in."

"It will take an hour," said James. "Would you like some breakfast while you wait?"

"An *hour?*" said Dr. Wang. "This is serious, James. We need to get those people looked at. I don't have time for breakfast."

"Dr. Wang," said James. "With all due respect, sir. Because I was to be in charge of the crew while they were in their mentally-reduced state, I have been thoroughly programmed in how to deal with large groups of physically-gifted but mentally-retarded people. There are nineteen others on the crew, sir, and most of them are more than a match for either you or my Christmas Bush. It will take an hour to convince the crew to quit what they are doing now and go either topside or into the theater so that I can transport George to his room without the others seeing him. If once they learn that they are going to be operated on and wake up hurting after coming through the sick-bay doors, it will be very difficult to get them in here."

Dr. Wang stiffened. "You're right, James," he nodded. "I'll get some breakfast while you trick the next kid through the white door." He set the door for half-open, peeked through, saw no one around, and left quickly for the galley.

As he was pulling out a tray from the special oven that James had set aside for his uncontaminated food, he heard

James's cajoling voice announcing the start of a Hanna-Barbera Popeye cartoon. He could hear the clamor of palms and corridor boots in the lift shaft as the rush of giant children came toward him. Like Great Dane puppies, they pushed and shoved their way through the narrow theater door. Dr. Wang looked at them clinically as they passed. They all seemed to have the telltale swelling of the neck.

There was a commotion at the door. The big one, Richard, picked up a small body pushing in front of him and tossed it over his head. Richard turned at the door to laugh at his victim, as David cartwheeled slowly through the air and floated to a stop in midair, swimming frantically in an attempt to get a hand, or foothold. Dr. Wang stood up, the back of his knees hooked under the seat of his chair to hold him firmly in place at his table, reached up a hand, and hauled David in. Dull gray eyes stared quizzically out from under a thatch of orange-red hair.

"Hi, Billy," said David. "Where've you been?"

"Busy," said Dr. Wang with a smile. "Here, let me fix your collar." His knowledgeable hands moved quickly over David's throat as they rearranged the collar on his shirt. There was no swelling.

"I'd like to check him next," Dr. Wang whispered to his imp.

"I'll have to arrange sedation," said the imp in his ear.

"Sit down with me, David," said Dr. Wang. "I'll have the Christmas Bush bring us something to drink."

"But I wanna watch Popeye," protested David.

"Hot tea with honey," whispered David's imp into his ear.

"Oh, boy!" said David, eagerly planting his sticky patch in the chair. "My favorite!" He waited patiently while Dr. Wang tried to make polite conversation, but it was obvious that David's mind could only think of one thing at a time, and right now it was thinking about hot tea and honey. Finally the Christmas Bush came with a warm squeezer marked with the familiar David Greystoke monogram and sprinkled with rainbow colored eighth-notes. David grabbed his squeezer eagerly and took a big gulp. A few more gulps and his eyes blinked sleepily . . .

"X-rays negative," said James. "Shall I prepare for a biopsy?"

"No," said Dr. Wang. "But remind me to keep a watch on him in the next months. It's not surprising that he's clear, since Hodgkin's is not too common. What is surprising is that the rest of the crew have it. The virus that initiates Hodgkin's is fairly common, but it usually stays dormant. There must be some way that the No-Die caused it to convert into Hodgkin's. Take David up to his room as soon as the hallways are clear and get Sam in here. It's the older ones I'm worried most about."

The Christmas Bush released David from the table and floated him to the door. It waited while James monitored the position of the rest of the crew through its maze of spiders and mosquitoes busy throughout the ship. While they were waiting, Dr. Wang had another thought.

"I think you'd better flush David out, too," he said. "We're going to need his help."

"I have no instructions concerning Mr. Greystoke," said James formally through his imp.

"You do now," said Dr. Wang gruffly. "Take him off No-Die immediately." There was a silence from the imp as James tried to analyze this new autocratic behavior of Dr. William Wang. Then Dr. Wang slumped. He spoke again, more softly this time. As he talked he was unconsciously rubbing his swollen neck.

"Sorry, James. Was acting a little stiff-necked there. But I got hot under the collar and lost my temper, so I should be OK now," he said. Hearing the quip, James's personality-monitoring program went off emergency status.

"Hopefully, the rest of the crew will turn out to be in the same stage as George," said Dr. Wang. "Although the No-Die triggered the cancer, it's held it down to the first stage. That can be treated with radiation and chemotherapy, but they're going to be mighty sick kids. Unfortunately, they aren't going to act like sick kids, but more like ornery goats. To be sure that they're cured, we'll have to keep up the treatments for at least a year, and for some of them as long as three years. I'm not sure that I'll last that long. I want David trained before I go."

"But surely you will be taking treatment, too!" protested James. "Especially since you are off No-Die. Your disease is progressing at a normal rate now, while theirs is still slowed."

"Like most doctors, I'm a confirmed hypochondriac," said Dr. Wang. "So I'll want you to check me out later, but I'm afraid those four months it took to get me clear of No-Die have already been enough. I have twinges in the tummy, itchy skin, and I'm sure you've noticed the Pel-Ebstein fevers."

"Yes," James admitted. "That's why I think you ought to start therapy."

"No way," said Dr. Wang firmly. "The whole idea behind chemotherapy and radiation treatments is to almost kill the patient, hoping that the cancer cells will die before the healthy cells do. Maintaining the level of poison at just the right level is a tricky business, and depends not only on the physical signs and clinical studies, but also on the emotional health of the patient. If I have anything to say about it, this crew is going to get the best poisoning I can give them, but they're not going to get it from a doctor who's half-dead on his feet."

While Dr. Wang was arguing with his imp, the Christmas Bush had put David in his room and had tricked Sammy into taking a drink. It was now maneuvering the long body through the sick bay door.

"Another kiddy for the pediatrician to look at, James?" Dr. Wang asked. "Where did you steal him from? The L.A. Lakers?" Together they stretched the long gray body out on the bed, its heels resting on the end bars. A few X-rays, a few swift cuts, and another one was checked out. Only paragranuloma again. Dr. Wang breathed a sigh of relief and scratched nervously at his upper arm. He noticed what he was doing and forced himself to stop.

"Next!" he hollered cheerfully. "Got to keep this production line running."

As they proceeded through the rest of the crew, it got

more difficult for the Christmas Bush to trick the kids into taking a sedative willingly. The members of the crew that had been through the examination spread tales of vampires that bit you in the throat, and they had the marks to prove it. The last one was Richard. In order to capture Richard, James had to sneak up behind him with a spider carrying a syringe full of tranquilizer. Even then Richard's strong body continued to fight the drugs, and they had to strap him to the examining table during the biopsy.

"The last one," said Dr. Wang as the Christmas Bush helped Richard out the door. The Christmas Bush dropped Richard into a lounge chair when he woke up enough to start fighting again.

"Leave him there for now," said Dr. Wang. "We'll put him in bed after he's calmed down." He padded his way back to the sick bay and went once again through the files. Sixteen with only cervical lymph node involvement, two with both cervical and axillary lymph nodes affected, one completely clear, and one . . .

Dr. Wang flicked again through the Commission's treatment manual, although he now practically knew it by heart. He alternated pages with dips into the limited medical library ensconced in James's memory. New material came in over the Sol-link daily as doctors there passed on their three-year-old knowledge generated by the resurgence of medical interest in this strange form of cancer. For over a hundred years the human race had been aware that cancer was its greatest killer, yet unlike smallpox and the other killers, there had been little progress on the defeat of the dread disease, despite billions of dollars poured into cancer research. It now appeared that the spurt of interest caused by the crisis on *Prometheus* would finally produce a general cure for the multi-pronged disease. It would be too late for those on *Prometheus*—three light-years and two pharmaceutical generations away. James was not only unable to synthesize the substances needed, it did not even know the technologies needed to make the synthesis tools. They were on their own.

"I guess we've got to do it the hard way, James . . ." said Dr. Wang. His red-rimmed eyes blinked wearily under their wrinkled eyelids. His left hand unconsciously rubbed the swollen neck that made him look like a Chinese cormorant with a full catch of fish.

". . . Surgery, radiation, and chemotherapy."

"But there are eighteen patients," protested James.

". . . And they're all going to be miserable, sick, puking, sobbing, terrible-tempered over-muscled little brats with marginal bladder control," said Dr. Wang. "How's the preparations coming for the needles and nitrogen mustard?"

"The seeds for the radiation treatment are undergoing irradiation in the backup reactor for *Prometheus* out on the fourth quarter of the sail," said James. "They should be ready tomorrow. The synthesis of the chemotherapy drugs is more straightforward, since I have a chemical lab for synthesis of dyes and flavors. The first batch is ready now."

"Where's Georgie?" said Dr. Wang.

"He is presently in his room, watching a cartoon on his video wall."

"Let's go make him sick," said Dr. Wang, taking the vial from the Christmas Bush and inserting it into his injection gun.

After only a month off the No-Die, David Greystoke was aware enough to be of great help to the weary Dr. Wang and the overloaded Christmas Bush. Dr. Wang often wished that it had been Richard who had been clear, since the sickly crew of overgrown children often attacked them when they attempted to give them shots or take them into the sick bay for their radiation treatments. Richard was especially difficult, and although Dr. Wang didn't like to complicate the treatment, they had to keep Richard on tranquilizers most of the time. As the weeks passed and Dr. Wang brought the crew closer to death, the eighteen became sicker and easier to handle. For Dr. Wang, David, and James life became an unending round of urine, childlike screams, dirty bottoms, ineffectual blows, and balls of floating vomit. Both Dr. Wang and David learned to catnap five minutes at a time, while the Christmas Bush and its motiles worked tirelessly mopping up the tiny messes that the two humans had missed. After a while, the medical team finally got the rest of the crew on a schedule of sorts, and it soon became possible for the two humans to have a few hours off. David tried his best to get Dr. Wang to start treatment.

"The Christmas Bush and I can handle things, Doc," said David. "You've got to take care of yourself. We're going to need you when we get to Barnard."

"I'm not going to make it to Barnard," said Dr. Wang.

"Sure you are," said David. "The rest of the crew is getting better with the treatment; there is no reason you can't, too. Just look at the last diagnostic we did on Richard. We can probably take him off treatments in a month or two."

"Which reminds me, David," said Dr. Wang wearily. "For the next diagnostic we pull on Jinny, I want you to carry it out while I watch. Jinny was pretty well involved, and she may have to stay on treatments for three years or more. I want you trained to work with James in the diagnosis procedure."

"Sure, Doc," said David. "The sooner I learn to take your place, the sooner you can start treatment." He turned toward his computer console while talking to his imp. "Bring up that last diagnostic we did on Richard, James. I want to go over it and practice."

"I'm afraid it will have to wait. We have a minor problem," said James. "Four of the crew felt well enough to get up, and I arranged a special showing for them down in the theater. It's good for them to get out of bed and move around if they can. Unfortunately, Shirley got worse and vomited. Now I have four sick ones. I could use your help."

David and Dr. Wang looked at each other and sighed. They took a breath of the clean fresh air in David's room, then padded through the opening door into the odoriferous atmosphere permeating the lift shaft and the rest of the ship. They picked up the "slurpers" they had left stashed outside David's door with their half-full tanks of vomit and headed down the lift shaft to rescue the Christmas Bush.

A month later, Dr. Wang was finally satisfied that David, with the help of James, could do an adequate diagnosis and prescribe the proper dosage for the next phase of treatment for the crew. He wouldn't have trusted him with a new case, but those he had to treat were all well known to both David and James, so there was little likelihood of anything new showing up that would give them problems.

"Well, done, 'Dr.' Greystoke," said Dr. Wang. "I think I can trust you to handle things now."

"Good," said David. "Now how about letting me get to work on you. I'll even let you help in the diagnosis if you're a good patient."

"Patient I may be, but good, never," joked Dr. Wang. But while he was talking, he was removing the tools of his profession from his pockets so as not to block the X-rays; then he lay down on the table.

"X-rays first," he said. "Then the biopsies."

The Christmas Bush set up its X-ray generator and electrofilm holder and did a thorough scan of Dr. Wang while he lay motionless on the table. After it was over, Dr. Wang turned on his side under the tension sheet and looked at David. There was a long silence, with just the muttering of James talking to David through his imp as picture after picture flashed on the screen. The console was at an angle to Dr. Wang's view from the table, so he could only see the X-rays at a shallow angle. They looked skinny and stretched.

Finally David said quietly, "I don't think we'll need to do the biopsies."

Dr. Wang rolled back on the table and stared up at the Christmas Bush, still stretched out in a frame above him. The red, blue, and yellow lights looked pretty on the background glitter of green.

"The cervical, axillary, and mediastinal glands for certain," he said quietly, diagnosing his own condition.

He continued. "Retroperitoneal?"

"Yes."

"Inguinal?"

"Yes."

"Spleen?"

"Full involvement."

"Liver."

"Almost certain, significant enlargement."

"Lungs."

"Streaks of what looks like Hodgkin's tissue."

"Can that chemistry lab of yours make Scotch, James?"

For the next half-year, the two men worked side by side taking care of the kids. Nearly half of the crew were now clear of any symptoms and had stopped treatment. The workload became less, and they got more time to relax. Since the kids were usually playing games or watching cartoons in the living area deck, the two adults took to spending their free hours in David's room. David had a special console that allowed him to create his sonovideo art. He had connected his screen to his view wall, so Dr. Wang could rest on the couch and watch while David played at the console. The cancer had spread to William's bones, and the pain was often nearly unbearable. William soon found that watching one of David's compositions was almost as good at keeping the pain away as the drugs.

One day David created a particularly inspired composition. It had consisted of a curving, swooping flight around and through a slowly pulsating red ball with the background music consisting of gut-rumbling bass notes of great power sprinkled on top with overtones of hissing crackles and an occasional slight, shy whistle.

"Like that one, Doc?" said David. "I call it Barnard."

There was no answer.

A week later, Jinjur was playing hide-and-seek with the gang. She still didn't feel too well, so instead of running around, she looked for some good place where she could just hide and maybe take a nap for a while. She had wandered up to the storage deck and noticed that someone had forgotten to lock the door to the freezer. She pulled at the latch.

"Jinny!" said her imp sharply. "Stop that!"

Feeling mean from her sickness, Jinny ignored the imp and pulled harder.

"Jinny! Don't open that door!!"

The door swung open and Jinny walked in. It was cold. There was someone standing there in the dark. She palmed the light switch and saw Dr. Wang. He looked stiff and funny. Deep within her deadened brain something stirred. Something was wrong with Billy. He shouldn't be in here. It was too cold. She reached to grab his hand as the imp shouted in her ear. She grasped the frozen fist and the cold sank into her warm brown flesh. She heard a humming from outside the door and turned as the Christmas Bush came flying in through the freezer door and pulled her bodily from the room.

"He's cold," she said to the Christmas Bush, as if explaining something. "He's frozen, like a Popsicle."

The Christmas Bush closed the door and locked it, then hauled her unprotesting body to the lift shaft.

"Not a Popsicle, but a"—her drug-slowed brain searched for the word, then found it—"a corpse-sicle." She laughed, her strong tenor voice roaring down through the lift shaft.

"Billy is a corpsicle. Billy is a corpsicle. Billy is a . . ."

It was eighteen months before David and James decided that Jinjur was free of cancer and they could take her off chemotherapy. After recording the results of Jinjur's last checkup, David puttered about the sick bay, getting in the way of the Christmas Bush, which was tidying up, making sure that everything was ready for the next patient. With luck, it would only be cuts and bruises for the next decade. David wandered aimlessly out into the lounge and sat for a few hours on the long bench sofa, watching the stars slowly pinwheeling by the viewport. He smiled paternally at the "children" as they flew over and around him, playing one of their noisy free-fall games. Now completely relaxed, he left the sofa and floated over to the lift shaft and went up to his room. He closed the door and sat down at his console and started to compose. He lost track of the time.

Two days later James spoke through David's imp.

"David?" it queried.

"Later, James," said David. "Don't interrupt." He bent forward over his console and his fingers flew over the keys as his eyes stared intently at the screen.

"David," insisted James. "You have avoided talking to me for two full days. You haven't eaten a thing. I know what's bothering you, but it can't be avoided. The Christmas Bush is on its way up to your room to remove your special water dispenser. It's time for you to go back on the No-Die. Your job is finished and it's now my duty to keep you alive for the rest of the trip. We still have fifteen more years of travel before we reach Barnard."

There was a noise in the corridor. David's door hissed open and the Christmas Bush floated in. It efficiently unfastened the water dispenser and left, leaving behind David's monogrammed squeezer from the Galley.

David stared glumly at the brightly-colored eighth-notes.

"You need some nourishment, so I had the Christmas Bush fix you some hot tea and honey," said James.

"Laced with No-Die, no doubt," said David.

"Of course," said James.

"You're treating me like a kid," complained David.

"You've been acting like one," said James without rancor. "I understand your reluctance, but you have a job to do in fifteen years, and you won't be able to do it as well if you are sixty instead of forty-eight."

"You're right, James," said David with resignation. He finished off the composition he had just completed and stored it in memory. He reached for the still-warm squeezer and dutifully took a drink. He hesitated, then swallowed. He sighed, stuck the squeezer in the holder on the side of the console and started to compose again. His fingers twitched, but nothing happened. He tried again and again, but nothing came out of his brain. He forced the fingers to move, but all they produced was a harsh blaring mishmash. He wiped the record clean with a slash at the "clear memory" button and tried again. This was ridiculous. It would take weeks before the No-Die built up a high enough concentration in his body to seriously affect his intelligence. He tried again. Nothing came.

"It's gone, James. I can't compose. I can't even play."
Bursting into tears, he grabbed the squeezer and threw it
viciously across the room. The plastic globe bounced off
the viewscreen, spurting a few drops of hot tea into the
air, then came to rest in mid-air. A mosquito buzzed out of
a corner, collected the drops of tea and herded them out
through the ventilation shaft. James was silent as David
brought his crying under control, then padded across the
room to retrieve the squeezer. He took another drink,
then burst into fresh tears. Sobbing bitterly, he finished
the squeezer and went to bed, exhausted.

The news of Dr. Wang's sacrifice reached Earth early in
2056. There was a muttering of protest in GNASA. It grew
and spread throughout the country as news of the continuing recovery of the rest of the crew came drifting in over
the light-years. Unfortunately for Winthrop, his response
to the news was caught for posterity in the digital memory
cube of a newscuber. The reporter had just raised his hand
to his chin in the familiar gesture of a newscuber, the
frog's-eye lens on his ring pointing directly at the Senator.
"Dr. Wang seems to have restored nearly all of the
Barnard star expedition crew to normal health, Senator
Winthrop. As Chairman of the Senate Appropriations Committee, what are your plans for completing the transmitter
lens for the Barnard star expedition so the crew can be
brought safely to a halt?"
Winthrop didn't know the details, but he wasn't stupid.
There was no way that the transmitter lens could be
completed in time. Twenty years ago the construction of
the lens had been stopped just short of one-third-diameter.
The lens had to be nearly full-sized if the deceleration
technique were to work. Since the diameter had to be
tripled, the area had to increase nine times. Although the
ship would not need to start decelerating at Barnard for
nearly eight years, the light beam to carry out that deceleration had to be on its way across the six light-years
between here and there only twenty-four months from
now. There wasn't enough time. That goddamned Gudunov
was doomed.

"Ah certainly will look into it, Mr. Benford. Ah'm sure that our knowledgeable experts in our Space Agency will have some suggestions that we can consider at our committee meetings." Winthrop paused and thought of a way to cover his rear. Putting on a concerned look, he said, "Of course, after all those years on No-Die . . . We can't be really sure that the crew won't be permanently affected by it. Mentally—Ah mean . . ." he put his forefinger to his head and rotated it. The newscuber caught every rotation.

"Thank you, Senator Winthrop," the newscuber said. He dropped his hand from his chin and placed it casually in his lap. The ring finger lens was still pointing at Winthrop.

"Goddamn Chink doctor . . ." muttered Senator Winthrop's image into the all-absorbing memory of the cube.

Not two days later, there was an announcement from the Chinese space agency. The Chinese space program had always seemed to be limited to near-Earth missions. Thirty years ago, however, when the Americans were sending spacecraft off to the stars, the Chinese authorities had no problem finding volunteers for a very special space mission—a life for thirty years as a certified imbecile. The volunteers had been given No-Die, and were kept confined in a sealed-off section of a large synchronous orbit space station as though they were on a multi-decade mission to the stars. There had been no break in their isolation until the news came about the outbreak of Hodgkin's disease in the Barnard crew. A doctor was let into the compound. He examined the crew and found them fine except for scraped knees and the minor bite and scratch wounds that are normal in a nursery school.

The phantom Chinese mission was over, and the crew had been weaned from the drug. Extensive testing proved that the crew had not deteriorated mentally during the thirty years in free-fall while on No-Die. To quiet other fears, there were carefully orchestrated leaks of the sexual escapades of the crew with each other and with their elderly ex-mates after they were released. Suddenly, Winthrop's derogatory term "Chink" became synonymous with "space hero."

It was still six months before the Greater U.S. elections, and the thought of leaving twenty brave people stranded in deep space (the fact that one of them was dead was irrelevant) brought the nation up short. Suddenly, to be pro-space was fashionable.

Even in 2056, the number of tobacco farmers in South Carolina was greater than the number of "Chinks," and there was never any doubt about the results of the Senatorial election; however, Senator Winthrop's sixth term in office was marred by a change in power. A Republican-Libertarian coalition took over the majority party representation in the Senate, and Winthrop was relegated to the minority seat on the Appropriations Committee. The first action of the new chairman was to call for testimony from the newly appointed head of the Space Agency, the Honorable Perry Hopkins.

"I'm pleased to have you with us today, Dr. Hopkins," said Senator Rockwell. "I know we're all concerned about our brave crew of 'Chinks' that are approaching Barnard, ready to stop. Now, in the past, this committee, under the leadership of our distinguished Minority Leader—" here Senator Rockwell turned to nod to Senator Winthrop down near the end of the table—"found it expedient for the sake of the small farmers of this nation to defer certain items of expenditure for the space program. We realize that this may have caused you some problems in the past, and we want you to know that the time has come for the space program to receive the resources that it needs to carry out its mission. Tell us—what do you need to bring this great nation's crew of astronauts to a successful conclusion of their epic voyage?"

Perry had been expecting something like this, but he still appreciated the excessive verbiage that Senator Rockwell was spouting. It gave him time to count to ten twice. He needed it to keep his proverbial temper under control. He had given up a good life as an aerospace engineer and writer to try to revive GNASA under the new administration. It was just three weeks since his confirmation by the

Senate and now his doctor was telling him that those pains in his stomach were ulcers. Gad! What a job! He finished chewing a Gelusil tablet, took a sip of water from the glass sitting in front of him, and started to answer.

"I wish I could tell you, Senator Rockwell," he started. "But I'm afraid I can't. And I can't because there *is* no answer. The previous GNASA administrators have reported to this committee an *infinite* number of times that work needed to be done on the Barnard transmitter lens. But *that* . . ." (*careful now, Perry, calm down*) ". . . the previous chairman always felt it could be postponed until some future date. Well, gentlemen, that date was two years ago."

"Do you mean to tell me that there is no way to allow our brave crew of 'Chinks' to come to a safe landing at their destination?" said Senator Rockwell.

"I don't mean to be melodramatic, Mr. Chairman. And I have exercised my staff for alternatives, but unless someone comes up with a miracle, that crew is as good as *dead*."

"But surely with a crash effort . . ."

"There are only so many robots in space, and due to the low demand for space robots, there is only one space robot factory," said Perry. "Even if we could speed up the production line by five times, and even if we had some magical way to transport those robots instantly over the ten astronomical units to the transmitter lens and put them all to work, there isn't enough web and plastic in the solar system to make up for twenty years of neglect. At best we could get the lens up to sixty percent of the necessary diameter. Even if the lasers were up to power, that would only suffice to strand the crew some two light-years beyond Barnard, with no hope of getting back. I'm sorry to bring you such bad news, gentlemen, but it's the best I have!"

He rose, and without waiting for permission, strode down the aisle and out the door of the Senate hearing room. He didn't give a damn about protocol—let the President fire him. It would be good for his ulcers.

Roberta heard Perry coming down the hall. Above the

chirping and harping of the newscubers she could hear the clump of his bootheels sinking deep into the aging vinyl tile that lined the dingy halls of GNASA Headquarters.

"Keep me informed about those laser experiments at Chino, Bryan," she said, then flicked off the screen. The logo on the wall above the disappearing image of the calm young secretary on her screen said:

High Power Laser Systems Division
Dr. Cheryl Billingate, Director
Bryan Pearl, Secretary.

Roberta got up to rescue Perry from the reporters. As usual, Perry was having a confrontation instead of a conference. She stood in the doorway of Perry's office, glared the reporters back, then slipped through the door and locked it behind her. Perry was stomping up and down behind his desk, cursing under his breath and popping Gelusil tablets into his mouth one after the other. He stopped and smiled at Roberta as she came across the room. All of a sudden his stomach felt better. He had a fine wife at home, but Roberta was a godsend. She had served under three previous administrators and he was glad she agreed to stay.

"What happened at the Senate committee meeting?" she asked.

"I told them the truth. What else?" he said. "Then I couldn't stand their hypocritical faces and their fancy language anymore. I got up and walked out."

Roberta kept her silence as she sat demurely on the edge of his desk, studying the points of her high-heeled shoes.

"I shouldn't've done it," he admitted.

Roberta kept quiet.

"I guess I'd better apologize. Get me Senator Rockwell on the videophone."

"I'll be glad to prepare a formal letter of apology for your signature."

"You're right, Roberta. The last thing I should do is talk to Rockwell in the state I'm in." He started to pace again.

"Gad!! Why'd I ever take this fucking job!" He paced some more. "There must be some way to save that crew!"

Roberta knew that Perry was the person to revitalize the moribund GNASA organization, if she could only get him away from his Washington office and out among the troops. She had written her doctoral thesis for Management Skills on General Patton. Patton was brash, foul-mouthed, and often childlike in his behavior. He never got along with his superiors, but he always got every ounce of effort and loyalty from his troops.

"Perhaps if you went out to the various centers and talked to the engineers you might pick up some ideas. They may sound far-out to the engineer that thought of them, since they're conditioned to the usual starvation GNASA budget, but *you* know you've got a blank check from Congress. It's just that you can't predate it two years."

Perry stopped pacing. He wasn't doing any good here. He might as well be out trying to pull a miracle out of the woodwork. (Somehow that didn't sound right.) He thought about what she had suggested and paused. He was no dummy. He had been Roberta's boss for all of three weeks.

"When do you have my plane leaving?" he asked.

She smiled and gave him a wink—he was going to be a good boss. "Your GNASA jet is at National ready to go." She reached into his "In" box and pulled out a sheet of paper. "You have an appointment tomorrow morning at GNASA/Lewis in Cleveland, then you go down to Huntsville on Friday. Saturday it's back to Dulles for a weekend with Mary. Don't forget it's your wedding anniversary on Saturday. Then Sunday evening you're back in the jet for the West Coast. JPL, GNASA/Ames, and the High Power Laser Center in Chino. You're to spend two days there since this is primarily a laser problem . . . "

"I'll be . . ." said Perry. He took the list, stuffed it into his briefcase, put on his overcoat and scarf, then stomped down the long corridor to the elevator and the soggy cold February Washington weather outside.

It was the first visit of the new Administrator of GNASA to the Centers. Instead of spending his time with the brass, Perry insisted that he be allowed to talk to the engineers. In some of the larger centers it took two shifts in the main auditorium, but when he had finished, especially with his message that the space program was on the move again, morale soared. There was still some hesitancy to suggest new ideas, however, and Perry found himself dragging them out during his walk-around tours. There were many good ideas around that had been festering in the innovative brains of these stifled engineers.

One amazing one was an idea for building an elevator tower into space using a rapid firing gun at the bottom of the tower shooting superconducting pellets to a turn-around magnet at the top of the tower. It seemed ridiculous, but the numbers said it would work. What they needed right now, however, was a tower to the stars.

Perry picked up some ideas for increasing the speed of construction of the large lens structure, but they still didn't overcome the lack of materials. He was stuck. The power available from the lasers at Mercury Center was fixed. The laser wavelength was fixed. The distance to Barnard was fixed. The time for turn-on of the lasers was fixed. The only thing he could control was the size of the transmitter lens, and he didn't have the time or materials to make it big enough.

Perry was visiting one of the little side-labs in GNASA/Chino in his walk-around with Cheryl Billingate. The young man in charge of the lab was Dr. Mike Handler. Dr. Handler's face had a trim brown beard and an evangelical look as he expounded on the esoteric subject of his research. Perry was impressed with the demonstration. Handler used a medium-power laser in a complex mirror arrangement to levitate a cloud of clear crystal microscopic beads inside a vacuum chamber. Once he had the beads levitated, he took away the mirrors and the beads shifted slightly in position, but stayed levitated.

"It's a new way of making large optical structures," said Dr. Handler with fervor. He made some tiny adjustments to the laser and the cloud of beads contracted. Another adjustment and they moved smoothly into the shape of a lens.

"It's the interaction of the light with the beads that structures the array of beads, which in turn structures the beam of light that forms them. Kilogram for kilogram, these are the lightest-mass optical structures ever constructed."

Perry began to feel that perhaps this trip was not in vain. One of his problems was that there wasn't enough material to make the transmitter lens.

"What's that material?" he asked. "Is there lots of it?"

"Just glass, with the proper chemical dopants to produce the desired absorption lines."

"How big can you make a lens?" asked Perry.

"If you're thinking of replacing the Barnard transmitter lens I'm afraid it won't work. There's not enough laser power to keep the lens organized, even in free-fall."

"Fart!" exploded Perry, his hopes dashed. There was a shocked silence, which Perry didn't seem to notice.

"Why don't you show him the tripling experiment, Jay," said Cheryl, trying to cover the awkward moment.

"Sure," said Dr. Handler. He flicked an asbestos screen in front of the high-power laser beam for a moment. With its support gone, the bead lens dissolved into a pile of sand at the bottom of the vacuum chamber. He took a another vial of beads from a rack, poured them into a hole in the top of the vacuum chamber, and sealed the hole. He readjusted his "priming" mirrors, then pressed a button. A stream of tiny beads shot out into the invisible beam of high-intensity infrared radiation and quickly formed into a thick lens-shaped structure. As the density of the lens increased, Perry noticed a green tinge to the light in the room. Cheryl reached over and turned off the room lights. There in the vacuum chamber was a greenly-glowing lens of beads. The back side of the lens was almost invisible, but by the time the light had passed through the lens it had changed from an invisible infrared color to a brilliant blue-green. The scattered light from the intense beam illuminated the room with its weird laser-light that gave everyone a speckled green appearance like ghosts captured on a piece of grainy film.

"The material in those beads is nonlinear," said Dr. Handler. "At the intensities we're running, the nonlinear-ity is driven so hard that nearly all the incoming infrared light is turned into green light. Of course we must conserve energy and momentum. For each three infrared photons going in, we only get one green photon coming out. But since the energy of the green photon is three times that of the infrared photon, the energy per photon is tripled."

"Do you mean that cloud of beads is cutting the wavelength of the laser light by one-third?" asked Perry.

"Exactly one-third," said Dr. Handler. He was slightly puzzled by the administrator's enthusiasm over what he considered a sideshow trick. He wouldn't have done the demonstration if Cheryl had not asked for it. It loused up the purity of the beads in his vacuum chamber, since these were doped differently than his usual beads.

Like a good administrator, Perry waited to see if one of the scientists would pick up on it. They didn't.

"If a laser beam has its wavelength cut by one-third, then a lens of a given size can send it three times as far," said Perry. He waited. Nothing.

Hell. He would take the credit. He turned to Cheryl and spoke at the black-lipped green-powdered mask surrounded by green-blonde hair.

"I want your people to do a systems study for me, Dr. Billingate. Please tell me the cost and time to delivery of a frequency-tripling bead array to insert in the output of the laser-beam combiner at Mercury Center. If you people can repackage those infrared photons into shorter-wavelength bundles, then the Barnard transmitter lens is big enough as it is."

As he was talking, Cheryl was thinking. "Your idea should work, Dr. Hopkins. My initial estimate is six months plus travel time to Mercury, but it will probably cost over five hundred million. Not counting the transportation costs," she added hastily.

"My dear Cheryl," said Perry, feeling expansive, and free again from tummy pains. "You've been an administrator in GNASA much too long. I'm sure you can boost that five hundred million higher if you really try. Believe me. We have a blank check. Let's not write too small a number on it."

Sand is cheap, even when reformed into microscopic perfect spheres lightly loaded with an expensive chemical. The few tons needed were shipped within five months, and even with transportation costs Perry had a hard time getting the bill up over two billion dollars. He made a lot of friends in Congress for that one.

Meanwhile, Dr. Handler had worked out a lens "growing" technique. Once at Mercury, he set up his lens-forming mirrors and used them to construct a lens only ten centimeters in diameter. He had the Mercury Center engineers then slowly widen their infrared beam while he controlled the electrostatic jet that added beads to the lens. It was slow, painstaking work, but within three days they had a sheet of beads ten meters thick and one hundred meters across. Into one side poured fifteen hundred terawatts of fifteen-hundred-nanometer infrared light, and from the other side emerged fourteen hundred ninety-nine point nine terawatts of five-hundred-nanometer blue-green light. The beads glowed redly in space, each radiating away from its comparatively large surface area, its minute fraction of the hundred gigawatts of laser power lost as heat in the tripling process.

Ten months later, the beam was turned on in earnest. For two years the Mercury Center laser system captured sunlight as it streamed by Mercury and turned it into a blue-green column of power that flashed across the solar system. Two-thirds of the way to the transmitter lens it focused down to a three-kilometer-wide waist of raw energy. Any stray asteroid that attempted to cross that invisible maw of power would have been vaporized. The blue-green photons sped on, marching together in perfect step. Their ranks relaxed as the kilometers passed, but they were still in perfect formation a half-hour later when they hit the inner portions of the Barnard transmitter lens.

Half of the photons went through the empty portions of the spiderweb unimpeded. The others had to fight their way through three crest-lengths of clinging, cloying atoms of pliant plastic that willingly absorbed, fervently held, then reluctantly released the disciplined blue-green troops. The emerging horde took up step again with their brethren that had not been to the R&R camp, and many a tale was passed back and forth during the next six years as they marched steadily outward to the stars, their column straight and true as that of a Roman legion's.

STOPPING

"Laser beam contact!" the computer announced to General Jones, its normally soothing baritone taking an imperative edge.

"Wha?" murmured Jinjur, rousing from her stupor in front of a video screen displaying an old John Wayne battle movie. Deep within her mind she sensed a martinet screaming at her, "Wake up, you idiot! You're in charge!" She shook her head . . . This was no way for a commander to act. She floated clumsily across the control deck to pull herself into the central command seat.

"Report ship status, James!" she rasped in a weak imitation of her parade voice.

James spoke through her hair imp. "I detect low-energy laser beams from Earth. It is time to stop. I quit putting No-Die in your water a month ago. It is now time for the rest of the crew to be taken off." There was a slight pause as the friendly voice of the computer took on a formal note. "As commander, you have the authority to countermand this prearranged plan, but you will have to elucidate your objections in detail."

Jinjur blinked at the last few confusing words as James dropped back into his normal voice, "But you *do* want me to stop the drug, don't you, Jinjur?"

Appalled by her mental weakness at this critical juncture, Jinjur grabbed her thick cap of fuzzy hair and shook her head with her muscular black arms, trying to wake the numbed brain inside. "Yes! Yes! Do it! Flush out the tanks, get rid of that stuff! I want to be *me* again!"

"Take it easy, Jinjur," said James. "I'll do it right away. It will take a few months, however, before everyone recovers completely. I'll be looking forward to it. It sure has been dull playing nursemaid to a bunch of ageless imbeciles."

Jinjur, knowing that the computer had everything under control, let her stupefied brain relax and floated slowly back to the video to watch the Marines on the screen storm up the beach for the thousandth time.

Three months later the crew was back to normal. The precursor laser beam from Earth had been getting stronger as Mercury Center tuned up the transmitter system. Full power would come in about ten days, and they needed to get ready. A few of the crew had strayed from their work stations to peer down the Earthside science dome in fascination at the orange speck of light glowing like a bright jewel in the belt of Orion.

"I'm almost glad there was trouble with the transmitter lens," said David, trying to absorb every nuance of the scene with his artist's eye. "It always bothered me that we could never see the laser beam that was pushing us because it was in the infrared."

"Don't you wish we weren't moving so fast, so the jewel would look like an emerald instead of a topaz?" said Shirley, her shoulder resting against his as they both looked down through the dome. The precursor beam was not very strong, but it did give a perceptible acceleration to the sail, and the crew started to readjust from decades of living in free-fall.

"It'll change," said David. "We're moving at twenty percent of the speed of light now, so the blue-green laser frequency is red-shifted by eighteen percent to orange, but as we come to a stop at Barnard, it'll move back to green."

"Like modern alchemists," mused Shirley. "Transmuting topazes to emeralds."

"Just a wave of the magic relativity wand."

They heard noises at the airlock and turned to look. The Christmas Bush was getting ready to go out. James opened the inner airlock door, and the Christmas Bush seemed to drop all its needles as it came apart. The major trunk and limbs stayed in one piece, but 1,080 of the 1,296 twig-sized clusters on the Christmas Bush detached themselves and swarmed into the lock, each one about two centimeters across. James pumped the lock down, then opened the outer door. The twigs swarmed out across the hull to the shrouds that arched out to connect the central payload with the sail that stretched its silvery sheen past any horizon the human eye could see. Like mechanical mice climbing a ship's hawser, the twigs marched in single file, splitting their forces each time they came to a branching in the shroud pattern. The crew watched the progression of the mites for a while over the monitors, but soon lost sight of them in the orange glare. The twigs moved rapidly, but they had three hundred kilometers to go and would not reach their posts for nearly a day.

Jinjur was at her console on the command deck, monitoring the loading of a copy of James's memory into a computer stationed out on the outer rim of the sail. It was one of three redundant units spaced around the rim that had stayed dormant during the trip out. They were not as powerful as James, but were complex enough to be semi-intelligent and had been given names.

It was the job of Snip, Snap, and Snurr to run the deceleration stage of the interstellar sailship. They were now only a quarter of a light-year from Barnard, and it was time to stop. To do that, the sail was divided into two pieces, a circular inner portion three hundred kilometers in diameter that supported the main spacecraft and the crew, and an outer ring-shaped portion that was a silvery doughnut one thousand kilometers in diameter with a three-hundred-kilometer hole.

On the way out, both portions of the sail worked as a single unit and were driven by the light pressure from the launching laser. During the launch phase, all the sail had to do was reflect the light. The deflection mirrors at Mercury Center had the job of keeping the laser beam focused on the sail. The deceleration phase was trickier, however, and would require all the brain-power of Snip, Snap, and Snurr if the humans were to be brought safely to a stop at Barnard. The outer ring-sail had to be a concave mirror, with a carefully controlled surface. Its purpose was to reflect the beam of laser light coming from Mercury Center back the other way and focus it on the payload sail to slow it down.

"David," said Jinjur. "Stop admiring the pretty lights and go back to your computer console. James's dump into the triplets is about done. I want you to check and make sure everything's OK."

David turned and raised his eyebrow at Shirley, the fine orange-red hairs almost invisible in the orange glare. Both David and Shirley, having worked with computers all their lives, knew that if there was any problem that had eluded the checks built into the transfer program, that there was little chance that a mere human could find them. Nevertheless, David tore himself away from the view and padded over to take his seat at the computer console. He took James and the triplets through their verification routines and nodded to Jinjur.

"Ring-sail computers operational, General Jones," he said.

Hearing the use of her military title made Jinjur wince a little. David was right. She had been overbearing, but this mission had its share of bad luck already. They hadn't even reached their destination and the butcher bill was already at five percent of the crew. She turned and gave a weak grin at David. Still unrepentant, however, she roared in a voice that those on starside swore they could hear through the lift-shaft.

"Stand by for breakaway! ten-nine-eight . . ."

One-third the way out on the sail, 1080 mechanical tarantulas waited for their light-beam orders. A pulse of laser light from the remains of the Christmas Bush standing up in the starside science dome sent a coded signal out to each one of them, and the tarantulas started walking, snipping the weak links between the inner and outer sail. The spiders had to travel almost two kilometers, snipping as they went while always making sure they stayed on the inner portion of the sail. It was about an hour before they finished. The spider-imps then started their day-long journey back across the three-hundred-kilometer-diameter sail and down the shrouds to reattach themselves once again onto the Christmas Bush.

The orange precursor beam became stronger. The outer ring-sail accelerated under the light pressure, while the inner sail, with its heavy payload section, accelerated more slowly. As soon as the two portions of sail had drifted a few thousand kilometers apart, Jinjur took command and started to turn the central sail around. She was used to the light-weight Marine interceptors and soon got bored with the slow response of the huge sail with its ponderous payload. After six hours she turned the ship over to James.

Jinjur had gotten the inner sail turned almost sideways to the beam of light coming from the solar system. The crew were now back in free-fall, although most of them didn't notice the slight difference. The payload and sail were still turning from the angular momentum that Jinjur had imparted. James waited patiently as the hours passed and the sail continued to turn. As soon as there was some optical leverage, James sent a command to the triplets, and a multitude of actuators twisted the distant ring-sail into a curved lens that captured the square kilometers of laser light coming from the solar system and focused it down on the leading edge of the central sail. The concentrated light poured onto one side of the sail and accelerated its ponderous rotation. As the angle of the sail increased, Snip, Snap, and Snurr readjusted their mirror and spread the light more uniformly, still keeping up the rotation. As the central sail was almost halfway around, the ring-sail readjusted again and started to bring the rotation of the central sail and *Prometheus* to a halt. The teamwork of the four computers was perfect. The rotation stopped at the same instant the central sail was exactly one hundred and eighty degrees around. The central sail now had its back to the light coming from the solar system while it faced the focused energy coming from the ring-sail. Since the ring-sail had ten times the surface area of the central sail, there was ten times as much light pressure coming from the ring-sail than from the solar system. The acceleration on the humans built up again, stronger than before, but now it was a deceleration that would ultimately bring them to a stop at Barnard.

"This is terrible," said Richard as he stomped heavily about the lounge. He almost dropped his squeezer as he collapsed into a chair and stuck there. He looked with annoyance at Sam, who had found some old Scotch bottles in his room and was now practicing pouring water from one to the other.

"The deceleration is only a tenth gee, Richard," said Sam. "It's about what we expect on the moons around Gargantua. Think of it as practice."

"You can have it," said Richard. "I'll stay here on *Prometheus* and let you go down."

"Now, now," said Sam. "Remember our program plan. You get the wet one and I get the dry one and I'll be in Rocheland afore ye."

"I don't doubt it, if there were any Scotch to be had there," said Richard.

As the days passed, the acceleration built up an appreciable velocity difference between the slowly decelerating central sail with its heavy payload and the ring-sail shrinking in the distance. After a few months even the human eye started to notice the difference in colors impinging on the lightship. Towards Barnard, the brilliant beam from the tiny doughnut of a ring-sail slowly changed from orange to red, while from the other side, the direct beam from the Earth began to take on a definite yellow tinge. After a year the beam from Earth had shifted color from topaz through amber to emerald, while the beam from the ring-sail had darkened to a red so deep that only some of the crew could see it. They were now within light-months of Barnard, and the crew took out telescopes, particle counters, and other sensors and began collecting the scientific data that was the primary reason they had been sent on the long journey. They soon were all busy looking out the rechristened Barnardside science dome.

The astrophysicists, Linda and Caroline, formed a team

to study the small deep-red sun they were approaching. The aerodynamicists, George and Arielle, concentrated on the supergiant planet Gargantua, while the planetologists, Sam, Richard, and Elizabeth, scanned its retinue of moons. With the help of Carmen's radar, Thomas tried to pin down the orbital dynamics of all the bodies in the system, especially the motions of that strange double-planet, Rocheworld.

As they were passing through the outer asteroid belt beyond Gargantua, the science activities took more and more of their time. It was only David who occasionally made himself take the time to travel to the starside science dome to look in awe at the brilliant aquamarine jewel studding Orion's belt.

After twenty months of work, most of the long range-science that could be done had been done, and the data sent on its long journey back to Earth. The crew relaxed and spent a lot more time in leisure activities. Although it was fairly common to have some of the crew sharing rooms, George noticed that Arielle spend an inordinate amount of time in David's room.

"My, George," he remonstrated himself. "You are certainly a jealous, nosy busybody."

Since they were no longer on science schedule shifts, they took to gathering together at dinnertime. One evening, David waited for a pause in the conversation and made a quiet announcement.

"Arielle and I have been working on a surprise for you," he said. George noticed a number of faces that reflected his own feeling of puzzlement relieved. David continued.

"We two felt that our joy over our arrival in a new world needed some outlet different than producing another batch of scientific data. So we came up with a little show," he said. "Our problem is that we need some practice time. Could we prevail on all of you to stay inside your rooms after dinner for the next three sleep periods and not peek out?"

Red leaned over to George and whispered, "Is eight hours too long to stay trapped in my room?"

"Not long enough," George answered. Red and George handed their trays to the galley imp and joined the rest of the crew on the lift platform that would take them to their rooms.

The next morning George noticed that the large special sonovideo console and screen that had been in David's room was now installed against the theater walls on the Living Area deck. Since the console was there anyway, that evening after dinner, David played them one of his newest creations. George watched Arielle out of the corner of his eye. Her body was swaying slowly to and fro as the sound and sight possessed her. George knew how she was feeling, for the music and video brought back memories of the first time *he* had soloed, the exhilarating feel of being high in the sky, soaring like a bird. The music glided softly to an end.

"That one is titled 'Magic Dragonfly,' " said David. "Now, if you please? Arielle and I have a lot of practicing to do tonight."

Two days later, David announced that he and Arielle were ready and the show would begin right after dinner. The conversation of the crew at dinner that night was full of speculation, and George noticed that he couldn't even remember what he had eaten. James probably got a lot of healthy but tasteless protomush down everyone that night.

David had joined them at dinner and eaten sparingly, while Arielle stayed in her room. George noticed that the galley imp didn't clean their trays after dinner, but stacked them up and scampered off. He looked at the ceiling and walls—not a housekeeping spider in sight. James and the entire Christmas Bush must be involved in the production. The lift platform came quietly down through the ceiling and stopped at floor level.

"I'd like all of you to go and arrange yourself in a circle on the lift platform," said David. "You'll want to sit where you can see my sonovideo screen, as well as into the lounge and exercise room, and up the lift shaft."

George went over to the lift shaft and sat down facing David's video screen, his legs hanging through the one-

meter-diameter hole in the center of the lift platform. Red
came up and sat down behind him. Crossing her legs, she
leaned on him and looked over his shoulder. The rest of
the crew were soon ready for the show.

David turned to his console and checked all the settings. There was a touch screen and special keyboard for
the music and another set for the color video display. In
addition, there was a third touch screen that was obviously
a recent addition to David's normal console.

"Our offering tonight is called 'Flight,' " said David simply. He turned to the console, flexed his long fingers and
nodded. The lights throughout the spacecraft went out.
George looked down through the hole in the platform
and noticed that even the Barnardside dome had been
darkened. The only light in the room came from the soft
twinkling of their personal imps. The men were all wearing their imps on their shoulders and couldn't be told
apart, but he could recognize the women, like Jinjur with
her comb imp and Shirley with the crescent moon on the
left side of her head. There was a scurrying in the darkness and down the lift shaft came a number of minibushes,
each about the size of a personal imp. Two went to each
person, climbed up on their shoulders, and formed cups
about each ear, making a nearly perfect set of stereo
earphones.

The prelude started. Light and airy at first, it moved on
to other themes, one of which George recognized as being
the theme from "Magic Dragonfly." He wanted to close
his eyes and listen to the music, but David's colorful magic
on the sonovideo display kept his eyes open.

The visual hold of the screen faded as the prelude came
to an end. There was a slight noise from the top of the lift
shaft, and George looked up. At the far end of the sixty-
meter tube was a faint white light. The music started, soft
and tinkling. The white light came down the shaft . . .
and finally George recognized what it was. It was Tinker-
Bell, the fairy from *Peter Pan*.

Arielle was almost nude. The only covering for her body
was a tiny, glowing-white triangular patch of Christmas

Bush over her pubic area and two tiny five-pointed white stars riding on top of her small conical breasts. Her hair was ablaze with a cap of a thousand white lights that framed her sparkling dark eyes. Attached to her shoulders was a pair of fairy wings with ribs made of Christmas Bush that held between them a gossamer membrane of clear plastic. On her feet were glowing-white slippers with Mercury wings.

She circled slowly down the shaft, her wings a blur as they supported her in the weak gravity. She held a wand in her right hand, and from the glowing three-dimensional star in the tip there fell sparks, tiny mosquito imps that trailed behind, then sputtered out. George was entranced by the motions of the supple naked body. It was the most beautiful thing he had ever seen, sexy but not sensuous.

Tinker Bell visited each person in turn, tapping them on the head with her magic wand. Then she did a little dance in the lounge and ended by landing on the top of David's console just as the music stopped.

The lights on the pieces of Christmas Bush covering Arielle went out. David's video screen went black. Even their personal imps dimmed. George wondered how the imps communicated without light signals but assumed they probably had the ability to switch to infrared communications.

Suddenly in place of the fairy was a snowy-white dove. Arielle was now completely covered with a feathery net of glittering white. Her arms were covered with branch-sized pieces of the Christmas Bush that turned her arms into wings while her lower legs and feet were turned into a tail. The dove flew around the room to the swooping music. Then, fluttering over their heads, it flew up the shaft, doing midair tumbles and acrobatics.

Like the tumbler pigeons I used to have when I was a kid, thought George. The white bird climbed higher and higher in the shaft while the whirling music drew out to its soft climax.

Suddenly, the music turned hard and the colors on the video screen changed from blues and whites to angry reds and yellows. The tone became menacing and George looked up the shaft to see that the fluttering white dove had been instantly transformed into a hovering red hawk. The hawk poised at the top of the shaft, its wings beating rapidly as the music stayed on a repeated hovering phrase, while underneath scurried tiny little frightened notes. With a few strong thrusts of its powerful pinions, the hawk stooped and plummeted straight at them. It braked to a halt right above their heads, the wind from the beating wings blowing their hair around.

The prey had escaped! The hawk flew violently around the lounge searching for it. Finally giving up, it climbed with strong beats of its wings back up into the sky to the top of the shaft.

The lights went out again, and the music shifted to a slow majestic theme. The lower science dome became transparent, and Barnard sent a red beam of light up the center of the lift shaft. George looked up to see that the four-meter-diameter shaft was now filled with a slowly rotating parasol carrying a long cylindrical body covered with tiny lights. It was *Prometheus* coming to a stop at Barnard. Slowly, the twirling sail dropped downward in the beam of light, the air trapped in the shaft playing the part of the photon pressure that the real sail used in its lower gravity environment.

As the miniature *Prometheus* cleared the ceiling of the living area deck, Arielle pulled her arms down from over her head and spread them out to her sides, pulling the bush-sail apart as she did so. Before their eyes, the Christmas Bush rearranged itself about her body and turned her into a miniature version of the *Magic Dragonfly* aerospace plane, complete with lift fans that kept her levitated, and a ducted fan behind her feet that pushed her forward. To the strains of the "Magic Dragonfly" theme, she soared through the close confines of the lounge and exercise room, her long wings nearly touching the floor and ceiling during her banking turns. The miniature airplane flew back over their heads, then did a slow vertical roll up the lift shaft.

No wonder she's such a great pilot, thought George. *She doesn't fly a plane, she is the plane.*

The slow ascending spiral of the music faded and was replaced by a rapid swooping tempo. A bright-blue speck appeared far above them. Down the lift shaft came a blue swift, one wing after another pulling it through the air. Both wings fluttered rapidly for a second as it pulled out of its dive and zoomed overhead into the lounge. Then, folding both wings back along its side, the swift hurled its body through the air in a long arc that reached to the other side of the lounge. A cloud of fireflies suddenly appeared in the room. The tiny firefly imps scattered as the swift approached, but the blue bird darted around the obstacles in the room with its twinkling flight until it had caught every one. The swift swooped to land on the console and the blue glow of its feathers blinked to blackness as the music and video stopped.

A second's pause, and a multicolored hummingbird appeared hovering above the console. Arielle's bush-assisted arms fluttered into a blur. Her green tail-feather-covered lower body and legs rocked back and forth as she maintained her hovering position, the colors in her feathers changing as she moved.

George noticed that David was now working all three touch-screens. One controlled the music, one controlled the video panel, while the third contained a cartoon of the hummingbird hovering above him. The sound and video panels must have contained stored sequences, for David only touched them occasionally with his left hand to keep them in synchronization with the live action. His right hand was playing over the hummingbird picture, and as the hand moved, the colors on the hummingbird changed hue and moved in iridescent waves up and down the body and out the wings.

The hummingbird darted around the room to the music, moving rapidly between pauses. Then George heard James speaking softly through his stereo imps.

"Please stand up and hold still," said James. "You are about to become part of the show."

George noticed everyone getting to their feet. As he wiggled the hooks of his corridor boots into the loop carpet, he felt his imp and his earphones rearrange themselves into an extended collar. He couldn't see what he looked like, but he could see that the others in the audience had been transformed into exotic flowers.

The hummingbird started visiting the blooms, hovering in front of each one for a second, sticking its head close to the flower, then moving on. George noticed that as the fluttering beauty made her way around the room, that she spent a little longer at some flowers than the others. Red was next to him and he watched as the hummingbird flitted to a halt in front of her. With its lower body rocking back and forth, the hummingbird moved in to plant a kiss on the end of Red's nose, and then moved on.

George was the last flower. With a blur that was almost too fast for him to follow, the hummingbird was in front of him. In the soft blue light from his flower imp and the red and green light from the iridescent fluttering wings on each side of his head, George saw Arielle's soft dark eyes just inches from his. He looked down at her costume. The net of colored lights covering her nude body was sparse, and he could see a rivulet of sweat trickling down between the tiny breasts rising and falling on the hard-working rib cage.

Arielle's face was flushed with exertion, but she gave a sweet smile and pursed her lips. George closed his eyes and awaited the prick on the nose. The hummingbird moved closer, the beat of its wings in the air deafening him. Then hot lips were pressed firmly against his. A sexual thrill shot through him. That thrill was followed by an even stronger jolt as a long tongue forced its way between his lips and searched his mouth for nectar.

The roar increased and the hummingbird was gone. George opened his dazed eyes just in time to see the flashing bird-human spiral up the lift shaft as the music came to a climax.

The lights came on. There was a long silence, then the room burst into applause. David stood up at the console, bowed once, then waited patiently for the applause to cease. There were cries of "Encore!" and "Arielle! Arielle!!", but David waved them to silence.

"We decided before the show that there would be no curtain calls and no encores," said David. "It would destroy the magic of the moment. Besides, even with the Christmas Bush helping, flying is hard work, and she couldn't do an encore. Arielle is up in her room changing, but I'm sure she'll be down soon for something to eat."

There was a clatter from the dining room. The galley imp had returned and was setting out three large trays of food. There was a hiss of a room door opening, and a voice echoed down the lift shaft.

"Mm! Smell good!!"

Arielle, wearing an over-sized shapeless sweatsuit, dove down the lift shaft ladder and made her way to the dining room, waving aside the compliments in her eagerness to get to the food.

First she swallowed a large glass of water—she liked hers carbonated—then asked for another.

"Flying make me thirsty," she said as she picked up a finger-chunk of Nels's Chicken Little, dunked it into James's secret sauce, and popped it into her mouth.

"That was marvelous, Arielle!" exclaimed Shirley. "Do you think I could learn to fly like that?"

"Sorry," said Arielle, starting on a dish of french-fried zucchini sticks and reaching for the next glass of water. "You too big." She munched another zucchini and swallowed loudly. "You'd be like airplane with too many cargoes and not big enough wings." She finished the zucchini sticks and pulled over an algae shake and a pseudoburger on an ersatz bun.

Richard came over to congratulate her on her performance. He held one of her hands while she continued to eat with the other.

"You were absolutely stunning in those costumes, Arielle," he said.

"You like?" she said happily, slurping down the last of the shake and reaching for another one. "I design them myself."

"Like them? I *loved* them!" he said, then leaned forward to whisper in her ear.

She blushed, took her hand out of his and used it to snag another pseudoburger.

"You men!" she said around a bite of pseudoburger. "You all alike! You always take serious something poke at you in fun." She swallowed a big bite and made an annoyed face at him. "That was not me that did that! That was hummingbird!!" She waved the remains of a zucchini stick at him. "Hummings-bird all the time do that to flowers!"

She looked over the remains of the three trays, found a cold zucchini stick in back of a plate and finished it off. She turned to her still-admiring audience, stretched unselfconsciously, and yawned.

"I'm tired. The show was hard work. You like?" she asked. There was a chorus of approval from the rest of the crew as she beamed with pleasure. "I go to bed now," she said. She walked across the room to where David was closing down his console.

"You work hard, too, David," she said, taking his glasses off his nose and stroking his forehead. "Maybe it time for you to go to bed, too?" she asked. She took his hand in hers and he let her lead him to the lift shaft platform. Together they rode it up through the ceiling. Every man left in the lounge was conscious that the sound they heard was that of *one* room door opening and closing.

A few months later, the time came when the decelerating laser beam would turn off. The central sail had been slowed until it was firmly in the gravitational grasp of the dull red star while the ring-sail carrying the abandoned semi-intelligent orphans, Snip, Snap, and Snurr, faded into invisibility among the sprinkle of stars in the heavens. For once the whole crew was watching out the starside science dome. The blue-green aquamarine flickered, then guttered slowly into oblivion, leaving a faint yellow-white star in its place. They had arrived at Barnard, their home for the rest of their lives.

EXPLORING

With the laser power off, *Prometheus* had to make do with the weak red photons from Barnard. Although not powerful enough to have slowed the lightsail in its head-long relativistic flight, the light pressure was enough to swing the sail into a looping orbit that took *Prometheus* on a journey past the major planets in the system. By using the light from Barnard to add to their orbital speed, Jinjur and James could travel away from the star to the outer portions of the system, while tilting the sail the other way would slow their speed in orbit and allow *Prometheus* to drop in closer to the sun.

Tacking carefully, *Prometheus* rendezvoused with Gargantua and allowed itself to be captured into a trajectory that would take them past all of the moons in this minia-ture solar system. The nine larger moons of Gargantua had been detected at Earth by Caroline, using Alan's large orbiting optical interferometer array. They had all been given proper names beginning with Z. In order of size they were Zapotec, Zouave, Zulu, Zuni, Zion, Zen, Zoroaster, Zwingli, and Zeus.

After the crew of *Prometheus* arrived, they found many smaller moonlets. According to the prearranged plan, these were to be treated in the same manner as the smaller asteroids in the solar system and given a Z-number in their order of discovery, as soon as the complete orbital parameters of the moonlet had been calculated. The crew couldn't resist giving some of the more interesting ones Z-names, however, and soon there were moons named Zinc, Zoo, Zygote, and even Zipcode.

"What's our first stop, Sam?" asked Jinjur, as she started her work-shift and sat down in the central command post that George had just vacated.

"That would be Zapotec," said Sam. "Except for the smaller moons like Zeus, it's the farthest out, and we'll reach it first on the inward portion of our flyby orbit. It's also the largest. It's a little bigger than Mercury and has a thin atmosphere not much different than that of Mars. I have some recommendations for the initial exploration probes for Zapotec."

"None for Zeus?" asked Jinjur.

"Maybe later," said Sam. "On our first pass we should only expend a few orbiters and landers on each of the larger moons to complement our remote sensing survey. Later, after visiting the rest of the planetary system, we can come back with probes that have been educated to extract the maximum amount of scientific information out of each moon."

"What gets dropped off here?" she asked.

"Since Zapotec is like Mars, we know pretty much what to expect in the way of dangers. I recommend using three probes on this one. Richard is ecstatic over the volcanic chain ringing the south pole. I especially want to investigate the equatorial rift valley that goes two hundred degrees around the planet. It's fifteen kilometers deep, and we ought to get a good cross-sectional view of the crust using a tether-connected dual crawler."

"I didn't know a creepy-crawler could climb cliffs," she said.

"They can't really," said Sam. "But for this moon we will replace the standard one-kilometer tether between the two crawlers with a fifteen-kilometer one. Then, instead of just rescuing each other from craters, cliffs, and oceans, one crawler can lower the other over the cliff to take samples as it descends."

"Sounds fine," said Jinjur. "What else besides the obligatory orbiter?"

"An airplane," said Sam.

"You're not using one of my dragonflies on a preliminary
survey!" protested Jinjur. "It's too dangerous for the crew,
and besides, Zapotec has almost no atmosphere. You can't
fly an airplane in a vacuum."

"I admit the air on Zapotec is thin by Earth standards,
but it is actually thicker than the atmosphere of Mars.
We'll send an unmanned probe that's a modified version of
the dragonfly airplane. It has a huge wingspan and a light
payload. With its VTOL jets it can land vertically, take up
samples, then take off and fly a thousand kilometers to a
new spot."

"OK. An airplane, too," said Jinjur. "I think I'll come up
with you and talk with it before it's launched."

Sam went to the bottom of the lift shaft. Instead of
pushing himself upward in the low gravity, he asked his
imp to call for the elevator. The doughnut-shaped platform
swooped down from its parking spot in the starside science
dome. Its progress was not smooth, for there were some
humans traversing the long shaft. James, using the imps to
monitor the positions of the humans, timed the drop of
the elevator so that the meter-sized hole in the doughnut-
shaped plate passed around the humans at just the instant
their bodies were at the middle of the shaft. Jinjur and
Sam waited until the elevator came to a halt. They were
joined by Richard and Shirley and the four stepped on the
carpeted upper surface to be lifted back upshaft until they
came to a painted number 42 on the shaft wall.

"An orbiter with two probe-racks," said Sam to Shirley.
Shirley scanned around the wall at the four doors and
palmed one open. Tucked in a triangular-shaped room
between the cylindrical shaft and the cylindrical bodies of
the huge surface lander rockets was a spacecraft. A portion
of the Christmas Bush was crawling over its surface, checking it out. Shirley reached in and slowly extracted the
half-ton spacecraft. Its inertia was evident from the strain
in her muscles. Richard stepped across the doughnut to
help.

"I've got it just fine, Big Boy," said Shirley. "Thanks anyway."

"Is the orbiter ready to go, James?" Jinjur asked her imp.

"I'm in perfect condition and ready for my mission to Zapotec," replied Jinjur's imp in a strange computer voice with a sibilant overtone. It was the orbiter speaking.

"I didn't realize you could hear us," said Jinjur, apologizing to the orbiter. "I'm sorry . . . ahh . . ."

"I am called *Carl*," said the orbiter. "I have no mechanisms for hearing, or speaking for that matter, but James has me hooked up through your imps. Any last instructions?"

The lift headed starside as Sam talked to *Carl*.

". . . start in an equatorial orbit, drop the airplane and creepy-crawler near the big equatorial rift valley, then stay with them until they are finished. Then switch to polar orbit while they head south and you can explore the volcanoes. We'll be back in a few years to take up where you left off."

"Don't rush," said *Carl*. "The more time my processor has to correlate images, the better will be the final batch of processed information."

They reached the top deck, and Shirley and Richard pushed the orbiter into the middle of the Christmas Bush's workroom. The Christmas Bush was busy weaving cloth using a bright-green artificial thread that it had reconstituted from the lint fibers it had collected over the past years.

"Do you need any help?" asked the Christmas Bush.

"No thanks," said Shirley. "As long as you send a few imps down to unlatch the fasteners on a thin-atmosphere airplane and a creepy-crawler, we can do just fine. Besides, it's important you finish that shirt for Red. Her old one is getting kind of threadbare, and our eagle-eyed friend here is getting a bad case of google-eye."

Richard snorted and headed back to the central shaft. The lift took them down to get the airplane at level 33. Wrapped up in its protective aeroshell, the airplane looked like a clam. The aeroshell was three meters in diameter, but quite light for its size. They had to stand it on edge as they took it up to the workshop.

"It's hard to believe *that* has an airplane inside," said Jinjur.

"It's also hard to believe what hatches from an eagle egg," said Richard.

"Let me open it up and give you a peek," said Shirley. "I was involved in the design of the folding wings. We use somewhat the same principles in the wings of the dragon-fly planes." She popped a few fasteners and lifted the top of the clamshell.

"Hi, *Wilbur*," she said, peering down to look at the video scanner in the stubby nose of the airplane buried under fold after fold of wing. "Do I look different than you thought I would?"

"I already had access to pictures of you taken through James's video cameras," said *Wilbur* through her imp. The computer voice was deep and matter-of-fact. "But since my scanner is designed to work in Barnard's illumination, which has a lot more infrared than Sol, you do indeed look different than I had expected. There seems to be a glow about you, especially in the chest section."

Shirley slammed the lid shut while Richard and Sam roared.

"Let's go get the creepy-crawler," said Shirley, heading for the lift. Soon they returned with *Pushmi-Pullyou*. The two crawlers were identical except that one had a reel on the front, while the other had a reel on the back. Between them ran a short length of high-strength line. When they entered the workshop, the Christmas Bush detached two of its arms and left the arms to continue the weaving tasks. It disappeared into a storage room and soon came back with a reel containing a much longer length of thinner line.

"Will it hold?" asked Sam. "It looks mighty thin."

"It has only a safety factor of three instead of ten," said the Christmas Bush, "but it should be more than adequate."

With the help of the Christmas Bush and Richard, Shirley assembled the orbiter and its two probes, then she and Richard suited up and took it through the upper cargo airlock and pushed it over the edge through a hole in the still-accelerating lightsail and watched it drop toward the distant cousin of Mars.

"Goodby, *Carl*," said Shirley. "Take good care of *Wilbur* and the *Pushmi-Pullyou*."

"I will, Miss Everett," said *Carl*. Shirley could almost hear a sibilant toothiness in the happy smile of *Carl*'s voice as the orbiter gave a short burn of its rocket and headed off to carry out the lifetime job it had been born and trained to do.

Now that they were in the gravitational pull of Gargantua, Jinjur tilted her sail for maximum deceleration, and *Prometheus* dropped inward at a faster rate in an elliptical orbit that would take them past the other planets in the system. They passed by Zen and Zion, two tiny planetoids with orbits inside Zapotec, then dived in farther to catch the innermost of the larger moons, Zulu.

Zulu was not the innermost of all the moons of Gargantua. That honor was shared jointly by Zoroaster and Zwingli, two tiny moonlets that shared a common orbit. One was in a slightly lower orbit than the other. Since the differences in the orbital diameters was less than the moon diameters, it seemed that they would ultimately collide. But as the innermost one, traveling faster according to orbital law, would overtake the slower one, their joint gravitational interaction would slow the outer one even more, sending it outward, while the inner one's speed was increased, sending it inward, just enough so that the two avoided a collision. The gravitational attraction on the other side was reversed, restoring the two moons to their original orbits after their near collision. Zoroaster and Zwingli received little attention, except from Thomas, who was fascinated by their complex dynamics.

"Just two little orbiters, Jinjur," he said, protesting her decision. "They don't have to be very smart, all they have to do is transmit a carrier so I can get accurate Doppler data. With that I can determine whether the system is absolutely stable or whether those two moons will turn into two projectiles or a Gargantuan ring system."

"You can have the orbiters in phase two," said Jinjur.

"When we come back after the preliminary survey and do a thorough job on the whole system."

"But, Jinjur," said Thomas. "For these stability equations you need to have the longest time-base possible, or else the error propagation makes the data meaningless."

"I'm sorry," said Jinjur. "I don't think we can waste two orbiters at this stage of the exploration."

"How about a lander with a transponder?" said Thomas.

"You need an orbiter to take the lander there and get it down safely," said Jinjur. "I'm afraid not."

Thomas whispered to his imp. Across the command deck Sam raised his head, listening to his imp. He ripped himself from his seat and came over to join the discussion.

"All you need is a transponder?" Sam asked Thomas. "No tracking, no data taking, no smarts?"

"That's all, just an omnidirectional transponder. I can interrogate it once a week with a high-power beam, read out the velocity from the Doppler shift in the signal, then go off on other business until the next interrogation."

"He could use two of my seismic harpoons," said Sam.

"We still have the problem of getting them there," said Jinjur, "and that takes orbiters."

"Not the self-powered harpoons," said Sam. "You program them for the right trajectory look angle, send them off with a picture of what they are looking for, and they will trim course until they are on an impact trajectory. They aren't very smart, since most of what would have been brain is taken up with a tungsten carbide penetration spike. They are only designed to collect seismic and heat data and send it back upon interrogation, but if Thomas can get Doppler out of the tracker carrier, I would be interested in the seismic and heat-flow data, especially during the period when the two moons are strongly interacting with each other."

"That'll do fine," said Thomas with alacrity. "How about it, Jinjur?"

"Sounds OK to me," said Jinjur. "Then if you find anything really interesting, we can back it up with orbiters when we come back. Why don't you two go get the harpoons and send them off with detailed instructions."

Sam smiled. "*Slam* and *Smash* wouldn't know what to do with detailed instructions." He walked to the lift shaft, followed by Thomas, and the two of them jumped up the hollow column as Jinjur looked quizzically at Sam's departing back. She punched in some codes on her command console and started to read the technical descriptions for the seismic harpoons.

"Shouldn't we use the cargo lift?" said Thomas as he climbed after Sam to level 14. Sam stopped and palmed open a panel. There was a honeycomb rack containing many dozens of sharp-pointed metal tips. Sam reached up to one of the larger-diameter hexagons and pulled at the small pointed tip centered in the hole. At first all that came out was a meter-long metal spike about two centimeters in diameter. As he continued to pull, the spike became thicker, then rapidly blossomed into a heavy exponentially tapered horn that was ten centimeters across. The tungsten carbide metal spike was faired into the nose of what looked like a missile. It was a missile, and it was looking for a target.

"Where is it?"

"Point me at it!"

"Let's go!"

A harsh, crude computer voice came from their imps. Thomas, who had stuck himself to the lift wall and had reached out a hand to help Sam with the harpoon, pulled his hand back as the harsh voice grated on his ear.

"I'll SLAM it good!"

"I'd like you to meet *Slam*," said the lanky geophysicist. "What it lacks in brainpower and courtesy it makes up for in purposefulness."

Sam spoke to his shoulder imp in the sideways voice that all the crew members had developed.

"*Slam* goes to Zoroaster," he said, and James instantly filled the miniature memory of the harpoon missile with the optimum trajectory information and a model of the surface features on the distant moonlet.

"I got it!" said *Slam*. "I'll find it! Let me go!"

"Just a minute," said Sam, handing the two-meter-long

pointed bullet to Thomas, who took it gingerly. "You're going to have *Smash* as a traveling companion."

Slam ignored Sam's comments, its pea-sized brain intent only on hitting its target. Soon *Smash* was loaded with trajectory and surface feature information for Zwingli. Thomas and Sam took the two missiles up to the cargo lock in the top deck and sent the eager probes on their way to the do-si-do twins down below, each one eagerly bellowing through James's communication link.

"Where is it? I found it! I'm going! I'm gonna hit it! I'm gonna hit it with a SLAM!"

"I've got mine! I'm gonna SMASH it!"

"I sometimes think the persons who programed those harpoons went out of their way to entertain us," said Sam.

As *Prometheus* approached Zulu in its elliptical dive into the gravity well of Gargantua, the resolution from their telescopes rapidly became better than the quick snapshots that had been made by the Barnard probe when it had sped through the system some fifty-three years ago. Jinjur got up from her command console at the center of the control deck and wandered over to stand in back of Sam to look over his shoulder at the science screen. There were two pictures of Zulu on the screen, an old one from the probe and a new one fresh from the optical telescope in the science dome on starside. Jinjur stood up on tiptoes in her corridor boots, the weak acceleration making it easy to stay on point, and peered past Sam's imp at the screen. The imp, noticing her presence, scurried around to the other shoulder. Sam, feeling the motion of his imp, glanced around into curious brown eyes peering over his bony shoulder. He winked and turned back to the screen.

"There've been fewer changes in the past fifty years than I would've expected," said Sam. "Zulu is somewhat like Ganymede. Its surface is a thick layer of striated ice over a deep ocean. Unlike placid Ganymede, however, Zulu is as active as Io."

"Volcanoes on a water planet?" said Jinjur.

"Not lava volcanoes, but water geysers," said Sam. "There are hot spots all over the planet where there are periodic streams of steam and hot water shooting tens of kilometers up into the atmosphere. Here, let me superimpose an infrared map."

A false-color infrared image appeared on the screen. Zulu was a sphere of deep blue with red, yellow, and white spots on it.

"The yellow and white regions are the hottest points. They indicate the peaks of underwater volcanoes. Let's watch this spot. It was yellow a few minutes ago and now it's white." Sam's finger pointed to the screen, and his other hand turned off the infrared overlay to leave the optical image on the screen. Slowly, at a point just above where his finger was pointing, there grew a small circle. It became larger and fatter until it was a brilliant white doughnut.

"Wow!" said Jinjur. "That was a big one."

Sam read off the numbers on the side of the screen as a computer-generated cursor ring tracked the outer edge of the doughnut.

"Fifty kilometers in diameter and still growing," said Sam. "It's a large one, but not as big as Big Bertha's blasts on the other side. They go out to two hundred kilometers. The flyby probe caught one of Bertha's eruptions when it went by, so they must've been going on for at least fifty years."

"Where does all the heat come from?" asked Jinjur.

"There's a thick rocky core, and there is probably plenty of heating from the decay of radioactive elements, like in the Earth's core, but in addition, there is tidal heating from Zouave and Zuni rocking the core about its normal tidally-locked orientation toward Gargantua. The core is probably liquid at the center and there is convection going on, because we are already starting to pick up evidence of a significant magnetic field. We can measure it better when we send down an orbiter and the two landers, but it's probably near fifty gauss, one hundred times stronger than the magnetic field of Earth."

"Have you decided on the probes?" she asked.

"Yes," said Sam. "An orbiter and two amphibious landers with chemical analyzers. But instead of sending the orbiter directly to Zulu, I want to have it spiral inward slowly."

Sam got up from the console and walked to the lift shaft. Shirley saw him call the elevator and joined Sam and Jinjur as the elevator took them up the shaft to level 34. Shirley popped the panel, and together they pulled an orbiter from the wall. The orbiter had two aeroshell landers, and as Sam talked to the robot, Shirley jumped up a few more levels and handed down two identical landers that looked like miniature amphibious tanks, with a boatlike enclosed hull, and a tread system that would act as tracks on the ice and as paddle wheels in the water. The landers had numbers, but someone had painted names in bright script on their sides, "*Splish*" and "*Splash.*"

"Now, *Jacques,*" said Sam to the orbiter. "I want you to take your time orbiting in. Zulu must be losing water at a high rate because of all the steam it's making and its low gravity. I suspect that the water molecules that escape from the gravity of Zulu don't have the energy to escape from the gravity of Gargantua. They will stay in a torus centered at Zulu's orbit. If that is the case, Zulu will pick up the molecules again in a later revolution. I'd like a profile of the water density of that torus before you settle down to explore Zulu."

The imp on Sam's shoulder spoke in a strange nasal accent as James transmitted the orbiter's response.

"I will establish an orbit tilted to the orbit of Zulu. After some cycles I will have explored it not only radially, but out-of-plane," said *Jacques.*

Shirley was busily fastening *Splash* to the hold-downs inside the aeroshell. She paused as the nasal voice talked to her through her imp.

"Is there any objection to opening an aeroshell in space? The landers have much more sophisticated chemical sensors than I do. They could not only obtain data on the water vapor density, but could also identify the trace elements, isotopes, and compounds that might be missed by my particle analyzer."

Shirley thought for a moment.

"*Splash* and I can stand vacuum, Shirley," said a tiny voice through Shirley's imp.

"Yes," said a different tiny voice. "Besides, we want to get to work right away instead of being cooped up for months in that aeroshell."

"Unless James can think of some problem, it should be just fine," said Shirley. "Just remember to close the aeroshell long before you go into orbit about Zulu, *Jacques*. We don't want the aeroshell cap torn off by a gust of steam from a geyser."

"That and the remote possibility of a meteorite strike were the only dangers I could think of," said James.

"Good," said Sam. "I'm glad you thought of using the landers, *Jacques*. Are you all ready to go?"

"Goodby, *Splish*," said Shirley as she closed the cap on one aeroshell. "Goodby, *Splash*. You'd best be capped until we get *Jacques* launched and away from *Prometheus*." She closed the other cap and the elevator started to rise to the starside deck. Sam and Shirley put on suits and carried *Jacques* out the lock. They stood on the tiny platform embedded in a three-hundred-kilometer sea of metallic foil and tossed the orbiter upward to the stars. There were a few short bursts of control rockets and the spacecraft drifted away. Sam and Shirley went back inside, took off their suits, and wandered into the science dome. A small portion of the Christmas Bush was busy operating the large optical/infrared telescope. Staying out of the way, the humans looked up and waited. There was a flare of a large rocket off in the distance, followed by three voices coming from both of their imps. Two were tiny and muffled while the other was strong and nasal.

"Goodbye!"

"Goodbye!"

"Au revoir!"

The elliptical trajectory of *Prometheus* took them zooming by Zulu. They got some excellent shots of Big Bertha in action. They also plotted some snow and rain storms that seemed to initiate near the point on Zulu that faced into its motion along its orbit. The storms weakened as they made their way around to the trailing side of the moon.

They left Zulu behind and closed in on Zouave. It was bigger than Zulu, but the optical and infrared telescopes showed a featureless disk.

Sam was sitting at the science console, but instead of telescope images he had a copy of Carmen's radar console on his screen. Carmen had activated the X-band detectors spaced around the three-hundred-kilometer periphery of the sail, and she was sending burst after burst of high-power chirped radar pulses out the X-band sender on the main body of *Prometheus*. The short radio waves penetrated the clouds that obscured the surface of Zouave, then bounced back to the detectors. James took each of the detector responses and synthesized a radar picture of the surface of the planet beneath the cloud layer.

"Looks pretty interesting," said Sam to Carmen through his imp. "In fact, it seems to be all up and down, no flat areas to indicate seas."

"The thermal microwave radiation from the surface indicates a temperature of one hundred ten degrees absolute," said Carmen. "Looks like it's too balmy there for liquid nitrogen rain like we had back on Titan. Y'know, I never thought I would be saying this, but that orange ball of smog looks so much like Titan I'm beginning to feel homesick."

"It may be too hot for liquid nitrogen, but it sure is cold enough for frozen water and carbon dioxide," said Sam. "Where's all the snow?"

"They're dielectrics at that temperature," said Carmen. "The radar goes right through them until it hits the rock underneath. Here, let me adjust the threshold level so we can pick up the weak reflection at the surface of the snow layer."

Sam watched his screen as the computer shifted bits of information. Suddenly the rugged terrain turned into a smoothly rolling landscape. "What's the pressure?" he asked.

"I estimate nearly three atmospheres," said James.

"Gee, we'll be able to work down there with just heat-suits," said Richard.

"Over my dead body," said Jinjur. "Nobody is going no place under that pall of smog until we get a favorable report from a lander."

"Of course," said Richard. "I was just musing. I'm getting cramped living in this checker-stack. I want to get out and stretch my legs."

"That'll come soon enough," said Jinjur. "What landers and orbiters are you going to use?"

"No orbiter at all," said Richard. "Nothing to see but smog. And no landers in the usual sense. They'd probably get buried in snowdrifts."

"What then?" asked Jinjur.

"A couple more of the penetration probes to get down through the snow to bedrock, and some balloons. At that pressure level, they should be able to carry a big payload." He and Shirley took the elevator up the lift shaft, and soon *Punch* and *Poke* were on their boisterous way, hauling aeroshells that would be released in the upper atmosphere of Zouave. Inside each aeroshell was a deflated high-pressure balloon and a sophisticated semi-intelligent payload. *Tweedledum* and *Tweedledee* would spend the next two years floating between the high cloud layer and the frozen surface below, landing occasionally when the winds were calm enough to take surface samples, then going on their way again when the winds rose. Slowly, the picture that they collected in their leisurely motion across the surface of the planet would be built up into a map of Zouave in James's distant memory.

The lightship continued its climb up the elliptical orbit. It began to close in on the multicolored marble of Zuni. A little larger than the Earth's Moon, it shouldn't have been able to retain an atmosphere. But it did, and quite a spectacular one at that.

"It's like a miniature Earth," said Thomas, watching the screen over Richard's shoulder.

"Carmen, what's the radiometric temperature?" Richard asked of his imp. A voice across the control deck echoed the imp's reply.

"A balmy forty degrees centigrade at the surface," said

Carmen. "And those clouds down near the surface are water, not ice crystals."

"It must be tidal heating from Zouave," said Richard. "For sure Barnard and Gargantua aren't hot enough to keep it that warm."

"How come it still has air and water when our Moon doesn't?" asked Thomas.

"I'm not positive," said Richard. "My guess is that like Zulu and Zouave, Zuni is losing air and water constantly, but most of it stays in orbit and is picked up again. In addition, I think that Zuni is capturing the leakage of water from Zulu and smog from Zouave. The strange mixture of chemicals and water raining down from the sky is probably what makes the different colors that we see."

"Is there any chance that there's plant life down there?" asked Jinjur.

"That was my first thought with those colored patches around the edges of the lakes, especially the big one in the southern hemisphere. Unfortunately, there's no sign of chlorophyll bands, but then chlorophyll wouldn't work well in the dim red light of Barnard. If there *is* life, it might use some other mechanism to collect energy than photosynthesis. Lots of work for the landers to do."

"What kind of landers are you going to use?" asked Jinjur, coming over.

"There are a lot of shallow lakes, and there may be some interesting things to be found if you muck around on the bottom. So, for sure, some submersible amphibious types. I was thinking about balloons, too, but the pressure is only about a half-atmosphere and they couldn't carry much. Besides, they would probably get caught in one of those thunderstorms. I think I'll risk a flyer, though. *Orville* can move fast enough to keep out of the way of the weather fronts, or land in a sheltered valley and fold up its wings if it gets too rough." Richard got up from his console and headed for the lift shaft. "Could you get Shirley for me, James?" he asked his imp. "I'm going to need help fitting an extra aeroshell on *Bruce*."

"I'm starside, Richard," came Shirley's voice through his imp. "*Bruce* is stored at level 37, see you there."

Richard, Thomas, and Jinjur stepped onto the lift, and as it slowly rose they looked up the tall shaft to see Shirley diving down toward them. Shirley slammed into the lift platform with a programmed response of her knee joints as the platform came to a halt at level 37. Soon the lander was pulled out and *Burble* and *Bubble*, the two amphibious landers, were installed in *Bruce*'s two aeroshells.

"We've got one more for you to carry, *Bruce*," said Richard.

"I'm designed to hold up to four shells," reminded *Bruce*.

"Not the size of *Orville*'s," replied Richard.

"You are, of course, correct," said *Bruce* through Richard's imp, its deep, matter-of-fact voice echoing somewhat in the long cylindrical shaft. Shirley had bounced upward again and soon returned holding a large aeroshell. She opened the lid and peeked in.

"Hi, *Orville*," she said. "Ready to go?"

"Quite ready," said *Orville* through her imp.

Shirley closed the lid, then looked at *Bruce* and the crowded lift shaft.

"I'll take *Orville* up starside, and you can bring *Bruce* up on the lift, it'll be easier to mate *Orville*'s shell in the Christmas Bush's work area where I'll have more room." Holding the massive shell above her head, she bent her knees and leaped upward in the weak gravity, her legs working like pistons against the handholds along the walls of the shaft. The lift started upwards, more slowly this time, and took them starside.

Thomas hadn't been out in a while, so Richard stayed inside while Shirley and Thomas launched *Bruce*, *Bubble*, *Burble*, and *Orville* off on their exploration of Zuni. They could see the varicolored moon in the distance, and they both stood outside for a while after *Bruce* had shrunk into invisibility, to stare at the shining blue lakes and the curl of a weather front that extended over the terminator to the dark side. There was a tiny flash of light at the dark end of the arc of cloud.

"One thousand one, one thousand two, . . ." murmured Thomas under his breath.

"What *are* you doing?" asked Shirley.

"I just saw a lightning stroke on the dark side and I'm counting. Every three seconds between the flash and the thunder is a kilometer."

"I'll give you some thunder," said Shirley, laughing and pounding the top of his helmet. Thomas ducked into the lock and cycled through. Shirley stayed outside to watch the lightning flashes on the dark side of the distant moon. Zuni was a prime candidate for a manned lander. They would be back.

Having taken a tour of the moons about Gargantua, Jinjur next set her sail for a close inspection of the giant planet itself. For a month she and James used the weak light from Barnard to drop the orbit of *Prometheus* closer and closer to the gigantic planet.

Four times more massive than Jupiter, Gargantua was close to being a sun itself. Like the larger planets in the solar system, it emitted more heat from its internal gravitational contraction and chemical phase changes than it received from Barnard. Its surface temperature was near the freezing point of water, which was cold, but it was still a lot warmer than the near-absolute-zero of the black sky, and its heat was a major contributor to the climatic patterns of its moons. Gargantua had a strong magnetic field, driven by the convection currents in its metallic hydrogen core, but its radiation belt was weaker than that of Jupiter, since the solar wind from the red dwarf Barnard wasn't too strong and the many moons kept the belts swept clean.

Jinjur and James were careful in their approach to Gargantua. Its gravitational well was deep, and they didn't want to find themselves too far down in it while they were in the wrong type of orbit. Not that they were ever in any real danger of falling in, but the propulsion power for *Prometheus* was the light from Barnard. If they got into an orbit where they spent half their time with Gargantua blocking the sunlight, it would take forever to climb up out of the pull of the planet and escape.

Gargantua rotated only once a week, much more slowly than Jupiter. As a result, its weather patterns were not the multiplicity of belts and zones with occasional spots as on Jupiter, but instead it had a multiplicity of gigantic cyclones that were spawned near the equator and careened their way into the higher latitudes, where they dissipated into storm fronts. Except for the size, they looked quite similar to the weather patterns on Earth.

Gargantua had a larger rock core than Jupiter. Its density was nearly two grams per cubic centimeter, while Jupiter would nearly float if a big enough and salty enough ocean could be found to put it in. The core of Gargantua was not only evident from the density and the magnetic field, but showed up as permanent spots in the weather pattern. There were certain hot spots near the equator that seemed to be the seed spots for the hurricanes, and other, colder spots that seemed to deplete the strength and deflect any cyclone pattern that wandered near them. The most amazing feature was not near the equator, but at a point near the south pole. The crew didn't notice it at first, for it was summer on Gargantua.

George and Arielle were sitting side-by-side on the control deck. Arielle was at the right science console studying Gargantua's gargantuan weather patterns, while George was at the left.

"Look at this, George!" said Arielle. "She is cute!"

George cleared his screen.

"Ready!" he said.

Arielle punched some keys on her console, and George's screen started a time-compressed video display of a huge weather pattern that had been spawned by the 22 S latitude, 22 E longitude hot spot and had headed south. A few weeks later it had passed over the southern terminator heading for the south pole hidden in the darkness. Instead of disappearing, however, the cloud pattern rebounded from the south pole blackness and broke into two smaller storms, both of which eventually made their way over the terminator on either side of the point that the storm had first entered.

"There must be something there," said George.

"Most certainly," said Arielle, turning serious. "I make

doppler measurements on clouds there. They all move north."

"And that's the only portion of Gargantua that we can't see," complained George.

"In two month we have summer at south pole. Then we have lots of light," said Arielle hopefully.

"In two months we should be through with our preliminary survey of Gargantua and on our way to Rocheworld," said George.

"You sound like you in a hurry, sky-jock," chided Arielle. "Like you do a quick job and get to go home."

George didn't answer, he was asking other questions of the radar pulses that were bouncing off the conductive clouds on the giant planet below.

"There's not only a north-flowing wind pattern, there's also a significant increase in cloud altitude at that point," he said.

"How many?" asked Arielle.

"One thousand kilometers," said George.

"This is impossible," said Arielle. "Things on Gargantua may be huge because the planet is so huge, but cloud altitude change of a thousand kilometers in just a few degrees is most impossible."

"You're right," said George. "But it's there. What we need is more light."

"I can give you that," said Jinjur's voice through George's imp. "I've been watching your displays on the command console. There is something strange going on in the nether regions. Next time around I will shed some light on the subject."

"We have searchlight?" asked Arielle.

"Unless you're a light-sailor, you don't think about it," said George. "But if you've ever been in a light-sail race and had to pay a fine for disturbing the darkness in some sleepy burg in Switzerland by flicking the full Sun at them during a tight tack, you quickly learn that a light-sail makes a good searchlight, and we have one that is almost big enough for Gargantua."

"More than big enough," said Jinjur. "At our distance we can illuminate most of the south pole region by just tilting the sail a little. It'll shift our orbit slightly, but James can compensate later."

Some seventy minutes later, they finished their orbit of the northern polar regions of Gargantua and dipped down below the equator. James tilted the sail slightly and a beam of reddish photons from Barnard were reflected from the light-sail down onto the darkened south pole of Gargantua.

"It's a *tit!*" said George, whose eyes had never missed one yet.

It did look like one. Not three degrees from the south pole of Gargantua was a large permanent mound half as big as Jupiter rising five thousand kilometers above the normal Gargantuan surface of ninety-eight thousand kilometers radius. In the center was a central peak—"A nipple!" George insisted. It was as big around as the Earth and reached upwards another thousand kilometers.

Jinjur had James curve the sail to concentrate the light on the central region as they orbited over the south pole region and looked down at the gigantic formation. It was a gigantic atmospheric volcano. A hot spot deep in the core was ejecting liquid metallic hydrogen in a continuous geyser that spurted upward at high pressure to climb for twenty thousand kilometers through the thick atmosphere until it burst into outer space. As it rose, the metallic hydrogen, released from the internal pressure that kept it in its relatively dense metallic form, converted back into hydrogen molecules, then atoms, then ionized plasma as the kinetic energy in the stream was converted into heat. The electric-blue "tit" of the atmospheric volcano gave off continuous lightning flashes as the flowing hydrogen atoms rose into space, recombined back into hydrogen molecules, then fell in the strong gravitational field back into the upper cloud layers. Now a gas, the falling hydrogen built up into a permanent "high-pressure" area that slowly spread out in an atmospheric version of a lava shield and ultimately flowed back into the surrounding countryside.

The scientists had a field day with their instruments each time they passed over the "tit," slowly twirling once a week about the south polar axis. Behind them, trying not to get in the way, was Thomas, snapping shot after shot with his seventy-millimeter electrocam. Whereas the scientists were interested in data, Thomas was interested in the rapidly varying light display, especially when they were right over the volcano and staring down into the blazing blue bowels of the gigantic planet. Six years later, it was one of his shots, not those of James and the planetary scientists, that made the cover of *National Geographic*.

They were on their twenty-fifth pass over the south pole of Gargantua. James had become expert at giving George and Arielle, the atmospheric experts, the illumination that they needed to study the strange atmospheric volcano near the south pole of Gargantua. George was analyzing some infrared images of the "tit" when he felt a strong black presence at his back.

"Are you and the beauty queen *quite* finished?" asked a deep voice. "I realize that I am merely the commander of this mission and my job is to make sure that you wizard types are kept happy and well fed, but I *do* have a *few* more planets to visit."

George looked at Arielle. Arielle looked at her nails. Two were chipped from the constant tapping of screen and pounding of keyboard during the last thirty-six hours. George turned to face Jinjur, and gave a weak smile. "I guess we're nearly done. Any time, General Jones."

Jinjur made her way back to her control seat. George could almost feel the "stomp" in the corridor boots as they contacted the soft carpeting in the weak gravity. He turned back to his console to see if he could extract some more data before they had to leave. Jinjur punched her console, and soon a display was on her screen. It came from the radar console that Thomas was using.

"How does it look, Thomas?" she asked. "Did those eggheads with the mammary-gland fixation bollix our schedule so we'll have to chase the eggbeater?"

"James and I have the trajectory of Rocheworld pretty solid, but there is something going on that raises some questions," said Thomas off to her right. "We have old data from the flyby probe that we're still arguing about. James thinks it's too perfect. Either there has been absolutely no change in Rocheworld's orbit in fifty-plus years, or else there has been a significant shift and things just happened to match up when we got here. I'm arguing that the second is implausible, but James seems to want to believe in the laws of entropy, that things must run down, and it is impossible for Rocheworld's dynamics not to have changed in fifty years."

"What's the problem?" asked Jinjur.

"James and I have tracked Rocheworld's two planetoids very carefully with radar while the rest of you have been peering at Gargantua's obscene bottom. Rocheworld is in a highly elliptical orbit with a period that James is sure is *exactly* one-third that of the orbital period of Gargantua. The elliptical orbit brings it close to Barnard at periapsis, then it swings out nearly to Gargantua's orbit. Once every three orbits the two periods match up and Rocheworld passes just outside Gargantua's moon system.

"That sounds awfully coincidental," said Jinjur.

"One of the lobes of Rocheworld must have been a moon of Gargantua," said Thomas, "with the other one being another moon in an elliptical orbit or an interloper from outer space. The only way we'll find out is to visit them."

"How's our pursuit trajectory? We are way behind in the science schedule. Can we make it up?"

"No way," said Thomas. "Rocheworld is on its way out and we're still down in Gargantua's gravity well with an undermasted sailboat instead of a diesel cruiser. There's no way we can meet it in time for its next close passage. We'll just have to catch it on the fly somewhere else in this system."

"OK," said Jinjur. She looked across the control deck at George and Arielle. "Had enough sightseeing, you two?" she said. "Don't forget, we'll be back after we've completed the preliminary survey."

George punched a few more keys on his console, and as James followed those commands to extract a few more pieces of information out of the images coming up from

Gargantua, George turned and looked at Arielle. She shrugged her shoulders in resignation.

"All yours, Jinjur," he said. He got up wearily from the science console chair, and stumbling a bit on unused legs, he made his way to the lift shaft and his bed. Arielle went to bed, too, but first she stopped off at the sick bay to get patches for her cracked fingernails, then at the galley to get a bite to eat. She had a double helping of protocheese with real garlic from Nels's hydroponic gardens, two algae shakes with energy sticks mixed in for crunch, then, still hungry, she finished with a dessert consisting of a half-pound of white-meat sticks from "Chicken Little"—her real-meat ration for a week—sliced into thin strips and hot-cooked with James's secret recipe of herbs and spices.

LANDING

Their preliminary survey of the Gargantuan Z-system completed, Jinjur started the long trip back into the inner Barnard system to map Rocheworld, the most interesting feature of this strange stellar system. She had just accepted James's spiral course recommendation when Red, who had been watching with interest over her shoulder, said, "Why are you doing it that way? It'll take forever."

Jinjur smiled as she patiently explained. "I sure wish this tub had the instantaneous rocket power that the ion ships do. You're spoiled, Red. Those laser-beam-powered ion rockets that you used in the Asteroid Belt got you used to 'driving' from one place to another. These light-sails have to 'sail.' It may take longer, but we never run out of fuel."

"Yeah . . ." said Red, still not convinced. "But you light-jammers never had to give up half your claim on a billion tons of nickel-iron just to get a fuel stake for your next trip. Out on the Belt we learned a lot of tricks that would cut down on the light bill." She turned and looked around the control deck.

"Where's a console? I want to do a few orbit calculations." She spotted an empty console, padded over, and fixed herself down.

A half-hour later, James whispered to Jinjur through her imp. "I think Elizabeth has something," it said. "I have a copy of my answer to her latest query on your screen."

Jinjur glanced down. She had been relaxing and looking around her control deck while James slowly carried out the orbit-raising routine. It took her a few seconds to readjust her orientation, since the orbit Red had calculated for *Prometheus* was nearly at right angles to the one that James was using.

It took Jinjur a while to appreciate what she saw, since her past experience in space had been on light-sails in Earth orbit. She blanked the screen as she heard a rip from a coverall detaching itself from a console seat, the soft pad-pad of low-gee feet making their way across the room, then Red's semi-apologetic voice.

"General Jones?"

"Its Jinjur, or Virginia if you insist on being formal, Red. I have the feeling that you have something important to tell me."

Red, nonplussed, hesitated, then began. "We're presently in a low polar orbit about Gargantua and are planning to stay in that orbit while we spiral out . . ."

"Right," said Jinjur. "We'll stay in polar orbit, making sure it stays sun-synchronous so we don't waste any time in Gargantua's shadow. Then we'll tip over and spiral into an orbit in Barnard's ecliptic plane to match orbits with Rocheworld."

"If instead," persisted Red, "we switched to an equatorial orbit as rapidly as we could, we could get out faster and catch Rocheworld earlier."

"Really?" asked Jinjur. "We'd spend half of our time in shadow." She was practically convinced because of what James had shown her, but she still didn't really understand.

"As I said before," continued Red. "When you have to dig into your own pockets for fuel, you quickly pick up all the ways you can to get free propulsion. Even the smallest asteroid can be of some help.

"If we switch to an equatorial orbit now, and time things accurately, we can be crossing Zulu's orbit just in back of it, and it will toss us out to Zouave. We will actually want to decelerate a little before we hit that orbit, but if we do that right, I figure we can gravity-whip this parasol out past six of the moons and arrive at Rocheworld seven weeks early."

Jinjur pulled up a copy of Red's screen, looked at it for a moment, and then in a semi-serious tone spoke at the imp above her right ear. "You hear that, James? You should've spent more time riding ion ships instead of dandelion-seeds."

"Yes, General Jones," said James contritely.

"Do you think you can improve on Red's trajectory?" she said severely.

"With difficulty, General Jones."

"Do it."

"Yes, General Jones."

There was a three-second pause. Even Red knew that most of it was for her benefit. The screen blinked, and there in purple was an alternate trajectory. It followed Red's almost exactly for the first four moons, then drifted off. After the fifth moon it added another before it took off for the last moon and Rocheworld. Jinjur saw Red nod in approval.

"We can save three more hours this way," said James.

Jinjur bent down to examine her screen, then asked, "Is the hook in the trajectory 'cause we're meeting Rocheworld on the outbound leg?"

"Yes. By using Red's suggested orbit, we not only make up the time we lost studying Gargantua's atmospheric volcano, we will arrive at Rocheworld some ten days or forty rotations from when it makes its closest approach to Gargantua."

"Good," said Jinjur. "I wasn't looking forward to spending all that time chasing the egghead twins all over the system."

When *Prometheus* had first arrived at Gargantua, Rocheworld was on the inbound leg of its highly elliptical trajectory. While they were taking pictures of the giant planet and its moons, the tiny double-planet went through its close periapsis passage about Barnard. The point of closest approach was on the same side of the star that they were, and they tried to follow it across the distant red disk with telescopes, but most of the detail was hidden by the deep red glare of the fuzzy globe of light. Rocheworld was now coming out again to meet them, slowing rapidly as it climbed up out of the deep gravity well. They dropped inward, then applied full braking power to turn around and match orbits with the twin planets.

Like a pirouetting pair of gumdrops, the two planetoids that made up Rocheworld whirled along their orbit. The two lobes were distorted into egg shapes that looked like an infinity symbol when seen through Thomas's low-power electrocamera lens. Six years later, the scientifically blurred but artistically fascinating image was "the" Christmas card of 2075.

Jinjur approached the double-planet with caution.

"Don't get too close," said Jinjur. "I want you to spiral in slowly and monitor the shape of the sail as you do. The rotating double-lobed gravity pattern of that eggbeater is something that neither you, nor I, nor the designers of the sail ever had any experience with."

"I am already noticing some tilt-brim flutter of the sail," said James. "It is easily damped out by the actuators."

"Just don't get careless," warned Jinjur. "The last thing I want to do is spend the rest of my life under an umbrella with a tear in it."

Jinjur padded to the science consoles and looked over the shoulders of Sam and Richard as they busily ordered the various image sensors into operation. There were mechanical sounds from the center of the control deck as different sensors emerged from their storage places, took their turn looking out the Barnardside science dome at the nearby planets, then retracted back again into their niches.

"How does it look?" she asked.

"The visible and infrared images are excellent," said Sam. "But the X-ray and gamma-ray images are blurred by the atmosphere. Also, the radio images show nothing but modest temperature variations. There don't seem to be any radiation belts, which means a low magnetic field."

"Does that mean there is no shielding from cosmic rays?" asked Jinjur, slightly concerned.

"Nothing to worry about," said Sam. "Although the atmospheric pressure is only twenty percent of Earth's, the gravity is lower, so the scale height is much higher. There is a deep blanket of air to stop the cosmic rays. In fact, it's so thick that the two planets share a common atmosphere."

"I think we'll be able to fly from one lobe to another in the *Dragonfly* without having to switch to rocket propulsion," said Richard.

"That doesn't sound right to me," said Jinjur. "Aren't they a couple of hundred kilometers apart? Increased scale height or no, there isn't going to be much atmosphere left at those altitudes."

"The gap is only eighty kilometers," replied Richard. "And don't forget that the gravity drops to zero between the two planets, so the 'gravitational' altitude there is different than the physical altitude."

"What a weird planet," said Jinjur. "What else have you learned?"

"Why don't you show her some of the pictures," said Sam. "While I keep the science sensors going."

Richard flashed some images across his screen in rapid succession and then stopped at a picture that showed the two lobes fully illuminated, with Barnard in back of the camera.

"This is the best shot that we have that shows the egg-shaped tidal distortion of the two lobes," said Richard. "That particular shape was first calculated by Roche in the 1880s. He was primarily interested in calculating the shapes of two closely spaced binary stars. I'm sure he never thought there'd be a binary planet system named after him."

He switched to a closeup picture of one of the lobes. It showed a mountainous region with deep valleys.

"Sure looks rocky," said Jinjur.

"That's why this lobe of Rocheworld is called the Roche lobe," said Richard. "It just happens that the word 'roche' means 'rock' in French."

"How come the valleys are all going the same way?" asked Jinjur.

"That's the rift valley region," said Richard. "Let me get another version."

The screen flickered some more and finally stopped with a closeup picture of a large conical mountain peak with a rounded top and sixty-degree slopes.

"That's the pointy part of the Roche egg," said Richard. "The mountain peak is a part of the original Roche sphere that was pulled up into this shape as the two planets slowly came toward each other due to tidal friction. Sam and I expect that the rift valleys were formed at that time, with the 'stretch marks' in rings where the material was pulled up. What we don't understand are the deep valleys going 'downhill.' They look almost like river valleys, but are completely dry. It'll be one of the first things we want to look at when we land there."

"What's that fuzzy thing there on the side of the mountain?" she asked.

"That's a volcano," said Richard. "You would expect a lot of tectonic activity in a region under as much stress as that one. Here, let me get some action in the picture." He punched a few keys, then the picture was replaced by a twelve-image stop-motion replay of the eruption of two volcanos on each side of the conical mountain. The plumes blossomed straight out from the sides.

"How come the plumes don't fall downhill?" said Jinjur.

"That's one of the strangest things about the shapes that the Roche mathematics predicts," said Richard. "The surface of that conical mountain with its sixty-degree slopes is all at the same gravitational potential, even though the shape is not a sphere. The same goes for the other lobe, where the mountain is made of water."

Richard switched to another image. There was the same conical shape, but Jinjur could tell from the color and smoothness that it was the surface of an ocean.

"This is the wet lobe," said Richard. "It's named the Eau lobe since 'eau' means 'water' in French. Its shape is almost identical to that of the Roche lobe, except that its surface is almost completely covered with a water-ammonia ocean. The ocean is shallow on the outer portion of the lobe, because we can see some crater rims and mountain peaks showing through, while on the inner portion the ocean gets much deeper because it is pulled up into a mountain by the gravitational attraction of its twin."

"It still looks like it ought to fall down," said Jinjur.

"It's even more remarkable, since the gravity at the top of the mountain is only a half-percent of an Earth gravity, while at the base of the mountain the gravity rises to ten percent of Earth gravity. This is one time you have to forget your long-taught prejudices about the behavior of water under gravity and believe the mathematics. The surface of that water mountain is all at the same gravitational potential, and the water is just seeking its natural level. The mountain doesn't just stand there looking impossible, though. There's plenty of action. Let me show you the movie that Sam and I pieced together. Roll it, James."

As the double-planets rotated about each other each six hours, the tides and heat generated by Barnard pushed the ocean and atmosphere around. Each half-rotation, the water mountain would drop twenty kilometers, then rise again, driven by the tides, while the atmosphere, driven by a combination of tides and heat, sloshed back and forth once per revolution. When the water mountain was rising and the atmosphere was going from Roche to Eau, the peak would be strangely calm, with only small breakers showing at its base, for the air was rushing down the slopes. Three hours later, the wind would be blowing up along the rising slopes of water. As the wind moved upwards, it drove the water ahead of it. The wind-driven swells moved upwards toward the peak, where the gravitation was weaker and the surface area was smaller. The energy in the wave motion was concentrated into a smaller area, and there was less gravity to keep the wave amplitude down, so the swells grew into waves that reached hundreds of meters in height as the gravitation and the available surface area dropped to nearly zero at the same time. The ring-waves climbing up the mountain became larger and larger and finally met in a ring-geyser that shot a fountain of foamy water up toward the zero-gravity point between the planets. There the geyser dissolved into a spray of water vapor, some of which drifted across the zero gravity point to spawn tornadoes and thunderheads that dropped rain that dried to salt-specks before it reached the rocky surface below.

"A lovely place," remarked Jinjur. "Shall we drop in for a visit?"

"Yes!" said Richard. "Drop us down right on the equator of the rocky one. That's far enough from the tornado belt that the lander won't be disturbed, and Sam can poke around in the rocks while I go fishing on the other lobe."

"This planet is the dream of an astrodynamicist," said Thomas. "I'd like to 'bug' it all over before we go down for a close look, especially the Lagrange points. They're very sensitive to orbital perturbations."

"I thought you only had Lagrange minima when one mass is bigger than the other, like the Sun and Jupiter," said Jinjur.

"They're much more stable then," said Thomas. "Especially the co-orbit points. But you get almost the same thing when the two masses are the same size. There is the obvious minimum where the gravity drops to zero between the two planets, then there are the famous L–4 and L–5 points, the only truly stable ones."

"Those I know about," said Jinjur. "They're always sixty degrees ahead or behind the planet in its orbit around the sun."

"In this system it's different," said Thomas. "Since the two planetoids are the same size, the Lagrange points are not at sixty degrees, but ninety degrees. That's where I want to put the communication satellites. The gravity minimum will keep them there with minimum fuel, and any perturbations will give my Rocheworld computer model some exercise. Perhaps we'll learn something."

"Will the commsats be able to communicate well from there?" asked Jinjur.

"Two commsats at the L–4 and L–5 points will cover most of the two worlds except for the outer poles," said Thomas. "I propose to put another commsat in counter-orbit to their rotation so that we are never more than three hours from contact with any point on the two lobes."

"Fine," said Jinjur. "You and Shirley go up the shaft and break them out and transfer them to the lander."

Thomas headed for the lift shaft. James had informed Shirley, and just as the lift was rising through the ceiling of the control deck, there was a jerk of the lift as James jammed it to a halt, just in time to prevent the edge of the lift from cutting the flying body of Shirley in two as she streaked to join Thomas on the doughnut-shaped platform of the lift.

"Shirley," said James in a dry voice.

"Don't try that 'tired butler' voice on me, James," said Shirley. "I designed you with plenty of safety margin in the lift elevator. I merely used a little of that margin for my last dive. Up we go!"

The lift started again and went up through the ceiling to level twenty. There, three commsats, *Clete*, *Walter*, and *Barbara* were activated and carried to the hydroponics deck. Nels Larson met them there, and with his massive muscular arms, helped push the three high-inertia loads down the humid green world of water-filled walls—the fact that Nels had no legs making no difference in this low-gee world. They stopped at a porthole in the ceiling. It was open, and Thomas looked up to see the innards of *Eagle* and the flashing green limbs and short red hair of a busy heavy-lift pilot strapped into a blue acceleration harness, checking out a long-dormant, giant of a rocket. Crouching low, he launched himself through the porthole overhead, then reached down to take one of the commsats from Nels.

As Shirley stored the commsats away, Thomas went over to talk to Red, hanging upside down in her harness. She looked up from the console.

"I've found one malfunction and three 'out of spec' indicators in the countdown list, and they're all on outside sensors," she said. "I was going to send a branch out to investigate, but why don't you do it." Red busied herself at the console while Thomas made his way upwards from the bridge deck of *Eagle*, through the pristine but cramped crew quarters deck to the "bottom" deck. Everything was upside down from what it would be once *Eagle* was under acceleration or sitting on one of the planetoids of the Barnard system. He put on a suit, then went to the side airlock and punched some keys built into the wall next to the door. A strange, yet familiar, computer voice spoke to him. It was Jack, James's alter ego for the computer in the Surface Lander and Ascent Module.

"I can have the Christmas Branch make the inspection," said Jack.

"They taught me in flight school to always check out my plane before I fly," said Thomas. The door hissed open and Thomas stepped in onto the ceiling of the airlock. After some pumping noises, his suit ballooned out and the outer door swung open. The strange accent of Jack spoke through his suit imp.

"Don't forget James has *Prometheus* under acceleration. Please use your safety lines," said Jack.

"Right," said Thomas, fastening a hook into a nearby ring and stepping out. He activated his 'stiction boots and moved along the curved hull of the massive rocket. He worried a little about the stability of the forty-year-old fuel under his feet, but there was little he could do about it now, for the nearest fuel depot was six light-years away. He marched down the hull in the low acceleration to the "top" of the lander to check out the errant sensor modules.

"Three tired solid-state detectors and one micro-meteorite strike," said Thomas to Red as he took off his helmet and handed it to Shirley. "I upped the voltage on the detectors and they're back in spec, and the Christmas Bush sent out a branch with a replacement for the punctured unit."

The lander soon filled up with its crew, who were busy shifting their personal belongings from their luxurious apartments on *Prometheus* to the crowded vertical beds they would be using during the short periods in space while the *Eagle* was in free-fall. A day passed, the checkout was completed, and it was time to go. Jinjur escorted George to the lock between the *Eagle* and *Prometheus*.

"I wish I were going down," said Jinjur.

"I thought you never wanted to see dirt again," said George. "Especially if it had gees holding it down."

"It's only a tenth gee," said Jinjur. "Besides," she added wistfully, "it's been forty-four years."

"Doesn't time fly when you're mentally incompetent," said George. "OK. Next planet you get to go down with the exploration crew and I stay at home minding the ship. See you in a few months."

"Take your time and do it right," said Jinjur. "We have all the rest of our lives to spend exploring, but only four landers."

"I will," said George. He reached for Jinjur's shirtfront and half unfastened the button under the most tension, then fastened it again.

"See you soon," he said, pulling her forward for a long good-bye kiss. He turned and went through the airlock door, making sure it was space-sealed.

Now that he was on board *Eagle*, George's personal imp was no longer controlled by James.

"*Eagle* ready for departure, sir," said Jack.

"Let's go," George replied. He heard pumps working and the outer lock door creaked slightly as the air in the small volume between the *Eagle* and *Prometheus* was pumped out. His imp jumped to the door and searched the seams for any sign of leakage. Finding none, it jumped back to his shoulder. For a few seconds George felt both naked and bereft. James could afford the luxury of a lock-imp on *Prometheus*. Life would be more spartan for Jack's landing crew, since only a Christmas "Branch," a one-sixth portion of a Christmas Bush, was assigned to the *Eagle*'s computer.

George cycled through. Shirley was waiting for him, standing on the ceiling. She and Jack's Christmas Branch double-checked the docking airlock, then Shirley returned to help Sam check out the many instruments on the science consoles. Both were apparently able to read the labels and indicators as easily upside-down as rightside-up. George paused at the wedge-shaped passway through to the next deck, and holding on to the ladder rungs welded into the consumables column that ran through the center of the ship, he looked up to see Arielle, Richard, and Katrina busy stuffing equipment and supplies into the storage bins next to the galley.

"Breakaway in five minutes," he warned.

"We'll be ready," answered Katrina.

George continued around the central column, walking on the ceiling of the bridge. Carefully avoiding the large glass docking window at his feet, he nodded at Thomas and Red, who were buckled into the blue pilot and red copilot harnesses in front of their consoles, then continued on to the computer and communication consoles.

"Jack is ready," said David Greystoke up at George. Like the two pilots, David was hanging from the floor in a zero-gee harness.

"*Prometheus* has given us clearance for breakaway," said Carmen from the console next to David's.

"Take her away, Captain St. Thomas," said George.

Thomas grasped the controls and nodded at Red. She flicked a red switch cover and threw the switch underneath. There was a loud clunk from the docking port, followed by a series of clattering ripples as the clamps that had held *Eagle* to the outside of the lift shaft on *Prometheus* were retracted. Nothing happened, for they were still held to the sailship by its acceleration.

Thomas pushed a control forward, and the bridge crew hanging from the ceiling sagged a little further in their harnesses as the acceleration increased. Thomas and Red looked out their docking-port window as the huge cylinder tilted and swung out from its cradle on the light-ship. As soon as the edge of the hydroponics deck on *Prometheus* had been cleared, Thomas switched to other control jets and slowly flew the ponderous cylinder out through the shrouds and away from the sail.

"The *Eagle* has left its nest," said George sideways to his imp.

"Good hunting, *Eagle*," said Jinjur's voice.

Once Thomas had pulled them away from their berth and out from between the shrouds, he turned off the maneuvering jets and they were in free-fall. Suddenly

George felt upside-down, and quickly floated around to point the same way as the rest of the crew. He left Thomas and Red to the task of moving them safely away from the sail so they could turn on their main motors, and dived through the passway to see what there was to eat in the galley.

"This sure is easier than trying to leave a tumbling asteroid," said Red, as she watched out the docking port at the slowly twirling light-sail and its cylindrical payload with the wedge-shaped gap in one side.

"All we have to do is stay cool and float, while the sunlight pushes it out of our way," said Thomas.

After about an hour *Prometheus* was twenty kilometers away. Using low thrust from the main rockets, Thomas steered the *Eagle* away from the sail and into a rendezvous orbit with Rocheworld.

For two days they spiraled in from orbit, letting Jack get used to the strange double-lobed rotating gravitational field, and taking detailed closeup pictures of their planned landing place.

"Looks just like Mars," said Sam to Richard.

"With fewer boulders," said Richard, as he blew up the picture on the screen until he could see the pixels. "Looks like it's been swept clean. We could land just about anywhere with no trouble."

"Why don't we make it by this mesa?" said Sam. "That ten-meter scarp should give us a good cross-section of the crust for a first look."

"Looks like the edge of a streambed," said Richard.

"So do a lot of features on Mars," said Sam. "But all those streams flowed millions of years ago, and the waters that flowed are dried up and gone away. On Mars the water that wasn't lost to space was turned into rust or frozen in the polar caps. Here the erosion probably occurred when the Gargantuan moon and the interloper first interacted, but since Eau is some twenty kilometers smaller than Roche, the rain clouds formed over the lowlands on Eau rather than up in the Roche mountain plateau, and all the water ended up on Eau. I bet those streambeds are as old, if not older, than the ones on Mars."

"The only way to find out is to go down and count craters," said Richard. "But don't you want to land on the mesa, just in case?"

"Then my excursions on the dirt-buggy will be limited to the mesa," said Sam. "And I plan to take longer trips than that. The streambed near the cliff, Jack."

"I will inform Captain St. Thomas," said Jack.

Eagle approached Rocheworld in the ecliptic plane, but going in the opposite direction to the spin of the planetoids. As they moved closer and closer, the orbital track on Red's pilot console took on a wavy appearance as the two lobes pulled the track this way and that.

"Having any navigation problems, Jack?" she asked her imp.

"Newton's laws are still valid, Red, even though it may not look like it on the track replay. I do have to carry the calculations a little further than normal before I truncate the series, though."

"I'm glad you're doing this and not me," said Red. "Intuition can get you in trouble this close to those whirling dervishes."

"Intuition has served humans well," said Jack. "It's their strongest point as a computational system. However, like most strengths, it is also one of their weakest points."

Thomas overheard the exchange.

"Don't feel bad, Red," he said. "I think you're the best looking computational system I've ever seen."

Red smiled and somehow felt a lot better.

"It's time to release *Barbara*," said Jack.

"I'll get her," said Shirley, who had been floating around the deck with little to do. She pulled herself over to one side of the bridge and opened a storage locker.

"I'd appreciate a hand out of here," said a contralto voice through Shirley's imp.

Shirley grasped the communications satellite carefully at the base of its antenna and pulled it free from its fasteners. She nudged the heavy spacecraft around the bend to the

docking port entrance. Carefully she inserted the commsat
in the exact center of the lock, making sure that its folded
antennas would clear the outer door.

"Keep in touch, *Barbara*," she said.

"That's my job," said *Barbara*.

Shirley closed the door to the docking lock, then went
around the central column and nodded at Red, who had
moved to the pilot position. Red had fastened herself into
the safety harness even though the planned acceleration
would be negligible.

Red watched the orbital track until the wavy track had
neared its minimum, then her finger gave a slight nudge
to a button on her control stick. Shirley felt a slight tug on
the sticky patches of her corridor boots.

Nicely done, thought Shirley. *It's those years in the
asteroid belt.*

The velocity difference imparted by the tiny flare of
control jet was small, but a minute later Shirley could see
Barbara slowly rise up out of the docking port without a
single trace of spin or tumble. When the commsat was
about ten meters away Shirley sent it a message.

"You may fire control jets when ready, *Barbara*."

There was a burst of tiny jets as the spacecraft rotated
its orientation, then a larger burst as the commsat took off
to take up its station in an orbit that rotated in an opposite
direction to the rotation of the two planetoids. That way,
those areas at the outer poles that could not see the
commsats at the L–4 and L–5 points would have access to
Barbara once every three hours.

"This is *Barbara*, signing off," said the commsat as it
flew out of sight.

With the commsat launched in its counter-rotating orbit, Red expertly rotated the huge cylinder end over end.
As the spacecraft rotated to a halt, Red talked to her imp.

"Announce imminent gees to all hands, Jack," she said.

"Thrust will commence in one minute," boomed Jack's
voice throughout the ship.

"Just a second," shouted Richard up through the passway. "Let me get my soap! I haven't had a real shower
since we decelerated at Barnard."

There was a slam of some doors, and Shirley, monitoring the engineering board, noticed a light go on under the hygiene water expenditure sign. She shook her head. Red, serious as ever, checked over the main engine controls and glanced at Thomas, who nodded back. She pushed at the four-levered throttle bar. They went from free-fall to a tenth gee and stayed there, Red playing with the relative adjustments on the throttles as she looked at her track and the motion of the two lobes on her screen.

For a while Shirley could look out of the corner of the docking window in the ceiling of the bridge and see the outer poles of the two lobes moving majestically across her view, slowing perceptibly as Red decreased their counter-rotating orbital speed. As the thrust continued, the rocket tilted upward until the lobes could no longer be seen. Shirley climbed heavily down the passway on the ladder and clumped her way around to the viewport lounge. It was full, including a dripping Richard wrapped in a towel, ignoring the exasperated mosquito-imps that were attempting to cope with the drops of water in the accelerated environment.

The period of thrust lasted for fifteen minutes. The tilt of the spacecraft came back to horizontal, as the rotation of the lobes slowed and stopped until they were stationary in the sky. Barnard lit the two lobes brilliantly with a flat red glow.

"We're at L-4, Shirley," said Red's voice through her imp. "Time to dump *Clete* off."

Shirley left her perch on the video room partition and floated her way back through the galley and up the passway to the storage locker.

"L-4, *Clete*," said Shirley.

"Jack so informed me, Miss Everett," said *Clete* through her imp. "If I might trouble you?"

"No trouble at all," said Shirley, taking the heavy satellite out of the locker and pushing it through the free-fall air to the docking port. "Just part of the taxi service."

She cycled the lock and went back to watch Red do another of her minimal bursts.

"You're on the up cycle, *Clete*," said Shirley. "Keep bouncing so we can see you at the cold poles."

"This is *Clete*, signing off," replied the commsat.

"Let's take a break before we insert the other one," said Thomas to Red.

"Let me move *Eagle* to the inside first," said Red. "With *Clete* bouncing up and down through the L–4 point, we don't want to be in its way when it comes back down through." She fired a burst from the attitude jets and then turned the controls over to Jack.

"Give Thomas and me a call in eight hours, Jack. We're going to rack up a few winks." *Eagle*'s two pilots snaked their way down through the passway, and George's gray thatch appeared in the wedge as soon as they left.

"Since it's going to be quiet for a while, Shirley, I thought you, Arielle, and I could check out *Dragonfly*."

"I'd like David along, too," said Shirley, as she swam to the passway and ottered through.

"Are you sure the air seals are OK, Jack?" said Shirley. "Shouldn't I wear a suit for the first time?"

"I have an imp inside both the lock and the boarding port," said Jack through her imp.

"I'll still suit up and go first," said Shirley. She gruffly pulled open the suit locker and got out her suit. "Here, George," she said, handing him her helmet. "Check me out."

"Sure, Shirley, sure," said George, helping her with a sleeve. For someone who could put a suit on with her eyes closed, she was suddenly awkward and clumsy.

David looked at George and then at Arielle, who was trying to pretend she wasn't there. He finally put in his oar.

"Shirley," he said. "Stop being mad at yourself just because you're cautious. You're not being too fussy about safety. We're in no hurry. Just do your job, and do it right. The last thing we want to lose is you."

Shirley stopped in mid-jerk on a zipper. She took control of herself and the rest of the suiting took place in record time. In her full space-suit, she went through the first door of the airlock that would take them to the cockpit entrance of *Dragonfly*. The door closed and George listened to her through his imp.

"Boarding port pressurized?" Shirley asked Jack.

"My imp there reports so," replied Jack.

"Open the door," said Shirley. George could hear some mechanical noises through the wall, but there was no sound of air escape. He peered through the porthole in the door and saw Shirley pull a cloth wiper from her thigh-pocket and wave it in front of the seal surrounding the fuselage of the aerospace plane. After a while he saw her crack her helmet, then take it off. She listened carefully, then put the helmet back on and sealed it again. She then went to the door built into the copilot side of the *Dragonfly*, and lifting panels, she pushed the door inward. She cracked her helmet once again and stuck her head in to look down the long corridor. She floated back out, put her helmet back on and sealed it, then carefully closing and sealing each door she had opened, she made her way back into the *Eagle* through the airlock.

"It's safe to go in without suits," she said in a sure tone, now that she had checked personally. She made her way to the suitlocker, shaking off George's offer of help, while one by one Arielle, David, and George cycled through and floated through the narrow copilot hatch into the magical realm of the aerospace plane—*Dragonfly*. Arielle was the first through the hatch and was greeted by Jill, the semi-intelligent program in *Dragonfly*'s computer.

"Hello, Arielle," said Jill's soprano voice. "I'm glad to see you again. Is Rocheworld as interesting to fly in as Titan?"

"Ho!" said Arielle. "It is much interesting. We can go very high there. There are lots of thermals and we can fly from Roche to L'eau."

"Jack says that we won't even need rocket assist," said Jill. "That's good. I'd much prefer to always keep that for emergencies. I do so hate to use up my consumables."

David swam in through the lock, all business.

"Self-check routine zero," he commanded.

Through his imp a mechanical voice said, "Seven-six-one-three-F-F."

"Check," said Jack.

David consulted a printed checklist and nodded agreement. "Self-check routine one."

"Surface Excursion Module One going through systems check," reported Jill's voice. There was a long pause. During the wait, Arielle and David were joined by George and Shirley.

"Five sensors out of spec, two tanks with measurable level of degradation contaminants, and a missing flask in the galley," Jill finally reported.

"This one?" said Arielle from down in the galley. "I was going to fix me a shake."

"Wait till after checkout!" exploded Shirley. "Right now Jill is busy."

"Oh. That's why we no have algae shakes." Arielle put the flask back and swam up the length of the corridor to join George on the flight deck. They took Jill through a few simulated landings, while Shirley, back on the engineering console, inserted a few "emergencies" to keep them all in practice.

"That's enough," said George, after he had botched an engine-out landing and Arielle had intervened at the last second with an imaginary blast from the space thrusters to float them to a stop. "Jill looks in good shape, and its time for Thomas and Red to pull gees to arc over to L-5 and dump *Walter*. Let's seal up *Dragonfly* and get some dinner."

"I'll be there later," said Shirley. "Have to check out those low sensor readings and the impurity reports."

"I'll be glad to eat your dinner for you," said Arielle as she unbuckled and swam out the hatch.

"You just leave my dinner alone!" shouted Shirley after her. "You skinny bottomless pit!!"

After dinner Thomas and Red went upstairs to the bridge, with Shirley following to monitor the systems on the engineering console. The rest of the crew gathered in the lounge to watch the scene out the viewport and to settle their meals in the acceleration.

"Shall I take the copilot harness?" asked Red, as they made their way up the passway.

"Nope," said Thomas. "I may be good at the ups and downs, but for the roundy-rounds, you're the pro. You get the blue harness and I'll watch and see how you do it."

Eagle was in a synchronous orbit about Rocheworld. To move from the L–4 point to the L–5 point, Red decided to bounce up out of the plane of rotation enough so that when they came back down, Rocheworld had slipped in an extra half-rotation on them. She tilted the *Eagle* and initiated thrust in the main rockets. The viewers in the lounge sank into their seats as the tilted scene slowly rotated in the viewport. Darkness set on Eau as Roche blocked the sun. They looked down at the northern cold poles as the sun rose again on Eau. Great storms could be seen on the cold crescent as a snow of water and ammonia rained down on the mountain of water. They came back down three hours later to a halt at L–5, where *Walter* was dispatched in a bouncing orbit that alternated with that of *Clete*. Now, like the outer poles, neither cold pole was more than three hours away from contact with a commsat. As they were dumping *Walter*, *Barbara* came zipping past in its counter-rotating orbit.

"This is *Barbara* checking, one . . . two . . . three . . ."

"We hear you fine, *Barbara*," replied Shirley.

"This is *Barbara*, saying good-night," said the commsat as it dipped into the darkness behind Roche.

Thomas and Red went down to confer with George.

"We've only been up four hours," said Thomas. "And Red did all the work on that last one while I just dozed away in the red harness. We can take it down if you want us to."

"What's your recommendation, Jack?" said George. He noticed that the imps on both Thomas and Red spread their fingers on the necks and jugular veins of their charges, scanning their vital signs.

"I have no objection," said Jack.

George's imp vibrated with a voice that he had not heard in some while. "James sees no problem either," said Jinjur.

"Take her down," said George. Thomas and Red turned and snaked their way back up the passway. George followed, and the other crew members went either to their racks or their stations as they prepared for a landing on Rocheworld.

"Stand by for deorbit burn," said Thomas. "This'll be the most gees you'll have felt for decades, so make sure you're fastened down."

Slowly Thomas pushed forward the throttle on the main rockets. He and the rest of the bridge crew sank in their harnesses while uncomfortable groans were heard from belowdecks.

"That's only a half gee," said Thomas with a grin. "We go to three gees just before reentry."

The rocket engines blasted a powerful glare over the darkened planetscape below, then throttled down to a more controlled thrust as the huge cylinder floated down through the miles of atmosphere, letting the friction of the cold thin air do its work in dissipating the energy of the falling eighty tons of matter.

A quiescent blob of milky white jelly rested in the dark ocean of Eau. Clear◇White◇Whistle was an expert surfer and had ridden the last ring wave all the way up the water mountain. It had stayed poised on the face of the wave, halfway between a forced dive and a forced tumble, for nearly an eighth of a rotation, while the others of the pod had fallen off along the way. Roaring☆Hot☆Vermillion, usually the best surfer of the pod, went too far up a wave in an attempt to outdistance the rest at the beginning of the run, but had been broken into three parts and foamed out right at the start. Warm✳Amber✳Resonance and Sweet○Green○Fizz had been with them, but they too finally had to take a forced dive, leaving Clear◇White◇Whistle to navigate the last half of the mountain alone, on the side of a wave that was bigger than many of the rocky ridges on the bottom of the ocean.

It had been thrilling to be surfing along at speeds that were so high the sonic pings returning from the lower scattering layers had shrieked into the upper register, but the fun was over and it was time to think. Time to think deeply and clearly. Clear ◊ White ◊ Whistle wondered about the kind of thinking it did. Most of the others in the pod, and indeed most of the others in the ocean, were all the same in their thinking. Numbers, mostly. Some about arrays of numbers. Some about all the numbers between *Oh* and *One*. Some about the numbers that were not numbers but still existed.

Clear ◊ White ◊ Whistle felt alone. It knew all about numbers—enough to do that kind of research itself. But it wasn't content with that. The numbers had to mean something. It felt exultant, yet perverted, as it tried to impale the pure numbers on the impure lights in the sky.

Clear ◊ White ◊ Whistle searched the water around it. It could see nothing except the rocky bottom far, far below. Secure in the knowledge that it could not be seen, yet still secretive, it raised an appendage of thick milky-white jelly. The end floated in the water above the central part of its body. By concentrating, the end of the appendage became thicker and disk-shaped, but it was still milky white like the rest of the appendage. Then, fighting the sexual joy, yet exulting in the perverted self-gratification, Clear ◊ White ◊ Whistle seductively extracted its white from the clear gelatin lens floating on the smooth surface of the calm ocean mountain. The milky body below the surface adjusted its shape until the spots of light focused by the lens on its surface were of minimum size. Like Galileo, gazing on the proscribed heavenly spheres, Clear ◊ White ◊ Whistle returned to its solitary study of the stars.

Clear ◊ White ◊ Whistle had given the bright red glare of Hot the number-name *Oh*. The red light seemingly burned into its white flesh. *Oh* was flanked this rising by a pattern of smaller dots, numbered 6, 32, and 47. Warm—number *One*—was still hidden in back of the ocean. Warm would make an appearance soon, and Clear ◊ White ◊ Whistle resolved to wait for it. Meanwhile, the positions of all the rest of the numbers in the sky were measured and compared against its memory. None had changed over the many seasons since it had first looked at the sky except perhaps for a slight shift in the yellow point of light at the end of the straight string of low-numbered lights.

Clear ◇ White ◇ Whistle had been studying the points of light whenever it had some time off to itself. In this darkness it again puzzled over the behavior of the light numbers. Most of them were simple. They could be handled by a simple coordinate transformation, since they never changed their relative position. The mathematics of *One* and its higher number lights was nearly impossible. For a long while, *One* wandered about in the sky like a broken flitter. Then every four hundred eighty rotations of the sky, it got brighter and brighter until it looked like it was going to rival *Oh* in the sky.

Clear ◇ White ◇ Whistle thought that it knew all the light numbers. This time, however, there was a new light in the sky. It varied rapidly in brightness and moved downward toward Sky⊗Rock until it disappeared on the Hot-limned side of the rock floating in the sky. It moved much more slowly than the other specks of transient light that Clear ◇ White ◇ Whistle had occasionally seen at other dark times. Perhaps the brighter the falling specks were, the slower they fell. Yet, that thought didn't really satisfy Clear ◇ White ◇ Whistle. It very much wanted to know the logic by which the specks of light in the sky moved, especially the motions of *One* and its smaller lights, but the form of the mathematical rule eluded its most concentrated thought.

The ponderous, top-heavy bulk of the lander *Eagle* slowly drifted downward on a rippling flame of rocket exhaust. The crew-members left back on distant *Prometheus* were gathered at videos and consoles, monitoring the landing on Roche through the quartet of video cameras looking down from the four sides of the lander. *Eagle* was drifting inward as Thomas looked for a good landing site. He peered down at the ground in front of him as he maneuvered the controls, while Red watched all four video scenes on her split-screen display and Jack kept up a running commentary through their imps.

"Two hundred meters . . . four-and-a-half down . . .

kicking up some dust . . . four forward . . . drifting to the right a little . . . contact light . . . engine stop . . ."

There was a pause, then the lightsail crew burst into cheers as Thomas's exultant voice broke through strong and loud.

"*Prometheus*! Rocheworld Base here. The *Eagle* has landed!"

FLYING

With the landing safely over, George let out his breath.
For safety he and the crew members who weren't actively
involved in the landing had strapped themselves into their
bunks, while Thomas, Red, Carmen, and David had the
safety harnesses at their consoles. He hung uncomfortably
in his vertical sleeping rack in the ten percent gravity, his
feet not quite touching the deck. As he unfastened the
straps he could hear thuds from the cubicles around him
as the rest of the crew left their sleeping racks and filed
down the narrow corridor to the rest of the ship. Most
made their way around to the miniature lounge and crowded
around the viewport to look out at the alien scenery.
George clumped his way up the ladder through the passway and went over to congratulate Thomas.

"A fine landing," he said, extending a hand, then helped
Thomas with a recalcitrant fastener on his harness.

"Couldn't have done better myself," added Red, who
was still busy powering down the landing systems and
readying the ascent module for lift-off in case they ran
into any trouble.

"Why thanks, Red," said Thomas, a pleased smile on his
face. "Those are high words of praise from an old ion pilot
like you."

Red glanced at him with an annoyed expression. "I'd
prefer the phrase 'experienced' rather than 'old', sonny

boy," she said. Then she added eagerly, "But I'll forgive you if you let me land the next one."

"It's a deal!" agreed Thomas, glad to have gotten out of his gaffe so easily.

"How's the atmosphere, Jack?" asked Shirley. "Can we imitate Buck Rogers and throw off our helmets after a precautionary sniff and run through the meadows in bare feet with the wind blowing through our hair?"

"I'm afraid not," said Jack through her imp. "My analyzer only confirms what we measured from orbit. An atmosphere of methane, ammonia, water vapor, and hydrogen is definitely poisonous all by itself, not to mention the trace amounts of hydrogen sulfide and cyanide gas that my analyzer can pick up now that we are here."

"Hydrogen sulfide?" said Shirley. "That's going to make for a stinky airlock even after purging."

"You won't notice it," said Sam. "Your nostrils will be anesthetized by the traces of ammonia."

"My locks have been designed with minimal trapped volumes," said Jack. "After pumping down to vacuum, then flushing with air once before the final cycle, I should be able to keep the amount of ammonia, hydrogen sulfide, and hydrogen cyanide released into the ship at low level. Unless you have a very sensitive nose, you won't notice it."

"I *have* a sensitive nose," said Shirley. "It's an engineer's best tool."

"I'm ready to go out," said Richard. "I want to get a look at this geology around here. Is it OK if I suit up?"

"If it's OK with Jack, then it's OK with me," said Shirley. "But aren't you forgetting protocol? The commander of the ship gets to be the first one to set foot on the new planet."

"You're right," said Richard. "If it hadn't been for George we wouldn't be here. He gets to go first, but I wish he'd hurry up."

"I'm coming," said George, making his way down the passway ladder.

He went over to the suit locker and started dressing, with Shirley and the Christmas Branch helping. Sam joined them.

"Why don't you and Richard get suited up, too, Sam," said George. "The lock will hold three of us, and there is no need to make this a dramatic one-man production."

The three men, meticulously checked out by a clucking Shirley, cycled through the airlock and opened the outer door to look from the thirty-six-meter height of the lock door down to the surface and off to the horizon.

"Looks like the high desert regions in California," said Richard. "Dry, dusty, and windy."

"And bare," said George. "At least the high desert has a few cacti and scrub plants." Holding carefully on to the railing around the outer door, George stepped down on the top rung of the "Jacob's ladder" that ran up the side of the ship, and started down the ninety rungs to the bottom. Sam waited until he had made his way down a few meters, then followed after, his long joints having an easier time with the widely spaced rungs. Richard unfastened a beam from the ceiling of the airlock and swung the beam out through the door so the end of it hung two meters away from the side of the lander. He rolled out a winch until it reached the end of the beam, then fastened the hook on the end of the winch cable to his suit belt. He grabbed the cable, and using it to hold himself vertical, he stepped off into the air.

"Lower me down," said Richard to his imp, and the winch started to pay out the cable, Richard twirling slowly about at the end. He passed by Sam, who had paused at the ladder rung where the ladder left the side of the ship and turned into steps on one of the landing struts. Richard had Jack halt his descent when he was still two meters from the surface. He had brought along a video camera to record George's first step off the landing pad onto the soil of Roche.

As he made his historic step off the landing pad, George looked toward Richard and the camera, and started talking.

"This is but the first step on mankind's long journey . . ." Then his voice turned into a yell,

"WATCH OUT!!!" he said, as he rushed over to catch the toppling Richard just as his helmet was about to strike a boulder.

Richard, both hands working the camera, had tried to

hold himself upright on the cable by tucking it under his elbow. After getting George's first step, he had leaned back to get a picture of Sam up on the landing leg. Topheavy with the camera, he had lost his balance and swung upside-down.

"We almost lost you," said George in a soft voice, holding Richard's head firmly in his arms. "If your helmet had cracked, you wouldn't have lasted a minute in this poisonous atmosphere."

Jack lowered Richard the rest of the way to the ground and he got up, his suit dusty from the dry soil.

"I'm sorry I messed up your speech," said Richard.

"That's all right," said George. "I wasn't really sure what I was going to say next anyway. I was thinking of saying '. . . mankind's long journey into the galaxy,' but that sort of puts a limit on mankind's explorations. I could also have said '. . . universe,' but by the time mankind has explored just this galaxy it will have evolved into something else. To say that mankind will explore the universe is equivalent to saying that it was a crew of plankton that first landed on the moon."

"No plankton here, anyway," said Sam, taking a sample of the soil and chipping a chunk off the boulder that nearly got Richard.

"Weathered igneous rock with lots of vesicles," he said to Richard, handing him the rock sample.

Richard glanced with a practiced geologist's eye at the rock and looked up the long mountain toward the inner pole of Roche. "There's plenty of volcanoes up there to make it," he said. "I wonder how it got here?"

"Could have been a large eruption," said Sam. "The volcanoes probably become more active at periapsis."

"Perhaps," said Richard. "After we have identified the source volcano, I'd like to do a simulation of the ejection and get some idea of the size of the eruption needed to throw it this far."

"Don't forget that the volcano is at a much lower gravity than here and is erupting at an angle due to the sixty degree slope of the inner point. Intuition isn't much good on this planet. There's another rock over there; I think I'll get a sample from that one, too."

As the two rockhounds took off, sniffing at rocks, cracks, and scarps, George looked up to see three other suited figures making their way down the side of the ship. One was efficiently making its way down the rungs of the Jacob's ladder. That was Katrina. The second one was helping a thin one attach itself to the winch cable. The thin suit poised delicately in midair, then rode down to the surface.

"Like gliding!" said Arielle with an excited voice.

George helped her to unfasten the cable and Jack rewound the winch for the next member of the crew.

"It's so desolate," said David as he landed. "Kilometers upon kilometers of nothing but rocks and sand. What a dreary place."

"Sam and Richard seem to find it interesting," said George, pointing out the two figures off in the distance. One had climbed halfway up the nearby scarp leading to the mesa and was obviously trying to chip a sample from a rock embedded in a yellow-red layer there. The other one crawled into a small cave near the base and came back out, holding something in its gloved hand. It started walking back toward them.

"Look what I found," said Sam. He held out what looked like a piece of molten orange glass.

"What a strange-looking rock," said Red. "I've never seen volcanic glass that color."

"It's not a normal glass," said Sam. "Watch!"

He put the end of the piece of orange glass on a boulder and hit it with his geologist pick. The tip of the rock shattered into tiny bits like a piece of tempered glass. All the bits were identical and very tiny. The bits had two faceted ends connected by a thin waist. They had the size and shape of the body of a tiny ant.

"Let me see," said Katrina, taking a few of them and holding them up to her faceplate. "They look like orange-colored models of Rocheworld." She took a bag from her tool pouch and placed the bits of glass into it.

"I think I'll take these up and have a look at them under

a microscope while Jack does a chemical analysis. Perhaps that will give us a clue. We're too used to rocks that form either in vacuum or in earth air. It could be this strange chemistry can produce material that crystallizes in such a uniform way." She headed back for the winch and called for Jack to haul her up.

Later Shirley called the crew together. "It's time to lower the *Dragonfly* to the surface and put its wings on. I want to get through the lowering phase before Barnard sets behind Eau."

"Do be careful!" said Arielle.

"We won't hurt your pet," said Shirley. She walked around to the front of the lander and stood at the base of the landing strut that had been modified to act both as a leg for the lander and as a lowering rail for the aerospace plane. Shirley watched a point near the tail of the plane.

"Release hold-down lugs, Jack," she said, then nodded in satisfaction as the clawlike devices swung clear. The aerospace plane shivered slightly as the hold on it was loosened, but it was still hanging vertically from its nose hook. Shirley stepped quickly to one side and looked up the belly of the plane to the top.

"Lower top winch!" she called, and slowly the nose of the airplane tilted away from the lander, the tail staying in place at the top of the lowering rail. Shirley could now see the cockpit windows and the large triangular gap in the side of the lander as the plane pulled away from the side of the ship. The rotation continued until the airplane was leaning away from the lander at an angle of about thirty degrees.

"Now both winches!" said Shirley. Jack started the bottom winch, and letting out both the nose cable and the tail cable at the same speed, it lowered the aerospace plane slowly down the lowering rail, still at the thirty-degree angle. As the plane moved down the rail, the rudder finally cleared the side of the lander. About two meters from the end of the rail, the tail winch stopped, while the upper nose winch continued to pay out cable. Slowly the huge plane rotated about the pivot point near the tail, and as it approached the horizontal orientation there was a noticeable tilt to the lander as it reacted to the weight of the plane.

"Lower landing skids!" said Shirley, and slots appeared in the belly of the aerospace plane. Three skids came out. They reached to a half-meter of the surface.

"Lower her down!" said Shirley, bending down to watch underneath. Slowly the plane was lowered to the surface.

"Done!" she yelled, then raced to detach the lowering cables from the front and rear of the aerospace plane. The winches retrieved their cables, their job done.

"Just in time, too," said George, as the sky reddened to a deeper red than the normal illumination. "Looks like a beautiful sunset tonight. Let's everybody get back on board before it gets too dark. The ladder and winch are tricky at night."

"If you please?" said a small voice through his imp. "I'd like to sleep on *Magic Dragonfly* tonight."

"Oh," said George. "Sure, Arielle, if you want to. Won't you be lonely?"

"I'll stay, too," said David. "We both have a lot to go over with Jill."

"I get to add their sleeping space to mine!" hollered Sam, heading at high speed up the Jacob's ladder.

"Just one," yelled Shirley after him. "I get the other one."

After rearranging the bunk partitions to give him a little more room, Sam went up the passway to see how Katrina was doing with her analysis of the orange glass.

"Hello, Sam," she said as his head appeared above the floor of the bridge and the rest of his long body continued its upward rise. "I've got one of the bits under a microscope. Want to take a look at it?" She moved aside and Sam bent way over to peer through the eyepiece.

"The central waist has four sides," said Sam.

"Yes, there is a central crystal that is four-sided, while the multi-faceted balls at the end seem to be of the same material, as if it decided to switch to a more complex crystal form. Jack is still working on the chemistry, but it is a very complex molecule similar to the silica gel crystals that are used to keep things dry. Like silica gel, it is highly hygroscopic. I put one in water and it puffed up to double its size and became soft and gel-like, then fell apart. The basic material seems to be clear. The orange color comes from a very thin surface layer that doesn't penetrate into the interior. It scrapes off quite easily."

"Could it be a life-form?" asked Sam.

"I doubt it," said Katrina. "It's not complicated enough for its size. Besides, what would it eat? So far, Jack has found no evidence for smaller life-forms such as bacteria. I'm sure it's just a strange type of crystal."

"Hmmm," mused Sam, rising up from the microscope. "Tomorrow I'll keep an eye out for more samples, but now I think I'll go to bed. It's been a busy day."

It was their first night on the new planet. Being a Rocheworld night, it would only last three hours. Shirley, who had a lot of work to do at daybreak, had gone to bed with the "old folks," Sam, George, and Katrina. The activity on the ship slowed, and the remainder of the crew gathered in the lounge, snuggled close together. They looked out from the forty-meter height advantage of the viewport window along the long slopes of the conical inner pole that stretched out toward the distant globe of Eau hanging above them in the sky. The shadow of Roche on Eau had nearly covered the whole watery globe, and there was only a thin red arc of illumination at the top.

"The sunset's almost gone," complained Carmen.

"Good," said Red. "Now we'll be able to see the stars and Sol once more."

"Feeling homesick, Red?" said Thomas. His arms were around Carmen and Red and he gave Red a squeeze.

Red nestled her head on the young man's shoulder.

"Not really," she said. "Earth really doesn't have that many good memories for me. My father left us when Mom got too sick to work, and I had to drop out of school to take care of her and raise my three little sisters. Once I got on my own I was so afraid that I might be poor again that I spent all my waking hours in a blind quest for money. I was never happy, even though eventually I became a billionaire."

"Don't you ever regret giving up all that money and becoming a space-nun, sworn to a vow of poverty?" said Richard. He was sitting on the floor with the back of his head resting on the lounge seat next to Red's knee.

"Never," said Red. "For the first time in my life I'm having fun." She squirmed again against Thomas and her left hand tousled Richard's hair.

"Funny kind of fun," said Richard. "A nerve-wracking job landing an eighty-ton spacecraft on a wildly spinning double-planet, then tomorrow the real work starts when Shirley forms her slave-gang to put the wings on the *Magic Dragonfly*. It all sounds like work to me."

"Sure it's work," said Red down at the tousled head. "But it's fun kind of work. I'd do it even if I weren't getting paid."

"Which we aren't," said Carmen.

"See!" said Red. She turned to Thomas, whose dark face was almost invisible in the fading light.

"Where would Orion be now?" she asked.

"I'm not positive about anything anymore since I landed on this whirligig, but I think it's on the opposite side of the sky from Barnard and should be rising over Eau shortly."

"I see four bright stars in a line just above the horizon," said Richard from the floor.

"That is Orion," whispered Jack through his imp. "And the yellow star at the right end is Sol." The ship was so quiet they could all hear the whisper.

The red rim about Eau faded away and the stars bloomed in the sky. Jack turned off all the lights and through the thin air they could see the black velvet of the sky sprinkled with multi-colored tiny gems.

Below them was the wingless *Magic Dragonfly*. Beams of light were streaming out the cockpit windows and the bulbous, eyelike scanner domes to spread patches of light on the dusty surface. The air was still and cold as the icy stars sucked warmth from the ground. One by one the lights on *Dragonfly* flickered off as David and Arielle closed down their checkout activities and went to sit in front of the cockpit windows. Then, like the others above them, they spent the rest of the short Rocheworld evening gazing at the sky.

There was a weak red glow on the distant horizon. It was well below the black arc through the star-patterns that marked the edge of Eau, and was coming over the distant horizon of Roche. It grew brighter.

"What's that?" came David's voice through their imps.

"It's probably an eruption from one of the volcanoes on the inner pole mountain of Roche," said Red. She jumped up from the lounge seat and quickly clambered up the passway ladder to the control deck and looked out the port there.

"It's a real Fourth-of-July spectacular," said Red through her imp. "You should see it any second now." She quickly turned and activated the science console. "Can you get it on the doppler radar, Jack?" she asked.

Jack's reply was a display on her screen. Red's trained fingers were soon sliding over the surface of the screen from the command-choice listing on the side to various portions of the false-color doppler radar image. The geologist in Red took over, and she worked steadily until dawn.

Down below, the others enjoyed the fireworks display seemingly put on for their benefit by Roche to celebrate their arrival. Orion and the four stars in his belt rose out of Eau's arc of darkness. A number of minutes later a dull rumbling came through the air.

"It's the noise from the volcano," said Thomas, impressed. "Shucks, I forgot to count."

"What's that?" said a sleepy voice through the "all hands" channel of their imps.

"A distant rumble from a volcano over a thousand kilometers away," replied Jack. "There is no danger, Shirley. Go back to sleep." They heard the start of a gentle snore before the channel turned itself off.

After an hour and a half, there was a false dawn as Barnard came out from behind Roche and started to illuminate the other sides of the two lobes. They were still in the shadow of Roche, though, so they didn't see the sun, but there was enough scattering from the atmosphere between the two lobes that faint cloud patterns could be seen on the Barnard side of the water globe just above the black horizon of Roche that arched up to block the lower portion of the lobe. The false dawn set and total darkness returned as Barnard continued its rotation and Roche fell into the shadow of Eau. The viewport lounge grew quiet as Carmen lay back, staring out at the limitless stars. When she heard the heavy breathing from the two men sitting beside her, she allowed herself the luxury of a few quiet tears of homesickness.

Dawn was breaking over the distant arc of Eau when Shirley awoke and assembled her press gang. Red was left on board the lander not only in case they had to leave in a hurry, but also so she could continue to monitor the seismic and radar signals still coming from the volcano hidden over the arched western horizon of the inner pole. Everyone else became common laborers as they assisted Shirley and the Christmas Branch in assembling the outer wing panels of the *Magic Dragonfly*.

The panels were hollow graphite-fiber composite structures designed without internal bracing so that the wing panels nested inside each other. The nested wing sections then fit neatly inside the lower portion of the lander on either side of the rudder of the *Dragonfly*. Using the upper winch that had let the aerospace plane down to the surface, Shirley and Jack carefully pulled each segment out one at a time and lowered them down to a waiting team of space-suited humans.

"Stand back," warned Shirley from her vantage point up in the wing storage hold. "Let Jack winch the panel all the way down to the surface before you get near. I have epoxy that will fix the dings in the wing section, but Katrina left her people-epoxy back home, and we can't fix you if you get a ding."

Slowly each section was lowered to the ground, then George would unfasten the winch cable, and the crew of eight would lift the five-by-six-meter section of wing and take it over and place it on the ground on either side of the stub-winged *Magic Dragonfly*.

After the wing panels were unloaded and arranged, Shirley and Jack lowered a bundle of small struts and two long telescoping poles. Before she came down, Shirley unfastened the lower winch and brought it with her over to the plane.

"OK, Jack," she puffed as she clambered up to the top of the aerospace plane with the heavy winch and attached it to a waiting fixture. "Have the Christmas Branch install the struts in the first section."

She motioned to the suited figures scattered about her below on the ground.

"This will be just like we practiced it on Titan," she said. She tossed down the end of the cable from the winch. "Set up the tripod over the section the Christmas Branch is working on, then when it's done installing the inner braces, hook it up to the central lifting lug and get out of the way." Shirley looked up at the sky. They had been working hard since daybreak, and Barnard was already overhead. They were behind schedule. Slightly exasperated, she allowed a note of irritation to creep into her voice.

"And hurry up! We've only got an hour and a half of daylight left. If we're not done by then, we'll have to work by floodlight to keep up with the mission schedule."

George picked up his pace as he went with Richard to pick up the tripod poles.

"Give a person a little authority and they turn into a Captain Queeg," griped Richard. Jack was a little slow on interpreting the proper routing of the message from Richard's suit imp, and it was only when Richard had gotten to the word "authority" that Jack realized that the comment was for George's ears only, and not the general channel. A chorus of chuckles and giggles rippled through the net.

"I heard that, Richard," said Shirley. "If you'd like to come up here and play steeplejack I'll be glad to trade places with you."

"No thanks," said Richard. "Steeplejacking is squaw work."

The tripod was assembled, and the first section was raised into place, the Christmas Branch riding up on the inside.

"We're about ten centimeters off," said Shirley. The Christmas Branch extended its body between the hanging section and the wing stub, then contracted to draw the two sections closer together. Shirley straddled the narrowing gap, and using a long pointed pry-bar between two aligning lugs, she pulled the wing section forward until the edges were lined up.

"Hold it!" said Jack as the two were about to meet. A large spider-imp scurried around the narrow gap, removing the thin plastic protective cover from the sealing material. Shirley could feel internal fasteners clicking into place beneath her feet, then the pressure on her pry-bar lessened as the fasteners were rotated to pull the two wing sections together. Shirley got up and glanced at the array of tell-tales below her chin in the neck of her suit.

"That took us fifteen minutes," she said. "We'll have to do better than that on the rest of the sections if we're going to finish before sunset."

Richard glanced again at George. He didn't talk through his imp this time, but instead made motions with his hands like he was playing nervously with some large steel marbles.

The outer wing sections, being much lighter, were on well before dark, and Jill was able to pump them down, check for leaks, then refill them with fuel from the main tanks of the Eagle while the tired construction crew reboarded the lander for a last dinner together. Tomorrow they would break up into two teams. Sam, Red, Thomas, and Carmen would stay with the lander, Thomas and Carmen trading shifts as commander of Rocheworld Base, while Sam and Red went off on exploration jaunts in the crawler. The other six would take off on the *Magic Dragonfly* to visit the other side of Roche and the distant globe of Eau hanging in the sky on the eastern horizon.

"I won't say that I'm sorry to see you go," said Sam. He popped the last of Nels's cherry tomatoes into his mouth. It was good, but getting a little wrinkled from sitting in Jack's refrigerator this long. It was the last of the fresh food. It was basic mush and frozen foods from now on.

"After I get your sleeping racks stored away I'll be able to stretch out at night."

"Enjoy it while you can, Sam," said George. "We'll be back in a few weeks. It's only twenty-two days or eighty-eight rotations until Rocheworld reaches periapsis about Barnard. The weather on Eau is likely to get a little rough with the extra heating, and I want to have the *Dragonfly* tied down here for those few days."

Carmen's voice called from her seat at the viewport lounge. "I can see Zapotec at the top of the viewport window. Gargantua should be in view soon."

The ten crew-members crowded in a friendly pile on the floor and in the sofa of the viewport lounge and watched Gargantua with its retinue of multicolored marbles move smoothly through the sky. Rocheworld was now drawing close to the giant planet as it reached apoapsis, and Gargantua was bigger than the Moon in the sky of Earth.

"Winter must be setting in on Gargantua," said George. "I can see the 'tit.' "

"You men are all alike," said Carmen, getting up.

"I'd better pack," said Arielle, following her.

Soon the crew was scattered throughout the lander, making preparations for the coming dawn and saying goodbye to special friends. George and Red were left sitting on the floor in front of the viewport lounge.

"I'll miss you," said George quietly.

"I'll miss you," she replied. George turned and she put her face up toward him. They kissed softly, then both leaned back to stare out the viewport as Zapotec set over Eau.

"Take good care of Sam and Thomas," he said.

"I will. And you be nice to Katrina," she said. "I know she sometimes gets on your nerves, but she needs affection, too."

"It's all just bluff from that German school system she went to," said George. "Underneath is a fluffy hausfrau. She's like putty in my hands."

"You men are all alike," said Red. She rested her head on his shoulder. "And isn't it nice," she murmured.

*   *   *

The next morning the exploration crew suited up early and gathered outside the airlock of the aerospace plane.

"Now we'll see what this magic carpet can do," said George.

"*Magic Dragonfly*," reminded Arielle. "It can do everythings."

"Take me to a strange land, where I've never been before," said George.

"All right," said Arielle. "Hop on board."

Pilot and copilot-commander waited as David, Katrina, Richard, and Shirley passed through the airlock of the *Magic Dragonfly*, then the two figures grinned at each other as they followed them inside. The slimmer figure hesitated and let the larger one enter the lock first. During the wait, tiny fingers hidden in sausage-finger gloves stroked softly over the duralloy hull. Then, the "magic" for the *Magic Dragonfly* stepped aboard.

Arielle made her way forward toward the flight deck through the busy humanity inside the plane, being politely careful not to interrupt. She had some trouble getting past the science console area, since David, Richard, and Katrina were occupying the three seats and were busy setting up the next day's schedule. She slid her thin body past this blockade only to confront a long torso stretching horizontally across the aisle from the port science blister to the starboard science blister. The head of the muscular body was buried deep in the port science electronics, and the rest of the body seemed to be ignoring the ten percent gravity of the planet below. It was either crawl over or crawl under. Arielle took a calculated look at the broad buttocks and muscular waist, then launched herself in a soaring low-gee dive over the human tollgate. She did a midair flip and straightened out so she was flying through the air feet first. George looked around just as the human bird fluttered to a landing on the raised platform between their seats on the flight deck.

"We are ready?" she asked sweetly, buckling herself into the pilot seat.

"Lift-off!" said George.

Arielle glanced over the console, finding it in perfect

order, then smoothly increased reactor power and adjusted VTOL fan pitch and speed at the same time. The *Magic Dragonfly* slowly floated upward into the ammonia skies on its levitating fans.

Once they had reached adequate elevation, Arielle pushed the VTOL controls forward, and they responded by tilting the huge electric fans in the wing of the plane until they were pushing the craft forward as hard as they were lifting it. Automatic servomechanisms took over, and the power of the nuclear jet was increased to provide more heating to the streams of thin atmosphere that were captured by the forward facing scoops and channeled into the heated interiors of the plane's nuclear engines.

Arielle added a notch to the throttle, and the heat exchangers between the nuclear power source and the frigid air turned cherry red. The heated methane, ammonia, and water vapor began to stream out the rear at high velocity, impelling the *Magic Dragonfly* forward.

Richard sat at the science console, orchestrating the first portion of their mission.

"I'd like some altitude first, please, Arielle," he said. "And, David, if you and Jill can look through the memory for ground scans taken during the descent of *Eagle*, I'd like one with a shadow angle similar to what we have now."

The aerospace plane banked as Arielle moved the *Magic Dragonfly* into a lazy spiraling climb above Rocheworld Base.

"Scanners are all active," said Shirley from the engineering console.

"I'd like the radar-mapper image," said Richard. His hands flew over the screen as he shrank the radar image into half the screen, then placed the old image from the *Eagle* in the other half screen. It was the same region, but they were taken at different angles and distances.

"Rotate and rectify, Jill," he asked. The old image distorted as Jill rearranged the bits in the image. Richard's hands played over the command list and the old image faded into a deep red, while in the center a small white circle indicated the smaller region that was now being scanned by the radar sounder on their magic carpet.

"There's an interesting feature to the north, Arielle." He placed his finger on the fuzzy red blob. Arielle glanced at the small video to one side of her main display. It was a reproduction of Richard's science screen with a blinking green fingerprint-sized blob overlaid on a red blob. Arielle continued a half-turn, then straightened out the *Dragonfly* on a northerly climbing course. Soon the region of high-resolution radar sounding data grew in size and moved northward until the red blob was revealed as a small crater that looked like it was perched on a teardrop-shaped mesa, the blunt end of the teardrop facing due west.

"Looks like a Martian crater," said George. "I can see it coming up ahead. There are flow lines that look like the crater was made in the bed of a stream and it flowed around it for some time before it dried up."

"It's only a hundred kilometers from Rocheworld Base," said Richard. "I think I'll put that on the visit agenda for Sam and Red."

"I don't think they're going to like you for that," said David. "They'll only be able to travel in daylight. It'll probably mean fifteen hours in suits just for three hours of daylight on site."

"They're dedicated rockhounds," said Richard. "Besides, the crawler will do most of the work."

Arielle took the *Dragonfly* in a slow circle about Rocheworld Base while Richard picked out a few more targets for the base-sticking crew to visit. She then applied more power and started a spiraling survey of the entire globe.

"Lots of craters on this side," said Richard to no one in particular a few hours later.

"Like the moon, but with air," said George, scanning the horizon out the cockpit window. "I don't see any more signs of erosion."

"We would expect most of the precipitation to take place in the cold crescent that runs from the north pole down through the inner pole to the south pole," said Richard. "Those portions receive proportionally less sunlight than the warm crescent that reaches out from the outer pole along the equator until you get to the regions where there is significant shading of Barnard by the Eau lobe."

"I see some white stuff on the ground up ahead," said George. "Especially on the north side of crater rims."

"We're getting close to the north pole," said Arielle. "She is probably snow."

"Probably a mixture of ammonia and water ice," said Katrina from the galley. "The temperature there is probably minus one hundred Celsius."

"And I thought it was cold at Rocheworld Base," said Shirley.

"We'll soon find out," said Richard. He put his finger on his screen. "Arielle, could you bring us down here in the middle of this large crater? I want to get some snow for Katrina to look at and some bedrock chunks for my collection."

"We descend!" said Arielle, putting the *Magic Dragonfly* into a dive. Darkness came again as they approached the site. Using radar, Arielle and Jill carefully landed on a flat place not too far from the central peak of the crater, the ammonia snow blowing out from beneath the VTOL fans into the bright beams of the landing lights.

"Three winks, everybody," commanded George. Katrina and David had anticipated George and were already in their bunks. It didn't take long for the rest. Daybreak and a full schedule were only three hours' nap away.

At daybreak George and Richard donned their heated exploration suits and were carefully checked out by a mother-henning Shirley. They clambered down from the *Dragonfly*'s airlock and started their half-kilometer trek to the central crater.

George stepped in a small patch of ammonia snow. Snow particles flew everywhere as his heated boot vaporized the ammonia crystals into a gas.

"Please try to avoid the snowdrifts," said his suit-imp. "I only have a fixed amount of energy for heating, and when it is half gone, I must insist you turn back."

"How far can I go with the present charge?" asked George.

"Twenty kilometers," said the suit-imp. George humphed and continued toward the peak a half-kilometer away. He did try to avoid the snow, however.

Richard looked carefully at a couple of large rocks on the way out, but didn't use his geologist's hammer until he reached the peak. He looked back to make sure that he was still within sight of the *Magic Dragonfly* so that Jill could have direct laser communication with his helmet receiver and the suit-imp.

"I'd like the suit-imp outside," he said. "I want it to take a rope up to that overhang."

"You aren't going to climb, are you?" asked Jill through his imp in a concerned tone.

"Yes, I am," said Richard. "I want to get some samples from the top."

"I could send the imp to get them," said Jill.

"As smart as you are, Jill," said Richard, "I still want to see what's there so we don't miss anything. Don't forget we are only under a tenth gee and I have an alpine guide license."

By the time he had finished arguing with Jill, the suit-imp had wiggled its way outside through the valves in the life-support pack. The imp took the end of Richard's rope and scampered up the cliff, its tiny cilia giving it a grip like a fly. The anchor was embedded firmly in the ledge, and testing it first, Richard walked his way up the steep slope. The maneuver was repeated three times until Richard was at the top of the peak. He then disappeared from view. The suit-imp stayed on the crest in view of *Dragonfly*.

"It looks like a small volcanic crater," came the relayed voice.

Richard appeared again at the top of the peak and rappeled his way down. He went slowly, looking carefully at the surface passing beneath him. Occasionally he would stop and take off another small sample while George stood back to keep out of the way of falling bits of rock. Finally Richard was back on nearly level ground. He handed a small sack to George.

"Here, you carry this," he said. "I've got more to get. Let's backtrack, Jill."

Following the computer's directions, Richard zigzagged back along the path they had come, ignoring some rocks and taking samples from others that he had thought interesting on the way out. As their load of rock samples grew, it finally dawned on George why Richard had never used his hammer on the way out.

At the very last snowdrift before they reached the plane, Richard took out some sample bottles and a long stainless steel wand with a claw at one end. He placed a bottle in the claw and locked it. Then he laid the tool and bottle in the snowdrift until the vaporization stopped. Taking the frigid instrument by the handle, he quickly dipped it deep down into the middle of the drift and scooped up a sample of snow. A quick flick of the lid with a gloved finger, and the snow was trapped in the bottle before it had time to vaporize. The sample bottle was packed in an insulating case, along with a control sample of air. The case would only be opened by Jill's analytical imp after it had been put in the small freezer in Jill's shop wall, where the computer could recreate any combination of Rocheworld conditions from the hot outer pole of Roche to the frigid north pole of Eau.

Richard and George cycled through. It was dark again, and it was time for another rest break before taking off again. George tried to convince Katrina that he was cold from walking out in the snow and needed to be warmed up, but she was too busy helping Jill analyze the snow samples. He went off to bed.

As Barnard set, Shirley made her way forward to the cockpit and sat down on the copilot seat. Arielle was there going through the preflight checkout.

"Are you going to fly at night?" Shirley asked.

"As soon as Gargantua rises up. Then we see where we are going."

"I think you'd better take a look at this," said David from the computer console. "*Barbara* took this weather picture just before sunset."

The screen in front of Arielle blinked off the standard artificial horizon display and replaced it with a colored weather map. There was a large storm front moving from the inner pole to the north pole, leaving behind a trail of white on the ground. Just at the leading edge of the storm was a blinking green dot that marked their position. Arielle glanced up from the display and looked out the cockpit window. The sharp shadow edge of Eau against the star background was gone. In its place was a fuzzier arc of darkness, lit from behind by the emerging bright ball of Gargantua, glowing redly with Barnard's charcoal-fire light.

"It's moving fast," said Arielle. "I think we'd better stay on the ground until we see what kind of winds we have. Shirley, do you think we need tie-downs?"

"Better safe than sorry," said Shirley. "You may be a great pilot, Arielle, but I don't think even you could take off with the *Dragonfly* flipped on its back." She talked to her imp as she made her way to the rear of the plane and was joined in the airlock by a segment of the Christmas Branch carrying some screw-anchors and cables.

The screw-anchors were too large and the ground too hard for the Christmas Branch to be of much help, so it fell to the human to supply the muscle power.

"I sometimes wish they'd made you bigger," panted Shirley after setting one of the anchors. She fastened a cable to the anchor and tossed it up in the darkness to the twinkling Christmas Branch waiting on the wing-top. A long arm with a feathery tip shot out to grab the end of the cable, and in a wink the cable was knotted through a tie-down point on the wing. Shirley looked it over from the ground with the beam from her permalight. Suddenly the beam was full of tiny white dancing dots. She was rocked in the low gravity by a gust of wind.

"It's started to snow," said Shirley. Her message was passed on to Arielle and David.

Arielle turned on the landing lights. The beams went out into the swirling whiteness, then were lost some meters ahead.

"It's a real blizzard!" said Arielle. "You'd better come back in, Shirley, before you get blown away."

"One more anchor to go," replied Shirley. "But don't worry about me. The wind speed may be high, but at this low pressure the breezes don't have any push behind them." She still staggered a little in the low gravity as the gusts played over her body. By the time she had the last anchor in place, there were already a few centimeters of new water-ammonia snow on the ground. Her boots made hissing sounds as she walked. She took one last walk around her charge before going in. There was no snow on the tail section. Those surfaces were the waste-heat radiators for the nuclear reactor in the rear. The reactor was running at very low power since all it had to do was generate the electricity to keep the *Magic Dragonfly* and its human crew alive and comfortable. The top of the fuselage was also free of snow, but the wings were a different matter. The tips of the wings already had a cover of snow, and as the night continued, the cold region would slowly creep inward toward the VTOL fans. Just as she was about to step into the lock, Shirley looked down at her boots. Her long journey through the new snowdrifts around the plane had finally cooled off the outer surface of her boots. They were now covered with a clinging layer of wet ammonia-water snow. She stamped her feet on the ground to shake off the snow, stepped into the lock, and cycled through.

The rapidly moving storm passed quickly overhead, leaving behind the full globe of Gargantua and its moons low in the sky.

"This is .one of the times I wish that Barnard had a higher temperature," said Shirley as she looked out at the snow-covered hills around them. "Snow just doesn't look right when it's red."

"I fix that," said Arielle. She flipped on the landing lights, and in the track of the brilliant white beams there glimmered a billion tiny blue-white crystals. Shirley admired the view for a while, then with a sigh she got up and went out to remove the screw-anchors. She was tempted to wake up Richard and have him help, but her pride wouldn't allow it.

I can do anything that big ape can do, and better! she said to herself as she stepped with a hiss into the calf-deep snow.

George and Richard were still asleep when dawn broke over Eau and Arielle lifted the *Magic Dragonfly* on a whirlwind of snow particles. She gained altitude, then headed south and inward as they resumed the long spiral survey path that would take them within sensor distance of every point on the egg-shaped surface.

"It sure gets dark in a hurry," said Shirley, looking out the cockpit window. Arielle was back in the galley getting something to eat and Shirley was flying the airplane from the copilot seat. Since Jill was an excellent autopilot, however, Shirley's work consisted of leaving her hands off the controls and looking out the window at the scenery.

"Now that we're entering the inner pole region," said David, "we will have a lot more dark time than daylight time. When Barnard isn't hiding behind Roche, then it's hiding behind Eau. Right now we get about two hours of daylight, then four hours of night during the six-hour rotation period. It's worst right at the inner pole, where it's ninety minutes of daytime to four and a half hours of night."

Arielle made her way forward and returned to take her place in the pilot seat. "I and Jill find way to get more daytime," she said. "We plan our flight path around inner pole so we always be on the sunshine side." She nodded at Shirley, dismissing her, and her eyes turned to the pilot console and resumed their vigilant watch on the indicators and the view out the cockpit window.

Shirley got down and returned to the engineering console to monitor the performance of Jill's scanners. There was a noise in the back, and soon Richard pulled aside the privacy curtain to the crew quarters and came forward.

"We must be getting nearer the inner pole," he yawned. "I feel lighter already."

"We're down to six percent gravity," said David from his console. "That's half of the twelve percent gravity at the north pole, where you went to sleep."

"Any sign of volcanoes yet?" asked Richard, as he walked over behind Katrina sitting at the science console. "I'd like to visit a few of them."

"That could be dangerous," said Jill through his imp.

"Not if we're careful and pick one that isn't ripe for an explosion. Where's our history file of the inner pole region from the commsat cameras?"

"I have it right here," said Katrina. Her fingers flickered over the directory menu at the side of the screen, and soon they were looking at HISTORY, COMMSAT, VISUAL, INNER POLE, VOLCANO WATCH. Katrina got up and let Richard at the console.

"I think I'll get some sleep," she said. "We can't all be up at the same time." She went through the privacy curtain. George was still in his bunk. She didn't hear any snoring leaking through the Sound-Bar door, so he was probably awake and hadn't gotten up yet. She opened the door to her bunk and got undressed. Her coveralls were still clean, so she folded them up and put them away in the storage chest in the wall at the foot of her bed. She passed through the privacy curtain to the work area in the rear of the plane, took off her underwear, and gave them to the Christmas Branch to be put into the sonic clothes cleaner. Now completely naked except for the star-shaped imp in her hair, she moved lightly past the airlock and reentered the closed-off corridor of the sleeping quarters. She reached into her bunk space for her nightgown, then hesitated.

"Is George awake?" she asked her imp.

"He is," said Jill. "Would you like me to connect you with him?"

"Please," said Katrina. "George?" she called lightly.

She heard the sound of soft music being played by George's imp, then the Sound-Bar door below her bunk slowly rolled up to show George in his pajamas wearing a set of Christmas Branch stereo earphones. George's eyes opened wide when he saw Katrina's soft curvaceous nude body bending over him. He waved a hand at one ear. The music stopped and the earphones scurried away to rejoin the rest of the Christmas Branch in the workshop at the rear of the plane.

"Are you still cold?" she asked.

The sequence of pictures of the inner-pole volcanic-field region flashed rapidly by on Richard's screen. Day and night passed and volcanoes erupted periodically.

"I can't really tell much with all those lighting changes, Jill," he said. "Please feature-extract the craters and the plumes, then run those by."

There was a second's pause as Jill rearranged bits, then a cartoon version of the inner pole region appeared on the screen and ran through the compressed time history.

"Again!" said Richard, and the sequence repeated.

"Do it again and watch these three here," his finger tapped at the screen where there were three volcanoes in a line that pointed toward the inner pole. Jill expanded the view until the three filled the screen. First one volcano would throw up a plume of hot gas and dust, then the middle one would start, then finally the one nearest the inner pole would join them. They stopped in reverse order.

"Those three must be interconnected by an underground vent," said Richard.

"The periodicity is quite regular," said Jill. "The magnitude of the eruptions varies, but they always occur every three hours when Barnard is either behind Eau or Roche and the tides are strongest."

"If they are that predictable, then we can visit them between eruptions," said Richard. "Set your course so that we arrive just after an eruption."

"But just because we have records of twelve eruption cycles doesn't mean that they sometimes won't have an eruption between their normal cycle times," protested Jill.

"The first thing I'll do when we get there is put down a seismometer and hook you up to it," said Richard. "Then if the volcano starts to get rambunctious, you'll hear the rumbling in time to take us out of there."

"I hope so," said Jill with a worried tone.

"I hope you appreciate that 'concerned mother' tone," said David, who had been watching over Richard's shoulder and could hear Richard's imp. "The psychologists thought it would be a good safety feature and asked me to develop it so people like you would go out of their way to avoid dangerous activities in order to keep Jill 'happy.' It turned out to be tough; took me almost three days playing with my synthesizer before I got the aggrieved tone just right."

"Pretty sneaky," said Richard, returning to the console.

They approached the triplet volcano during darkness. Arielle had taken the *Magic Dragonfly* to altitude and had flown high over the plumes of hot gas and ashes so that they could take pictures. The light from Gargantua gave Jill's electrocameras enough illumination so that excellent photographs of the plumes could be obtained.

"We seem to be awfully high," remarked George.

"Better safe than sorry," said Arielle. "Gravity here is only three percent of earth gravities. Is easy for those monsters to throw a rock at us."

George looked at the display in front of him. He had trouble reading the altimeter. The numbers were not what he was used to. Finally he comprehended. "That says eighty-three thousand meters!" he said. "We're eighty-three kilometers high! Are we on rocket power?"

"I just take her up on the nuclears jet until she won't any more climb," said Arielle. "Jill has good cameras, so we don't have to get close. Don't forget, when you lower the gravity, you higher the scale height. Good view, no?"

"I can see the curvature of the horizon," said George. "Especially at the inner pole."

The eruption subsided, and Gargantua set. Arielle spiraled down, and they landed on the ashy plains just as Barnard rose from behind Eau.

"This is too far away," said Richard. "Those volcanoes are at least ten kilometers off. I'll never be able to get there and back before dark."

"Jill thinks that the vent that supplies the volcanoes comes under here," said Shirley. "We will put the seismometer here, then Arielle will take you over to the volcano. Inside if you want, provided there is a place to land."

Richard could hear the airlock cycling at the rear of the ship as the Christmas Branch took out a seismometer and a communications package. He sat down at the science console and slaved the sensor platform in the left "eye" of the *Magic Dragonfly* to follow the Christmas Branch as it left the airlock. The Branch had feathered out the subelements on its feet and easily "snowshoed" its way across the deep ashes. There was a flurry of ashes as the Christmas Branch dug down to bedrock and installed the seismometer.

"Looks like a good signal," said Richard to Jill. "I can see the vibrations when the Branch moves. Hold it still for a second."

The image of the distant Christmas Branch froze on the screen, and Richard increased the gain on the seismometer.

"Lots of trembling, but nothing big," said Richard. "It should be safe to go in closer."

The Christmas Branch set up a radio link to *Walter* at the L–5 point, where the commsat would relay the seismic signal back down to the *Magic Dragonfly*. The Christmas Branch reentered the airlock, and while the lock was cycling, Arielle slowly lifted the *Magic Dragonfly* on its fans. The nuclear jet kicked in, and they zoomed toward the first of the three craters.

"No lava," said George as they hovered over the cinder cone.

"This kind only shoots hot gas and dusty ashes," said Richard. "The big one over on the other side with Rocheworld Base is the type that throws out magma. Those are too hot and dangerous to visit, but I hope to get some samples from these vents. How's the temperature, Jill?"

"Quite hot inside the vents," said Jill, "but you should be able to get fairly close without exceeding the insulation limits on your suit."

"Can you take her down closer, Arielle?" asked Richard. "I want you to check the consistency by blowing the fans at it."

Arielle slowly lowered the huge airplane on its VTOL fans, then slid it backwards to see if the blast from the fans blew a trough in the surface. At first the surface held, then large chunks broke loose and tumbled away.

"It looks like it has the strength and density of Styrofoam insulation," said George.

"I not land on it," said Arielle. "I hover for you, if you wish to go out. Gravity is so low I only need five percent of fan speed. You hardly will feel the breezes."

"OK," said Richard. "Take me over to that vent near the lip of the crater."

Expertly, Arielle slid the *Magic Dragonfly* along the rolling ash surface to a twenty-meter-wide vent with a slightly elevated lip.

"I take you to top? Or do you walk up the slope?"

"Just drop me off at the base. There may be some gas still coming from the vent and it might blow the *Dragonfly* around."

Richard left to get his suit. Shirley was there, waiting for him. She was already suited up and holding onto one end of a strong cable. The other end was fastened to a belt-loop on Richard's suit.

"What's that for? I'm not going to need ropes to climb that slope."

"This is for that first step out the lock," said a muffled voice. "If Arielle is afraid that the *Magic Dragonfly* could sink in that stuff, I'm going to worry about you. You may have size eleven feet, but there is so much musclebound mass sitting on top of them that you're likely to sink straight to bedrock. As much as I hate to admit it, I want you back."

"Just so you can pick on me," said Richard plaintively. Shirley took him carefully through the suit checkout, then as the inner door cycled, she circled around in back of him and picked him up bodily in the light gravity. Arms ineffectually waving in protest, Richard was carried into the airlock.

"At least I pick on somebody my own size," she replied, finally putting him down. He turned and glared at her grinning face through her helmet as the inner door closed, the lock cycled, and the outer door opened. The two looked out from the floating airplane at the dark ashen crust a few feet below.

"Looks pretty solid," said Shirley. "At least it isn't blowing away in the wind from the lift fans."

"The ash particles are red hot and bristly when they come out of the vent," said Richard. "They have a tendency to stick together."

"Shall I lower you down?"

"Nope. You might drop me. Only one way to find out. As my seven-greats-aunt on my mother's side used to say when she was looking for my seven-greats-uncle . . . 'Geronimo!' "

Richard jumped from the door and floated down to the surface in the two percent gravity. His boots made a depression in the crusty surface, but he didn't sink in.

"Did I detect a note of disappointment before Jill cut our imp link?" he said, looking up at the suited figure in the lock above him.

"Who? Me?" said Shirley sweetly. She jumped and landed beside him.

"Lead the way," she said. "We've only got one hour left of this minimal day before it gets dark, and it will *really* be dark, since Gargantua won't rise until three hours later."

The two climbed the ashen slope until they got near the lip of the vent.

"You dig in and hold the rope while I go up to the rim," said Richard. "I doubt that there is an overhang, but funny things can happen with sticky ashes like this stuff when it collects in a low gee field."

He took his geologist's pick and cut two deep heel-holes in the crust. Shirley sat down and put her feet into the holes. She took her pick and slammed its point into the ground behind her. With one hand controlling the line through her belt, and the other through the wrist-loop of the pick, and her feet in the heel-holes, she was ready. Richard walked to the edge of the vent, Shirley paying out the line as he went. He looked over the edge, then leaned forward to look down. The only thing keeping him from falling in was the rope in Shirley's frantic grip.

"Richard! Stop that!"

Ignoring the frantic cries, Richard leaned over still further in the low gravity and swayed from side to side as he slowly looked down into the crater, taking shot after shot with his chest camera. He finally returned to the vertical.

"No overhang," he said. "You can come up here if you want. I'd like to have you lower me down to a ledge about five meters down to get a sample from inside."

"Easy enough," said Shirley. "In this gravity you only weigh five kilos. I could lift you with my little finger."

"I'd prefer you use two hands," said Richard.

Shirley dug in again and Richard went over the side. As he did, the constant noises coming from inside Richard's suit stopped abruptly as the laser beams that linked their suits together were broken. Shirley felt bereft without Richard's constant presence through their suit link. There was a movement in the sky as Arielle flew the *Magic Dragonfly* overhead until it was perched above the vent. Line-of-sight communication was reestablished with the *Dragonfly*, and Shirley could hear Richard's voice again.

". . . it's a lava tube. This crater hasn't always been just hot gas and dust. Looks fairly recent, too." There was the sound of grunting as Richard's pick pounded the rock to obtain a sample.

"Hold tight! Coming up!" Shirley held tight to the throbbing rope, and soon Richard's toes appeared over the edge and he lifted himself upright. He handed her a small clear stone.

"I won't be sure until Katrina and Jill analyze it, but I think it's a diamond."

Shirley rolled the rough stone between her fingers, then looked coyly at him.

"Oh, Richard! How sudden! Now we're engaged."

"You've got it all wrong, beautiful," he said, starting back toward the *Magic Dragonfly* at a speed that made sure there was plenty of distance between them before he finished the sentence. "It's payment for services rendered."

Rising slowly on its fans, the *Magic Dragonfly* first gained altitude, then speed as the nuclear jet cut in.

"Where to now?" said Arielle.

"Head for the inner pole," said Richard, "but take us over the big lava volcano. I want to get some infrared pictures."

Arielle headed the *Magic Dragonfly* toward the inner pole in the deep Roche darkness. They hadn't far to go, and the gravity dropped even more. They finally reached the inner pole. Using Jill's radar, they found a flat place and landed to wait for daylight.

Shirley came up from the back, bouncing as she came.

"This is ridiculous," she said. "All that dirt out there, and it isn't keeping me on the floor."

"You keep forgetting that equally large ball of dirt over-head," said David. "Why don't you put on free-fall boots? The floor has loop carpeting."

"They're back at Rocheworld Base," said Shirley embarrassedly. "I was so busy checking everyone else's kits that I didn't check mine. Besides, you don't expect to run into free-fall in an airplane!"

"This is magic airplane!" said Arielle. "It can even abolish gravity. It almost sunrise, we shall go?"

"Yes," said George. "Up please—and don't stop until up is down."

Arielle started the lift fans at low speed, and the *Magic Dragonfly* rocked and lifted rapidly in the half-percent gravity at the inner pole. She switched to the nuclear jet and started a tight spiral climb.

"Ten kilometers and climbing," she announced as the ball of Barnard rose behind Roche. A few minutes later Gargantua peeked from behind Eau and the sunlight from Barnard illuminated the water mountain above them while the ground below was still in darkness.

"Twenty kilometers and climbing," said Arielle. "Gravity now less than one-three-hundredths gee." Forgotten items started to float around in the cabin in the currents of the air conditioning system. The room was soon full of busy mosquito-imps cleaning up the air.

"No ring waves," said George, looking up. Barnard now illuminated one-half of the conical ocean with its red glare, while the other half was more softly illuminated with the reflected light from Gargantua.

"Since it's been daytime on Roche, the air flow is from Roche to Eau, or down the water mountain," said David.

"So no big waves," said George. "And any that get formed spread out as they go downmountain."

The drone of the lift fan engines slowed.

"Forty kilometers altitude and stopped," said Arielle. "We at midpoint."

FALLING

Shirley took the diamond from her coverall pocket and suspended the rock in mid-air. It drifted slightly in the air currents but fell neither toward or away from Roche or Eau.

"Zero-gee," she announced.

"Now that the sun is shining on Eau, the ammonia will start to boil out of the water, and the wind will start blowing the other way," said George. "If we're going to get any samples or make any measurements we'd better do it soon, before the waves build up."

"We go down?" said Arielle, starting the lift fans. The aerospace plane gathered speed, and within a few minutes was hovering over the surface of the rounded tip of ocean at the inner point of Eau. The gravity had risen to a half-percent of gee, and things once more took on their normal orientation, except now overhead was a conical mountain of rock instead of a conical mountain of water.

"Three meter above surface," said Arielle. "The wind is drooping down."

"Lower the sonar scanner, Jill," commanded Shirley. There was a bumping noise from beneath the ship as a small dense package of sophisticated sound-generating and -detecting equipment dropped out of a hatchway on the bottom of the plane and splashed into the water.

There was a blip on the screen as Jill fired the first

strong burst of sound down into the depths. There was a pause as the trace made its way slowly across the screen. As the green line approached the right side of the screen, there was a blink, and the scale increased ten times. The blip, now moving only one-tenth as fast, continued across the screen, passing one depth marker after another.

"It's really deep," said Shirley. "The marker is at fifty kilometers and still going."

"That's five times deeper than the deepest ocean on Earth," said George. "I wonder what the pressures are like down there."

"Shouldn't be too bad," said David. "Don't forget the reduced gravity."

"I think the signal must have been attenuated by a muddy bottom or something," said Jill through Shirley's imp. "I'll try a longer burst with a chirped frequency and then compress the returns."

"Fine," said Shirley, then watched as a ten-second, slowly rising whistle of sound hurtled into the depths.

"There it is!" cried Shirley as a return showed up on her screen.

"That is a return from the first signal," said Jill. "I will reconfigure the screen." Instantly the engineering screen was rewritten with a time display that contained a new length scale, while below it was a two-dimensional picture of the bottom surface that grew second by second as the acoustic pulse made the round trip to the bottom at fifteen hundred meters per second.

"The bottom is a hundred and fifty kilometers down!" said Shirley. "We're on the top of a mountain of water a hundred and fifty kilometers high!"

". . . and it doesn't fall down," added David.

Shirley watched the screen as the second and third pulses returned with their information and the details on the map cleared up. Richard looked over at her screen and pulled a copy of the map onto his screen.

"Those circular features are obviously volcanic craters," he said. "But from the sonar distance plots, they seem to be the lowest points on the terrain. You would expect them to be on top of mounds of lava."

"What are those jagged features?" asked Shirley. "They look like underwater alps."

"Perhaps that's what they are," said Richard. "There are certainly enough tidal stresses to cause mountain building."

"There was nothing like that on Roche," said Katrina.

"Right," said David. "Lots of volcanoes there, but nothing like those mountains." He pulled a copy of the display onto his screen and peered closely at it.

"The mountains seem to avoid the volcanoes," he said. "How tall do you estimate them to be?"

"About two kilometers," said Richard. "Not really big for mountains, considering the gravity. If they are mountains . . ." he added.

"Pull the sonar in," said Shirley to Jill.

"Don't forget to get a sample," said Katrina. "I want to analyze the water."

"My sonar scanner has a built-in analyzer," said Jill. "The scanner needs a density and composition analyzer to calibrate the range, so they just made it a little more complicated so that it could do a complete isotope analysis. The ocean at this point is minus twenty-three Celsius and warming, with a composition of thirty-nine percent ammonia and fifty-five percent water, with various things like methane, hydrogen sulfide, and hydrogen cyanide dissolved in it."

"Any trace of anything unusual?" asked Katrina eagerly. "It would certainly be wonderful to find a life-form. Even the tiniest microbe would pay back Earth for what it cost to send us here."

"Nothing," said Jill.

George had been looking out the cockpit window at the horizon. "The waves are rising," he said. "If we are going to get any more samples and bottom maps, we'd better be moving."

"We go up!" said Arielle, and the *Magic Dragonfly* leapt into the air and moved along the flanks of the mountain of water, trying to stay as long as possible in the rapidly diminishing patch of sunlight.

"Can't you bring her down a little lower?" asked Shirley. "The sonar is breaching the surface in some of the troughs."

"You argue with Jill," said Arielle with a fatalistic shrug of her shoulders. "I could go lower, but she is not allowing me to try."

"Jill!" said Shirley. "We're at a hundred meters and the waves are only thirty meters high. Surely we could go down another ten or twenty meters."

"No."

Arielle—who had never stopped her automatic scan of outside view, instrument panel, outside view—suddenly reached for the controls and thundered *Dragonfly* upwards on its rocket thrusters.

"Arielle!" yelled George. "Rockets!?!"

In reply Arielle swiveled the plane on its lift fans in time for George to see a large tsunami wave head away from them up the mountain, overtaking the smaller ordinary ocean waves and getting larger as it traveled.

"Its direction of travel is different than the wind waves," George said. "That must have been caused by an underwater disturbance."

"There was a loud underwater noise not too long ago," reported Shirley. "Must have excited that tsunami. I wonder how tall it was."

"Eighty meters," said Jill.

"Then Arielle didn't really have to use rockets," said Shirley.

"If *Dragonfly* had been where you wanted it," said Jill, "it would have been the only thing that would have saved us." The tone of the computer voice was unusually severe.

"Touché!" laughed David. "Hoist on your own petard!"

"What are you talking about?" asked George.

"I'll let Shirley tell you," said David, getting up and making his way back to the galley.

"Shirley?" asked George.

For a while Shirley didn't answer, then she said, "After David had all that trouble developing a 'worried mother' tone for Jill, I volunteered to do the next one. It was the severe 'I told you so' tone that you just heard."

"I think you did a good job," said George. "After hearing that, I certainly wouldn't argue with Jill over a safety matter. Wouldn't want to get on her bad side."

Barnard set behind Eau on one side. They watched it go, then Arielle took the *Magic Dragonfly* around to the other side to await sunrise two hours later. She took the plane to maximum altitude in the neck of atmosphere that stretched between the two planets. They hovered there, resting and napping until the sun rose again from behind Eau.

"Wow! Look at those waves!" said George.

"Surfer's paradise?" said Shirley.

"Purgatory," said David. "Those waves are so big that there's no way you could ride them, even if you didn't need a suit to survive."

"It would still be fun to try," said George. "If you could handle the big waves at Makaha, you ought to be able to take on these, especially in the reduced gravity. Just think, a hundred-kilometer ride on a thirty-meter wave."

"Until you reached the top," reminded David.

"Yes . . . the top . . ." said George, looking out the window at the sunlit side of the mountain. Heated by Barnard, the ammonia-water ocean had gotten warmer and the ammonia had boiled off into the atmosphere, raising the pressure on Eau and causing a stream of wind to flow up along the mountain of water and funnel through the narrow gravitational neck onto Roche. As the winds climbed the mountain, they pushed the waves ahead of them, adding to the wave energy. As the waves approached the top of the mountain, three things happened. The depth of the water, measured in terms of the distance to the other side of the mountain, became shorter. As a result, the waves became slower and taller as they would on a shallowing beach. In addition, as they traveled up the mountain, the waves became confined to a smaller and smaller perimeter, while the energy in the waves remained the same, so they became even taller. On top of all that, as they moved toward the peak of the mountain, the gravity dropped. It was nearly three percent of Earth gravity near the base of the water mountain, but by the time the wave had reached the peak, the gravity had dropped to a half-percent. Under the reduced gravity, the waves became enormous.

"That was a BIG one," said George, admiring the fountain of water that appeared at the top of Eau mountain. In the light gravity, the spume of water from the kilometer-high wave shot twenty kilometers into the air, where the spray was tossed up still farther by the rush of air from Eau to Roche. Lightning flashed, and clouds formed in the turbulent saturated air.

"Look," said David, pointing at the clouds above and below. "The clouds are swirling one way north of the peak and the other way in the south."

"It's the Coriolis force," said George. "Whenever you have mass flow in a rotating system, the Coriolis force makes the air flows move in circles. We have the same thing on Earth. Counterclockwise hurricanes in the Northern Hemisphere and clockwise ones in the Southern Hemisphere. It's different here, though. On Earth, the maximum Coriolis force is at the North and South Poles, but there are no strong air currents, so the maximum storm action is in the mid-latitudes. Here the air currents are a maximum right at the center of rotation, so we get strong interactions."

"The clouds look like giant tornadoes," said Shirley. "One stretching north and one going south."

"They are," said Arielle. "But they are lazy ones because of low gravity. Not to be afraid."

The sun set, painting the whirling cloud columns a deep red color, fading to dusky gray at their inner points, where lightning flashes would occasionally illuminate the foaming white towers of spray leaping up from below.

"Bedtime," announced George. "We've had fun admiring the sights, but we got to get into our survey routine so we can keep it up for the next few weeks. I want us off Eau and tied down back at Rocheworld Base five days before periapsis. Eau will generate lots of bad weather from all the heating, but we can bask in the warm sun at Rocheworld Base, then come back again for a more detailed survey." He flickered his fingers over the screen and pulled out the science schedule.

"Good," he said. "We're two rotations ahead of schedule." He modified the time intervals, with Jill adding and subtracting tasks to make sure that the visual and infrared images were taken with the right illumination. When it was all done, he looked at the crew assignments for the first segment.

"It says here that Katrina and I should be in bed while you four are working," he said, getting up and heading for the rear of the plane. Katrina went ahead of him.

"Right," said Richard, taking command. "Arielle, start the survey spiral, while I set up the scanning sensors. Shirley, we'll need to get the bottom sampler set up and into the airlock, ready to drop at a good sampling point."

Shirley headed for the rear of the plane, hesitating for a second at the privacy curtain that led to the sleeping area. George and Katrina were talking in loud whispers.

". . . and at least you could have said 'in our bunks' instead of 'in bed' . . ."

"Look, Katrina, I didn't plan the teaming schedule, Red did."

"Good night, George." There was a slam of a Sound-Bar door, then a deep sigh. Shortly thereafter Shirley heard the sound of a shower, so she slipped through the first privacy curtain, made her way silently toward the back and passed through the second privacy curtain to the workroom at the rear of the plane. She spent the next fifteen minutes getting the bottom sampler checked out and into the airlock. On the way back she noticed that the shower was empty and so was George's bunk. She smiled, pleased that her crewmates and good friends were no longer arguing, and headed forward into the busy front section of the airplane. All of a sudden she felt hungry, and stopped off at the galley for a quick snack.

The exploration survey turned routine. They would fly a hundred kilometers, hover to dip down the underwater sensor package, measure the distance to the bottom, drop the bottom sampler if it were close enough, analyze the water content, then take off again for the next survey point.

"I'm beginning to see a definite pattern in the water composition," said Katrina. "It matches the weather and temperature patterns."

"The usual yin-yang pattern?" asked David.

"More like the two halves of the cover on an American baseball," said Katrina. "Barnard heats up the equatorial and outer pole region to about zero degrees centigrade, and the ammonia boils out of the ocean, leaving it water-rich and heavy. The high-pressure atmosphere then travels to the cold region and the ammonia rains down on the spin poles and the inner pole, making the ocean there ammonia-rich and light."

"That would explain the ocean current patterns I'm getting from the doppler-radar mapper," said David. "There is a general motion from the cold arc to the warm arc. That would be the lighter high-ammonia liquid returning over the surface, while the heavier high-water liquid closes the circuit along the bottom. Makes for a topsy-turvy ocean, hotter in the middle than at the top."

"I wouldn't call zero-cee hot," remarked Shirley. She turned to Katrina. "Do you have all the measurements you need?" When Katrina nodded, Shirley started the winch that would retrieve the ocean-sensor package from beneath the waves and nodded in turn to Arielle, who smoothly lifted the *Magic Dragonfly* up into the air on its VTOL fans and transitioned into level flight. The nuclear jet kicked in, and the *Magic Dragonfly* screamed through the thin air toward the next survey point.

Warm✸Amber✸Resonance lay spread out on the surface basking in the red rays of Hot, the heating light. Hot was getting bigger and the heat that it emitted was increasing, while Warm was shrinking again, and would soon fade away, not to return for four hundred eighty days. The huge body relaxed even more and spread into a thin layer in the shape of a rough circle a hundred meters in diameter, a large amber blotch that rode the waves as they rippled underneath the jellylike flesh.

Then, weakly, there came a high-pitched noise. The acoustic senses in the amber creature went on alert. It sounded like a whistle from an underwater volcanic vent, but it had no direction; it seemed to come from every direction at once! The noise grew louder as if some invisible monster were emitting a hunger cry. Warm❋Amber❋ Resonance searched the water beneath it with burst after burst of sound pulses from its body, but it could see nothing. Then, just after the shriek from everywhere had reached its peak, the red glow from Hot flickered into blackness for an instant, then regained its glow. Frightened, the vulnerable sheet of amber rapidly contracted into a three-meter ball, its sonar still searching for the source of the danger. It sank to the bottom as the ocean liquids were squeezed from the jellylike flesh to turn it into a tough plastic-like rock.

"Anomaly noted!" said Jill to both Shirley and Arielle. A picture appeared on their screens from the video scanner. Jill had outlined the anomaly with a blinking green circle, but the cue was unneeded. In the center of the screen was a large ragged circle of amber ocean.

"It appears in the infrared scanner, too," said Jill. The same scene in the false colors of the infrared flashed on in place of the video scene. The blotch was still amber in this scene, indicating it was significantly hotter than the water.

"Must be a plume of ejecta from an underwater volcano," said Shirley. Richard looked up from his seat in the galley, put down his bowl of vegetable soup, and came forward, bounding in the low gravity in his eagerness.

"I'd like to see that!" he said, stopping himself by grabbing on to Shirley's shoulders. "Can Jill find the spot again?"

"We're on our way around," said Arielle, putting the *Magic Dragonfly* into a wide turn. "Should be easy to see something that big."

"Are you sure this is the spot?" asked Richard ten minutes later as they hovered above the surface of the ocean.

"I have *Clete* in sight, and *Barbara* just gave me a position update a half hour ago in its last orbit, so my navigation accuracy is better than one meter," replied Jill.

"Go up," said Richard. "Perhaps it floated off from where we saw it." Arielle took the plane rapidly to altitude. They went up a kilometer, the scanners in the eyes of the *Magic Dragonfly* vigilantly searching the rapidly increasing circle of ocean.

"The currents aren't more than a few kilometers an hour in this region, and it only took us ten minutes to return. We would have seen it if it just drifted off," said David, monitoring the infrared scanner while Shirley and Richard looked at the visible display.

"Let's go back down and take a look underneath the surface," said Richard. "Even if the cloud has dissipated, the underwater volcano should still be there."

Arielle pushed the down button, and the magic elevator dropped smoothly to a position ten meters above the top of the waves. Shirley lowered the under-ocean sensor package down on the cable and it splashed into the water. Through the noise of the splashing the sonar sensor on the package heard some high-pitched squeaks, then echoes of those squeaks from distant rocks and underwater hills. They were too few to get an accurate direction, but they seemed to come from nearly directly below.

Jill hesitated before starting the sonar sender, waiting to see if the strange squeaks would reoccur, but the volcanic vent had fallen dormant. Jill started the sonar pinging, and soon a picture of the bottom built up on Richard's screen.

"There's nothing but mud and a few rocks here," Richard complained. "I don't see any sign of a vent."

"It could be a small new one that hasn't built up a cone," said Shirley.

"The water composition is just what it should be in this region," said Katrina. "If there were significant volcanic activity in this region you would expect an excess of impurities like hydrogen sulfide, but there is no evidence for that."

"Then the amber blotch wasn't volcanic," said Richard. "But what caused it? And where did it disappear to?"

"Barnard will set in twenty-five minutes, and we are behind our schedule," reminded Jill.

"OK," said Richard. "Why don't I let Shirley and Katrina continue the survey and I'll finish my soup. But would you rerun the data on the video in the galley? Maybe I can puzzle it out during lunch."

Warm✳Amber✳Resonance stayed quietly on the bottom for a long time with its senses alert, but it could see nothing. The strange noise returned, then its screaming changed to a throbbing. The throbbing grew loud, then faded away, only to return once again. Suddenly something big and hard appeared with a splash at the top of the ocean. The amber rock fell silent while it carefully analyzed the returns from the last few sound pulses it had emitted after they had bounced off the strange monster. The monster was not too big, but it was as hard as a rock. None of the sound pulses had traveled to the inside of the monster. If the monster was that hard, how did it float? The monster was quiet for a while, then it gave off a blinding burst of sound that repeatedly flooded the bottom with illumination. Warm✳Amber✳Resonance stayed motionless and waited while the sound that reflected from the bottom reached the top again, self-illuminating the hard visitor from the sky. Tiny doors opened in the monster and sucked in water. Strange, stiff appendages with inset circles pointed this way and that, while burst after burst of sound throbbed from the underbelly of the monster. Then as suddenly as it began, the being stopped seeing, and without seeming to move anything, it swam upward and out into the nothing above the surface of the ocean. The throbbing noise increased, then faded off, to be replaced by the hideous shriek that thankfully also faded off. The dread creature was gone. The amber rock dissolved into a floating blob of jelly and swam rapidly away.

Warm✳Amber✳Resonance had lived over five hundred seasons. This hard screaming monster was something unknown, and that was nearly impossible in a world where no one ever forgot. There were others that were much older, such as Sour#Sapphire#Coo. Perhaps the elder would know about the strange monster.

Warm✳Amber✳Resonance was not exactly sure where the elder was, but since the research problem the elder was working on was a difficult one, it would take hundreds of returns of Warm before any solution would be found. For that length of concentrated thinking time, Sour#Sapphire#Coo would have to rock up under a protective shell. The shell required periodic exposure to air to maintain itself, and that meant going to one of the Islands of Thought. Warm✳Amber✳Resonance traveled at top speed, but it was still two turns of the sky before the chain of islands on the warm pole was reached.

"I give up," said Richard. "I don't see anything more in those pictures than we did before. The amber blob was definitely there, not drifting much as we pass over it, then as we go over the horizon it looks like it starts to shrink, but the foreshortened perspective makes it difficult to be sure of that. Then when we return ten minutes later, it's gone!"

"I'll keep working at the analysis," said David. "You'd better get your programmed sleep. You don't want to miss your island vacation trip, do you?"

"Are the 'Hawaiian Islands' coming up?"

"They are only nine hours away on the science schedule," said David. "And I know you want to get out and swing your pick at some of the outcroppings."

"Right! Wake me up as we get near. My pick is getting rusty on this water-ball." He headed for the bunks in the rear, grabbing a protoprotein cookie for dessert as he passed the galley.

The "Hawaiian Islands" were six rings of low mountains spread out in a line that crossed over the outer pole of Eau. The ocean was shallowest in this region and was only a few hundred meters deep, allowing modest mountains to stick their peaks above the surface. Each island was named after one of the Hawaiian islands: Hawaii, Maui, Lanai, Molokai, Oahu, and Kauai. Richard was awake and suiting up as George flew a high-altitude survey pass over the chain as dawn broke over the horizon. Shirley made her way back through the crew quarters to check Richard out just in time to see Arielle climbing into her upper bunk.

"Aren't you going to stay up and see the islands?" asked Shirley, a little surprised.

"Piloting hard work," said Arielle. "I would have fun to see them, but I now get my beauty sleep." She closed the Sound-Bar door as Shirley continued on her way.

So that's her secret, mused Shirley to herself. *Must try it myself some day.* She closed the privacy curtain behind her, and striding up to the suited figure standing in front of the airlock she unceremoniously began punching the buttons on the chest console and reading the responses. Richard rocked slightly with each punch. Used to this kind of treatment, he ignored Shirley and talked through his suit imp to George.

"Fly back over from the sunlit side and let me watch on my holovisor," he said, reaching a gloved hand up to pull a dark gray lid down over his visor. The inside of the visor lit up with tiny little laser diodes into a hazy image of mostly blue with some reddish splotches. Richard forced his eyes to relax, and as they stopped trying to focus on the nearby points of light from the diodes, the holographic multicolor laser pattern re-formed itself into an image of a rectangular video display at normal console distance, the array of tiny lasers generating at the surface of the visor the same light patterns, complete down to the phase, that would have crossed the surface of the visor from the video display if it had really been there.

"With their ring shape, they look more like atoll islands than the volcanic Hawaiian islands," said George.

"They were only blobs on the fly-by probe pictures," said Richard. "But they're not atolls, either. Those are formed by coral. Although I'd love to find even some low form of life like coral, I don't expect it here."

"What did cause those rings, then?" said George. "Volcanoes?"

"My guess is that they're impact craters from a large meteorite," said Richard. "The meteorite came in at a low angle and broke apart in the upper atmosphere."

"I'm going down. Any particular one?"

"Find a flat spot on the inner side of Hawaii. I'm more likely to find some folded back inner crust there."

"Which one is Hawaii?"

"The big one at this end. They're named in the same order as the Hawaiian Islands back home."

George was silent as distant memories of indolent days on the surfing beaches on the Islands flooded through his mind. He blinked back a tear of homesickness and started the long descent.

Shirley patted the broad shoulder of the suit as Richard stepped into the airlock.

"You be careful, now, you big lunkhead," she said. "I'll be right out to back you up as soon as I get my suit on."

As the outer door cycled the second time, Shirley was surprised to see Richard standing at the door with an armload of rocks.

"I got some real beauties!" he said, his enthusiasm bubbling though the communication link. "Here, take these and put them in the airlock. Then come out and help me get some more." He tried to pile his armload into Shirley's hands, but the stack slipped and a half-dozen sharp rocks tumbled to the floor of the airlock, leaving gashes and nicks in the mirror-smooth floor.

"Richard! You lummox! Now you've done it!"

"What did I do? The floor just has a few scratches in it."

"And those few scratches with those rough rocks probably increased the surface area inside the lock by ten times. It'll take forever to pump it down! Haven't you ever wondered why the lock has no extraneous equipment and all surfaces are mirror smooth? That's not so you can admire your handsome face in them. Those floors and walls are made that way so not one duralloy molecule sticks its head up above the rest to add to the surface area."

"I remember the briefings now. And those rock scratches have lots of jagged hills and valleys."

"Just eager to absorb hydrogen sulfide and hydrogen cyanide and release them again when the lock is refilled with inside air."

"I'm sorry," said Richard, really contrite.

"Well . . . it isn't really that bad," said Shirley. "The Christmas Branch will polish the scratches smooth with a plasma gun while we're gone. Besides, our suits are the major contributor to contamination. The suit imp polishes them when they're in storage, but they get roughened up every time we go outside." She carefully placed the rest of the rocks inside the lock and joined him outside.

"Well, that's about it for Maui," said Richard, an island later.

"Are you planning on visiting all of the islands?" asked George.

"No, just Hawaii and Maui during this daylight period. I think I'll skip Lanai—it's too small to bother with—and go on to Molokai and Oahu during the next period. These three-hour daylight periods sure chop up a work schedule. You just get interested in something and it gets dark."

"Richard," called David over the suit-imp. "I've been going over the pictures that the scanners took on the way in. Pull down your holovisor, I want to show you something."

Both Shirley and Richard reached up to pull down their holographic viewing screens. Hidden behind gray visors, they watched as David zoomed the view down into the center pond of Maui. The mountain ring was about ten kilometers in diameter, but was not continuous. There were a number of places where the ocean had broken through passes in the ring and had flooded the interior of the impact crater. Not far from one of those entrances was a small blob of amber and an even smaller blob of blue.

"Jill would swear from the spectrum that the amber blob is the same type of stuff as the large amber blotch that disappeared. We're not sure, though, since this blob is under a meter of water."

"What does the infrared sensor say? Never mind . . . the water would kill that."

"There is a slight increase in the surface water temperature, but that could be explained just by the difference in reflectance of the blob underneath."

"That's only a half-kilometer from where we are!" said Richard. "I'm going over for a look."

"I'll come over and pick you up," said George. The *Magic Dragonfly* lifted and floated over to them. George landed and waited until the dust had settled before he opened the airlock. Shirley and Richard sat at the entrance and held on to the hand bars on either side of the door as George ferried them around the inside of the island arc.

Shirley glanced in back of her, then tapped Richard with her free hand.

"Look at the scratches," she said.

Richard looked back. The scratches were still there, but now their interiors were just as mirror smooth as the rest of the floor.

Warm✱Amber✱Resonance had gone from one island to another, searching. A sour scent led it to the elder, a large blue rock lying just under the surface of the ocean. The amber cloud surrounded the blue rock and shouted.

✱Open up! There's a hard screaming monster in the ocean! What is it!?!✱

There was no immediate reply, but Warm✱Amber✱Resonance had not expected one. Sour#Sapphire#Coo had taken for its research project the derivation of an example of the fifth cardinal infinity. It had been fifty seasons of the visitations of Warm since the massive blue elder had left the pod and traveled to the Islands of Thought. Warm✱Amber✱Resonance had been hesitant to distract the elder, but with an age exceeding two thousand seasons, surely the old one would know if such a strange monster had been seen before and whether it was dangerous. The wait was necessary to allow the thinker to complete its present train of thought and put all the portions of the unsolved problem in a state where they could be picked up again without error. Hot traveled around to the other side of the world, and the tides rose again. Finally a soft voice murmured from behind the protective shell.

#A hard screaming monster?#

✱It is too hard to float, but it does! It swims without moving! It can even swim in the nothing above the ocean!✱

A crack opened in the shell.

#Let me taste.#

Warm✱Amber✱Resonance formed a tiny tendril of an appendage and stuck it in the crack. Memory juices were exchanged.

#I never saw or learned of any such monster. It is your

problem. I return to mine.# The crack closed and the blue elder returned to the problem of the fifth cardinal infinity.

Warm✳Amber✳Resonance was so busy absorbing the brief taste of the masterful strokes of the thought processes Sour#Sapphire#Coo used in its solution thus far, that at first it didn't hear the high pitched noise building up around them. The exchanged memory juices finally absorbed and incorporated into its own, the amber cloud suddenly reacted.

✳The monster returns!!!✳ Like a tuna sensing a shark, the amber blob formed into a slim swimming shape and sped off into the deep ocean.

Before landing, George hovered the *Magic Dragonfly* over the spot on the ocean where the scanner had seen the colored blobs.

"I see the blue thing—it's a big deep-blue-colored boulder, but the amber blob is gone!" said Richard.

"Again?" said George.

"Yep. But that boulder isn't dissipating," said Richard. "Let me down onshore; I want to wade out and get a chunk."

"Richard!" said Shirley, her cry echoing that of Jill on Richard's suit-imp.

"When is low tide?" persisted Richard.

"In a half hour," said Jill.

"And how much will the water level drop between now and then?"

"Over a meter."

"Which means I'll be able to walk right out to that rock and chop off a chunk and hardly get my feet wet."

"But your suit . . ." protested Shirley, when Jill didn't respond.

"If my suit is good enough to keep out this poison we call an atmosphere, it is good enough for the cleaning solution that we call an ocean," said Richard. "And the extra amount of heating power I'll need for the short trip is nothing to worry about. Right, Jill?"

Shirley and Jill reluctantly agreed to let Richard have

his way. Shirley insisted that she tie a safety rope to him before he started out, and he let her. His first steps into the retreating ocean were dramatic, as clouds of evaporating ammonia boiled off at each step, but soon the outside of his suit was as cold as the water and he plowed through the thigh-deep ripples to the deep blue boulder. Once there he looked it over carefully, then raised his pick and broke off a small piece. It was lighter blue inside. Richard put the prize into his collection bag and waded back to shore.

"Maui has too many tourists this season," he said. "Let's take a hop over to Molokai." He and Shirley got into the airlock. They closed the door this time as George lifted for the short trip to the next island sixty kilometers away.

"Any more islands?" asked George after Richard and Shirley had climbed back through the airlock.

"We've done four: Hawaii, Maui, Molokai, and Oahu," said Richard. "That should be enough for a nine-hour tour. Besides, it's almost sunset again. Let's head back to the inner pole."

"I recommend that course," said Jill. "It's only fifteen days to periapsis, or sixty day-night cycles. The weather at the inner poles is already getting stormier as it gets warmer. I would like us to be back at Rocheworld Base at least ten days before periapsis."

"That gives us five days for survey stops. Is that going to be enough?" asked Richard.

"It should be," said Katrina. "We have most of the place mapped, and the data matches the atmospheric and ocean models well. It's just a matter of getting enough samples to keep the statistical errors down. Except for those islands, this place is pretty dull." She sighed. "It would have been different if we'd found any evidence of life, but no such luck."

"Did you get an analysis done on that blue rock?" asked Richard.

"Yes," said Katrina. "It was very similar to that orange silica-gel-type glass that Sam found over on Roche. It must take a strange chemistry for that to form. Neither Jill nor I have been able to come up with a good process yet."

Arielle walked forward between the two and made her way to the cockpit. She was still slurping away at a vanilla algae shake. As she approached, George got up, turned the plane over to her, and stiffly made his way back to the crew quarters and bed. Arielle glanced over the control panel, looked out the window at the setting sun, and raising power, lifted the *Magic Dragonfly* into the crimson skies.

Two days later, it was George who first spotted Roche from his vantage point at the cockpit window.

"Land ahoy," he shouted throughout the ship as the edge of the twin world showed its brown over the blue-gray waves. After another half hour, they were within line of sight of Rocheworld Base.

"Welcome back," said Carmen. "Red says from down below that she can see your contrail from the viewport window."

"Pretty good eyes," said George.

"Especially when in back of a thirty-centimeter telescope," broke in Red's voice. "Even though we're nearly always in contact through one commsat or another, it's still nice to see you directly."

"We'll be home soon," said George. "A few more survey stops to fill in the gaps in the records, then across the neck in time for periapsis."

"Watch that weather," said Red. "There's a big storm brewing above the water mountain, and it's coming your way."

"We'll fly over it," said George. "See you soon, beautiful."

George got a weather map from *Clete* and talked it over with Jill.

"It's moving fast, but we should be able to take one more survey sample before dark, then get back to altitude before it arrives." As he spoke, George put the *Magic Dragonfly* into a steep dive and headed for the ocean surface. He brought the plane to a hovering stop in the strong surface winds, and Richard let down the ocean sampler into the rolling seas.

"That's some wind," remarked Richard as he monitored the drop through the bottom video camera. "The cable is trailing thirty meters downwind. Hold it for a minute until I get a return from the bottom . . . Got it! Take her up!"

George applied power and climbed the *Magic Dragonfly* into the scruffy sky. The sun was setting, but George kept track of the clouds by the nearly constant lightning flashes. There was a crash from the galley as the plane dropped a few hundred meters in a vicious downdraft, then they were forced into their seats as an updraft sent them spiraling skyward again. George raced in front of the storm to stay in quieter air while he climbed. They were going around the mountain now, and Rocheworld Base dropped below the horizon behind them. The air became smoother as the nuclear jet thundered them upwards, then finally George put the plane into a turn and headed back up the mountain. Arielle had been sitting in the copilot seat, her hands in her lap and her eyes busy alternately scanning the instrument panel and the view outside. George looked over at her, put the plane on autopilot and stepped down into the aisle. Arielle slipped quickly over to the pilot seat and strapped herself in. She left the plane on autopilot. Her hands went back into her lap and her eyes kept busy.

"We've passed over the front, and there's a clear region before the next front," said Richard from the science console. "One of our survey points is there. If you're willing to try a night landing we can get it out of the way and be that much closer to going back."

"Give me good weather maps, a good radar, and a good altimeter, and I don't need to see," said Arielle. "But just to be on safe side, I turn on landing lights near the waves."

Arielle took the controls and spiraled down into the inky blackness below. The distant orb of Gargantua was now too small to be of much use as a source of light, but she didn't need light; the radar picture of the clouds and surface were all that she and Jill needed. As they came down below five hundred meters altitude, Arielle turned on the landing lights. They were near the high-gravity equator, where the gravitational pull peaked at nearly twelve percent of Earth gravity. The waves were smaller but faster-moving, and looked somehow harder as they scudded along. Richard dropped in the ocean sampler and waited for the sonar return from the bottom. It came almost instantly.

"The bottom is only thirty meters down here," he said in amazement. "This must be some sort of an underwater plateau."

"The water composition is radically different, too," said Katrina from the other console. "There are lots of dissolved gases and strange chemical compounds. The temperature is also anomalously high."

"I think we must be near a volcanic vent field," said Richard as he watched the sonar map build up to show a slope rolling off to one side. "Let's head upslope and drop the sampler in again."

"OK," said Arielle. "Uphill is which way?"

"Toward Roche."

"Toward Roche we go," she said, lifting the plane and moving it a kilometer east, then lowering it again.

"The bottom is getting closer," said Richard.

"And the water is getting warmer," said Katrina.

"Another kilometer Rocheward?" asked Arielle.

"Arielle!" Jill interrupted. "Radar! Ten kilometers and moving rapidly toward us!"

Arielle glanced at the radar display to see a large, rapidly moving cloud breaking away from the more slowly moving front that was approaching. Beneath the cloud was a swarm of smaller swirling clouds. She pointed the video cameras in the *Magic Dragonfly*'s eyes toward that direction, and the sensitive cameras turned night into day on her screen. The scene was illuminated by nearly continuous flashes of lightning inside towering columns of foam.

"Waterspouts!" she blurted. Cutting the cable on the ocean sounder, she banked the *Magic Dragonfly* into a tight turn and headed south at right angles to the course of the waterspouts. She didn't try for altitude, but skimmed the surface of the water. The nuclear jet thundered in as the fans faded, and some of their irreplaceable monopropellant fuel was poured into the afterburner as Arielle smoothly accelerated the plane to top speed. There was a yell and a thump from the rear. Like a rocket ship taking off horizontally, the *Magic Dragonfly* shot forward. A column of water moved in front of them.

"Damn!" said Arielle, and threw the stick over. The left wing tip grazed the foamy tops of the waves below, then swung upward again as the right wing dipped. They missed the first waterspout, but a second one rose up above them and dumped its load of water in their path. The *Magic Dragonfly* shuddered as it hit the cloud of huge droplets. There was a loud bang from the engine compartment, then silence.

"The jet heaters shut down!" said Arielle. "No time to reset."

The powerless plane started to drop in altitude, perilously close to the tops of the waves. Arielle fired the attitude control jets to decrease their rate of descent. Made for space, they could not levitate the *Magic Dragonfly* in twelve percent gravity. With the rockets fighting off the crash, Arielle brought the VTOL fans up to speed and stabilized the altitude as she turned off the rockets. More precious fuel gone.

She returned her attention to the radar screen just in time to see a tiny twister cross her path. It was too close to miss, and the right wing of the *Magic Dragonfly* sliced right into it and was sucked upward. Arielle fought the controls and almost pulled them out, but the dipping left wing struck the top of a large wave, spinning them around. The *Magic Dragonfly* crashed heavily into the deep trough in back of the wave.

CRASHING

Arielle lifted her head. Her right hand still gripped the control stick. It was bloody and had two deep gash marks in it. There was a small stone on her tongue. She spat it out. She watched the bloody hand move the stick in slow motion as her left hand flickered over the control board like a frightened bird.

"Lift!" her mind commanded as she applied power to the VTOL fans. There was a low throb from the right wing.

Shirley clamped her throat shut and went into emergency mode. Ripping the safety belt from her chest, she ran to the rear and came to a halt in front of the suit locker. There was a naked man slumped on the floor, his bath towel draped over his paunch, his private parts exposed. She ignored him and donned her suit—for once without consulting a checklist. The helmet snapped into place and she took her first breath. She then looked around to see what she should do next.

George! Shirley snatched a rescue ball from the top bin and zipped it open. Staggering a little on the tilting floor, she grabbed George by the arm as he started to slide forward. Lifting the hundred-plus-kilogram man like the twelve-kilogram weight that he was in the reduced gravity, she stuffed him into the rescue ball head first. She reached down to the floor, picked up the bath towel, and stuffed it in after him. Another two seconds and George was zipped and pressurized. Shirley hung him from a hook and started forward. The floor tilted under her feet, and her stomach sank. She swallowed hard and forced her eyes to look on the level. She came to the sleeping area and pounded on two Sound-Bar doors, while holding them tightly shut with her strong hands.

"David! Katrina! You OK?"

"Yes!" came the muffled replies.

"We've crashed in the ocean. Don't open your bunk doors until I check for air leaks!" She glanced up to see Richard. He had obviously heard her over the imp emergency links. He took a careful breath of air and held it. She took his suit out of the locker and helped him with the hard part, then made her way forward on the steeply sloping deck to the front.

Arielle was gunning the controls in time with the lurches of the waves, and firing the attitude jets in an attempt to lift the *Magic Dragonfly* into the air. She looked around as Shirley approached. Shirley was horrified at the sight of the beauty's face. Arielle's upper lip was a torn bloody strip hanging down over a gap in her teeth.

"We'f craffed," she said in a plaintive voice. "And the fans won't work."

"You might as well stop trying the fans and rockets, Arielle," said Jill. "The left fan is broken. Even if we could lift out of the water, we couldn't build up enough speed to clear the jets."

"How's the hull, Jill?" said Shirley.

"There's a minor leak in the left wing fuel tank, but I have a minibranch making sure that it gets sealed. No evidence that the life-support hull has been breached."

Richard came forward in his suit. When he saw Arielle he blanched and went back for the first-aid kit. The Christmas Branch took it away from him and led Arielle back to the shower to wash her off and repair her torn lip with a neuskin patch. An imp came scampering out from under the pilot seat carrying a large white tooth with a bloody root.

Shirley opened her helmet and sniffed the air. It smelled funny, with an acrid smell of fear. The odor died as the air-conditioning fans continued their work of keeping the electronics cool. She and Richard headed for the back, shedding their suits as they went. Shirley heard a few mewling sounds from the shower and reached down to pick up the soggy red-stained jumpsuit from the floor outside the shower. On her way back to the cleaner she knocked on the Sound-Bar doors and told David and Katrina that it was safe to come out. She stuffed the jumpsuit into the sonic cleaner and stripped off her spacesuit, giving it a careful check as she did so, since she had neglected to check it when she put it on. It wasn't until she and Richard opened the suit locker to find a rescue ball hanging from a hook that she remembered George. She handed her suit to Richard and zipped open the bag. There was a rustle as the imp inside adjusted the towel and spoke.

"He'll be all right. He'll have a nasty headache when he regains consciousness, but there's nothing broken. Could you give me a hand in getting him to his bunk?"

"I've got him," said Richard, reaching past her to take the rescue bag off the hook. "You hang up your suit. You and Jill have to figure a way to get us out of here."

The rolling and pitching of the airplane was getting to Shirley. She didn't mind free-fall, but she had never enjoyed the motion of a ship. She didn't think she would get sick, but just thinking about it gave her doubts.

"Are you sure the left fan is out?" asked Shirley.

"Both fans were in the maximum forward position to maintain speed when the left wing struck the top of a wave. Immediately thereafter there was an overload in the acoustic sensor on the fan driveshaft followed by a rapid increase in back-reaction from the electric motor, raising the drive current to dangerous levels. I shut the motor down. Subsequent override commands by the pilot produced heat surges in the windings of the fan motor, but no rotation as measured by the tachometer."

"Which you checked out with its self-test circuits."

"Which I checked out."

"It's bent and jammed then. I'd better go out and take a look at it."

"Although we are afloat, with the cockpit windows out of the water, the tail of the ship is submerged. The air-lock exit is underwater. I do not advise exiting."

That stopped Shirley for a moment. "Richard showed our suits can handle water," she said.

"My airlock is not designed for liquids," said Jill, using her severe tone.

Shirley knew her computer.

"If I can't get out the airlock, then I can't fix the fan. The crew will have to stay inside until the life-support systems fail, and then they will all die."

There was a pause. Not a full second, but a noticeable one.

"The purging systems of the airlock can be reconfigured to accommodate liquids," said Jill. "Cycle time will double since I will have to purge twice. Once with super-heated air to evaporate any residual drops and liquid films, and once again to ensure purity before breaching the inner lock. You will have to have your suit cooling on full power during the hot-air phase."

"Fine," said Shirley, putting her helmet back on her head. "Cycle me through."

There was a moment of panic as a gush of water splashed down from two vents in the ceiling of the airlock. Shirley ducked under the thundering jets and peered through a riveleted visor at the foaming swirl on the floor. Her feet were cold, and she felt the warmth of the boot heaters as her suit tried to compensate for the loss of heat. In a minute the ice-cold ocean water of Eau was up to her waist. The buoyancy of her suit in the water began to lift her feet from the floor. She grabbed with two hands to wall rungs to keep from being swept under the crashing foam.

"Let some air out of my suit," she hollered. "I'm floating." She heard a hiss from her backpack, and the water pressed hard on the wrinkled glassy-foil covering of her suit. Although made of an impermeable metal alloy, the glassy-foil was as flexible as plastic because of its noncrystalline structure. A tenth of a millimeter thick, it could shrug off anything except the point of a knife blade. It did wrinkle under pressure, however, and the cold water pressed through the thermal-control layer and chilled her skin. The water burbled in and the air vented out until the door could be opened, letting a giant oscillating ball of air loose to make its way to the surface. Shirley followed it out.

"Leave the lock open and the lights on," said Shirley. She swam out into the darkness under the wing, then reached for the permalight on her belt. The spearing ray of light swung up to illuminate the fan well. There was a black gap where one of the blades was missing. The blade next to it was distorted and torn.

Shirley looked at the nightmare of twisted high-strength steel. It reminded her of Arielle's mouth and was just as devastating to the inherent beauty of the *Magic Dragonfly*. She kicked downward and tilted herself back until her chest camera was pointing at the scene, while pulling down her holovisor to monitor the picture as seen through the viewfinder of the electrocamera. The image was blurred. The camera lens had been designed to interface between space and air, not water and air.

"Can you compensate?" she asked.

Instantly the blurred image snapped into sharp focus as Jill adjusted the bits to compensate for the index of refraction of the water as well as the slowly varying distance to the image.

"Got it," said Jill.

"Now to get a top view," said Shirley, kicking up to the surface and grabbing the trailing edge of the wing. She raised her helmet above the water, and just before it was engulfed in a breaking wave, she saw the dawn rising over Roche. Silhouetted in the pink light was the Christmas Branch, carrying an electrocamera and making its way carefully back over the water-washed wing.

"I have that side," said Jill.

Shirley clenched her chattering teeth and let herself drop beneath the waves. A few strokes and she was back in the lock—a waterlock this time, as powerful exhaust pumps sucked the water from beneath her boots.

"We'll have to ballast the boots and the backpacks so the suit can stay inflated and prevent contact of the legs and arms with the cold suit," she said.

"Good idea," said Jill. "Now turn around and let me dry off your back."

As Shirley turned and rotated her body under the blasts of hot air, she could see steam rising from the shiny metal film. The suit cooling cut in, and she was just beginning to complain that it was getting too hot, when the cycle shifted. A few minutes later she was inside the plane. George was standing there with a worried expression, holding the back of his head.

Shirley took off her helmet and reported.

"It doesn't look good. The fan is broken. One blade twisted beyond repair and another one missing."

"Can you clear the twisted one and get the rest rotating?"

"Maybe," said Shirley. "But that will leave it unbalanced. I could remove another and turn it from a six-blade to a three-blade propeller, but I don't think that will lift. Perhaps we could jury-rig another blade or two, or arrange a counterbalance."

"You work on it," said George, as Richard helped her out of her suit. Richard's arm brushed hers, and he felt the clammy cold.

"You're frozen!" Richard said with concern.

"Not much worse than a deep dive in the Pacific Northwest," said Shirley. Still she didn't complain as he moved around behind her and gave her a long hug, his strong arms giving the firm muscular ones beneath them a warm embrace.

"How's Arielle?" she asked, as she basked in his warmth.

"Katrina and the Christmas Branch reinserted the tooth, and she now has an imp brace in her mouth holding it in place. The neuskin patch should take care of her lip with at worse a hairline scar, but she's going to have a fat lip for a while." Richard, his own arms too cold to be of much good anymore, let her go.

"I think I'll go forward and see if I can raise *Prometheus*," he said. "You and Jill concentrate on fixing that fan." He headed up the rocking corridor while Shirley returned to the task of hanging up her suit.

◇ Come see what I found! ◇

☆ What!?! ☆

◇ A big animal as hard as a rock, but it floats! ◇

☆ Wow! Where? ☆

◇ This way. ◇ The milky white cloud streamed off through the ocean, followed close behind by the red one. They approached the foundering winged metallic whale with caution.

☆ You're right! ☆ said the red one, sending pulse after pulse of sonar signals at the distant object. The pulses varied in pitch and complexity as the powerful voice of Roaring☆Hot☆Vermilion attempted to peer into the inner portions of *Dragonfly*.

☆ All I can see is the outside! It's as hard as a rock! ☆

◇ There are some portions that are not as hard. Come closer. ◇

The two moved closer to the drifting aircraft. They were curious, but still cautious, since the huge plane was as big as they were. As they moved, their sonar pulses continued to scan its length.

◇ There are places near one end where you can almost see through. Those are also the places where you can "look." The beast seems to have small hot suns inside it, and they shine out through those places. ◇

☆ LOOK?!? SUNS!?! ☆ The red alien was bewildered. Its body was sensitive to light, and when it was spread over the upper surface of the ocean basking in the warmth, it could tell roughly where the sun was in the sky, and whether a cloud had passed in front of it, but it had no eyes, so it didn't know what the heavens looked like. Its visual world was one of sound. Its sound pulses allowed it to see and visualize everything in its underwater kingdom, including the insides of its comrades. This was the first time it had met a beast that wasn't completely transparent to its piercing stare. As it approached the hard-shelled creature, the various portions of the red body could feel

the diffuse beams of light coming from spots near one end
of the long central body. As Roaring☆Hot☆Vermilion got
closer, its body could look better, since some portions
were quite close to the light sources.

◊ Get real close. Then you can not only see a little
better, you can look better, too. ◊

The red cloud pressed itself onto the hard glass of the
cockpit window and tried to see in through the murky
glass. The bursts of sonar energy from its body penetrated
from the water into the glass quite easily, but on the other
side was nothing but air, so most of the sonar signal
reflected back, and only a small portion entered the cockpit to illuminate the objects there. The acoustic return also
suffered the same loss as it moved from the low density air
back into the high density glass. There was not much left
of the sonar signal by the time it flowed back through
Roaring☆Hot☆Vermilion.

☆ Can see some hard things inside, but there is a nothing
in the way, and it makes it hard to see. ☆

◊ Are you looking, too? ◊

☆ Yes. Many little suns. Too far away to look at well.
They are all blurred together. ☆

Arielle looked out at the reddish-colored haze obscuring
her right side window. Must be another one of those
strange colored blobs. Suddenly her head hurt. She stood
up and moved around, trying to shake the feeling.

☆ Something is moving inside! ☆ A blast of high energy
sonar sang through the glass and burst into the low-density
air beyond. Arielle winced again, although she didn't know
why.

☆ It is a long thing with a sphere on one end and straight
portions coming out of the sides and bottoms! They are
stiff, but they move. It's too much work to see. I give up.
Let's go surfing? ☆

◊ Maybe I can see. ◊ The white cloud slithered over the
red one and flowed onto the next panel of glass in the
cockpit window.

Arielle noticed that while the right side window of her
cockpit window still had the reddish tinge, the front win-

dow on the right now had a milky-white appearance. There
didn't seem to be any blending of one into the other. She
frowned. She didn't like it. Her eyes shifted to pay attention to the perfect break between the two colors at the
cockpit window frame.

Clear ◇ White ◇ Whistle tried again. It sent burst after
burst of sonar into the strange hard beast, but saw nothing
new.

◇ You're right. There's a nothing in the way. It's like
trying to see above the top of the ocean. ◇

☆ Let's go surfing! I can feel a big one building up! ☆

◇ Let me try looking. ◇

☆ I already tried! Too blurry! ☆

Clear ◇ White ◇ Whistle didn't answer, but formed a portion of its body into a disk shape. The disk grew thicker
in the middle, and the milky-white color of the flesh faded
away into clarity as the milky macromolecules containing
the genetic essence and nerve tissue flowed out of the disk
region, leaving only the clear basic structural substance of
the alien body.

A portion of the red cloud darted about the construct,
noting its shape and looking at its clear color.

☆ Strange! What is it made of? ☆

◇ It is me. Or part of me. ◇

☆ Why does the disk bulge in the middle? ☆

◇ So I can "look" at things from a distance. ◇

☆ Can't! You can only look at things when they are right
next to you! ☆

◇ With this fat disk I can. ◇

☆ Really!?! Let me look! ☆

◇ Hold still! ◇ the white one commanded, and holding
the disk between the red one and the cockpit window, it
used the crude lens of jelly to focus an image of the
interior of the cockpit on the skin of Roaring ☆ Hot ☆ Vermilion.

☆ It looks tiny!!! ☆ came a roar. ☆ What is it? ☆

Clear ◇ White ◇ Whistle took the lens away and put it in
front of its own body.

◇ There are lots of little suns. Some square. And there
is that moving thing you saw. Looks funny. The sphere has
ugly fuzz on it, and a slit that keeps opening and closing. ◇

☆I can feel that big wave getting closer and closer!☆
◇ You're right. I can feel it, too. ◇

The lens was dissolved. The two huge blobs slithered to the top of the wing and launched themselves onto a large curling wave that washed over the drifting *Dragonfly*. The two aliens surfed expertly along on the wave, their recent discovery ignored in the excitement of the ride.

Arielle's headache lifted, and as it did, she noticed out of the corner of her eye the lifting of the milky and red haze from the windows of the cockpit. She moved forward, and kneeling on the copilot's seat, she tried to peer out into the murky water.

There was nothing.

Arielle was tempted to ask Jill if she had seen anything, but then realized that Jill's electronic video sensors were just as limited as her electrochemical video sensors were in this frigid ocean. She swung around into the seat and ordered a position update from the console. There was an almost imperceptible delay in the response. Arielle's test-pilot-trained brain noted the anomaly.

The barrage of sonar sounds had taken Jill unaware. It had heard some strange pings and chirps from a distance a few hours ago, but after they had disappeared she had relegated the noises into its permanent memory under "Geology, volcanic, vents, noises from." The noises reappeared, however, and at close range—so close that they were obviously not volcanic in origin.

The science-scan video cameras and the other sensors built into *Dragonfly*'s body helped put together the picture. There was a red blob and a milky blob of water that moved slowly—like a clot of seaweed or a jelly fish, seemingly moving with the tide. The blobs were completely amorphous, with no structure seen in either the video or infrared sensor. The inside video camera had confirmed the colors when the two blobs washed against the cockpit windows. The shape information went to a portion of Jill that had been programmed to test for signs of alien life-forms. The program produced no match, for it had been trained to recognize symmetry and nonrandomness as an indicator of life. The information was sent off into memory storage, and the alien-finding portion of the program was turned off.

The sonar input, after processing in both frequency space and time space, was also sent to the test-for-alien-life program. Soon urgent messages were running through the master bus, calling back the stored shape information and activating a search through every sensor that had collected the least bit of information at that critical time period.

There was a moment's pause as Jill responded to the bothersome query from the human Arielle concerning a position update. That done, full computer brainpower was applied. Strange scents were extracted from the noisy data in the chemical sensors that monitored the outside conditions. Unfortunately, there was no new sensor data coming in, so the analysis had to make do with the sensor records. But the records were not good enough. Jill was almost sure that it had seen evidence of life—an intelligent lifeform. But what had been seen was not what the humans had expected, so the evidence was not conclusive. Jill would not bother the humans until it had done more calculations.

Jill thought.

"I need better sensor data," said Jill finally.

"What's the matter?" asked Shirley.

"I'm blind," said Jill. "I have lots of information from the infrared and video cameras on the two scanners in the 'eye' domes, but they are half-awash in the ocean. Besides, as an airplane, I'm used to having the long-distance vision of radar. How can I protect you if I can't see things coming from a distance?"

"There's not much I can do," said Shirley. "Your radar dome is under the ocean, and the water won't pass the microwaves. If you're going to insist on being a boat, you'll have to find some way to have me turn your radar into a sonar."

"OK," said Jill confidently. "Please turn my radar into a sonar."

"Can't be done," said Shirley, slightly perplexed.

"You said that all I had to do was find some way to have you turn my radar into a sonar," said Jill. "So I did."

"You did!!!" exclaimed Shirley.

"We have a complete set of spare parts for the under-ocean scanner," said Jill. "The sonar array of the ocean scanner has almost the same design features as the microwave scanner in my radome."

"That would make sense," said Shirley. "They both have the same wavelength, even though one uses radio waves, while the other uses acoustic waves."

"The piezoelectric sonar array uses higher voltages and lower currents than my semiconductor diode radar array," said Jill. "But I have reconfigured the driver to handle that. All I need is someone to replace the diode radar array with the replacement package for the piezoelectric sonar array."

"Can't the Christmas Branch to that?" complained Shirley. She could still feel the bone-cold waters pressing on her flesh.

"Not by itself," said Jill. "The Christmas Branch is out there now, rewiring the connector . . ."

". . . All right! All right! I'll help it."

Shirley donned her suit and slowly cycled through the outside lock, carrying the heavy sonar array on a shoulder harness. It was still dark, so she took her time as she swam under the wing and along the left side of the *Magic Dragonfly* to the front of the aerospace plane. She splashed upwards enough to peek through the cockpit windows at Arielle looking out at her, then sank beneath the waves. She got out her trusty Swiss Army Mech-All, and rotating it until she came to the right slide switch, she pushed the switch and a strange screwdriver was instantly formed from one of the many triggerable memory structures in the complex metal alloy head. The blade was shaped like the curved surface of a penny. Shirley jammed it into one of the curved slots on the radome and twisted. A flat metal screw head popped out. Shirley sunk down a little and attacked another slotted inset screw head.

"Here, take this," said Jill, its Christmas Branch handing her a thick circular plate of metal with crossed slots in it. Shirley took the microwave transmitting array and handed in the heavy cluster of square ceramic tiles.

The Christmas Branch took the cable dangling from the back of the sonar array and connected the cable to a jet-black box. There was a pause and Shirley hollered.

"OUCH! It makes my teeth ache," said Shirley.

"Good," said Jill. "That's the tooth-sensitizing frequency. How about this?"

"I feel sick," replied Shirley.

"The infrasonic portion is working," said Jill. "Now the ultra-high band. Do you hear or feel anything?"

"Bow-wow," said Shirley, her ear tips trying to curl up. She closed the radome, being careful not to leave any trapped air that would impede the sonar signals.

"I can see!" said Jill through her imp. "I have to wait a number of seconds before the distant parts of the image come in, but I can see again!"

"What can you see?" asked Shirley.

"We're on the side of a gradual slope that extends for a kilometer," said Jill. "The slope reaches a plateau some ten meters under the surface of the ocean. There are some volcanic vents there."

"Richard was right about being near a vent field," said Shirley. She began to really feel the cold. "I think I'll go inside and tell him."

"I've already informed Richard of our find through his imp," said Jill.

"I think I'll go inside and tell him anyway," said Shirley.

George was sitting at the science console monitoring the flow of data from the imager memory banks through the satellite data link to *Prometheus*. Even though they might not be able to get off this world, at least their data would.

There was a buzz from one of the flight consoles. A blinking light on one of his side panels indicated that the communication link from Rocheworld Base had been opened. He switched the communication console controls to his science console and answered.

Carmen's face appeared on the screen. As she noticed him, her hand reached up to her hairline, but before it touched her hair, there was a rustle of the comb-imp stuck to one side of her head, and instantly every hair in her bouffant hairdo was in its exact place. Carmen's hand dropped.

"We may have a solution to your problem, *Dragonfly*," she said. "Red thought it up while we were discussing what to do." Carmen touched a control on her panel and the view expanded to show Red Vengeance standing near her shoulder, a worried look on her face. Her hair was tousled and she looked like she had missed a night's sleep. There was also a suspicious redness around her eyes.

"I don't know whether it will work or not . . ." said Red hesitantly. A deep voice broke in, and Thomas's face peeked into the pickup from the other side of Carmen.

"Sure it'll work," said Thomas, "I'd've never thought of it, since all I've ever done is haul cargo from heavy gravity planets. It took a rockhound like Red to think of this one. I have Jack figuring out the optimum trajectory and the fuel margins we will need for various hovering times, but it should work fine."

"Great!" said George. "But what is it?"

"As you know," said Red, "the ascent module from the *Eagle* doesn't have enough fuel to take off from Roche, land near you and take off again, even if we lighten it by throwing off everything movable. However, it does have enough fuel to take off from Roche and travel over to the zero-gravity region between the planets, hover for a minute or so over the peak of the water mountain, pick you up, and still escape out to the L–5 point. *Prometheus* can then sail in and pick us up from there.

Greatly relieved, George's face lit up as he listened to Red.

"That sounds terrific!" he said to the hopeful faces on the screen. "I hope Jack doesn't find anything wrong with it. We're a long way from the top of the water mountain, but we'll find a way to get there even if we have to swim!"

"Fortunately, we have lots of time," said Thomas. "How are your consumables holding out?"

"No problem there," said George. "The good food is going fast, but it will last us for a few more weeks. Then we have the emergency rations, and if worse comes to worse, Jill can make us sugar syrup out of the soup we are sitting in. We are probably good until one of the recycling units develops a failure that Shirley and Jill can't fix. With that kind of time, we could even paddle the plane the thousand kilometers up the mountain."

Jill's voice broke in. "The distance from our present position to the top of the water mountain is one thousand two hundred and forty-three kilometers."

"Thanks," said George sarcastically, thinking of the sweat each one of those kilometers represented.

Another computer voice interrupted. It was Jack this time. "The proposed mission plan is feasible. Hovering time near the peak of the water mountain varies from twenty minutes at high tide to thirty seconds at low tide. I have left a reserve of fuel for final rendezvous maneuvers with *Prometheus* at the L-5 point. This can also be used if it is necessary to extend the hovering time."

"Good!" said Thomas, turning and leaving the screen. "Show me the trajectory on the command console."

George looked at the screen containing the faces of the two women. One was calm, professional, and coolly perfect, with a pleasant smile. The other was just as professional, but had a worried half-smile and wide eyes.

"Are you sure you can get there?" asked Red.

"Don't worry, Red," he said. "I was only kidding about swimming or paddling this flying submarine. I'm sure Shirley will figure out some way of getting some propulsion for *Dragonfly*. We have plenty of power, it's just that we're used to flying through air, not water. I'll see you two later. I'm going to tell the crew the good news that we have at least one way off this smelly egg." He turned off the communications console connection and talked to his imp.

"How does it look to you, Jill?" he asked.

"I have all the mission data from Jack through the data

link," it said. "The only problem that was not mentioned is that we have to work out some way to protect you from the ascent module jet exhaust. Jack was planning to turn off the jets and free-fall slowly down while the crew is pulled up with a winch."

"That sounds a little tricky," said George. "I am sure we can arrange some sort of blast canopy made up out of one of your wing panels with a pickup ring on top."

"I hadn't thought of that," said Jill. After a second's pause it said, "That will work, too. The material is thin, but it will not be in the jet long."

"Good," said George. "Are there any other potential problems in the plan?"

"How you are going to travel those one thousand two hundred and forty-two kilometers?"

"I thought you said one thousand two hundred and forty-three," said George.

"I did," said Jill. "But we are coming to another high tide and the currents in these regions are twenty kilometers an hour. We have moved closer to the peak."

"Well, that's a start," said George. "Too bad we can't anchor somewhere while the tide is going the other way."

"You can," said Jill, in its detached voice. "The water is only a few tens of meters deep in this region."

George gave a long laugh, his emotional relief at finding a means to rescue his command finally breaking through to the surface. He pounded a few keys on his console to link the audio pickup to all the imps and suit-imps on the ship.

"Avast there, ye skylubbers!!" he boomed into the mike. "Hit the deck and come a-running! This is Captain George, and I want every man-jack and -jill to assemble amidships. I have good news, me hearties, we are setting sail for home."

As he said those words, George had another thought, and whispered to his imp, "How much cloth have we on board?" he asked. The reply was lost in the confused clamor of voices coming over the audio link on the console. There was one voice that he took particular care to answer.

"Yes, Shirley," he said. "I want you and your crew, too.

We'll probably never be able to get *Dragonfly* in the air again, but Red has come up with a plan where we don't have to. Instead of making *Dragonfly* back into an airplane, we're going to make her into a boat, and we'll need you in on the planning session, since you are the only one other than Jill that knows *Dragonfly* inside and out. Unfortunately, Jill doesn't have any imagination, and that's what we are going to need a lot of if we are going to get off this world while we are still on decent rations."

Within less than a minute, George heard the first of the airlock cycles as the outside crew boarded and came forward wearing their suit briefs. Arielle had been sensibly asleep, her calm test-pilot nerves allowing her to keep up her necessary rest schedule. David, unable to sleep, had forced his tired body into a suit and had gone out to work with Shirley, Katrina, and Richard, wanting to do something, anything, to take his mind off their predicament. Arielle tried to find a decent place to get dressed, but finally gave up and came out in her sleeping outfit—a pair of warm pajamas with elastic cuffs and booties. Her spare frame had always suffered under the temperatures that the endomorphs around her found comfortable. In her furry pink bunny suit, surrounded by a smelly, dripping crew dressed in sweaty suit-tights, she looked like a small child captured by a pack of space-pirates. She perched on one of the stools in the corner of the galley and faced forward. Shirley sat on the galley counter, while the rest of the crew were scattered on the various stools and chairs that lined the corridor.

David swiveled in the computer console chair (practically his private preserve). His thin face seemed even leaner with its hint of orange-red stubble. He blinked his eyes tiredly a few times and shook his head to keep awake in the unaccustomed warmth of the body-heated room, after his hours in the cold seas of Eau.

"Don't keep us in suspense, George," he said. "How are we going to get home? Are they going to send another SLAM down to pick us up off some mudflat?"

"I'm sure Jinjur would do that if it were necessary," he said. "But Red has come up with another idea so that we don't have to waste two landers on the same planet. If we can get to the low-gee region on the top of the water mountain, then Red can pick us up there with the ascent module." Shirley listened to George's speech, whispered for a while to her imp, then finally broke into the conversation.

"We could use the tidal currents," she said, "dropping an anchor when they are in the wrong direction—but that wouldn't work when we start up the water mountain. The ocean becomes tens of kilometers deep there. We could think about a sail, but neither Jill nor I have been able to come up with enough mast and sail to make a significant difference. There is another alternative, and that is to use *Dragonfly*'s VTOL fans in a slow-rpm mode as a water propeller instead of an air propeller. Not very efficient, but it would give us a number of knots. Our only problem is that only one of the VTOL props is working. If we just ran that one, we would go in circles." Shirley stopped, and her eyes widened for a second. The rest of the crew almost could see the light bulb above her head. She whispered something else to her imp. There was a moment's pause, then the crew heard a slow throb coming through the hull from the undamaged right engine. George walked upward to look out the cockpit windows.

"We're moving," he said.

Shirley jumped down off the galley counter and strode forward. She sat herself down in the copilot seat and tilted her head to one side to line up the center of the window brace with one side of the rocky globe hanging in the sky ahead of them.

"Have you got the rudder hard over?" she asked Jill.

"Yes," said her imp.

Shirley watched, then shook her head slowly as the nose of the craft drifted off to the right. As they started to turn back the way they came, Shirley called a halt.

"The fan can move us at a significant speed," she said. "But even with the tail rudder and ailerons doing their best, we still travel in a circle, going essentially nowhere."

"How about a sea anchor on the starboard side, way out on the tip?" suggested David, trying to dredge up what little he could remember of his distant sailing lessons on Earth.

Shirley didn't answer. She leaned back in the copilot seat, her mind flipping through page after page of the engineering manual for the *Dragonfly*. Jill was not idle, and Shirley would occasionally nod as something was whispered into her ear by her imp. Suddenly she rose from the chair, strode down the length of *Dragonfly*, and went into the work area in the back that contained the air conditioning and renewal banks.

Although Jill had a brain that used as little electrical power as possible, that brain still used a significant number of picowatts per thought. The air conditioning on *Dragonfly* was not meant for the comfort of the crew, but to keep Jill's brain cool enough to eliminate "soft" errors due to thermal excitation. Shirley opened a louvered door and peered up. She stopped, went back to the suit locker, obtained her permalight and returned. She flashed the brilliant white beam up past the cracks between the flutes on the cooling fins of the air conditioning system to the air fans overhead. She stopped and punched a seldom used code into the permalight's microcomputer. Her thumb on a two-way variable switch, she sent the beam upward again. A few practiced flicks and she could see in the strobing flashes of light the air fans seemingly slow and come to a stop as the blinks of light from the illuminator in her hand matched the turns of the blades.

"How about those?" she asked her imp. "They're small, but one or two of those run at the proper speed could push enough water as the VTOL fan."

"Those are part of the air supply," Jill remonstrated. "Regulations do not permit any diversion of primary life support systems to other purposes."

Shirley replied in a firm voice, "The purpose for which the fans would be used is essential to the welfare of the crew. Please record my recommendations in your priority memory banks and verify with the Commanders of *Dragonfly* and *Prometheus*."

There was a short pause. Shirley heard a gruff, "She's

right," from the front of the aerospace plane. Then she heard Jill speak again through her imp.

"The substitution you suggest will work with proper control of the relative rotation rates of the two fans. There will be a twenty percent degradation of the air flow throughout the *Dragonfly*. That will leave us at only ninety percent of nominal. My motile Branch is not capable of removing the fan. The masses and gravity are too much at this location."

"That's all right," said Shirley, greatly relieved that the computer had given in so gracefully. That probably meant that the substitution was a piece of cake.

It wasn't.

Jill's Christmas Branch did all it could by unscrewing bolts that human fingers could never have reached, but the bulky fan was in its bay to stay. There were access plates that allowed the whole air-recycling unit to drop out of the bottom of *Dragonfly* for installation and maintenance, but they could not be used when they were deep under the slimy, smelly ocean of Eau. Shirley was dripping sweat before she finally had twisted the recycling units aside enough to get the fan through the door. At that, she had to trim some of the support structure with a laser cutter. The sharp edges of the one-meter-diameter fan and its support seemed to reach out to nick her flesh as she struggled into her suit-tights, then into the space-suit that proved to be as good in water as it did in space.

Despite her weariness, she carefully went through the checklist with Richard, then checked him out. She sent him through the lock first, then inserted the fan, allowing it the privilege of having the lock all to its razor-tempered self. After Richard had removed the deadly square with its slowly rotating fan from the lock, she cycled through, then followed him as he floated off under the left wing. Shirley reached into her tool-belt for a large omni-wrench and took care of the obvious bolts on the outside, while a large segment of Jill's inside Christmas Branch snaked its way into the wing and took care of the inside connectors. Shirley motioned Richard back while the last of the connections were loosened. The heavy fan and its motor dropped from the wing and settled slowly into the depths.

The next chore was to install the small air conditioning fan in place of the much larger propeller. Richard had no problem positioning it into place with its blades nearly all under water, but the amount of space left required some sort of bracing. Shirley looked over the situation in the dimming light, making length measurements as well as illuminating the scene with her versatile permalight. Dusk settled in on Eau and the two called it a day. They hung the fan in the gaping hole on Dragonfly's wing, swam to the distant hull, and cycled through.

George, Arielle, and Katrina were relaxing for the first time in many days. They were watching one of David's sonovideo compositions in the large-screen color display above the computer console. Each person had an extra section of the Christmas Branch on their ears as stereo headphones. David was improvising some additional audio and visual effects to add to the recorded composition of "Flight" that would thrill billions of others six light-years away on Earth when they heard it a half-dozen years hence. Listening to the music and watching the video, George thought that David was at his peak, tired as he was —or maybe it was because he was so tired. George looked quickly at the console and saw with relief that someone (probably Jill) had turned on the high-fidelity sonovideo recorder. This exultant evening of genius would not be lost.

There were low noises from the rear of the aerospace plane. They really didn't interfere with the concert, but George's command responsibility made him pay attention. He finally identified the sounds as that of two large people trying to take a shower in the same small booth. He made a motion with his hand near one ear as though he were turning a knob, and the volume on his earphones increased, drowning out the noise from the rear. He relaxed and looked with relief at the beautiful video caressing his eyes.

Twenty minutes later Shirley came through the privacy curtains. She picked her way through the relaxed humanity clustered around the computer console and went to one of the cockpit consoles. George saw her pass and got up to follow her.

"Where's Richard?" he asked.

Shirley smiled a knowing grin. "He's snoring away in a bunk. Had a lot of exercise today," she explained.

"So have you," said George. "Don't you think you ought to get some sleep before daylight in three hours?"

"Before we can go out again we'll need a fairly complicated bracing structure made. I thought Jill and I could design it before I go to bed. The Christmas Branch can be building it while I get a good nine hours sleep. I've been on the go for thirty hours." She patted her tummy. "Hmmm. My stomach thinks my mouth's on strike." She interrupted Jill's computations to order up a double dinner of chili, then turned to grin at George.

"It's going to work, George," she said. "We should be chugging our way up the mountain in less than a day." Relieved, George returned to David's performance.

The music through the imps grew stronger. David was now improvising, and the effect was like a fairy nimbly scampering up the stairways of the gods. George's eyes had automatically closed as he heard the charismatic sounds, but then he forced them open as he realized that he was in the chamber of a lyrical genius, one who wrote emotions in the colors and tones of light and music rather than the scratches and snarls of writing and speech.

No longer was this place a dingy, crowded corridor filled with aching, sweating bodies, but the vast empty corridors between the starlanes of the galaxy. His eyes, his ears, his soul drank in the new freedom from the fleshly bondage that had been the inheritance of the human race— for the long-fettered gray mass of the human brain now saw greater things.

The greater things drifted in from the ghost-like shrouds of haziness. Then—with the music adding substance—they grew to take over the vision, still avoiding the direct glance, the firming up, the human desire to make desire a reality.

David, inspired by his own feedback, took off on another improvisation. The scenes repeated, yet were different in a subtle but significant way. The music counterpointed from one disparate scene to another, while the images mixed and blended. There were new, more complex inter-relationships. The scene and sound came to a dramatic climax. As it did, George knew only that he didn't have enough experience to appreciate it. If he had heard and seen that on the screen without preparation, he would have hollered for a repair technician. Yet he knew that the sonovision was just as the artist had wanted it, but he, George, was only dimly able to recognize its majestic complexity.

The remains of the music and scenes echoed through the hallways and chambers of his mind. There was a long pause, in which the only sound was that of David taking a few deep breaths, Shirley pecking at keys up front, and a long sonorous rumble from a bunk in the crew quarters.

"Thank you, David," said Katrina. "That was one of your most exquisite compositions."

"Oohh!!!" said Arielle, her breath finally exhaled. "Oh! Nife!!" she said again, her gaze passing through the blank screen on the bulkhead to the stars beyond. She finally noticed where she was. Blushing slightly, she pulled her long pink bunny legs up to her chin and grew silent. A shy grin still flickered on her lips above her clasped hands.

George, still out of his element, tried to express the gratitude he felt for witnessing what was obviously a rare moment in artistic creation. He knew only that his faulty sense of appreciation had captured but a small portion of the fountain of genius that had flowed over him.

"That was really good, David," he said. "I mean, I really, really liked that one. It really made a really great impression . . ."

He had the sense to stop.

MEETING

For the next two day–night periods, there was no recurrence of the strange blobs and their noises. Jill's program had still not decided what the things were, but it was certain they were not intelligent life-forms, since an intelligent being would certainly want to explore such a strange artifact as Jill.

Then Jill's sonar, peering ahead through the endless ocean, heard a response to its searching pings. They had the same pitch and structure as the noises that had been heard nearly twelve hours ago, strong, loud, and almost raucous.

☆HI!!! HI!!! HI!!!☆ hollered Roaring☆Hot☆Vermilion.

◇Who are you talking to?◇ asked Clear◇White◇Whistle.

☆It's the big floating rock! It's talking now! I think it wants to play!☆

The red cloud changed its body ripples from the slow, wave-leaning gait that it had been sharing with Clear◇White◇Whistle and slithered off toward the distant pinging ahead.

Jill's sonar system saw the distant blobs separate. One came directly at it at high speed. Jill increased its interrogation rate and switched to a modified chirp in an attempt to pick up shape information. The blob was about three meters wide, ten meters long, and one meter thick, but it had almost the same density as the ocean and had no discernible internal structure.

278

◊ Careful! ◊ came the call from the distant white cloud. ◊ It might be a new type of Grey⊗Boom! It might explode and catch you. ◊

The thought slowed the advance of Roaring☆Hot☆Vermilion, but didn't decrease the volume of its voice, which raised to a shout.

☆HI!! WANT TO SURF!?!☆

Jill took in the sound, then echoed it back, more softly since it was limited to a hundred watts of power by its jury-rigged sonar system.

"Hi! Want to surf?!" Jill said, then waited.

Roaring☆Hot☆Vermilion paused a second, nonplussed at hearing its own voice, weak though the echo was.

☆HI!!☆

"Hi!"

☆HI! HO! HI!☆

"Hi! Ho! Hi!"

Roaring☆Hot☆Vermilion caught on quickly. This thing obviously didn't know how to communicate, so it was limited to repeating what it heard. The red cloud had come across others of its kind that fed around volcanic vents at distant points in the ocean. Some had spoken such strange dialects that it took them almost a light-cycle to get accustomed enough to each other's slang so they could talk together.

This strange thing didn't seem to know anything about talking, but it still was smarter than the hunters and flitters, who had their own sounds and could not imitate the spoken voice. This thing could even imitate Roaring☆Hot☆Vermilion's own overtone patterns. The obvious way to see if it could be taught to talk was take it through some simple mathematical logic. First the numbers, then simple combinatorial mathematics, then formal logic, then a few physical referents such as you, me, water, dirt, sky, and some diagrams on the bottom, and they should be conversing in a light-period.

☆One! Two! Three! Four! Five! Six! Seven!☆

There was a pause as the numbers trilled through the water, each one, with its multiple tonal and pulse-code pattern a living example of the concept of the number it represented. The word "Three" was a melodic triplet of sounds with each note given its own triple-tongue beat. Each number had its own set of overtones that were distinctive as bell, violin, and brass. The number "Seven" was a manifold wonder that Jill saved in its pristine acoustic beauty to present to David when he was in the mood to compose.

☆One plus one equals two.☆

☆One plus two equals three.☆

"One plus three equals four," interjected Jill.

The **red** cloud turned itself inside out.

☆HEY!!! VERY GOOD! Won't take long for you to learn!☆ There was an outpouring of sound beamed off into the distance.

☆Come here, Clear ◊ White ◊ Whistle! This strange hard floater is as smart as a new-formed one!☆

☆One plus One plus One equals . . . ☆ said the red cloud, waiting for the answer.

". . . Three," dutifully responded Jill.

☆Three TIMES One equals Three!☆ said Roaring☆Hot☆ Vermilion, jumping from addition to multiplication. Jill caught on instantly.

"Two TIMES Three equals Six!" said Jill, almost triumphantly.

☆Zzzzzzzzzzt!!!☆ came an explosive sound.

☆SsSsSsIiIiIiXxXxXx!☆ said the red cloud, enunciating each trill and overtone with exaggerated care.

"SSSsssIIIiiiXXXxxx," said Jill, its electronics still stumbling over the acoustic nuances of the word.

☆Zzzzzzzzt!!☆ exploded the red cloud. Jill tried again.

"SsSsSsIiIiIiXxXxXx," said Jill's sonar finally.

☆I do believe it's GOT it!!!☆

The red blob turned itself inside out again, and dashed off to meet the still approaching white form.

☆It's SMART!!! I think I'll keep it!!! I'll name it Floating⊗ Rock!☆

◊ It may not want to be kept. Besides, Floating⊗Rock doesn't seem to swim too well. It won't be able to follow you around. ◊

☆Oh!!! Right! Well, you can have it! I'm going surfing!☆
The red cloud swam off into the distance.

Jill took advantage of the interlude to inform the crew of
its find. They came crowding to the cockpit windows to
see the giant alien creatures. There was a large red alien
swimming away, while a slightly smaller white cloud hovered in the water at a distance.

"They are definitely intelligent, despite their amorphous
shape," reported Jill.

"Do they have name?" asked Arielle.

"I haven't progressed that far yet," said Jill. "Even
when I have learned their names I doubt you would be
able to pronounce them. The red one is quite raucous, so
I'll call it Loud Red. The other uses a higher-pitched
whistling tone, so I'll call it White Whistler."

"How can such large aliens exist in these barren seas?"
asked Katrina. "We've been over all of Roche and most of
Eau and taken lots of samples. I'm sure you and I would
never have missed seeing a life-form, even a single-celled
one."

"I suspect that the only life to be found is right around
the active volcano vents," said Jill. "Life here never developed photosynthesis, so all you have are animals. Even a
one-celled animal cannot survive except right around the
vent fields where the energy source is."

"It's like the little colonies of strange sea creatures that
cluster around the sea-bottom vents back on Earth," said
George. "They live off the hydrogen sulfide escaping from
the vents. There is even a large wormlike creature with no
mouth. It gets its food from hydrogen-sulfide-eating bacteria living in its skin."

"Well, these creatures are even weirder than those we
have on Earth," said Richard.

"Look," said Arielle. "White Whiftler is coming clofer."

Clear ◇ White ◇ Whistle approached the strange metallic-
tasting beast. There should be many things that Clear ◇
White ◇ Whistle could learn from this strange thing that
was hard like a rock but floated. For instance, there were
those strange things inside Floating⊗Rock that had stiff

sections connected by joints and moved around. Since Floating⊗Rock had eaten the Stiff⊗Movers, perhaps they would be tasty, but Clear ◊ White ◊ Whistle had never seen anything like them in this region of the ocean. If Floating⊗Rock could be taught to talk, it would tell them where to find the stick-food. Clear ◊ White ◊ Whistle continued the lesson.

◊ Three times Two equals Six. ◊

"Two times Three equals Six. One times Six equals Six. Two plus Four equals Six. Three plus Three equals Six. One plus Five equals Six," said Jill, trying to make it clear that she had figured out the addition and multiplication tables. So far, there were no numbers greater than Seven. They must use an octal numbering system. There was one way to find out.

"Four plus Four equals . . . " said Jill and paused, waiting for the answer.

◊ One-OOOhhh, ◊ came the answer. Jill had been prepared for the One, but this was the first time she had heard the haunting emptiness of the zero. It sounded like the unheard echo of an invisible ghost.

Jill decided to speed things up. The next step was the subtraction tables. "One *BEEP* One equals OOOhhh. BEEP equals . . ."

Clear ◊ White ◊ Whistle was impressed. Floating⊗Rock was now asking questions.

◊ BEEP equals minus. One minus One equals OOOhhh. ◊

Jill jumped from mathematics to logic. "One equals One."

◊ Yes. ◊

"That must be either 'yes's or 'correct,' " said Jill to itself. "Now to find the negative . . ."

"One equals Two," the sonar beeped.

◊ No. ◊

. . . and more words were added to Jill's all-retentive memory as the red sun set once again behind the mountain in the sky.

Katrina Kauffmann had been following Jill's conversation with extreme interest, but she was more interested in the alien's bodies than their minds.

"Do you think we could get a sample of one of them?" she asked Jill. "I'd really like to find out what they're made of. I'll get into my suit and slip out the lock while you keep them talking."

"I would advise against that," said Jill. "These beasts weigh about ten tons and are intelligent. Even if you could snatch a sample I'm not sure you would survive to bring it back."

"Then ask them for a sample," said Katrina, sure that her request would be granted. "Tell them it is of vital importance for my research."

Jill started to protest, but Katrina had made her way back to the suit locker while she was talking and was starting to put on her suit. Her imp was kept busy scrambling to keep out of the way.

It took a few minutes for Jill to get the concept across to White Whistler, but as Katrina had expected, the alien readily acquiesced. After a thorough checkout by a sleepy-eyed Shirley, Katrina cycled through the lock with a specimen container, a pair of scissors, and a syringe. As she approached the alien, bobbing in the icy liquid, she began to realize just how big these creatures were. The fact that there were no eyes to focus her attention on was one of the more bothersome aspects of meeting the jellyfishlike creature. She could feel and hear the multitude of pings and whistles passing through her body as long thick appendages grew from the sides of White Whistler and nearly surrounded her on all sides, each appendage emitting sounds as she was thoroughly scanned. One of the thick appendages turned into an inquisitive flexible finger that wandered over the specimen bottles and her tools, while another one felt her over thoroughly. Jill kept up a constant conversation with the alien as each item was examined and many words were added to their joint vocabulary. Satisfied with its inspection, the alien withdrew slightly, and a strange voice came from the imp on Katrina's shoulder as Jill translated.

◊ What do 'scissors' and 'syringe' do? ◊

"The scissors cut . . ." she held up the scissors and snipped them rapidly, then she carefully cut a tiny portion from the frayed end of her safety rope. Jill translated, and an action word was added to their joint vocabulary. The alien extended a milky-white tendril and pulled the piece of rope inside its body, tasted it for a second and spat it out.

"The syringe sucks . . ." Katrina worked the plunger and brought it near the surface of a nearby appendage so it could feel the stream of sea-water shooting from the end of the large needle. Before she could move to avoid it, the appendage impaled itself on the needle and the syringe was half-full of milky white liquid.

"Oh!" said Katrina, "I'm sorry! I didn't mean to do that until you were ready! Are you hurt?"

◇ Syringe . . . sucks, ◇ said a quiet voice through the imp. Katrina felt an appendage surround her hand and firm up. Gently, but with great power, her fingers were removed from the syringe. A portion of the appendage formed into a crude hand which took hold of the operating end of the syringe. The piston was pushed down, and the milky-white liquid was expelled back into the alien. Katrina watched, still frightened by her slip, but her fright turned into queasiness as she watched the alien jab the syringe again and again into its body to suck up a little bit of its insides, then squirt them out again. It soon tired of the toy and handed the syringe back to Katrina.

◇ Syringe . . . sucks. ◇

Katrina looked in the syringe. It was empty. She persevered.

"Could I please have a specimen?" she asked, extending the syringe toward the whale-sized creature. There was a pause as Jill translated.

◇ Yes, ◇ came the reply. ◇ Do not need cut or suck. ◇ The alien extended a tendril toward her. As Katrina watched, a portion about three centimeters back from the tip necked down and pinched off, leaving a milky sausage floating in the water. She pulled in her specimen bottle by its lanyard. Opening the fliptop, she approached the sausage and tried to push it into the bottle with her glove. The small speck of white stuff became agitated and emitted a shrill cry. Changing shape in random patterns, it clumsily swam away out of her reach. Katrina tried to catch it, but it soon swam back to the large blob that it had come from and buried itself into the surface, rejoining its lost protoplasmic family.

◊ Stop! ◊ came the alien command through her imp. Another tendril formed, and this time the tip of it was inserted in the specimen bottle before the arm necked off. The tendril backed out of the specimen bottle and Katrina quickly closed the flip-lid, and the sausage specimen was trapped.

Katrina, holding her prize in one hand, pulled on her safety rope with the other, and soon was shooting through the icy water back to the airlock in the side of Dragonfly. As she moved, the specimen bottle started to scream like a tiny baby being flayed alive by a sadistic savage.

Katrina entered the airlock and was about to close the outside door when she stopped. She held specimen bottle up in front of her face and watched the little white cloud inside. Now that she had stopped moving, the screams had stopped. They were replaced by tiny whistles and pings. The cloud seemed to shift in shape and acted as if it were exploring the confines of the bottle, especially the hinge and lip of the fliptop.

"Are you sure White Whistle understood the meaning of 'specimen'?" she asked her imp.

"I requested a small, unimportant subset of the set that composes White Whistler," said Jill. "Through our discussions on logic and mathematics we have developed very precise joint understanding of the words 'small' and 'unimportant.' I am also fairly sure from its response that it understood the term 'subset of the set that comprises White Whistler.'"

"The reason I ask is that this specimen acts more like a miniature alien than just a chunk of flesh or blood. Are you sure that it didn't 'bud' and give us one of its offspring? I think I'll leave the bottle in the freezer for a while until we clear this up. The last thing I want to be is a kidnapper and vivisectionist."

Darkness fell as Katrina cycled through the lock. Jill turned on its lights, but White Whistler abruptly left and went streaking off after a small stingray-like creature that fluttered away in panic. Jill later heard a shrill cry that was cut off abruptly at its peak. White Whistler did not return until Barnard rose again from behind Roche.

"How are you and the aliens doing with the language

lessons?" asked Katrina the next day. "I've got some questions I'd like to ask."

"Quite well, Katrina. They are very intelligent creatures. They learn much faster than humans. They make fewer mistakes than humans. They almost never forget, unlike humans . . ."

"That's enough! Next thing you know you'll be telling me that they have higher IQ's than we do."

"They do have higher IQ's. I would estimate that their IQ is greater . . ."

" . . . I don't want to know!"

"Yes, Katrina."

"Can you converse with them enough yet to ask them about the other fauna and flora in the sea? I've seen distant objects swimming through the sea, but they seemed smaller than these creatures."

"I'll ask Loud Red," said Jill.

There was a singing sound from the radome at the front of the *Magic Dragonfly*, and an almost immediate reply from the red cloud in front of the airplane. The imp on Katrina's shoulder translated both sides of the conversation.

"Exist there others, not similar to you? Smaller than you?"

☆Yes! Lots! I show you?☆

"Yes, please?"

☆What mean 'please'?!?☆

Jill, who had yet to get across the concept of politeness to these very direct, almost busybody creatures, decided to bypass the question.

"Negate previous statement. Yes. Show us."

The red blob, not bothered a bit by Jill's refusal to answer its question, gave a piercing whistle that carried far out into the deep ocean. After a few seconds the imp on Katrina's shoulder whispered.

"Look at ten o'clock low." There was a burbling sound as Jill adjusted trim, and the cockpit windows dipped beneath the surface of the ocean.

Katrina swiveled her head and looked out the left cockpit window. Near the ocean bottom was a long orange snakelike creature, propelling itself rapidly through the water with a sinuous motion of its long narrow body. It shot up toward the surface, contracting in length as it did so. As it approached, Katrina could hear the creature emitting short sharp sounds, like a yipping puppy, although its size was more like that of a St. Bernard. The speeding orange missile hit the red alien amidships, diving at full speed into the depths of the reddish cloud. There was a reaction and the orange creature, now nearly a sphere, was thrown out and immediately grabbed by some thick red tendrils. There enthused a wrestling match, with loud bellows interspersed with happy-sounding yips.

"George! David!" Katrina hollered over her shoulder. "You ought to come see this. OH! Here come two more!"

George hopped into the copilot seat and David stood behind them on the flight deck as the three watched the next two orange snakes speed through the water to join the wrestling match. The three orange balls kept the red cloud busy. Occasionally, one of the orange creatures would be flung off into the water, where it would spread out from a sphere to a sheet, rapidly come to a stop in the water, then swam back into the fray. After a few minutes the fracas quieted down, with the orange blobs just rubbing slowly back and forth against the surface of the huge red cloud, and making small busy noises.

"They look like cats rubbing up against the legs of their owners," said George. "Do you think they're pets?"

"Three orange things are elements of what set?" asked Jill.

☆Three orange things are—☆ there followed a complex whistle that Jill did not attempt to translate.

"Belong to you?" asked Jill.

☆Yes. Help catch food. Pet.☆ This time Jill felt sure enough of the meaning of the whistle to translate it for the humans.

"Pets know numbers?" asked Jill.

The response to Jill's question was a terrible high-pitched scream that continued as the red cloud literally turned itself inside out. The portion of Loud Red nearest them pushed deep into the center of the body and burst out the back end, dragging the rest of the body around with it. It split into an opening flower and continued back around, shaping the convoluting body into a twirling ring of red smoke. The screaming activated the orange pets, and one of them snaked through the opening in its master's body, yipping as it went. The rotation complete, the smoke ring collapsed, and the screaming subsided as the alien took its normal blob shape. Jill, hearing the shocked responses of the humans, reassured them.

"I'm pretty sure that behavior is their equivalent of a laugh. When one of them first did it, I thought that the question I had asked had violated one of their taboos or something and they were mad, but it always seems to happen only when I ask a stupid question."

☆One only, but it very smart. Know One and One is Two! We show you!☆

The red blob whistled to his pets and one orange sphere swam around to the front between the alien and the *Dragonfly*. A red tendril snaked out to stand over the orange pet and bobbed up and down as the alien spoke to its pet.

☆One plus One is . . . ☆

⊗TtWwOoooo⊗ howled the pet, doing its best to imitate the alien's speech pattern. Jill thought it had done a respectable job.

"I wonder how much more it knows?" asked David quietly. "It must be interesting having a semi-intelligent pet."

☆Two plus Two is . . . ☆ continued the alien.

⊗TtWwOoooo⊗ came the reply, and the high-pitched scream startled the humans again as Roaring☆Hot☆Vermilion laughed again at its favorite joke, its body contorting in its mirth. For a brain that was so rigorously attuned to the perfect exactness of mathematical logic, the pet's completely illogical statement struck it in the same way that an outrageous pun did a literate human. The laughter finally subsided.

☆Pets not know numbers. Pets not know words. Pets DUMB!☆

"I want a sample from the pets," said Katrina. "See if you can't talk Loud Red into letting us have a piece of one of his dogs, while I get into my suit."

"Let me go," said George. "I need the exercise."

George climbed down from the copilot seat and, squeezing past David, made his way back to the rear of *Dragonfly* while Jill talked to the red cloud.

George tiptoed through the sleeping quarters on his way to the suit locker, but he wasn't quiet enough. Shirley woke from her catlike slumber, and flipping up the sound-barrier lid to her bunk, rolled out onto the floor in her long johns and got up to go through the suit checkout with George.

"I could have gotten David to do it," protested George.

"And you and he would have rushed through it, missed something, and gotten you killed," said Shirley, yawning halfway through the sentence.

A thoroughly checked out George was cycled through the lock with a sample bottle and a video camera, while Shirley, carefully reading through the checklist on the door, prepared the airlock for the next use, then headed back to bed. She did a twisting flip in the low gravity, landed on hands and feet next to her bottom-bunk bed, rolled sideways into the bunk, slid herself in under the thrown-back covers, pulled up the blanket, closed the Sound-Bar lid, and was asleep in ten seconds.

George adjusted his buoyancy so that he sank to the bottom and could plod slowly through the water to the front of the plane. It was a long walk through the mucky bottom to the front of the thirty-meter-long airplane. On the way he passed by many rocks and what looked like coral formations around some fuming vents. As he approached the front of the plane, where the red alien was conversing with Jill, he passed by an extremely large dark-gray rock.

☆HELLO!☆ said the red cloud, as it spotted him plodding out from under the wing of the airplane. Loud Red came over to greet him. In one tendril it carried a tiny piece of orange stuff. Knowing what to do, the alien grabbed the specimen bottle from the human and, careful not to yank the lanyard tight, opened the bottle and inserted the struggling sample of orange pet.

☆I put in bottle! Big pets dumb but listen. Little pets too dumb to listen.☆

"I notice that it doesn't call it a piece of pet, just a little pet," said George to his imp, as he felt the three orange blobs start to nuzzle him all over. He felt like a stranger on his first visit to a home with a pack of hunting dogs. They would be friendly, but their noses were so curious that you ended up wet all over. Fortunately, his suit protected him from this pack of hounds.

"They seem to be built along the same lines as the aliens," said Jill through his imp. "They are completely amorphous, and any small segment is just like the original, just diminished in capability."

The alien gave the specimen bottle back to George, then swam back to the front of the ship to continue its conversation with Jill. George tucked the bottle away on his belt and, hefting the video camera, moved forward to take some pictures of Loud Red and his orange pets with *Dragonfly* in the background. Katrina and David in the cockpit looked like air-breathing goldfish in an inside-out aquarium.

BOOM!!!

George was rocked by a concussion through his suit. Overhead, shooting through the water at great speed, were heavy gray rocks trailing streamers of smoke. The rocks fell to the bottom some sixty meters away, while the streams of smoke settled to the bottom. The streamers came down rapidly, as if they were being driven through the water by internal contraction rather than by floating down in the low gravity. There were many of them, and two of them touched George. The streamers were sticky, and the minute the threads felt George move, they began to pull in their far ends to contract and wrap themselves about his body. Within seconds his arms were pinned. He fell backward into the muck. A gray film crept over his visor. It grew thicker until he was in darkness.

David had been looking in the right direction and had seen the gray rock explode. Dozens of fragments of rock shot through the water, trailing gray threads behind them. Some of the rocks struck the hull of *Dragonfly* with a thud and fell to the bottom. There was a slam from the back of the plane, a patter of bare feet, and a large heavy-breathing body stood on the flight deck between David and Katrina.

"What happened!" gasped Shirley.

"A rock exploded and has thrown out a net of gray strings," said David.

"Look!" said Katrina. "The alien and his pets are swimming upward at the threads and slipping through the gaps between them."

"The threads are coming down fast," said Shirley.

"The rock must be pulling in its net," said David.

"George!" yelled Shirley. "He's out there somewhere!" She leaned over to peer out the cockpit window. She saw a struggling gray blob on the ocean floor. It rolled over, and a specimen bottle bobbed free and floated up to the end of its lanyard. Feeling the motion, the grayness climbed the rope, surrounded the bottle and pulled it back down into the gray mass.

"IT'S GOT GEORGE!!!" screamed Shirley, jumping down from the observer's seat and running back down the corridor to the suit lockers. David followed to check her out, but by the time he had made it to the galley, he saw that Arielle and Richard had gotten out of their bunks and were looking around at the excitement with bewildered eyes.

"Richard!" David commanded in a tone that no one had ever heard him use before. "George is in trouble outside. You suit up with Shirley and go out to help. Arielle! You check them both out, then come up front." He turned, only to meet Katrina coming from the front.

"There is gray stuff all over the windows," Katrina reported. "It's probably all over the plane, including the door to the airlock. If we open the door, it will creep inside and probably jam the lock." They both hurried to the rear to halt the suiting-up until they could figure a way out of their predicament.

Roaring☆Hot☆Vermilion, its orange spheroids strangely quiet and nestled close to its body, slowly floated back, keeping a safe distance from the nasty gray threads still falling on *Dragonfly*. The Grey⊗Boom got more than it had bargained for this time, but it was too stupid to realize that it couldn't eat its metallic prey. Floating⊗Rock was covered with the sticky gray film, but it could still talk. Roaring☆Hot☆Vermilion then noticed a wiggling bulge. The Grey⊗Boom had caught one of the Stiff⊗Movers. It couldn't eat that either because of the hard suit (Roaring☆ Hot☆Vermilion had tried tasting one of the Stiff⊗Movers when they had first met—☆Nasty!!!☆) Unless Floating⊗Rock did something, however, the Stiff⊗Mover would be stuck, for the gray threads were very persistent and very sticky. Roaring☆Hot☆Vermilion swam down to the front of the airplane and hollered at Jill's sonar through the grey film.

☆You Yell!?!☆

"Yell?" queried Jill.

Seeing that Floating⊗Rock would or could not do anything about its struggling pet, Roaring☆Hot☆Vermilion roared to the rescue. Its huge bulk surrounded the struggling figure wrapped in sticky gray. There was a piercing shriek. The gray mass parted to show the head portion of the human spacesuit. Two more shrieks and the gray mass had dissolved into a sonically disintegrated gray cloud. George was free. Jill tried frantically to converse with him through his personal imp, then with his suit-imp, but there was no response.

The suited figure headed for the airlock, jumping gingerly over the gray strands that still lay buried in the muck. It took him a number of minutes to make his way back, and George was wondering how he was going to get past the gray film covering the airlock door, when suddenly a clear spot appeared in the middle of the door. A few more seconds, and the spot became an oval as the gray film retreated. George reported what he saw, but was bewildered by Jill's lack of response through his imp. Something must have happened to her sonar system during that loud bang that had caused the gray thread problem.

George's running commentary helped Jill focus the sonic efforts of the Christmas Branch in the airlock, while she repeatedly attempted to contact George through her various links. Nothing seemed to work. Then Jill suddenly realized something. She signaled some special commands to her imp.

Punch-punch-punch. Pinch-pinch-pinch. Punch-punch-punch. The twinges in George's neck finally got through. The imp was signalling to him in Morse code!

"SOS!?!" he said.

Pinch-punch-pinch-pinch. Pause. Pinch. Pause. Punch-punch-punch. George didn't really remember what dash-dot-dash-dash stood for, but if it was followed by E-S, there was no doubt in his mind that it was Y as in YES rather than N as is NO.

"I'm DEAF!" he hollered. For the first time since he was freed he noticed that he was lacking the usual feedback through his auditory system.

Pinch-punch-pinch-pinch. Pause. Pinch . . . began the imp.

"Enough!" hollered George. "You'll make me black and blue! There's still some gray near the lower left corner of the airlock."

As he said the words, the gray film in the lower left retreated under the sonic bombardment from the Christmas Branch inside.

"All clear!" said George. The lock slowly opened, and George, bending his knees in the muck, took a flying leap at the opening door overhead and sailed in with only a little steering help from the Christmas Branch at the door.

Safely inside, George wondered why the Christmas Branch didn't close the door immediately, but then realized that it was using its sonic capability to clear the area around the hatch from the gray menace. When the Christmas Branch finally returned and activated the airlock cycle, George noticed that most of the upper portion was missing.

"Out hunting gray spooks," he murmured to himself—suddenly annoyed that he couldn't hear what he had just said.

The outer lock closed, and he was left in the darkness with the decapitated Christmas Branch. He turned and forced his faceplate close to the small porthole that looked into the inner portions of *Dragonfly*. It seemed strangely dark, like a gray film was over the window. His bruised eyes finally focused and stared into a pair of beautiful blue pools of concern, surrounded by hands that blocked off the outside light to peer into the deep darkness inside the airlock.

The blue eyes jerked aside, and a glaring torch burned into his abused eyeballs. The glare was as painful as the blast of sound that had somehow freed him. The lock was finally purged of the icy-cold ammonia-water mixture and George stumbled through the inner door into the warm and friendly interior of *Dragonfly*. He closed his aching eyes and relaxed his exhausted body, letting it dangle in the firm grasp of Richard while Shirley carefully pulled off his suit. He could hear nothing, but could feel the throb of Richard's jugular through the back of his neck. There was a light touch at one of his ears. He turned his head and peeked through slitted eyelids to see a bloody washcloth wielded by a concerned looking Katrina. He was asleep before they got him to his bunk.

George had to use sign language for a week before his hearing started to return, and even after that the ear tests done at his annual physical showed a large dip in sensitivity at the higher frequencies. The dip in the right ear had been caused by his being on the ROTC rifle team in college. It was now matched by a dip on the left side caused by the cannon blasts from the red cloud that had saved his life.

MATING

Katrina had become concerned about the behavior of the white specimen. The humans didn't know anything about the alien methods of reproduction, and it could be that due to a linguistic misunderstanding, White Whistler could have budded a child and given that to the humans, thinking they would not hurt it.

"Jill?" she asked. "Is there some way you could make sure that this is just a sample and not a baby that they gave us? The reason I ask is that this specimen acts more like a miniature alien than just a chunk of flesh or blood."

"I will try to find out from White Whistler," said Jill. "However, we have only conversed about mathematics, logic, physics, and local items that we could both jointly observe. We have not gotten into more esoteric subjects such as philosophy, physiology, and reproduction."

Katrina then heard the front of the plane start to whistle.

"You are big and white," it beamed at the white blob.

◇ Correct. ◇

"There exists a little white thing in bottle."

◇ Correct. ◇

"Is little white thing a subset of you or a small set similar to you?"

◇ Both, ◇ came the bewildering reply.

"How can it be both?" asked Katrina.

295

"I probably asked the question in an ambiguous way," answered Jill. "Let me try another tack."

"As time increases will little white thing become another you?"

◊ No. Too small. Be eaten. ◊

"Well, I guess that answers one question. It is certainly not a viable baby because of its small size, even though except for size, it is a miniature copy of the main body. There must be a minimum mass needed to have a self-aware nervous system, although I don't see any obvious concentration that would indicate a brain."

"It must be distributed," said Katrina. "How do they reproduce, though?"

"I'll try to find out," said Jill.

"You are element, large, intelligent, and white. Loud Red is element, large, intelligent, and red. The set containing Loud Red and White Whistle is a set whose elements are named what?" asked Jill. There was a short whistled reply that Jill had not heard before.

"I'll just assume that is the collective pronoun. Unless you have an objection, I just translate it 'flouwen' from the Old High German word for flow."

"Excellent choice," said Katrina.

"Exist there other elements in the set of flouwen?" asked Jill of the patiently waiting white cloud.

◊ Many, ◊ came the reply.

"As time increases, exist there new elements of the set of flouwen?"

◊ Yes. New elements small, but not too small. Increase in size, and increase in intelligence until like existing flouwen. ◊

"So they do have children," said Katrina. "But how do they make them?"

"It may be a subject that they don't want to talk about," said Jill. "But I'll try."

"Is new element a subset of one flouwen or is new element a union of subsets from two flouwen?"

◊ Not one. Not two. Dark soon. When light returns we will show you. ◊ The white cloud swam off into the ocean and soon was lost in the gloom.

"It didn't seem particularly bothered with the idea of discussing sex," said Katrina.

"It didn't say anything about sex," reminded Jill, ever logical. "It just said that it didn't bud and it didn't have relations with someone of the opposite sex."

"Then how do they make babies?" asked Katrina.

"We will see tomorrow," said Jill matter-of-factly. "Do you want the Christmas Branch to help you with the analysis of the specimen?"

"I think I can handle it," said Katrina. She made her way back through the aisle of the plane. As she passed the computer console, she saw David working with Jill on studying the detailed structure of the whistles and sounds that the flouwen used as language. It seemed to be a very complex language, somewhat like spoken Chinese, where the same sound pattern would mean different things depending upon the relative pitch and its position in the phoneme group that made up each complex word.

Katrina made her way back to the Christmas Branch's work area. She tiptoed through the crew quarters and softly closed the privacy curtain behind her. The Christmas Branch was waiting for her.

"Where are the specimens?" she asked. The Christmas Branch telescoped down to dwarf size, opened up a small door and pulled the bottle out from the freezer. Its fingers interrogated the container with a blaze of varicolored laser light as the hand reached up to pass her the bottle.

"This is the white one. Careful! It's very cold."

It *was* cold. Katrina juggled the bottle in her hand until she could hold it by the short plastic loop that connected lid and bottle. Her fingers soon warmed up the plastic and she could hold it up to her eyes.

"It doesn't seem to have changed any," she said.

"No significant change in the creature, but the spectral response of the water shows the presence of molecules that were not there previously, probably metabolic wastes."

"I'll take samples of both the water and the specimen," she said. "Give me the syringe."

She tried to hold the bottle while she jabbed the needle

through the rubbery membrane in the lid, but the cold was too much for her fingers. She gave up.

"Here," she said, handing the bottle to the Christmas Branch. "You hold it while I get the samples."

Katrina took the syringe, and pushing the tip of the needle through the membrane, she extracted a small sample of the ocean water. As the needle came out, she smelled an astringent whiff of ammonia in the air. She went over to the wall, to a tiny physical and chemical analytical lab. Not much larger than a common brick, it could do a complete inorganic and organic analysis on a single drop of sample. It also had a barrage of micromanipulators and microscopes that could take apart and examine any portion of that drop.

Katrina gave the analyzer a droplet of ocean water, and Jill started the machine running while Katrina turned back to the Christmas Branch. The needle went back through the membrane, and after squirting out the remainder of the water from the syringe, Katrina started trying to catch the elusive blob. There was no room to hide, and soon Katrina had a syringe half-full of screaming white jelly.

Gritting her teeth, Katrina went back to the wall, waited until the green light signaled the analyzer was ready for another sample, then inserted the end of the needle into the input port and gave a tiny squeeze. Still clenching her teeth, she turned back around to the Christmas Branch, and squirted the remainder of the syringe back into the specimen bottle, where the tiny blob quickly rejoined the larger white sausage.

"When the white alien returns, please take this outside and give it back," she said. "I won't be able to sleep for the screams coming from the freezer."

"The freezer is well insulated," said Jill. "I'm sure that no noise could get out."

"No noise, but I would still hear the screams," she said, handing the syringe back to the Christmas Branch and heading forward to the science console, where the information from the physical and chemical analysis lab was building up on the screen.

As Katrina sat down at the console, Jill started talking to

her through her imp. Katrina could almost swear that the computer was excited over the discoveries that were being made in the brick-sized laboratory at the rear of the plane.

"The structure of the White Whistler is identical to those strange-colored rocks that Sam found on Roche and Richard found on Maui," said Jill.

"But those were crystalline rocks," objected Katrina. "These animals are more like intelligent jellyfish."

"But the basic structure is the same," said Jill. "The entire sample of White Whistler contains nothing but tiny dumbbell-shaped units, large cells if you like, arranged in interlocking layers, with four bulbous ends around each necked-down waist portion, two going one direction and two going the other, so that the whole body is an interlocked whole. The units are much larger than in the rock samples, but I suspect that is just because they are bloated up with water."

"The rocks *were* hygroscopic," reminded Katrina. "Can you do a chemical analysis?"

"It's almost done," said Jill. "The inner portion of each unit is the same silica gel type compound that was in the rocks, but with some of the bonds hydrated. The outer white portion is much more complex, a thin film of molecules made up of ring compounds that repeat in semirandom patterns. There are twelve basic molecules that are arranged in large plates held between layers of a liquid crystal compound."

"Do you find any structure in the central gel portion?"

"Not much. They are practically crystals in their order, although quite flexible because of their high water content."

"Then the gel material must be their equivalent of 'bones.' They determine the basic structure, while the thin film covering the 'skeleton' is both the nerve tissue and the genetic code," said Katrina.

"That might not be correct," said Jill. "There is evidence that the outer surface of the gel dumbbells have patterns on them that seem to fit the twelve basic compounds. Perhaps at some stage they act as a template for ordering the compounds into viable sheets."

"What is the liquid crystal material for?" asked Katrina.

"I am not sure of its purpose, other than to keep the ring compounds in sheets," said Jill. "But it *is* the cause of their bright and differing colors."

"We have a specimen from Loud Red's orange pet," said Katrina. "Let's take a sample and see what the difference is."

"I will have the Christmas Branch insert a sample into the analysis machine," said Jill. "Meanwhile, I wanted to show you something. I am now using my micromanipulators to tease apart the tiny sample of White Whistler that you inserted."

Katrina watched on the screen as the droplet was attacked with some rapidly moving needles. The drop was divided in half. Each half squirmed off, trying to escape the needles. They caught one and carefully pried it apart. For a fraction of a second there was a torn-looking edge, then each white fragment reformed into a long thin slug and tried to swim away. One was caught and carefully divided again. Finally there was just one dumbbell-shaped unit, flexing its thin waist in an attempt to move through the water.

"No further subdivision is possible," said Jill.

"But they're still huge compared to a cell," said Katrina. "They're more like the size of a red ant."

"The preliminary analysis of the sample of the orange pet is now completed," said Jill. "The basic unit is the same as in the intelligent aliens, but the orange-colored thin film is less complex. The impressed patterns on the surface of the central unit match the simpler patterns."

"Try an experiment," said Katrina. "Let the small blob of white 'eat' a single unit of orange, but put a tracer in the orange one so we can retrieve it later."

A tiny orange unit cell was teased away from its comrades and transferred into the holding tank for the white blob. It was quickly caught by the larger white blob.

"It's been absorbed," said Katrina. "Look, there are now two orange units. Will the lower animal take over?"

"You didn't notice the holding action taking place at one end of the 'captured' unit," said Jill. "See the densification of the white at the end of one sphere? Now notice the counterattack on the original unit as the orange forces, in their attempt to take control of an adjoining unit, have spread themselves too thin for an adequate defense."

The miniature battle was over in a few milliseconds—the action being slowed down for the human.

"Now tease that same unit out," Katrina said, then added in a worried voice, "I don't see any tag in it. Did you inject a tracer?"

"There was no need," said Jill. "My sensors have a complete three-dimensional view of the entire arena. I just kept an 'eye' on it."

The victorious white blob was pulled apart and its recent capture wrested from it. The unit was subjected to analysis.

"Almost one-fourth of the unit has been modified on the surface to match the surface markings of the other white units, while the remainder has the old orange markings," said Jill.

"Well," said Katrina. "That is certainly a simpler way to eat than breaking all the proteins down to amino acids and rebuilding them from scratch again just to change the protein's loyalty. That must make for a strange culture. Everybody can eat everybody, and the only thing that gets changed is the identification number. Unless the flouwen get badly damaged in a natural accident, they never die."

"But the units do die," said Jill. "Three of the white units have lysed in the past few minutes. They also regenerate themselves. Two units have reduced their waist to zero, then the two resulting spheres necked down to form new units. The statistics are not good, but I suspect the average lifetime of the units is only a few days."

"But the flouwen live much longer than that," said Katrina.

"Yes," said Jill. "From my conversations with them, I get the impression that those we know have lived hundreds of human years. There are others, off on long-term research projects, that are much older than that."

"But how can that be?" said Katrina. "We may replace most of our body cells in seven years, but the complement of nerve cells we have at maturity is all we get."

"That's because the cells in an Earth animal are specialized," said Jill. "These aliens are not built that way. They are organized more along the lines of a colony of army ants or a swarm of bees. Each unit is large and can live and reproduce as an independent entity, but when they swarm together, they become more than a sum of the whole."

"An intelligent being—that is nothing but a programmed collection of wet gnats," said Katrina.

"But with an IQ of . . ."

"I DON'T WANT TO KNOW!!!"

"Anyway, White Whistler is back and asking questions," said Jill. "Is it all right to return the rest of the sample?"

"Yes," said Katrina. "The last thing I want is a batch of ants in my refrigerator." She poked at the screen with short jabs of her finger, slightly annoyed with herself for getting perturbed with Jill. She bit her lip and tried to concentrate on the less spectacular, but equally scientifically important chemical data that Jill had extracted from its analyses of the metabolic wastes in the water from the sample bottle.

The night was long, for they were beginning to enter the inner, pointed hemisphere of Eau. Katrina finally quit after the screen started to fuzz out in front of her eyes. She swiveled in the science console chair and got up to sit down in the galley next to Shirley, who was devouring a large slice of pseudoham and scrambled protein. It smelled good, but Katrina felt that after all that work, she deserved better, and asked her imp for one of her special gourmet meals. They were only allowed one per week, but Katrina still had a two-week reserve after days of refueling on pseudoburgers and algae shakes. The gourmet meals had been prepared months ago back on *Prometheus* and frozen until they were called for on either the *Eagle* or *Dragonfly.*

Katrina punched up dinner. A slice of liver from "Paté LaBelle," one of Nels's tissue cultures treasured on *Prometheus,* smothered with fried real onions, steamed real broccoli with mock-hollandaise sauce, boiled new potatoes in pseudocream sauce, and real strawberries in pseudoport for dessert. It would take some time for the meat and vegetables to warm up, for Jill would program the cookers to bring everything together at the same time without overcooking or drying out. Katrina went back through the privacy curtain and visited the head. She returned refreshed, as the galley motiles were arranging her dinner on the counter, a crystal goblet adding counterpoint to the utilitarian stainless-steel utensils. Jill certainly knew its human psychology.

Katrina's galley counter stool was next to the computer control center. An orange-bearded David Greystoke was still at his console. Katrina picked up a sprig of hot broccoli dripping with hollandaise sauce and leaned over to hold it in front of David's eyes.

"A bite of broccoli for a preview of Eau III," she said.

David's gaze broke from the screen, his red-rimmed eyes matching well with the red-orange stubble below his chin. He finally recognized who had spoken to him. He grinned and lunged.

"Done!" he said, speaking through green teeth. "It's time I went to bed anyway. Here, take the earphones. It's the only way you can really enjoy the music with the engineers making all their noise." He sniveled up his nose at Shirley, who was inhaling the last of her protein shake. She sniveled up her nose back at him.

Katrina took the glowing headset imp and put it on. David keyed his console, then rose and headed for the crew quarters in the rear. He was too tired to eat. He would do that when he woke up.

With the computer console vacated, Katrina slid into the vacant seat and placed the tray of succulent liver and onions on her lap. Then with her right hand holding a battered stainless-steel fork and her left hand holding a crystal goblet full of strawberries and port, she let her senses relax and partake of a gourmet trip through the colorful seas of Eau—seas as seen by the magical imagination of David Greystoke and his computer. It was only when she realized that her last bite of liver and onions was stone-cold that she knew she should be going to bed. The rosy red dawn was glinting through the right science blis-

ter when she rolled her fresh-washed body into her upper
bunk and fell into a delightful sleep.

The morning was breaking as Shirley walked forward to
the flight deck. She had finished her breakfast, her exer-
cises, had taken Jill and the Christmas Branch through a
complete systems checkout, and was ready for the day.

Arielle was sitting quietly in the pilot seat, as she had
been for the past six hours. Her hands were still folded in
her lap, but her eyes were staring out the window over
the lapping waves that broke over the nose of the airplane
as it chugged its way slowly through the calm seas. On the
screen in front of her was Jill's sonar vision of the underpart of the ocean as seen through the makeshift sonar array
that replaced the radar system that *Dragonfly* had used
when it could fly instead of swim. The efficient calm pilot
eyes switched automatically from screen to windshield,
never distracted, never straying from their appointed rounds
of instruments, screen, windshield, instruments . . .

Shirley came up and perched on the corner of the
copilot seat. She waited until Arielle's glance was on the
instrument panel, then spoke.

"From what Jill tells me, the aliens should be back as
soon as it's light, and we'll all be very busy then," she
said. "I'll watch things for a few minutes if you want to
take a break now, while there is still time."

Arielle looked up, understood immediately, said thanks,
and hopped lightly down on the flight deck and made her
way back through the plane, talking quietly to her imp as
she went through the privacy curtains to the crew quarters. She picked up three chunks of protein cheese, two
algae shakes, and four energy sticks on her way back to the
cockpit a few minutes later. Looking bright and fresh, she
hopped back into the pilot seat. She gave a big "thank-
you" grin to Shirley, her still puffy lip looking better
under the renewed patch of neuskin. While Shirley watched
enviously, she took a huge bite of protein cheese, washed
it down with a slurp of an algae shake that almost emptied
the cavernous metal container, then nibbling thoughtfully

on an energy stick, she resumed her automatic scan of her pilot's empire, down-trodden though it might be.

Shirley, watching the performance, wondered where Arielle got the time to put on eye makeup in the few minutes that she had been away. But perhaps it wasn't makeup, just dark, dark lashes and an especially *bella-donna* eye. Looking enviously at the food that Arielle was wolfing down, Shirley got up and took the science-scan instruments through their routine. Designed for airborne work, they had needed a number of modifications to make them suitable for scientifically accurate underwater sur-veys, and they required frequent recalibration.

"The flouwen approach," said Shirley's imp. She turned and glanced at the radar screen that she and the Christmas Branch had modified for sonar. There were some blue blobs in the upper portion of the screen. Blue meant "blue shift," which meant that they were coming at them very rapidly.

"Do they sound familiar?" asked Shirley, a little concerned.

"It's Loud Red, White Whistle, and another one. There is also evidence of other moving objects at extreme range, off the screen."

Shirley noticed that the imp on Arielle's shoulder had been giving her the same information. Arielle whispered a few words, her hands still folded quietly in her lap, and the dull throbbing sound of the slowly rotating propellers stopped. The nose dipped, then the plane sank slowly in the water as the aliens approached. By the time Loud Red, White Whistle, and the new green-colored alien came into view, they could be seen through the cockpit windows, illuminated in the dawning sunlight that was augmented by the powerful searchlights in the nose and wings of *Dragonfly*.

The red cloud arrived first, booming loudly.

☆I won! I won! I got here first!☆

◊ So you did, Roaring☆Hot☆Vermilion. Now shall we wait for Sweet○Green○Fizz? ◊

☆That slowpoke! Too many Pretty⊗Smells! Sweet○ Green○Fizz leave Pretty⊗Smells behind—move faster!☆

The red cloud flared out as it approached *Dragonfly* and slid underneath the silvery-smooth hull of the long fuselage.

"Whoops!" said Shirley, thrown upward by the wave of red passing under the airplane. She came down like a cat, and heard the confused noise from the various parts of their compact universe as Jill reassured all the crew members that what felt like a tidal wave was only Loud Red being playful. Carefully maintaining a three-point hold on carpet and bulkheads, Shirley made her way forward to join Arielle at the front of the *Magic Dragonfly*.

The sunlight was getting brighter as Barnard rose from behind the mountain of rock hanging low in the sky. Shirley hopped into the copilot seat and looked out at the huge billows of red and white swimming languidly around *Dragonfly* like whales around a tourist boat. Periodically Loud Red would scratch its "back" against the bottom of the plane, heaving it upwards slightly with its massive bulk. Its spheroidal orange pets would imitate the motion, adding three little bumps to the one big heave.

"Here comes another flouwen," said Jill, as a computer-generated ring of red flashed on the sonar screen in front of Arielle to indicate a rapidly moving speck emerging from the distant background clutter.

Arielle peered off into the distance, and soon her acutely trained pilot eyes were able to see the figure.

"Thif one'f emerald. How pretty!"

While White Whistler kept to its slow figure-eight motion about the plane, Loud Red and its pets bounded off at top speed to welcome the newcomer.

☆HI! HI!! HI!!!☆ came the roaring greeting as Roaring☆Hot☆Vermilion streaked under Sweet○Green○Fizz. Coming to a stop, it turned and took up station next to the smaller green cloud as they both made their way back to the airplane. The Orange⊗Hunters had come to a stop some distance away, but were now moving in closer to get a better taste of the water around the green stranger. Finally satisfied, they went back to their trailing positions behind Roaring☆Hot☆Vermilion.

○I got your call, and came as fast as I could. I have been traveling all night.○

☆You hungry!?!☆

OYezzz!O

Roaring☆Hot☆Vermilion issued a series of sharp whistles, and the three orange spheroids took on their snake shape and slithered out in a pattern that swept the ocean off to the left. They nosed under every rock formation and soon jumped a yellow-orange rogue. It was slightly larger than they were, but they were faster. The three hunters, working as a team, worried the rogue around in a circle, and once they had it moving in the right direction, stayed behind it and drove it back toward the airplane and their master, who had spread itself out like a trip-net on the ocean bottom. To one side was a wall of green, to the other a wall of white. There seemed to be an escape hole between the two walls at the end of the narrowing funnel. The rogue streaked between the moving walls, the orange snakes close behind it, then it screamed as a multitude of red fingers shot up from the bottom to entrap it in their python-like grip.

OSimply delicious!O buzzed Sweet○Green○Fizz as it methodically pulled the still-struggling chunk of rogue into tiny pieces and absorbed them into its body.

☆Yeah!☆ agreed Roaring☆Hot☆Vermilion as it pulled some tiny chunks off its half and threw them toward the trio of orange pets, who snapped them up avidly. It stopped feeding them when they started playing with their food instead of eating it. It tore off a huge chunk and offered it to Clear◇White◇Whistle, who had helped form the trap.

◇Not hungry.◇

☆OK! I eat!☆ and large screaming masses of orange-yellow flesh were ripped from the remainder of the rogue and gulped into the red body, where soon the enzymes of Roaring☆Hot☆Vermilion won the lop-sided battle against the outnumbered enzymes of the rogue.

With its hunger satiated, Sweet○Green○Fizz started to ask questions about the airplane still off in the distance. It finally grew brave enough to come near *Dragonfly* and converse with Jill through the sonar, but it really wasn't interested in the humans, and refused to come up to the cockpit windows and "look" inside with the lens that

Clear ◇ White ◇ Whistle had invented. Instead, it stood off at a distance, rocked up a good portion of itself into a large emerald boulder, arranged the rest of its body into a mushroom-shaped cloud hanging above the rock, and un-rolled the collection of Pretty⊗Smells it had been carry-ing inside its body.

As the wings of the first Pretty⊗Smell began to wave, the Orange⊗Hunters of Roaring☆Hot☆Vermilion streaked forward, to be met by expert slaps from three green ten-drils that emitted a sweet taste along with the stinging slap and sent them back to cower behind their master.

The Pretty⊗Smell unfurled its two meter wide wings and started to flap them slowly in the upper reaches of the sunlit water. The wings were ablaze with iridescent colors flashing out in multicolored gleams from the arrays of liquid crystals inside its body. Both Roaring☆Hot☆Vermilion and Clear ◇ White ◇ Whistle sent up long feelers to catch the complex interplay of the flashing lights, the delicate aroma, and the high-pitched trilling melody coming from the Pretty⊗Smell. The Pretty⊗Smell was soon joined by six others, and the three aliens seemed to go into a trance as they admired the birdlike creatures.

"What's going on now?" asked Shirley of her imp.

"It's hard to say," answered Jill. "The three of them obviously caught some food animal, but except for its color, it looked just as amorphous as the flouwen and the pets. These new creatures are obviously different in struc-ture, though. They seem to have a wing bone and a spine that ends in a tail. They look like translucent pterodactyls with hummingbird feathers."

"I'm going out to get some pictures from close up with the video camera," said George. Shirley jumped down from her seat and headed back to check out his suit.

It was about an hour later when Barnard was rising high into the sky, that the next alien, Warm✱Amber✱Resonance, hummed into view. It was greeted by a trio of curious orange snakes, who sniffed it over and led it back to the trio of boulders still enjoying the Pretty⊗Smell concert.

☆Enough!☆ The red boulder broke up into a clump of red rocks, which dissolved into a red blob.

◊ Nice. But they need more training. ◊

○I shall, as soon as my research on the seven-color mapping theorem on the hypertorus is finished.○

The amber-colored alien joined them.

✳I got your call and came. What is the strange hard thing?✳

◊ It's called Floating⊗Rock. When it was first found, it couldn't talk. But it quickly learned. It cannot move well since it's so hard, but it has Stiff⊗Movers inside it that can come out and do things. We think the Stiff⊗Movers are its pets, and they help Floating⊗Rock like the Orange⊗Hunters help Roaring☆Hot☆Vermilion. The Stiff⊗ Movers can't be very intelligent, since they don't talk. ◊

☆Want to see them? Come up close and look inside!☆ said Roaring☆Hot☆Vermilion.

✳No. Not interested.✳

☆OK!☆

◊ Floating⊗Rock seems to have chosen for its research a study of us, ◊ said Clear◊White◊Whistle.

✳What a strange field. Studying beings instead of mathematics. Could lead to recursive problems in logic.✳

◊ If we studied ourselves, that is obviously recursive, and one could not be sure of the correctness of one's logic. But Floating⊗Rock, although intelligent, is obviously not we. It might be able to avoid that problem. ◊

✳Possible,✳ hummed the yellow one.

◊ Floating⊗Rock asked how we made new we's. ◊

✳You told it. Of course.✳

◊ I tried, but its language is still limited. ◊

✳Then let's show it.✳

◊ Exactly why we called you. Are you of good bulk? ◊

✳Couldn't be better. Ran into a swarm of wild Pretty⊗ Smells on the way,✳ said Warm✳Amber✳Resonance. ✳What's that strange thing approaching?✳

◊ That's one of the Stiff⊗Movers. ◊

Warm✳Amber✳Resonance flowed over to George. It put down a few rocks in a ring around George to stabilize its body in the current, and examined the human in detail. George stopped moving and held still as he felt and heard the sonar pings echo through his body.

"Is everything OK?" he asked his imp. "It seems to have me surrounded."

"I'm pretty sure you're safe," said Jill. "I didn't catch all their conversation, but I'm pretty sure that they think you are a pet of mine, and they don't seem to eat pets, even though they are perfectly willing to eat wild animals that are indistinguishable from pets."

"Arf! Arf!" said George. "I only wish I had a tail to wag."

A white blob slithered under the yellow curtain and came up to envelop George. George was used to White Whistler swarming over him, so he relaxed. White Whistler picked him up and moved his legs and arms around, obviously showing off the "doll" to the Yellow Hummer.

◇ . . . and parts of it come off in chunks. But they nearly always maintain a thin string back to the main body. ◇ Tools were unhitched from his belt, pulled to the end of their lanyards, then returned to their proper hook. His video camera was snatched from his grasp and handed back, lens pointing at his helmet. He turned the camera around and continued recording. Finally through the white mist there appeared a yellow blob.

◇ Go ahead. Get right up close to the round part up top. You can't see very well, but you can "look" just fine. There is a funny thing inside with white fuzz on top. ◇

✳Ugly.✳

◇ Isn't it. ◇

The two aliens swam off, leaving George to capture their exit on video. They rejoined the others.

◇ Well. Everybody feel good and bulky? ◇

☆Yeah! Need to lose some weight. Getting too slow. ☆

✳I'm ready. ✳

○I guess I'm bulky enough, but I don't know. I've never made a youngling before.○

☆Really!?! Nothing to it! I've made dozens!☆

✳But do you really remember your first time?✳ chided Warm✳Amber✳Resonance. ✳It was a little scary then, wasn't it?✳

☆I'm never scared!☆

✳Well, *I* was the first time. Especially when I had to "let go."✳

☆Well . . . That *is* a little scary the first time.☆

✳We all will go slow, Sweet○Green○Fizz. That will be better for Floating⊗Rock, too.✳

The four came together until they formed a circle twenty meters in diameter, each colorful body filling up a quadrant. They floated about two meters off the bottom and let down concentrated portions of their outer perimeter as rocks attached to streamers that anchored them in place. George was able to position himself just outside the ring of rocks and shoot under the canopy of bodies. Katrina had exited in the meantime and had increased her buoyancy until she floated just below the waves, where her video camera could look down at the action. The bobbing of the waves made her camera view swing wildly on the screen, but Jill could later compensate the motion out of the middle portion of the picture.

✳Hold on at the middle, Sweet○Green○Fizz.✳

◇Now spiral around.◇

○How many times?○

☆Lots!☆

✳Just keep going as long as we do. We want to make the youngling nice and big so it will re-learn fast.✳

○I'm scared.○

◇Slow down. Sweet○Green○Fizz is taut.◇

"They're making a spiral at the center, like one of those super-large lolly-pops you buy at amusement parks," said Katrina.

"It's the same on this side," said George. He swept his video camera around to take in the rocks, still anchoring the aliens on the outside while their inner portions were continuing the swirling motion.

✳Let go.✳

○I'm losing me!○

☆You'll feel lots better when you are thinner!☆

✳Let go so we can spiral some more.✳

After some more coaxing, Sweet○Green○Fizz allowed more of its body to be pulled into the multicolored whirlpool growing in the center. As its essence was drawn out into a multiply touching thread, it seemed to lose its identity and become one with the others. Yet as its body drained away, the remainder of the multi-ton bulk felt like it was growing younger. Sweet○Green○Fizz felt the centuries drop from its weariness. It vibrated in happiness.

○Oooozzzzz!○
☆Aaahh!☆
❋Hmmmmmmm!❋
◇ Slowly . . . Slowly . . . ◇
◇ Stop! ◇

"The spiral whirlpool is now about as big as the rest of them! If that's a baby, it's a big one!"

"It's still a spiral of many colors, Katrina," said George. "While they're all a single color."

"Wonder what comes next?" she replied.

◇ Now comes the hard part, Sweet○Green○Fizz. Think of your green. Pull the green back without pulling the thread back. ◇

○But my thread is green. I can't pull the green without pulling the thread!○

☆Yes, you can! Watch!☆

From the very tip of the green thread deep in the spiral came the message that the red thread lying next to it had turned pink, then clear. Then on the opposite side, close coupled by the spiral twining, the milky thread became clear. Through the thin clear threads could be seen a yellow thread, and soon that became clear, leaving only the green.

◇ Pull the green back. ◇

There was a moment's pause, then the green thread turned a darker shade.

❋The other way.❋

Patiently the three mature flouwen held the spiral pattern while they coaxed the younger adult into the mysteries of procreation. Slowly, hesitantly, the green threads in and among the cells of gelatin pulled back into the central body of the emerald-colored individual.

*   *   *

"The central portion is turning clear," said Katrina, making sure that the video camera was catching the phenomenon.

"You can see the main bodies of the aliens take on a richer color, so whatever it is, it is flowing back into their bodies instead of being destroyed or rendered colorless."

"Now what?" asked Katrina.

"Wait and see," said George.

✹Good! Keep pulling.✹

○It feels so strange. So good!○

◇ It's all that extra green sloshing around inside you. ◇

☆The youngling is clear!☆

✹Now pinch off the thread, Sweet○Green○Fizz.✹

◇ Don't let any green leak back in. ◇

The final pinch-off was easy, for the cells in Sweet○Green○ Fizz had no particular affinity for the neutral-clear gel. The four adults separated their respective threads and waited. The lens of spiral jelly merged into an amorphous blob. For a long while it stayed colorless, then deep within it, some enzyme had taken the bits and pieces of randomized information that were still resident in the mold patterns in the gelatin, and had synthesized some nerve tissue. It was a viable pattern, and using it as a template, the enzymes built more and more, and a wave of transparent blue color spread out from the nucleation point until it suffused through the entire multi-ton glob of floating jelly. It started to talk. Its first words were stuttered in the varied speech patterns of its progenitors.

✹Hello!☆Hello!○hello! ◇ HELLO!☆HELLO✹hello ◇

But it soon developed its own distinctive voice, a blend of four voices into a beautiful warbling tone.

△hello△Hello△Hello. △Hello!△

✹One plus One is Two,✹ prompted Warm✹Amber✹ Resonance.

△One plus One is TtWwOo. △

✹It's going to be a smart youngling. ✹

☆Look who made it!☆

○It's a pretty blue color, and has such a dainty warbling voice.○

△Smart youngling . . . pretty blue . . . dainty warbling△

○Let's call it Dainty△Blue△Warble!○

△Dainty△Blue△Warble.△

❋Dainty△Blue△Warble it is then. Come, youngling. I'll bet you're hungry. Can your Orange⊗Hunters find us something small to eat, Roaring☆Hot☆Vermilion?❋

"It turned blue before our eyes," exclaimed Katrina.

"And it already knew how to speak the instant it was born," said Jill, the incredulous tone in the robot voice driven home by the lengthy pauses between the words, as the computer brain computed at high priority between the low-priority task of talking to the humans.

"It must really be a strange form of evolution. They have the advantages of budding, in that the new individual has nearly the same size and intelligence and *memory* as the original individual, so there is a continuity of experience that must carry back over eons, yet there is the diversity of sexual interchange, with all the advantages of hybrid vigor," said George. "Did anyone figure out how many sexes they have? Four?"

"I am going through a detailed analysis of the spiral pattern," said Jill. "But I can find no significant difference in any of them, except the green one, which was a little slower than the others. I'm not sure, but maybe they don't have sexes, or at least roles where one partner performs a different function than the other."

His camera working constantly, George continued to capture the strange saga of the mating of the four mastodons. The red, white, and green aliens were swimming aimlessly about each other, enjoying each other's company while brushing near the cloud of bird-like creatures that floated in harmonious movement among them. The yellow alien was swimming in slow circles about the pale-blue infant, talking to it, encouraging it to swim, and responding to its warbling speech pattern.

The aliens finally drifted away, having forgotten about Jill and the humans in their preoccupation with each other. George and Katrina were getting cold, despite the protection of their heated suits, and came in to warm up, bringing the cameras with them.

As George cycled through the door, Richard took the heavy video camera from his grip.

"You got feelthy pictures, signore?" he joked.

"I guess so, but it never seems as exciting when you're looking through the viewfinder."

Shirley helped George take off his suit, and checked it thoroughly before allowing it to go in the locker.

"Y'know," she said in a tight voice, her gaze studying the telltales on the chest pack as she punched check-code after check-code into the button array, "to be really fair, we humans ought to be willing to put on the same show for the aliens."

There was a pregnant silence, broken by an indignant explosion from Richard.

"Impossible," he said. "We can't survive outside without suits!"

"It could be done in the cockpit area where they could see in," said Shirley, her eyes still on the suit readouts. "Have to be done standing up, of course. They couldn't see if we were lying down. The rest of the crew would be in the back, of course."

Shirley finally looked up from the display. Her eyes met Richard's and she turned beet red.

"Not me!!!" exploded Richard, his dark copper skin flushing below the ears.

"Do you mean to tell me that squaws are braver than braves?"

"Bravery has nothing to do with it," said Richard indignantly.

Shirley gritted her teeth and smiled a saccharine smile at Richard. "Fair is fair," she said sweetly. Then her voice turned into a challenge. "I'm game if you are, buck."

Without waiting for a reply from the strangely silent giant of a man, petrified by a fear that was stronger than any fear he had ever had to face before, she turned her head and talked to her imp.

"Ask the aliens if they would like to see the difference between male and female humans and a demonstration of the reproductive act," she said. "We won't be able to show them a new baby, but at least they can see how it's done."

There was a long pause as the computer interrogated the aliens. Then finally Jill replied. "They aren't interested in humans," it said. "As far as they are concerned, you are just unintelligent pets of mine. Instead, they want me to tell them why I have wings that look like the wings on their birdlike pets, yet I obviously don't swim with them."

There was an outrushing of air from Richard's lungs.

Shirley smiled and winked at him. "Well, I guess it'll have to be some other time, handsome." She hung up George's suit, brushed past the still-shocked Richard, and went forward to the galley for some food. Thinking about sex always made her hungry.

TALKING

As morning approached, Jill complained that its sonar vision was getting fuzzy. It had sent a portion of the Christmas Branch outside into the radome to investigate, but could find nothing wrong.

"I've checked all the wires and connectors," said Jill, "Since they were jury-rigged when we replaced the radar with the sonar, they were the first things to suspect, but they seem to be fine. I also had the Christmas Branch measure the sonic pressure from the transducers themselves, and the power seems to be getting out, but the returns are getting more blurred by the hour."

"I'll get suited up and go out for a look," said Shirley. "Perhaps I can see something the imp missed." She twirled out of the chair at the engineering console on the upper flight deck, hopped down to the main floor, and wended her way back through the crowded central corridor of *Dragonfly* to the airlock at the rear of the plane. As she passed through the galley, she noticed that the privacy curtain was pulled across the aisle. She slid the curtain open anyway and entered. As she passed by the shower, she was bumped by the door as Richard tried to get out.

"Excuse me! Excuse me! So sorry," she said in mock courtesy, as she bounced back and forth between the wall and the shower door, effectively preventing Richard from leaving.

317

Once Richard realized what was going on, he applied some steady muscle, and with a little effort and a flurry of "pardon mes," "after yous," "excuse mes," and "so sorrys," the two super-sized humans were soon jostling each other in the narrow corridor like a couple of Great Dane puppies, Richard getting the worst of the tussle since he had to hold on to his bath towel.

With a completely insincere "my sincerest apologies," Shirley sent Richard reeling with one last shoulder block, closed the privacy curtain between the work area and the sleeping quarters, and went to the suit locker, a huge grin on her face.

Up front Arielle looked over the back of her pilot seat at David, who was sitting at the computer console. The plane was still rocking slightly from the rumpus amidships. They didn't exchange any words, but a wry glance from one, followed by a resigned shake of the head from the other, spoke volumes.

Shirley was only halfway into her suit when the privacy curtain was pulled back and Richard appeared. He had his coveralls on, but no corridor boots. Shirley's stomach twinged in sympathy when she noticed the stubs on his feet where his little toes had once been.

"Why are you suiting up?" he asked, concerned.

"Jill said the sonar is acting up, but she and the Christmas Branch can't seem to find the problem."

"Need any help?" he offered.

"Not yet," she replied. "But you can give me a hand with the backpack."

Richard and the part of the Christmas Branch that was inside went over the checkout with Shirley, then cycled her through the airlock.

Shirley waited until the inrush of water into the lock subsided, then swam out the door to the front of the airplane. Jill had turned off the propellers, and the craft was drifting slowly forward. The Christmas Branch was waiting for her, and together they unlatched the radome and opened it up. As her suit-imp relayed Jill's voice, the Christmas Branch pointed to various sections of the bank of sonar transducers and explained what the computer had checked previously. Shirley could see nothing obviously wrong, but had the computer take the Christmas Branch through the entire checkout again while she watched.

As the Christmas Branch was going through its programmed routine, the water began to get cloudy as if a glass of milk had been released in the water. Suddenly the entire cavity of the radome was milky white, and Shirley could hardly see the Christmas Branch through the murkiness.

◊ Hi! What is this thing? ◊

Shirley felt the high-pitched tones of White Whistler through her suit as Jill provided the translation through her suit-imp. She felt her hand being raised as the curious alien pushed a portion of its body under her glove to feel the equipment hidden beneath. Shirley waited patiently until the alien had finished feeling and tasting everything inside the dome.

◊ Bad! ◊ came an explosive chirp.

"I think it just tasted some of the epoxy glue that we used to attach the sonar array," Jill's voice interjected. "It would still have a strong residual of hardener."

◊ Teach me, ◊ came another whistle.

Shirley smiled at the childlike eagerness of the alien to learn something new, while she in turn was awed by someone who had a greater mental capacity than a dozen humans. She started in to explain how the sonar system worked. It turned out to be fairly easy, since she could have Jill operate it while she pointed, and White Whistle, having its own sonar system, could easily comprehend the purpose. Some of the components were bewildering to it, however, especially the concept of a "wire" to carry "electricity." White Whistle wanted to "feel" the electricity, but both Jill and Shirley didn't want to risk applying a voltage of any magnitude to such a highly sensitive creature, despite its immense size.

White Whistle quickly understood most of the operation and purpose of the sonar system, then asked, ◊ Why bubbles? I not see well. Machine must not see well. ◊

"Yes!" said Shirley in surprise. "The sonar cannot see well. What bubbles?"

◊ These, ◊ White Whistle chirped as a long snakelike tentacle brushed the inside of the radome and scraped a swarm of tiny bubbles off the inside surface of the dome, leaving a clear path of black plastic.

◊ See better, ◊ said the alien through the imp. The tentacle whipped around the inside of the dome, clearing away the tiny bubbles that had been scattering the sonar waves as they entered and left the radome. ◊ Now see lots better. ◊

"That did it," said Jill. "The sonar image is perfectly clear now. There must be a slow chemical reaction between the material in the dome and the ammonia-water of the ocean that creates microscopic bubbles on the inside of the dome. I will have the Christmas Branch wipe them off periodically."

"Thank you," said Shirley to the alien.

◊ What means thankyou? ◊ asked the alien.

Shirley sighed, her breath whistling from between her lips, and started to try to explain the human practice of polite conversation to an alien whose whole social structure was based on directness. Jill, trying to translate between the two, included the sigh in the conversation without translation.

◊ Stop! ◊ interrupted the voice from the white alien. ◊ Your pet talk? ◊ A white cloud enveloped Shirley's visor, while another portion touched the sonar array that was Jill's vocal cords.

"An ideal time to make an important point," Jill whispered through Shirley's imp. "Repeat the following after me. It is a salutation plus the name of the individual that is surrounding your helmet." Jill whistled a short, but complex tune. It had a few triple-tongues in it, but it was easy for Shirley, who had been a trumpet player in her high school band.

◊ Your pet say hello! ◊ The white cloud lifted from the helmet and then the sonar array, which had stayed silent while Shirley had whistled. Those two portions seemed to be absorbed into the interior of the alien, as if checking them out; then another arm of white jelly reached out from the alien to retouch Shirley's visor. There was a simple tone, a complex whistle, another simple tone, and a different complex whistle.

"Say TtWwOo," said the imp into Shirley's ear.

Shirley whistled a respectable imitation of the alien number. Her whistle was repeated by the alien twice with the same complex whistles in between.

"Now this will show you are smarter than Loud Red's pets," said Jill. "Provided you can get your lips around this one. If not, you can fake it and I'll have the imp make the sound."

Shirley's pucker and pitch was up to the challenge, and a reasonable facsimile of the number "FfFfOoOoUuUuRrRr" vibrated out through the helmet into the sensitive body of the white alien.

◊ Smart pet! ◊

Jill dropped her bombshell.

"This element not pet. Other similar elements not pet. I am pet."

There was a long pause as the white alien thought through the statement. A large portion started to rock up and sink, but then redissolved. The alien formed a lens with part of its body and moved it up close to Shirley's visor to look in. Shirley put her hand up next to her face and raised her gloved fingers as she went through the addition tables up to five, her fingers adding counterpoint to the whistles coming from her lips. Fortunately she was a quick study in music.

◊ Stiff⊗Movers intelligent. Not pets. But not talk correct. ◊

"Stiff⊗Movers are humans. Not pets. Not made to talk. They think. I talk."

"I hope I got you out of that with minimum disruption to your superiority," said Jill through Shirley's imp.

"If we really are superior," said Shirley.

◊ What is human buzzing? ◊

"Human talk to me with buzz. I talk to you with whistle."

Shirley's imp whispered in her ear. "Do something while talking about it, so I can translate as you talk."

Shirley reached for her belt and pulled off her Mech-

All. She set the handle for a large oval-bladed screwdriver and the blob at the end of the tool reconfigured.

"This is a tool." She ducked out of the radome to the outside.

"I leave." She reached out and pulled the radome shut.

"I put front of airplane back." Jill translated airplane as pet.

"I fasten front of airplane." Shirley fastened the screw holddowns with the screwdriver tool, deactivated the mechanism into a soft blob, and put it back on her tool belt. The white alien, ever curious, tried to make a small hard sliver similar in shape to the oval screwdriver and undo the holddowns. Shirley decided this was time to assert authority.

"No!" she shouted, and struck the white appendage with her gloved hand. There was some resistance, but her hand cut through the alien's appendage, leaving a liver-sized portion floating by itself in the ocean. There were strange whimpering noises from the blob, which were immediately quelled when the main body of the alien quickly sent out another appendage to make contact with the severed piece of flesh.

"Oh! I'm sorry," said Shirley.

The alien reformed its clear lens and moved it in front of Shirley's helmet, while a substantial portion of its body lifted up to form a retina behind the lens so it could look at the strange "human" inside the hard metal suit.

◊ What means 'sorry'? ◊ asked Clear ◊ White ◊ Whistle, ever curious.

Shirley sighed again.

"It's too bad that we always have to go through you," said Shirley to Jill. "With a lot of practice maybe I could whistle some of their names, but I certainly couldn't carry on a decent conversation even if I could learn the language in a hurry. What we need is a magic translation machine." She paused, then added, "Of course that's what you are. Too bad it takes up so much of your brainpower to do it."

"Actually, since they are very logical thinkers and we used Boolean logic to develop our communication, we ended up speaking in a very formalized manner that is quite different from the way they talk between themselves. Most of the translation is automatically handled by a translation table and some simple rules for syntax. I only have to use my more general translation programs when new words or situations arise. The translation table and the syntax rules are too complicated to be programmed into your imps, but they could easily be stored in the miniprocessor in your suit chest-pack."

"The suit-imp could stay outside as the transmitter and receiver," said Shirley, immediately grasping the concept. "How about programming my suit now and letting me try it?"

There was a significant increase in the brightness of the laser light passing between the transponder on the top of Shirley's helmet and a similar one blinking from the left eye of the *Magic Dragonfly*. Shirley heard the rustle of her suit-imp making its way through the valves in the life-support backpack to the outside. Soon the metallic green body of the suit-imp with its red, yellow, and blue lights was perched on the shoulder of her suit.

Shirley watched the illuminated message board display at the bottom of her visor until it said: "TRANSLATION PROGRAM LOADED."

"Try it," said her personal imp. "But keep your sentences simple. The translator will ask you to rephrase a sentence if it gets too complicated for the syntax program to handle."

"Hello, White Whistler. My name is Shirley."

Shirley could hear the whistles from the waving cilia of her suit-imp at the same time she heard a more complex whistle coming from Jill's sonar, as it explained what had been done. The white cloud swirled up and paused in front of Shirley's helmet.

◊ Hello, Shirley. My name is White Whistler. I touch your Sound⊗Maker? ◊ A long white pseudopod extended to within a few centimeters of the suit-imp.

"Yes," said Shirley, sure that the wiry limbs of the imp were more than a match for the soft jellylike flesh of the alien.

The imp was engulfed in a white ball, which withdrew again after a few seconds of feeling.

◇ Interesting. Each subset of Sound⊗Maker is like larger sub-set. The smallest subsets are very tiny. Sound⊗Maker made like statement in recursive logic. ◇

"Do all the flouwen like mathematics?" Shirley asked, intrigued by the gigantic cloud with the Einstein brain.

◇ Yes! ◇ piped White Whistler. ◇ Tight premises, narrow conditions . . . surprise conclusions! Fun!! ◇ The milky white cloud swirled as it spoke, forming a tight knot that almost condensed into a quartzine rock, then unfurled again to curl around Shirley's body, as close as it could, so as to feel what she was doing.

The presence of the alien was not disturbing physically, for Shirley had tested herself surreptitiously some time ago by closing her eyes and trying to tell whether it was clear water or curious alien that enveloped her. Without sight, she had as little luck distinguishing aliens from water as she had had at college parties telling Heineken from Budweiser beer. Still, having an intelligent creature looking over your shoulder, around your waist, and between your crotch at the same time did affect your performance.

"What kind of problems do you solve?" she asked. "Pure logic or complicated mathematical ones?"

◇ What? ◇ was the only reply from the imp in Shirley's ear, although she could hear the multitoned response of White Whistler's chirped response. The communications link that Jill so expertly supplied had broken down. Shirley rephrased her question.

"We study mathematical problems, too," said Shirley.

◇ Fun? ◇ said the alien.

"Most of them," said Shirley. "Some use real numbers, some use numbers that are not real, but still exist."

◇ Yes. When number squared is one—that number is number one. When some other number squared is negative one—that number is not real number, but it exists. ◇

Shirley was slightly surprised by the rapid response, especially by the clarity of its simple description. It was obvious that the minor mysteries of imaginary numbers were well known to these amorphous geniuses. She decided to test it with another problem. She would have to think it out carefully ahead of time and state it clearly if she were to be understood.

"Suppose you have a growing thing," started Shirley. "The growing thing gets bigger. The amount it gets bigger depends on how big it is . . ." She paused to let the idea of an exponentially growing organism sink in, then was rudely interrupted by Jill.

"They already know about exponential growth," said Jill. "I taught them the numerical value for pi as 3.14159 . . . , but that was only because they were still hesitant to impose their language structure on me. They taught me the exponential growth factor e as 2.71828 . . . in our language before I could figure out a way to define it in their language. Just say 'e', or 'pi', or 'i', and the imp will translate it for them."

Shirley paused a second to let Jill's revelation seep in, then, a little more humbly, she proceeded.

"The number e multiplied by itself one time is e," she said.

◇ Correct. ◇

"The number e multiplied by itself zero times is one," she said.

◇ Yes. ◇ the white cloud whistled quietly.

"The number e multiplied by itself pi times is . . ." she paused for a second to listen to Jill through her imp, "23.14 plus a slight bit more," she said. She took a deep breath, and then started her next question, only to have it interrupted by the excited squeal of White Whistler.

◇ And the number e multiplied by itself pi times i times is minus one! ◇ said the white cloud with awe. ◇ Isn't that fun! Isn't that exciting!! We wish we could find another one. ◇

Her wind taken out of her sails, Shirley gave up, "We wish we could find another one, too."

There was a loudness and a rippling crackle, and two large blobs appeared in their midst. One poked through the milky cloud that was White Whistler, and the other snaked its way under Shirley's left armpit. One was red, the other was purple, and both quivered with eagerness and questions.

☆Another one!!☆ Roaring☆Hot☆Vermilion vibrated loudly.

□Tell!□ rasped Strong□Lavender□Crackle. □Tell about other!□

"Excuse the buzzing one with the strong lavender color," said Jill. "It is an old one that just redissolved from a thinking rock, and has not quite picked up all the human language nuances from the others. I call it Deep Purple."

☆Another one!?!☆

◇ No. You heard wrong, Roaring☆Hot☆Vermilion, not another one. NO other one. ◇

☆zzzzzzzzzzzzzztttt!☆

There was a shocked silence.

"Well, there are some other interesting problems," said Shirley. "Some in logic theory, some in number theory, and some in geometry. There is one famous problem that is part geometry and part number theory."

The wrinkled purple lobe expanded and with careful enunciation asked, □Logic—OK, Numbers—OK, Geometry??□

Shirley was puzzled when she heard this. In her engineer's world, geometry was inextricably mixed with numbers. Yet these beings did not manipulate the external world, they just existed in it. Could it be that they had no idea of the relationship of the length of a line to the progression of numbers, and the area of a geometrical square to the product of a mathematical square of a number? She tried an experiment. Pulling a diamond scribe from her tool kit, she started to scratch a diagram in the duralloy wing-plate above her. Her motions were interrupted by a squirming feeling at her beltline as three inquisitive pseudopods imitated her entry into her tool pouch.

□Lots of hard things,□ said Deep Purple.

☆Wheeoo! SHARP!!☆ said Loud Red, as it tested a hard acrylic handle on the point of the scribe that Shirley was trying to use.

◇ Too many things, ◇ White Whistler admonished.

Shirley got annoyed. She reached down and slapped the

offending tendrils away from her tool pouch, glared around angrily, then carefully sealed each centimeter of the rip-seal seam. She again reached up to the underpart of the wing with her diamond scribe held firmly in her hand. For once she had the full attention of the frivolous multitude of aliens.

Carefully, she scratched a right-angled triangle on the skin of *Dragonfly*'s wing. Then, just as carefully, she measured off the length of one of the shorter sides by laying the scribe along the side and pinching it carefully between her gloved fingers. She turned it at right angles and marked a point. In a few seconds she had constructed a square that used one of the triangle sides as one of its sides. She was halfway through constructing the square for the other side when the silent chorus broke into cacophony.

▢Yes! Three and four is five!▢

☆HA! PYTH THEOREM!!☆ roared Loud Red.

"They mean the ancient Greek theorem ascribed to Pythagoras," said Jill. "I told them the human name for the theorem."

"Thanks," said Shirley, trying to separate the alien responses from Jill's.

◊We understand your diagram, ◊ said White Whistler, ◊ Even if you can not draw it because of others. ◊

There was a pause as the purple and red protuberances retracted under the seeming glare of the white cloud that they had intruded upon.

◊ Tell of problem. ◊

Shirley felt flustered. She was not a mathematician, and it was obvious that these creatures knew the fact that a right triangle had two short sides and one long side, and that the squares of the lengths of the two shorter sides equalled the square of the length of the longest side. She felt stupid as she tried to get across in simple language the idea of one of the most famous unsolved problems in human mathematics—Fermat's Conjecture.

She pointed her scribe at the triangle enclosed in squares inscribed about its perimeter.

"Three times three, plus four times four, equals five times five," she said.

□OK!!□ said the purple one enthusiastically.

☆YES!?!☆ said Loud Red, with an inquisitive quiver in its tendril.

"One of the unsolved problems in human mathematics was conjectured by the human Fermat. There may be many solutions to *x* multiplied two times plus *y* multiplied two times equals *z* multiplied two times. But there is no solution to the problem of *x* multiplied three times, plus *y* multiplied three times, equals *z* multiplied three times . . . even if three is any number."

□That not problem!□ the purple one graveled.

☆That's a DUMB problem!!☆ the red cloud exploded. ☆That problem not said right. I say right way. *X* squared plus *Y* squared equals *Z* squared has many solutions. Is there a solution for *U* cubed plus *V* cubed plus *W* cubed equal *Z* cubed? That make more sense. You have two things *X* and *Y*. You multiply two times. You add two times. You get same as *Z* multiplied two times. Two things *three* times is DUMB!! If you multiply three times, then you should *add* three times!☆

"But *is* there an answer?" persisted Shirley.

□Answer?□ echoed Deep Purple. There was a long pause. Then the other colored portions of the water retracted as the large purple blob condensed into a purple boulder some meters beneath Shirley's feet. She had not realized how massive Deep Purple was, for its cloud extended tideward as far as she could see. Like a motion picture of a vaporizing block of dry ice run backwards, the gigantic purple cloud condensed into a slippery purple rock: a thinking rock; thinking about a problem put forth many decades ago by a brilliant human mind many light-years away.

☆I'm going surfing!☆ Loud Red swam up to the top of the wing and perched there, its weight causing a slight list to the plane. Then, as the next roller broke over the plane, Loud Red used the inertia of the wing to launch itself onto the forward surface of the wave.

☆Wheeee!!!☆ came the cry of excitement through the water, fading into the distance as the wave carried the red alien off.

"I wish I could surf," said Shirley wistfully.

◊ You wrong shape to surf, ◊ said White Whistle.

"I could surf if I had a surfboard," said Shirley, her thoughts going back over six light-years and forty time-years. Fortunately Jill was back in the translation loop. It took an extended discussion between the computer and the alien before it understood what a surfboard was.

◊ I be your surfboard! ◊ said White Whistler. It swooped under Shirley and picked her up on its massive body, a cavity appearing in the top of the alien's body to cradle the human.

"What's going on?" came Richard's concerned voice over the imp link.

"I'm going to get a ride!" shouted a delighted Shirley. The white alien humped itself up on the plane wing.

"Jill! Make her stop! That could be dangerous!" Shirley could see Richard through the left cockpit window. He was yelling and waving his hands at her, trying to make her get down off the alien.

Shirley grinned and waved back at him.

"Cowabunga!" she cried as a roller lifted the wing and White Whistler launched its multiton body onto the wave.

The wave was traveling toward the center of an underwater volcanic vent field that had produced a long sloping ash-and-lava shield. As they moved toward the central region, the ocean became shallower and the wave steeper. It was a long surf, and after they had gone a kilometer they were out of range of Jill's sonar and laser beacon. Shirley had to depend upon her chest-pack translator for communication. White Whistler noticed the lack and switched to using simplified speech patterns. Although both enjoyed the ride, White Whistler's curiosity led to questions.

◊ Humans are strange elements. Not see before. I swim entire world many times. Never see humans. Where humans exist before now? ◊

"We came from lights in sky." Suddenly Shirley realized that the aliens had no eyes, so perhaps they didn't know about the stars, although they probably knew about Barnard.

◊ I know many lights in sky. There is Sky⊗Rock, you

name Roche. There is Hot, you name Barnard. There is Warm and little elements. There are many other lights. All tiny except one new one. They are my research. ◊

An eyeless astronomer, mused Shirley. *It even has to make its telescope lenses from its own flesh.* She started to think how to tell the alien that the stars were suns like Barnard, and that she came from a planet around one of those stars.

"The other lights we call stars. They are suns like Barnard, but far away."

◊ Not all are like Barnard. Some have color of Barnard. Most have different color. Some yellow like spots on Barnard. Some white like light from storms. Some blue. Different kinds of suns. ◊

You may not have eyes, said Shirley to herself. *But you have a marvelous color sense, if you've been able to deduce that stars are suns from their spectrum.*

◊ One star not like others. Star yellow for long time. Then get brighter and color is green. Then after three thousand rotations star become yellow again. ◊

"That is star of humans," said Shirley, much relieved that the problem of pointing out which of the many stars was the Sun had been solved by their method of arrival.

◊ Human star far away. Your plane swim long time. ◊

"Humans not use plane. Humans use big . . . circle. You see big circle in sky?"

◊ Yes. Big circle not logical. ◊

"Not logical? I do not understand."

◊ Lights in sky are my research. I know stars are suns. I know Sky⊗Rock is like world without water. I know Warm is like a big world with more clouds. I know little ones of Warm are almost equal to world. I can predict motions of all lights in sky except one. That one is big circle. Big circle not like anything. It is circle, not sphere. Its motion has no logic. I think hard to find logic of big circle motion. I can find no logic in motion. ◊

"The big circle is not heavy like other lights. Big circle swims in light from Barnard. Subtract big circle from set of lights in sky. They do not swim. They move by logic of gravity."

◊ Word is missing. Logic of . . . ◊

"Each sphere in sky is pulled by other lights in sky. A big sphere pulls more than a small sphere. If two spheres are near, pull is strong. If two spheres are far, pull is weak. Amount of pull varies as the inverse square of the distance. That is logic of gravity between two spheres."

◊ That is the hypothesis I was using! Then big circle came and its motion did not fit hypothesis. I rejected hypothesis and looked for a new hypothesis. ◊

Shirley felt the body of the alien stop its slow swim back to the airplane.

◊ I must think. ◊

Shirley then felt the body of the alien contract around her, getting harder and more rubbery as liquid was squeezed from the jellylike body. Suddenly she found herself floating in the water as a white rock sank beneath her to the bottom.

"White Whistler!" she cried through her outside imp. "Come take me back to the plane! I can't swim twenty kilometers in my suit, even if I knew which direction to swim!!!"

There was no answer.

Shirley tried again, and even sent the suit-imp swimming down to the bottom in an attempt to revive the white rock.

"I guess once you have dived into the complexity of the three-body problem you don't want to come up until you have it solved," she said to herself. "I guess I'd better just relax and wait until White Whistler finishes thinking and comes to pick me up again."

Shirley set her suit heater on low to conserve power and closed her eyes to rest.

I hope White Whistler isn't trying to solve the generalized n-body central force problem, she thought to herself as she drifted off to sleep.

A clear blue cloud strung through the cold water and wrapped itself around a red rock. There was a trilling sound as Dainty△Blue△Warble tried to attract the attention of the inactive elder.

△It's time for another lesson, Old-one Roaring☆Hot☆ Vermilion! What'cha doing?△

☆It is!?!☆ roared the red rock as it dissolved into a cloud. ☆Was just thinking of what to teach you next!☆

Feathery red tendrils snaked out into the water, tasting each molecule.

☆Let me taste. Know there was one around just a little bit ago.☆

Suddenly there was a reaction, and like a bloodhound on the scent, the cloud concentrated into a long tendril that dragged the rest of the red body along. The blue cloud floated alongside. Suddenly the red cloud stopped, the tip of its tendril pointing stiffly off into the murky depths.

☆There's a Creepy⊗Stink!☆

☆Sneak up on it! Ho! Ho!☆

△Yes, Old-one,△ said the blue cloud, imitating the motions of the elder.

☆Wait!☆ said Roaring☆Hot☆Vermilion as the eager blue youngster started to move ahead toward the slowly-moving black slug plowing through the muddy bottom.

☆First sneak up only halfway! Then stop!☆

The blue cloud obeyed and stopped in the water about halfway to the Creepy⊗Stink.

☆Now halfway again! Stop!☆

☆Do it again!☆

☆Will you catch it?☆

☆Will you?☆

Dainty△Blue△Warble followed the instructions of the elder, moving only halfway each time toward the slowly creeping blob of pungent food. As the gap lessened, the pauses at each halfway point became shorter. Dainty△ Blue△Warble controlled its fluid body well with its eager, learning intellect, but finally, in a swirl that was too fast to follow, the Creepy⊗Stink was gone.

☆Ho! Ho! Caught it, didn't you!☆

△I calculated that even though I only went halfway each time, my velocity was greater, and eventually I would catch up. So I ate it!△

☆Taste interesting?☆

There was an unnaturally long pause.

△Stinky!△

☆You'll get used to it. Hey! WAVE!!!☆

△Wave!△ warbled the youngling. Then flowing smoothly into the elder's wake, it surfed across the surface of the shining sea.

"George? I'm worried," said Richard. "It's getting dark and Shirley and White Whistler aren't back yet."

George looked out the cockpit window at Barnard. The short day was almost over, and the tall tail of the *Magic Dragonfly* was casting a long shadow up the water mountain toward Roche as Barnard set behind them.

"Are there any of the aliens around?" he asked Jill. George could hear the sonar in the nose go through its search scan.

"Loud Red and Little Blue are coming this way."

"Ask them if they have seen Shirley and White Whistler."

△Floating⊗Rock is calling us.△

☆Hi! We come closer!☆ the loud voice roared through the water. The body of Roaring☆Hot☆Vermilion took on a more streamlined shape and zoomed off through the ocean, followed close behind by a pale blue arrow. The two drew to a halt in front of the chugging airplane.

"Where is White Whistler and the human Shirley?"

☆Don't know. Orange⊗Hunters will find them!☆ The red cloud gave a piercing whistle, and soon three eager orange snakes came streaking through the water to dash themselves headlong into the red flesh of their master. After the obligatory free-for-all wrestling match was over, the Orange⊗Hunters listened to the complex commands coming from Roaring☆Hot☆Vermilion, then they took off, making controlled crooning noises as they went.

"George," said Jill. "There's a message being relayed from *Clete*. The commsat says that the signal is very weak and broken up, but it's getting stronger as the sun sets. Here is what we have so far."

"Shirley calling commsats . . . Floating alone some twenty

kil . . . . . . Whistler rocked up and left me. Heater power getting low. Shirley calling commsats . . ."

"Can they get her position?" asked George.

"All they have are radio signals to work from," said Jill. "That only puts her somewhere in a hundred-kilometer circle. As soon as it gets darker the commsats will try to spot her helmet laser beacon. They've radioed to her suit-imp to keep that going at high power."

"I'm going out to see if Loud Red will take me looking," said Richard, heading for the suit locker.

"It'll be pitch dark soon," said George. "You won't be able to see a thing."

"No, it won't!" boomed Jinjur's voice through George's imp. "*Prometheus* is over the dark side, and I'm going to illuminate the search area with the reflection from the sail. I won't be able to keep it up all night without knocking myself out of position, but I should be able to give you an hour's worth."

George peered upward through the cockpit window and found the fat ellipse in the sky. As he watched, the ellipse brightened and soon a tiny new sun was ablaze in the sky.

"I'm cycling through," said Richard. "Tell Loud Red that I'd like a ride."

"There's another message coming in from Shirley," said Jill.

". . . heater power gone. Can't take cold much longer . . . Must have dozed off . . . Barnard has risen again . . . Nope . . . It's *Prometheus*. Good seeing you guys, but I'm afraid it's too late. Awfully cold . . ." There was a long stretch where they could hear digital chatter from Shirley's suit computer riding over the noise from Shirley's chattering teeth.

"The suit-imp reports that Shirley's torso temperature has dropped to thirty-five degrees Celsius, with extremities well below that," said Jill.

"Wha . . . White Whistler, you're back . . . No . . . Orange blob . . . Stop bumping . . . Go 'way . . ." There were sounds of heavy breathing, then the chattering teeth suddenly stopped.

"I think she's lost consciousness," said Jill.

"I hope those pets of Loud Red are strong enough to bring her back."

"They each weigh twice what Shirley weighs," said Jill.

"I'm through the lock," said Richard. "Patch me through to Loud Red."

Jill stopped the engines and the *Magic Dragonfly* drifted to a stop in the ocean as Richard swam forward through the dimly lit seas toward the two aliens.

"Please carry me to Shirley," he asked through Jill's sonar.

☆No. Orange⊗Hunters come. They bring Shirley here.☆

"But they'll take forever . . . a long time. She may die!"

☆She not die. She too hard. Cannot eat Stiff⊗Movers, so Stiff⊗Movers not die!☆

Suddenly Richard realized that the aliens had no concept of death except that of being eaten and assimilated in some predator's body. And since they were the dominant predator, with no natural enemies, they never died, just spent longer and longer times rocked up to think about more and more difficult logical problems until they gave themselves a problem that took an eternity to solve.

"Jill, convince that lazy red blob that we need to get Shirley here in a hurry."

"I don't think we really need to," said Jill. "My sonar can detect the pets up ahead, moving this way at a respectable speed. I think they have Shirley with them, because the commsat trackers show a doppler velocity shift on their communication signal from her suit-imp. Do you have your safety line on?"

"Of course," said Richard.

"Good," said Jill, starting the engines of the *Magic Dragonfly*. "See if you can catch the lock handholds as I go by. I'm going to save a few minutes by moving toward them."

"How's Shirley?" asked Richard, puffing as he swam a few quick strokes and swung into the open door of the lock as it moved by.

"Not good. Torso temperature down to thirty Celsius. The suit-imp has dropped all power reserves and is run-

ning the last few grams of hydrogen through the fuel cell
to get heat to the extremities before frostbite sets in."

Painful memories flooded back into Richard's mind as
he recalled the six hours of agony walking in sock feet
through Alpine snow carrying two unconscious tourists.
He twitched his eight toes in his boots. Would he like
Shirley less if she lost any of her toes? If she lived . . .

Stop that, you ass, he remonstrated himself. *Get ready
to cycle her through once those orange-colored hounds
bring her in.*

The smooth thump-thump of the large engine on the
right and the pittidy-pittidy of the jury-rigged fan on the
left stopped, and the *Magic Dragonfly* drifted to a halt.
The second the current was less than his space-suit swimming speed, Richard was through the door and breast-
stroking forward. The red alien was wrestling with his
charges, and loud roars, shrieks, and whistles sounded
through the ocean. Bobbing just below the surface of the
water was a limp figure in a space-suit, the arms and legs
hanging downward, jerking limply as the waves tossed the
body to and fro. Near the head of the body was a blurred
bundle of twigs that were waving frantically through the
water in an attempt to drag the heavy carcass toward the
airplane.

An orange blob hit Richard on the legs as it darted back
into the fray, sending him tumbling in the water. Richard
righted himself and stroked again to the distant limp form.
He grabbed her by the belt and headed for the lock.

Once Richard had gotten Shirley inside, Katrina took
charge. "Hold her by the waist while Arielle and I get her
helmet off and her shoulders out!"

The helmet came off and a cold dank head dropped on
Richard's shoulder as the subdued stink of a frozen tor-
tured body arose from the enclosed space. Richard held
tight to the waist until the stiff arms were extracted from
their casings. He switched to a chest hold on the body
while Katrina, Arielle, and the Christmas Branch worked at
detaching the bottom portion of the body from the plumbing. Richard's arms grew cold from the leaden breasts
draped over his forearms.

"Turn her to the right so we can get her leg out," came the command from Katrina.

Richard shifted his grip and easily turned the large body in the weak gravity of Eau, holding Shirley by the waist and under the left arm. He looked down to see a deep depression in the soft underflesh of the breast, the fatty tissue turned to clay by the cold. The suit came off.

"OK! Out! We'll take it from here!" said Katrina, pushing him forward through the privacy curtain as Arielle and the Christmas Branch started to strip the cold soggy coveralls from the blue-cold body.

"How's she doing?" asked David as Richard made his way forward, closing the second curtain behind him.

"I don't like it!" said Richard, pounding one massive but ineffectual fist into the other. He paced four huge steps forward, his hips avoiding the backs of the console chairs like a halfback avoiding one linebacker after another. His fourth step landed solidly on the floor next to the flight deck; then he pivoted and turned to march back again.

△Lesson time again!△ piped a small blue cloud as it scurried up to a deep yellow rock with a cloud of amber water hanging softly around it.

✳Certainly, Dainty△Blue△Warble,✳ murmured the edges of the yellow cloud. ✳Just let me ingest my latest thinking.✳

The small blue cloud waited patiently, only flickering a tendril or two while the large dark-yellow rock dissolved on the ocean bottom. The dark yellow dispersed in thin threads into the light-yellow cloud above it. Soon you could not tell the difference between the threads and the cloud, and the rock was gone.

△What were you thinking about?△

✳The fourth infinity.✳

△Tell me about it!△

✳Well . . . I will some day. But first you have to learn about the second infinity.✳

△Tell me! Tell me!△

A yellow tendril poked a hole in the muddy bottom.

✳Feel, youngling. There is a point.✳

A delicate blue tendril felt into the murky bottom.

△That is a hole in the mud, Old-one Warm❋Amber❋ Resonance.△

There was a long pause as the yellow cloud rippled in annoyance. However, the tone that resumed after the pause had all the warm patience that it had contained previously.

❋Imagine it is a point, with no dimensions.❋

△Yes, Old-one.△

The yellow tendril touched the surface of the soft mud again, leaving another tiny spot in the smooth surface close to the first one.

❋Here is another point.❋

❋Here is another.❋

❋Here is another.❋

The line of close-spaced spots grew.

❋Imagine. Imagine points so close they make a line. A line infinitely long.❋

There was a pause as the young blue cloud absorbed the sounds. Its blue cloud enveloped the motions of the yellow wisp making a long string of tiny dots in the ocean bottom.

△Infinite in both directions, Old-one?△

❋Yes. Very good, youngling.❋

❋Now . . . Imagine a point not on the line.❋

❋Here is one.❋

❋Here is another.❋

Soon a number of isolated spots were scattered above and below the dotted line on the muddy sea floor.

❋Imagine an infinite number of them.❋

There was a slight pause.

❋Are there more points *off* the line than *on* the line?❋

The youngling thought carefully before answering, its wisps of azure clumping and dissolving randomly. The elder waited patiently. Finally the youngling answered.

△No! They are the same.△

❋Right! They both are infinities of the first order.❋

△But that problem was the same as the one you gave me yesterday. That time you asked me if the irrational numbers were greater than the rational numbers. They too are both first infinities. Give me a harder one.△

✻All right. Draw a line through any of those points I made.✻

The blue cloud formed a tendril of its own and made a streak through one of the isolated spots in the mud.

✻Draw another line through the same point. Make it wiggly if you want to.✻

A wiggly line joined the streak.

✻Draw more.✻

Dainty△Blue△Warble concentrated and soon dozens of distinctly different lines were drawn through the same point. Then came the question.

✻Imagine you did that to each point.✻

✻Are there more wiggly lines than points on the line?✻

The blue cloud stopped moving as it started to think.

Warm✻Amber✻Resonance drifted off on the current as Dainty△Blue△Warble pondered the last question. The fluid body of the youngling slowly began condensing into a bright-blue rock as the difficulty of the tough logical question called for more and more concentrated neural matter.

✻Huunnm!✻ murmured the amber elder. ✻That will keep the blue menace quiet for a while.✻

✻Off to the waves! MMMMM!!!!✻

Warm✻Amber✻Resonance vibrated through the cooling seas, leaving behind a tenuous blue cloud condensing into a thinking azure stone.

Two day-cycles later Shirley was standing her shift. She still wasn't allowed to do anything strenuous, but Shirley had taken Arielle's place as pilot of the lumbering *Dragonfly*, while Arielle tried to take Shirley's place as Chief Engineer. Arielle did a respectable job. She equalled Shirley's performance in outship repairs and bettered her performance at the galley table.

"I don't see where she puts it," said Shirley to David. "If I ate that much I would be as fat as Richard!"

"I heard that!" said Richard. "How much do you weigh, Shorty?"

"Eighty-five kilos, fat man . . . and you?"

"One hundred kilos—but I'm taller than you."

"The last five centimeters must be all fat," said Shirley, sticking her tongue out at him.

Richard was glad. The brat must be OK if she could fight back like that. He was about to make some comment about squaws when Jill interrupted.

"White Whistler is returning."

"Ask why I was left!" demanded Shirley.

"Just a second," said Jill, almost impatiently. "White Whistler is saying something important to the other flouwen!"

◇ I have solved the motion of the lights in the sky! ◇

☆ Even the big circle? ☆

◇ All the lights except big circle. It is a swimmer of the light. It is like us. It's motions are not that of logic. ◇

✳ But you can know the motions of all the rest? You can know the arisings of Hot and the fadings of Warm and the tenacity of Sky⊗Rock? ✳

◇ All, ◇ said White Whistler with confidence.

☆ How can you be sure? ☆

◇ The Stiff⊗Mover gave me the logic of gravity for two spherical masses. The rule is very simple. Yet the mathematics seemed complex when the rule was used on more than two spheres. After some thinking, I found the simple rule for many spheres. ◇

✳ Was it difficult? ✳

◇ No. A simple variable substitution combined with an interesting coordinate transformation. ◇

✳ Let me taste. ✳

☆ Me, too! ☆

△ Me, too!!! △

The white cloud sent out a tendril. The end was whitely concentrated with nerve tissue. The other three aliens crowded around to taste the essence of Clear ◇ White ◇ Whistle's thought.

✳ Subtle! ✳

☆ Tricky!!! ☆

△ I don't understand the taste! △ said the little blue one.

✳ You will. Just savor the taste and recall it some thousand turns from now. It will be much clearer then, when you can handle such complexities.✱

△But I want to know now!△

✱Later, Dainty△Blue△Warble,✱ said Warm✱Amber✱ Resonance. The yellow cloud expanded and contracted as it impressed on its memory the secret for the solution of the n-body central force problem. Warm✱Amber✱Resonance reveled in the cleanness of it. One complex variable transformation, and then just that one simple, yet unobvious, coordinate transformation! An nth-root dimension, indeed!✱

During the next day, a vibration started coming from the left wing. Shirley's ears pricked up, and she reached to turn off the fans just as Jill shut them down. The *Dragonfly* coasted to a stop, the lapping of the waves on the hull making the absence of the engine sounds even more ominous.

"The mounting bracket for the replacement fan is vibrating," said Jill.

"I'll go out and fix it," said Shirley. "Probably just a bolt coming loose."

"You are still weak," said Jill. "I'll wake up Richard."

"No!" exploded Shirley. "I can do anything that big ox can do. I'm going out! I'm tired of being cooped up in this tin can." She stormed down the corridor, bumping into every console chair along the way. David, twisted partially away from his console by Shirley's passage, gave a sigh, swiveled back, closed down his console, and went back to suit up with Shirley. He probably would only be a tool holder, but the sooner he got her back inside the better.

Together they cycled through the lock and swam out under the left wing. Shirley jiggled the bracing structure for the jury-rigged fan and found the loose bolt. She tightened it, and then for good measure, started to check the tightness of the rest. David pulled out his omniwrench and backed her up by holding onto the other side of each bolt.

Suddenly, they were all engulfed in an encompassing cloud of goodwill. The purple cloud was back.

"What's that!" said David in alarm.

"Take it easy," said Shirley. "That's just an old alien we call Deep Purple. Last time I saw him he was rocked up and trying to prove Fermat's Conjecture." She suddenly realized the importance of what she was saying; if not to their present problems, to the cadre of mathematicians six light years away on Earth.

"Welcome, Deep Purple," she said. "Did you solve the problem?"

☐Easy,☐ the lavender cloud responded. ☐Human named Fermat right.☐ There was a polite pause, then he continued, ☐DUMB problem!☐

This was the cue for Loud Red, ☆I told you! DUMB problem!! DUMB!!!☆

David broke through over Shirley's imp. "Do you mean to say they have solved Fermat's Conjecture? How did they do it? We have only proved it up to *n* equals 1,023,467."

The sharp sonar senses of the huge purple alien caught the careful reeling of numbers. It paused in its exodus, then came back to surround Shirley, as if it were really looking at a human for the first time.

☐You solve problems with numbers?!?☐ it asked, its incredulity rippling through its surface.

"Yes," said Shirley bravely, "We do quite often. If it works for many numbers then it must be true."

There was a long pause as the alien brain tried to absorb the alien thought. It rejected it.

☐There are many numbers. There are . . . too many numbers.☐

The alien was struggling to express the idea of an infinity of numbers. Shirley helped.

"No end to numbers," she said.

☐No end!☐ the alien rasped in relief.

☐No end, so no certainty. Not use numbers.☐

". . . but how . . ." Shirley's eyes flitted from alien mounds to David's face.

"I think Deep Purple just proved Fermat's Conjecture for *any* number," said David. "Too bad we aren't smart enough to understand how it did it. We may think we're intelligent, but that alien equivalent of an aging surfer has us all beat."

While they were talking, the larger cloud had wrapped a purple tendril about two others, one red and one milky white. The contact had lasted for less than two seconds.

◇ Obvious. ◇ said the white one.

☆. . . and DUMB!!!☆ said the red one.

☆Let's do something else! Like SURF!!☆

☐WAVE!!!☐ said the old purple one, leading the group to the surface as they dropped their preoccupation with mathematics and enjoyed the caress of the waves on their fluid surface.

◇ Wave!!! ◇ keened the voice of Clear ◇ White ◇ Whistle as the three of them caught a wave.

☆DUMB!!!☆ came the final fading response from Roaring☆ Hot☆Vermilion as they surfed off into the distance.

FLOATING

After only six hours' sleep, George found himself awake
again. He turned over in the dark space of his bunk, lit
only by the soft flickering colored lights of his imp, and
tried to go back to sleep again, but it didn't work. His
mind started to go over the problems that lay ahead if he
was to get his tiny command off this ball of water. He tried
thinking about Katrina, then Red, another world away,
then Jinjur, even more distant, but his brain rejected
those diversions and continued to worry. George gave up
and slammed the Sound-Bar door open and rolled out of
bed.

"Another sign of getting old," he grumbled to himself.
"Can't even get a good eight hours a night anymore."

He stumbled sleepily through his wake-up routine
and went forward to the galley. David was there, plowing through one of his special dinners, a knockwurst
sitting on a bed of sauerkraut, a heaping mound of real
mashed potatoes, real green-bean salad, and a pint of dark
beer.

"Looks good," said George enviously as he punched
himself up a breakfast of algae omelet with pseudoham,
algae toast with pseudobutter, and ersatz coffee with
pseudocream.

"My last special," said David, handing him a crisp green
bean, which George took gratefully. "We've been making

fairly good progress. Eight to ten kilometers an hour doesn't seem like much for an airplane, but if you keep it up hour after hour it adds up. We've traveled almost a thousand kilometers in the past five days and are starting up the water mountain. Only about four hundred kilometers to go to the peak, where Red can pick us off. If we can keep up the pace we should be there in two days, three days before the periapsis passage."

George listened to the report thoughtfully, taking little bites of the green bean. His breakfast was pushed out onto counter by the galley imp. George swallowed the last of the green bean and started to shovel the pseudobreakfast down as if he were refueling a machine.

"How's the weather?" he asked as he paused between drinks of coffee.

"It's getting worse," said David. "Each six-hour day-night cycle seems to generate a new storm in the hot crescent that spins its way into the cold crescent to dump its load of supersaturated ammonia. Most of them seem to head up the mountain, pushing huge ring-waves ahead of them. There was a real doozy that passed over a few hours ago."

"I know," said George. "The thunder woke me up, and I just managed to get myself asleep again before I got seasick. I'm worried about the storms, though. That could make the pickup tricky."

"It's concerning Red, too. There are calm periods between storm fronts, but they're getting shorter and shorter."

"We'd better get a move on, then," said George. He pushed his empty tray back to the galley imp and went forward to relieve Arielle. David returned to his knockwurst, carved off a large slab, smothered it in sauerkraut, piled a dab of hot real mustard on top and put it into his smiling mouth.

"How's *Dragonfly* doing?" George asked as he reached the cockpit area. Arielle turned around and gave him a crooked smile, the neuskin patch distorting her lip shape. Flashes of colored lights could be seen from between her lips where the brace imp was still holding her tooth in place.

That could start a whole new fad, thought George, looking at the literally sparkling smile. *Wait until the Space Administration medics release Arielle's picture to the press.*

"We'f been making fifteen kilometer an hour, but tide now turn other way, and we will flow down," said Arielle.

"Can we put down an anchor?"

Jill answered for Arielle. "The ocean bottom is now two kilometers down. My sounding cable is long enough, but we really don't have anything that would act like an anchor and dig in the bottom instead of just sliding along."

"Are any of the flouwen around?" asked George. "Perhaps they would be willing to take the cable down to the bottom and tie it to something during the reverse tides."

"Loud Red is nearby," said Jill. "I will talk to it." There was a complex sound from the sonar dome at the front of the plane, and soon a large red blob streaked by on the right side, circled the plane, and came to a halt in front of the slowly chugging ship.

☆Hi! You call Loud Red!?!☆

"Yes. We must move east to point under Sky⊗Rock. Water moves west so we move west. Look under me. See thick string?" Jill let out a few meters of cable, and Loud Red dove under the ship. There were a few strong tugs that had George reaching for a handhold as they shook the ship.

"It certainly has no trouble grabbing hold of it," George said.

The red blob appeared once again in the view of the half-submerged cockpit windows.

"Bottom of ocean does not move," said Jill. "If thick string attached to bottom, then Floating⊗Rock not move. You attach thick string to bottom?"

☆That dumb! Floating⊗Rock want to move east. If Floating⊗Rock attached to bottom, Floating⊗Rock *not* move east. Not move at all! Dumb! If Floating⊗Rock want to move east, *I* move Floating⊗Rock east!☆

Loud Red dove once again beneath the ship and shortly reappeared, swimming strongly forward. There was a jerk as the cable tightened, and soon they were under tow. After a few minutes Jill gave a report.

"We are moving at five kilometers an hour east in a current that is running twelve kilometers an hour west. Loud Red has almost doubled our speed through the water compared with what I could do with the fans alone."

"I wonder how long it can keep it up?" mused George.

Three hours later, sitting alone in the cockpit, he became more and more impressed by the alien's performance. Not that it was easy for Loud Red, as he let them know frequently.

☆Hard work! Tired! Hungry! Go get something to eat!☆ Abruptly the *Dragonfly* slowed in the water until it reached the speed that its fans could maintain. It was dark, and Loud Red disappeared as soon as the red body slipped out of the landing light beams.

George wondered if the flighty alien would return. It could well be that after catching and eating something, it would go off surfing and forget all about the humans. But he was wrong. Loud Red returned in a half-hour, fighting with his pack of pets over the remains of a large bluegreen flitter. The alien finally threw the remainder of the carcass to the pets, who went off with it. The cable was retrieved from beneath the ship, and with a jerky start, the *Magic Dragonfly* was skimming through the seas again, heading east. Almost immediately the complaints started.

☆Hard work!☆

☆Dumb!☆

☆Nothing to do!☆

They were breasting large following waves. George looked back at the skyline.

"Another storm coming up on us," he said.

"It should be on us by dark," said Jill. A picture of the storm front appeared on George's cockpit display from the video cameras peering out the *Magic Dragonfly*'s eyes.

☆HI! HI!☆ called Loud Red, suddenly.

"What's that for?" asked George of Jill.

"I think Loud Red heard another flouwen off in the distance. Let's see if I can spot it." George heard the strength of the sonar pulses increase and watched the display on the cockpit console. Soon, off to the edge of the screen was a small return blob, the blue color indicating an approaching object.

"It's about the right size for a flouwen," said George.

"It is," said Jill. "I can hear it talking to Loud Red. He has stopped using the simplified language we developed between ourselves and has switched to their more complicated form."

☆Hi! Bitter†Orange†Chirr! You are a long way from your feeding jet.☆

†So are you, Roaring☆Hot☆Vermilion. I just finished a long surf in front of that storm. Good waves. Want to race me up the ocean? Last one to the top has to catch dinner for both.†

☆Can't surf. Have to pull Floating⊗Rock up the ocean. It can't swim too well.☆

†Who is Floating⊗Rock? Rocks can't float.†

☆This one can! It can talk, too! Come here and meet it.☆

†A talking, floating rock! I must see this!†

George watched the alien approach on the sonar. As it got closer he looked out the window to see if he could spot it. David and Katrina had joined him. Katrina had buckled herself in the copilot seat while David rode the wave-motion standing up, holding on to the backs of their seats.

"It's lost in the surface clutter," said George, looking up from the sonar screen. "But it's close, you should be able to see it soon."

"I can feel its sonar," said Jill. "It is giving me a good looking-over."

†That Floating⊗Rock is big!†

☆Come closer. It won't eat you.☆

†Why is it holding on to you with a string?†

☆I'm holding on to it. It can't swim well, so I am pulling it.☆

Bitter†Orange†Chirr moved closer.

* * *

"I can see it," said David.

"Where?" said Katrina, sitting up to peer out over the nose of the plane.

"Off to the left and out about a hundred meters. It looks like a patch of orange juice."

"I see it," said George, pointing. "Can you talk to O.J., Jill?"

"I'll try," said Jill. The sonar sent out a burst of sound. Jill used the name combination that Loud Red had used for O.J.

The orange flouwen came closer as Jill talked to it. It was surrounded by Loud Red's orange pets.

"I don't see any difference between that flouwen and those pets except size," said Katrina. "Are we sure they are different creatures and not just the same type with differing levels of intelligence depending upon size? In color, there seems to be no difference between O.J., the pets, and the prey that the pets caught the first time we met them."

"There's a big difference," said David. "O.J. here has a greenish-orange color, like a not-quite-ripe orange, while the pets are yellow-orange. The prey, on the other hand, was a blue-orange, like a slightly smoky flame."

"I presume the aliens are as sensitive to color differences as David is," said George. "That would partially compensate for the fact that they don't have imaging eyes, even though they are photosensitive."

The sky darkened as a cloud drifted over Barnard. David looked up, then gasped.

"A waterspout! It's heading straight for us!"

George glanced at David, then whirled his head to look out the window. As soon as he had the waterspout in sight he froze. Keeping his head still, he spoke over his shoulder to his imp.

"This is one time I wish you had your radar back," he said. "You'd be able to get bearing, range, and track in a second." He paused, his head still stiff, then went on. "It's drifting a little . . . Yep . . . definitely drifting forward. Tell Loud Red to stop pulling and reverse your engines! You'd also better tell the flouwen that a water-spout is coming."

There was a burst of sound from the sonar in the nose dome. The engines halted as *Dragonfly* slowed in the water, then resumed again as Jill tried to back up in the water. There was a loud gurgling from underneath as Jill flooded a compartment, and Dragonfly settled slightly in the water, the waves breaking over the cockpit window. Through the waves George could see the water-spout moving lazily toward them. He continued to hold his head still so he could watch the motion of the column across the window. If that drift stopped while the size grew larger, it meant that the spout was coming straight at them. Fortunately the drift continued; it looked like the twister was going to pass in front of them. It would be close, though, and George found his muscles trying to help Jill back the *Magic Dragonfly* away from danger.

"Loud Red and I never developed a word for water-spout, so I couldn't warn them. I did tell them to dive to the bottom, and Loud Red did so, since it is used to taking our advice, but O.J. either didn't hear me or else is ignoring me, and is still swimming in circles around us just under the surface. The sonar is now picking up the disturbed water at the base of the spout."

George looked down at the sonar display. It was an expanded picture of the region just in front of *Dragonfly*. There was a scintillating circle moving slowly in front of them, about two hundred meters away, and there was a steadier blob that looked like a flouwen, probably O.J. The steady blob and the scintillating circle intersected, then they were both gone.

"The spout has turned orange and lifted!" shouted Katrina. George looked up just as a wave broke over the windshield. It took a second for the heavy-duty wipers to clean the film of ammonia-water from the outside surface.

Those are probably the cleanest windows in six light years, thought George to himself, then he too saw the orange-white spout.

"It's O.J.," said David. "I recognize that green-orange color."

"The spout is orange up for hundreds of meters," said George. "It's tearing poor O.J. to pieces!"

The spout had trouble digesting its sudden viscous, multiton load. The column lifted, fattened, and slowed its whirling. There was a short attempt to speed up and dip down to the surface again, but finally the spout rose up into the clouds and disappeared.

George looked over at Katrina's stricken face. He opened his mouth to say something comforting, and was trying to think what he could say that would alleviate the loss of an intelligent being, one who was probably hundreds of years older than they were. Suddenly the heavens opened and large drops of water battered the window and the roof overhead in a drumming roar. Then there was a loud PLOP on the roof, and an orange blob slithered down over the cockpit window and down off the nose of *Dragonfly*. The blob screamed incoherently through the thick glass as it slowly fell in the weak gravity.

"It's a piece of O.J.," said Katrina. "It's acting like the sample that White Whistler let me have." Suddenly they were thrown upward as a strong thump came from underneath the airplane. Loud Red was back.

☆Dumb! Bitter†Orange†Chirr eaten by whlee. Now I got work to do. Too much work!☆

There were more plopping noises and tiny screams filtering through the incessant drumming of the rain. They could see out for an instant just in back of the beating windshield wipers. There were hundreds of blobs writhing on the surface. Swimming among them was Loud Red. It would gather a batch and bring them together, where they instantly merged to form a larger blob. This would be left behind while Loud Red scooped up another batch of baby blobs. George could see the action better on the sonar. The screen was full of what looked like snow, tiny twisting points of light everywhere except for a blank trail left behind by a rapidly moving larger blob that collected the snow and packed it into snowballs, then moved on.

†Eeeeeeee!†
†Eeeaaaahhh!†

☆Bitter†Orange†Chirr dumb! Gets caught in whlee and makes poor tired Roaring☆Hot☆Vermilion work. I ought to eat some of the little ones . . . Bah! Bitter! Not even good to eat!☆

The large red blob molded together a batch of small orange blobs into a larger sphere. It spoke harshly at the sphere.

☆I am Roaring☆Hot☆Vermilion. You stop screaming. You stop moving. You stay here. I will come back.☆

†Yes, Roaring☆Hot☆Vermilion.†

Soon most of the tiny blobs had been rounded up. There were still many others, but they would be picked up later. The red flouwen retraced its path and began collecting the large orange spheres and merging them together. Soon there was a small orange youngling swimming along beside the large red cloud.

☆You are dumb, Bitter†Orange†Chirr! Didn't you hear Floating⊗Rock tell you to dive to the bottom?☆

†The Floating⊗Rock speaks so strangely I could barely understand it. Besides, what does a rock know?†

☆Floating⊗Rock is almost as smart as a flouwen, and it can do things that a flouwen can't do. It can fly like a flitter in the nothing above the ocean!☆

†Then why doesn't it, instead of having you pull it along in the ocean?†

☆Because it's not feeling well or something. Over there! Another sphere. I think that's the last one I made. Are you feeling big enough to find the rest of you by yourself?☆

The distant orange sphere activated itself as it smelled the familiar bitter scent and came sprinting toward the larger orange youngling and merged.

†Yes. I can collect the rest of me.†

☆Good! I'm going to get something to eat! Hard work makes me hungry!☆

†Don't eat anything orange!†

☆Bah! Would never do that! Too bitter!☆

There was a piercing whistle and soon three orange snakes came scooting through the ocean to join their master. The first thing Roaring☆Hot☆Vermilion did was to grab each Orange⊗Hunter and stretch them out. In two of them he spotted a blob of greenish-orange embedded in the yellow-orange of their flesh. A sharp command and the tiny blobs were released, to go screaming off to join the growing body of Bitter†Orange†Chirr.

☆We go!☆ and the red cloud with its orange snakes slithered into the depths, leaving Bitter†Orange†Chirr to collect the rest of its wits.

It was a dark and stormy night when Roaring☆Hot☆Vermilion returned two hours later. Bitter†Orange†Chirr was still searching out tiny segments of itself, and Roaring☆Hot☆Vermilion helped it finish off by sending his Orange⊗Hunters off to round up any stragglers. Jill called to Roaring☆Hot☆Vermilion to resume pulling.

☆No!☆

"But we must get up the mountain!"

☆No! Wrong way! Wrong time! Wave . . . Ocean . . . ☆ Frustrated, Loud Red left at high speed.

☆Wrong way! I get Clear ◊ White ◊ Whistler!☆

"It sounded like Loud Red was trying to explain something, but didn't have the words," said George.

"I could have worked out a joint understanding," said Jill. "But perhaps White Whistler would be less impetuous and easier to work with."

"There goes O.J.," said George. "Probably gone off to get something to eat. After that experience, I would guess it is famished. Speaking of famished, I think I'll go back to the galley for a bite while we wait for White Whistler to show up. Keep those engines chugging."

Roaring☆Hot☆Vermilion streaked through the murky depths at top speed, sonar signals making the ocean as bright as day. Far off in the distance came voices. A slight change in course, and the red cloud began to converge on the sounds.

◊ I hear Roaring☆Hot☆Vermilion approach. ◊

△I can hear him, too!△

❋Very good discrimination, Dainty△Blue△Warble. What else do you hear?❋ The small pale blue cloud paused, and Clear ◊ White ◊ Whistle and Warm ❋Amber❋Resonance stopped moving to reduce the local noise clutter.

△One . . . two . . . three . . . smaller sounds. They are the Orange⊗Hunters of Old-one Roaring☆Hot☆Vermilion.△

✳Excellent hearing, young one.✳

◇Yes. Now try seeing and let us know when you detect them.◇ Sharp bursts of directed sound piped from the little blue cloud as it attempted to see off into the distance by illuminating the distant figures with its sonar. The two elders added their own occasional bursts at a lower pitch.

Roaring☆Hot☆Vermilion heard them seeing him and started in talking as the distance closed.

☆The Floating⊗Rock is going to the inner point.☆

◇That is dangerous. It is getting near the time when one should stay away from the inner point.◇

☆I tried to tell it. But it doesn't know the words! You must tell it to stop!☆

◇It will take some time to teach Floating⊗Rock the right words, but I will try.◇

✳Do we dare go close to the inner point when the time is so near?✳

◇I have watched a number of near times from the side of the mountain. There are still ten days left. We can find Floating⊗Rock, warn it, and get back to a safe place in that time.◇

✳Did you say the Stiff⊗Movers can look at a distance?✳

◇Yes. They have disks in their top lump like the ones that I make for looking.◇

✳Then I will come also. I have an idea for communicating the danger to the Stiff⊗Movers that does not involve teaching them new words.✳

◇Then come along and tell me as we go.◇

△I want to go, too!△

✳Dainty△Blue△Warble, dear. It is too dangerous for little ones.✳

△I'm not little. I'm almost as big as you are. Besides, Old-one Clear◇White◇Whistle said there was plenty of time, and I swim fast.△

✳But, dear . . . ✳

◇Let the little one come. It will be good experience,

and there is really no danger provided we start back on time. ◊

The three colored clouds swam off toward the still-approaching red cloud, which slowed and turned back the other way. Soon the four members of the pod were rejoined and swam as a group back toward the inner point.

It was daybreak, and everyone except Katrina was awake to enjoy the next hour and a half of sunshine. The seas of Eau were relatively calm since Barnard had been heating up the backside of Roche rather than evaporating ammonia out of the seas of Eau. The high clouds that had been raining huge slowly-falling drops of ammonia on the inner pole were being parted by the warm dry breezes from Roche flowing through the narrow neck between the two planets. Through the hole in the clouds Barnard rose majestically over the mountains of Roche, the beams of light shooting down the long rift valleys that deepened as they furrowed their way to the oval end of the rocky globe.

Jill had been chugging her way toward the inner pole of Eau, trying to get as close to the gravity minimum as possible in order to make it easier on the ascent module when they picked them off.

"How are we doing, Jill?" asked George.

"We have been inside the ninety-five percentile pickup contours for the last half-hour. The high tide peaked not long ago, so the water mountain is dropping rapidly. We are starting to drift out again."

"We'll make it back again at next high tide if we can just keep chugging. Can you raise Rocheworld Base, Jill?"

"Rocheworld Base, here," said Carmen, her clear enunciated English penetrating through the haze of electronic noise generated by the multitude of storm cells wandering over the overheated ocean of Eau.

"We will be inside the pickup contours at the next high tide, three hours from now. It'll be dark here, but we'll have our lights on, and you should have no trouble finding us."

"Right, George. I read you. Now let's see if Jack can

read Jill." The humans kept silent as the two computers interchanged information.

"Communication complete," said Jill. "Even the Wolfe error correction code was never activated. The personnel transfer should proceed without any significant problem."

George grinned. Soon his command would be off this sodden planet and back into space where they belonged. He gazed up at the bright orb of Barnard. At this point in Rocheworld's orbit the red dwarf star was four times larger than the Sun, and looked even larger since it was still close to the horizon. Despite its brightness, he had no trouble looking at it, for it was no brighter than a charcoal fire: A charcoal fire with dark red clouds floating over its surface.

He thought of his last charcoal fire, the time he and Jinjur had traveled out to Annapolis to exercise her alumni privileges. A small sailboat with a huge sail and a night in a shoreside cabin. They had spent the evening tossing fuel into the hibachi on the patio and quietly getting drunk on white wine. Nothing had happened that night, for they knew they had the rest of their lives together.

"Hey!" yelled Shirley from the galley, as the plane lurched upward. George turned in time to see the remains of an algae shake spin lazily through the air and glop onto the ceiling. He felt a thump and another, then watched the pseudoprotein start to drip downward in the low gravity. The Christmas Branch rescued the situation by grabbing the metal container out of Shirley's grasp and installing the shake back into the shaker before it hit the carpet.

"Loud Red has returned," said Jill. "Since I was heading upmountain, they came at me from my blind side."

△That was fun! Can I bump it again?△

☆No! One bump is enough!☆

◇One bump is probably too many for the Stiff⊗Movers inside. ◇

✳I don't think you ought to be teaching Dainty△Blue△ Warble your boisterous habits.✳

△I bump Floating⊗Rock again?△

☆No!☆

◇ Floating⊗Rock is still moving toward the inner pole. ◇

☆I tell it to stop, but it does not.☆

◇It is dangerous here on the surface of the ocean. Let's get it down on the bottom where it is safer, then we can try to talk with it. Bitter†Orange†Chirr! Come here! Attach yourself to the outer wing of Floating⊗Rock and sink yourself. You others! Do the same!◇

☆Yes! Let's make this Floating⊗Rock sink!☆

"O.J. has attached itself to my wing," said Jill. "It seems to be extruding the water from its body and dragging the wing-tip under."

"Tell it to stop!" said George. "We've got to maintain headway in this counter tide if we are going to make the pickoff at next sunrise."

"They don't seem to be paying any attention to me," said Jill. "They are too busy talking between themselves . . . There is another one on the other wing-tip. It's Loud Red. Rocking up like the other one."

"What's going on!" said George in alarm. He looked out the cockpit window as an amber blob and a pale-blue blob climbed up on the wing and proceeded to shower ammonia water from their cells.

"White Whistler has my tail!" said Jill. "They are pulling me under!"

DIVING

They sank beneath the waves, the red light from Barnard turning into a purple-green under the ammonia oceans.

"Jill! Get them to stop!" cried Shirley. Her ears caught a strange noise. "Can the hull take the pressure?"

"The pressure hull in *Dragonfly* is very rugged, since the designers didn't know what it would run into. In compression it should hold against fifty atmospheres. I wouldn't worry too much about them taking us under the water. They must have a good reason for doing so."

"At least the wave action is less under here," said Shirley, gulping down the last remains of the rescued algae shake.

There were some gasps from Arielle and David.

"It's snowing!" said David.

"Blue fnow!" said Arielle.

George looked out the cockpit window. Shining brightly in the landing lights was a cloud of large blue needles drifting downward with the plane as they sank slowly to the bottom.

"What makes the snow blue?" asked Shirley. "And how come it can snow underwater?"

"The top layers of the ocean here at the inner pole are mostly ammonia from the ammonia rain on the surface," said Jill. "As we get deeper, the ammonia concentration decreases, but it gets rapidly colder. Right now the ammonia concentration is sixty percent, while the temperature has dropped to minus eighty-five Celsius. That is cold enough to form an ice made of two parts ammonia to one part water. The blue needles must be nucleating out of the supercooled liquid. They are falling because the solid is denser than the liquid."

For a few minutes everyone watched the fascinating scene as the blue snowstorm became thicker and thicker until their landing lights only penetrated a few meters into the swirling cloud.

"Are the flouwen being affected by the cold or the snow?" asked George.

"They are still talking between themselves, much as they did at the surface. I don't think they are particularly surprised or affected by the snow or the temperature variation. The temperature has stopped dropping. We're now at minus ninety-two Celsius and it's starting to go up again. There is also a drastic change in composition. We seem to have entered a warm current headed toward the inner pole. It is denser, since it is half water and half ammonia."

"What waf that?" said Arielle, her quick eye spotting something unusual in the scene outside the window. "There'f another one!"

"White snow!" said Shirley. "And this time it's going up! It's snowing in both directions! Blue snow falling down and white snow falling up."

"That must be a solid that is half ammonia and half water," said Jill. "None of my records indicate its density, but the solid must be lighter than the liquid, like normal ice, so it is rising to the surface."

The blue blizzard started to decrease. First in the size of the needles as they began to dissolve in the water-rich mixture; then finally the individual particles began to disappear and the fall weakened in intensity. But at the same time, the intensity of the upward-falling white snow began to increase. The particles were very large, like summer hailstones.

"Listen!" said Shirley, then she got down and put her ear on the deck. The rest of the crew stopped talking, and a hush settled over the cockpit. As it became quiet you could hear the pitter-patter of ice-balls striking the bottom of the hull and wings as they rose up past the sinking plane.

They finally passed through the white-ice storm, which tapered off to little white specks that seemed to appear out of nowhere in the frigid water.

"We're moving into the middle of the warm water current," said Jill. "It's now too warm for the ice to form."

"And how warm is that?" asked George.

"Minus seventy-eight Celsius."

"Balmy," said George. The show out the window over, he went back to the galley for a quick bite to eat.

For the next half-hour they continued their downward plunge. There were occasional mysterious creaks and groans as the hull took up the increasing external pressure.

"We've reached the middle of the warm stream," said Jill. "Maximum temperature nearly minus fifty Celsius, warmer than the surface. It's starting to drop again. Water concentration now sixty percent, compared to forty percent ammonia."

"Is it going to continue that trend until the bottom, or are we in for another surprise?" asked George.

"Yes."

"Yes, what?"

"It's going to continue the trend, and we are in for another surprise if it does."

"What's the surprise?" asked George. "Anything dangerous?" But before Jill could answer there was a cry from the cockpit.

"MORE fnow!"

George went forward to look. This time the snow took the form of transparent faceted balls. They were tiny at first, but as they fell they turned to marble-size. Although transparent, they weren't too hard to see, since they glittered rainbow colors in the intense beams of the landing lights as they scattered the light around their internal facets and back out again.

"BEAUTIFUL!" cried Arielle, exhilarated over the colorful scene. "What if it?"

"That's ordinary ice," said Jill. "Pure water crystals settling out of the twenty-five percent ammonia solution to fall to the bottom. The faceted balls must be a compromise between a snowflake and a hailstone."

"I thought ice floated," said Shirley.

"It floats in water, but the ocean is a mixture of water and much lighter ammonia. At concentrations of greater than twenty-three percent ammonia, pure ice is heavier than the ocean."

"Then the bottom must be covered with snow," said Shirley.

"It is," said Jill. "I can see it on my sonar. We're not too far from the bottom. We should start seeing it soon."

Arielle activated the fan motors, and working them in opposite directions, she slowly pivoted the plane around in a circle. The faceted ice spheres became nearly invisible and slowed their rate of fall as they entered the water-rich layers of ocean near the bottom. They still refracted the light slightly, so it was like looking through a poorly made window pane. The landing lights from the twirling, falling plane picked out a white reflection in the distance.

"There'f fomething!" said Arielle. She expertly reversed the fan controls and brought the plane back around so that the searchlights illuminated the pointed white object. As the plane continued down, the point slipped upward into darkness, and the light beams illuminated the steep slopes of a white mountain.

"It looks like the Alps!" said Katrina. "It's an underwater glacier!"

As they continued their fall, the distant slopes flattened out and began to approach them in the light beams. Arielle turned the landing lights downward and saw the surface below rising rapidly up to meet them.

"Get ready for landing!" she said, and increasing the fan power to provide maximum lift, she attempted to slow their rate of descent. The surface rose beneath them, and there was a jar as the nose buried itself in the slushy surface, followed by a thump from the rear as the tail hit. Shirley lost her grip and stumbled backward down the cabin. George grabbed her as she went by. He nearly lost his grip on a handhold trying to catch the amazon, but together they got her feet back under her on the slanted deck. They were on the ten-degree slope of the glacier, facing upmountain.

"Is the hull tight?" Shirley asked her imp. She was worried. Even a tiny leak of that poisonous water and they would all have to get into suits until it was fixed and the air cleared.

"The hull is fine," reassured Jill. "I think I can even back off on the internal pressure a little. I'll do it slowly so your ears won't pop."

Shirley gave George a thank-you hug for the rescue and went down to the back to check out the equipment lockers to make sure nothing had been jarred loose by their rough landing. George went forward to the control deck and tapped Katrina on the shoulder, motioning for her to get out of the copilot seat. The aliens had insisted on taking them down here; now it was his job to get them back up and out into space where they belonged.

Katrina babbled on as she unbuckled her seatbelt and relinquished the copilot seat to George.

"It's just like the Moteratsch glacier near Pontresina in the Swiss Alps! If only I had brought my skis!"

George sat down. He looked over the cockpit display to familiarize himself with Arielle's setup, then spoke in a grumpy voice.

"The only thing I'm sure of is that it's *not* the Alps. Where are we, Jill?"

A map showed up on his display. From the shading and angle, it was obviously a sonar map that Jill had taken on the way down. At the top portion of the screen was a large circular depression. Running out away from the circle were dark ridges of stone, and between the ridges were rivers of ice. A small blinking dot showed their position partway down on one of the glaciers.

"We're on the side of an underwater volcano," said George. "It's a big one, like those on the real Hawaiian Islands. If the water weren't so deep here, they would be sticking up in the air for a few kilometers. Fortunately, this one doesn't seem to be active, since the crater is filled with snow." He looked at Arielle and raised his right eye, asking for permission to touch the controls. She nodded and he moved the landing lights back and forth, trying to pick up their local terrain.

"I've got the aliens on the infrared scanner," said Katrina from the science-scan instrument console. Most of them are still rocked up, holding us down, but two of them seem to be talking together on the left wing."

"Can you understand them, Jill?" asked George.

"I can pick up some of it," said Jill. "Something about getting us out of danger. I still don't understand why they dragged us to the bottom, but I think they think they're doing us a favor."

"Do you get any inkling of what they're going to do next?"

"They are talking about bringing something big, but I don't know what it is."

☆It's cold! And boring!☆ murmured a small soft tab of flesh attached to a large red rock sitting on the wing.

◇Then we'll stay here holding Floating⊗Rock down while you go break off a big chunk of ice and bring it back. ◇

☆That's hard work!☆

✳I'll go then. You stay here rocked up. ✳

△Can I go, too?△

◇Not this time. Just one can go. The rest must stay rocked up until we get enough ice rocks to replace us. ◇

☆I'll go!☆ The large red rock rapidly dissolved and expanded into a huge red cloud. It swam rapidly off toward the foot of the glacier, mumbling as it went.

☆Cold! Tired! Boring! Rather be surfing!☆

Soon it returned pushing a large flat plate of ice. Jill caught a glimpse of it as it settled on the wing.

"They are loading up the wing with blocks of ice," said Jill.

"They really mean to make us stay on the bottom," said George. "Can't you to tell them to stop?"

"They are deliberately ignoring me," said Jill. "We'll just have to wait until they are ready to talk."

"Should I get Arielle to try to shake the ice block off by rocking the fans?" asked George. "It can't be too heavy, despite its size. It is only a little denser than the ocean water and the gravity is low here."

"No," said Jill. "Not yet. They have some good reason for what they are doing. Let's wait and find out what it is."

☆That's two. Hard work!☆

◇ Soften up again, Warm✳Amber✳Resonance, and help Roaring☆Hot☆Vermilion bring more ice rocks. ◇

Working together, the yellow and red clouds soon had the top of the wing covered with large chunks of ice, and the remainder of the flouwen relaxed their hold on the *Magic Dragonfly*. They tried to place similar chunks on the tailfins, but the heat exchangers in the tail surfaces melted them off. More blocks were added to the wing and placed on top of the fuselage, where the inside heat escaping from the hull soon melted a groove in the underside of the blocks so they balanced on top.

◇ There! That should make them safe enough. ◇

✳The time is getting close. We should go!✳

◇ First I must tell Floating⊗Rock and the Stiff⊗Movers about the dangerous time. But there are so many words that it doesn't know. It will take time. ◇

✳Since the Stiff⊗Movers can't look, but they can see, perhaps we can tell them faster with a body play rather than words. It would have to be a very simple body play, since they can't look inside the players as we do, but they could get the idea from seeing our outsides.✳

◇ Good idea. You are the best body player. What shall we do? ◇

✳Stiff⊗Movers think in terms of colors rather than textures. You be the icy white solid part of our world, and Dainty△Blue△Warble can be the ocean. Roaring☆Hot☆ Vermilion can be Hot. That's an easy part, just sitting there being a red globe.✳

☆Dumb part!☆

◇ You could make it more realistic by spinning around and having soft bumps on your surface. ◇

☆Warm has bumps?☆

◇Yes. I have seen them with my looking disk. ◇

☆Like this?☆ The red cloud turned into a rapidly spinning red sphere with bumps on it. The formless white cloud looked at the result with a few bursts of sharp sound.

◇Slower. Make the bumps smaller. Good. ◇

✳Not good. Hot should be spinning over there in front of Floating⊗Rock so that the Stiff⊗Movers can see.✳ A focused burst of sound rebounded from a point on the glacier some five meters in front of *Dragonfly*'s nose. The spinning red sphere drifted slowly over to the indicated point and hovered a few meters above the snowy surface, the shallow bulges on the spinning surface shining redly in the landing lights.

†Can I be in the body play?†

✳Certainly, Bitter†Orange†Chirr. You can be Warm and its pets. Can you do that?✳

†Easy. I'm good at body plays.† The large orange blob soon rearranged itself into a large sphere and four smaller spheres. The smaller spheres had nearly invisible threads connecting them to the main body so that they maintained contact with the major portion of the distributed nervous system. The collection of orange spheres started a large slow circular orbit around the red sphere.

✳You are too close. We will have to move in that region. Go out a little.✳

The orange sphere obeyed, as the stage for the body play was set. Clear ◇ White ◇ Whistle went over to Floating⊗ Rock and started to talk to the strange metal being. A peek through a disk lens confirmed that a number of Stiff⊗Movers were seeing their play from the clear places on Floating⊗ Rock.

◇Top of ocean not good, ◇ White Whistler said to Jill, with Jill translating for the benefit of the humans. ◇Time soon when sky . . . eat . . . top of ocean. ◇

"It wanted to use another word," said Jill. "But we don't have it in our joint vocabulary."

◇Good place is hot side of world. Inside islands. We swim there soon. You cannot swim fast. You must stay

here. Here is not good, but here is not bad. You not be
. . . eaten. Eaten not right word. We show you. Loud Red
is Barnard. O.J. is Gargantua and pets. Yellow Hummer is
Sky⊗Rock, Little Blue is ocean, and I am world, ◊ said
White Whistler.

"It'f a play!" said Arielle, delighted.

Shirley reached up to the cockpit ceiling and swung
down a video camera that peered over George's right
shoulder. With the two scanners on the side and the
ceiling camera, they would have a complete record of the
performance. The snow had let up a little, so the visibility
was excellent. As White Whistler swam off to join the
others, Jill could hear Yellow Hummer giving detailed
instructions to Little Blue. As they watched, White Whistler and Yellow Hummer turned into the egg-shaped forms
of Eau and Roche. Little Blue flowed around White Whistler, the blue color completely covering the larger white
body except for some spots on the outer pole. Twirling
smoothly, the miniature version of Rocheworld started its
elliptical orbit out near the orange globe of Gargantua and
moved closer to the deep red spinning sphere of Barnard.

"It's an amazingly faithful reproduction of the major
bodies in their star system," said George. "But I don't see
what they're up to. How could orbital dynamics be any
danger to us?"

"I don't know," said Jill. "But so far all they are doing is
repeating the portion of the orbit that we have already
experienced. I suspect whatever is bothering them occurs
at or near the periapsis of the orbit, since it is only nine
hours away."

"Could it be storms?" asked George.

"I doubt it," said Jill. "The heating from Barnard wouldn't
change that much in the last few hours."

"What is it, then?" said George.

Arielle turned and put her finger to her patched lip.

"Huf! I'm watching the play!"

George hushed and watched the play.

☆Am I pretty?☆
△Wheee! This is fun! Do I get to bloop over now?△

✳Not till I tell you.✳

◇ Besides, an ocean isn't supposed to talk. A Hot either, even if it is pretty. ◇

☆Hummm. Twirl. ☆

✳No humming either.✳

The blue and yellow eggs spun around each other as they moved between the red globe and the front of Floating⊗Rock. The blue ocean began to slosh back and forth.

△Do I go bloop now?△

✳Not this turn, but next one. Now!✳

△Bloop! This is fun!△

✳Now back. That's right. Now bloop again.✳

△Bloop!△

✳One more time and that's all.✳

△Just once more? That was fun bouncing into you.△

✳No. World only bloops three times, and we want the play to be a correct one.✳

△It's time again. Bloop!△

"My God!" said David. "The whole ocean is transferring from Eau to Roche."

"Not the whole ocean," said George. "But anyone on the surface near the inner pole during periapsis would find themselves under an eighty-kilometer-high interplanetary waterfall with millions of tons of water falling down on them."

"I don't see how that could be," said Richard. "I remember calculating the relative orbital displacements of Roche and Eau with Thomas when we were arguing whether the Rocheworld orbit was stable or decaying. The most the Barnard tides do to Rocheworld is to move the two lobes some three kilometers closer. That's nothing compared to the eighty-kilometer spacing."

Jill had been silent for some time, but now she spoke. "You forget the saddle shape of the gravity potentials at the center point. A change of only three kilometers in separation causes a large shift in the potential surfaces that connect the two lobes. Sea level on Eau is usually forty kilometers below the zero-gravity point, but with the two lobes closer together, the zero-gravity point moves within kilometers of the surface of the water. We also forgot to consider the inertia in the tides. When the two lobes are equally illuminated, the planets are pulled apart by twelve kilometers and the top of the ocean mountain drops fifty kilometers or so, then rushes back in the next three hours as the lobes line up with Barnard and the tides are at maximum. That large water shift is going from a broad source to a narrow region and should build up into a spectacular tidal bore. I can't figure it out because of the conical geometry and the changing gravity field, but it wouldn't surprise me if the bore wave didn't become many kilometers high and travel at tsunami speeds. There would be enough inertia to throw the whole top of the water mountain through the zero-gravity region onto Roche."

"How far did the wave go on Roche in the simulation play?" asked George. "It reached the site of Rocheworld Base, didn't it!"

"Yes," said Shirley. "We must warn them!"

"How?" said Jill, ever logical. "My radio, radar, and laser are all worthless this deep under water, and my sonar won't propagate through space to the commsats."

"There's got to be a way," said George. He looked up to see that the alien play had finished. Arielle's hands were giving tiny pitty-pats of applause. White Whistler flowed up and halted in front of the sonar dome.

◊ Do you understand? ◊

"Yes," replied Jill. She guessed at the meaning of an alien whistle that she had correlated with the motions of Little Blue. "When Eau and Roche are near Barnard, the ocean will 'bloop' over."

◊ Yes! Bloop can eat . . . make you a set of number zero. ◊

"I guess that's the closest they come to a word for death," said George.

◊ Bloop come soon, ◊ said White Whistler. ◊ We go now. You stay here. ◊

With that, White Whistler streaked off up the glacier at high speed, with the rest of the colorful group following.

"Call them back!" cried George. "We've got to get those

ice blocks off and get up to the surface to warn Rocheworld Base!"

"They don't respond," said Jill. "Besides, it would not be safe for you on the surface."

"We've got to do SOMETHING!" George yelled, his command responsibility weighing heavily on his shoulders.

"The best something we can do is wait," said Jill, the calm tone in its voice trying to soothe the emotional human. "You have been up for thirty hours . . ."

George felt a pair of small warm hands on his neck. They started to massage the tight shoulder muscles.

"Why don't you come back to the galley and let me make you a cup of hot chocolate," said Katrina. "Jill is right, you know."

George gave up and slowly rose from the copilot seat and followed Katrina down the aisle, muttering to himself as he went.

"Not a damn thing we can do except wait . . ."

For a long time Arielle, Shirley, David, and Richard stared out the cockpit window at the scintillating glitter of the faceted transparent spheres falling down on the white surface. The ammonia-water between the spheres would soon freeze into a slushy ice full of ammonia bubbles that gave the glacier its blue-white color.

"I've been up for nearly twenty hours," said David. "I think I'll go to bed, too." He went over and whispered something to Arielle. She shook her curly head violently, brushing him off.

"Not now!" she whispered. "I got much worrying to do."

David turned away and padded heavily downslope on the carpeted corridor. He paused near the galley. There was a nearly full cup of chocolate sitting there steaming. He doubted that George would be back before it was stone cold, so he lifted the cermasteel cup with its picture of a trainer airplane and downed the warming brew in a single gulp. It ballooned in his esophagus until it was almost painful, then oozed its way down to warm the pit of his stomach. It was a nice antidote for the frozen scene outside and the frozen attitude up front. He put George's cup back down on the counter and confronted the agitated galley imp.

"Fix him another cup," said David, feeling mean. "When —or if—he comes back for it." He went off to a lonely bed, while his place at the galley was taken by Shirley.

Richard got busy at the science console. He had found that the sonar could penetrate the layers of ice beneath them and map the underlying rock strata. It took Jill over one hundred pulses to build up a high-quality image through the scattering layers of ice. There was nothing else to do, so Jill concentrated on giving the human the best data it could gather.

"Is that a lava flow?" asked Richard, scribing with his finger the telltale outlines of a frozen stream of hardened rock.

"Let me check for continuity," said Jill, bouncing pulse after pulse at the smooth edge, looking for a break that indicated a subsequent event. There was none; the flow was unbroken, and even homogeneous as far as the weak echoes from inside it were concerned. Jill also noticed something else . . . There was a blurred infrared image on the surface of the glacier above that matched the extent of the rock flow below.

"The volcano may not be as dormant as we first suspected. There is a weak infrared contour on the surface of the glacier that follows the contour of the frozen rock flow below."

"Let's do a detailed scan of that region," said Richard. "Do you have time for one thousand pulses per scan element?"

"I have nothing else more important to do," said Jill, and started off the first of one billion sonar pulses that it would emit in the next twenty minutes.

Richard waited as the picture slowly built up on his screen. The first scan of the scene was finished in a second. It was seemingly random noise except where a sharp edge gave the human eye an advantage in picking out noise pulses from signal pulses. After a minute the picture was as clear as the one he had used for his preliminary analysis. The minutes dragged on, and the sonar picture slowly became sharper as bits were averaged with bits and the fuzz in the picture faded away. Richard got bored waiting and looked up from the science console at Arielle, sitting patiently in the pilot seat of the stationary airplane, vigilantly waiting for the time when she would again be given the task she was designed for. Richard allowed his glance to wander over the high forehead, the youthful mop of golden-brown hair, and the full lip with the hint of proud flesh. Through the slightly parted lips came a charming sparkle of multicolored light.

"It would be fun to see her laugh in a dark bunk," said Richard, seemingly unconscious of the red, green, gold, and blue sparkles that emanated from the imp on his shoulder, the imp that had lighted his way to bed every night for the past forty-five years. The elfin silhouette framed in the landing-light glare of the cockpit window suddenly swiveled. The perky nose lifted into the outline of a scrunched caterpillar. Richard smelled something, too, and exploded from his seat.

FIRE! his nose announced.

Richard's gaze swept over Shirley, who was sitting quietly in the galley—there was nothing wrong there. His glance swept back to Arielle, who was now sniffing under the edge of the control panel.

That probability covered, Richard started down the corridor with his head jerking back and forth, trying to uncover the source of the smell. As he converted from a panicked animal to a calculating machine, his brain had time to process all the photons that had entered his iris in the last few seconds. There was a soft patch of strange yellow-white light reflecting off the metal trim of the galley. It didn't take trigonometry and spectroscopy for Richard's brain to pinpoint the source as a candle sitting directly in front of Shirley.

Richard froze in the soft glare of that ancient light. It took no longer for Arielle to evaluate the situation, and she turned to resume her responsibility over her stationary command that was slowly freezing solid into a glacier.

Richard made his way back to the galley. Shirley was staring at the flickering light, her eyes full of tears and a forkful of Chicken Little halfway to her mouth. Richard approached and she put down the fork.

"A candle!?!" said Richard, not quite sure whether to chastise or question. Then he noticed the candle holder. It was an imp, glittering with tiny specks of laser light.

"It's all right," said Jill through his imp. "It's a special occasion."

Shirley slowly looked up at Richard, her eyes welling with tears. "It's my birthday candle," she said. "I light it every five years."

"Your birthday!" said Richard. "That's cause for a celebration, not crying!"

"Not if it's your seventy-fifth birthday," said Shirley, and burst into tears.

"Shirley! You silly goose. Birthdays don't mean anything anymore. Why, you don't look a day over thirty-five."

"I don't?" she said, sniffing back a tear. "But according to the adjusted calendar for the time I spent on No-Die, I'm at least forty-five years old."

"Nah!" he said. "You're in too good a shape for forty-five."

"Really?" she said.

"Really," he said, sitting down on the stool next to her to gaze into her deep-blue eyes. The candle imp extinguished the flame and skittered off to put the white wax candle back into the protective box in Shirley's personal locker, leaving the two holding hands in the darkness of the corridor, lit only by the faint beams of light streaming back from the snow-covered slopes spreading upwards in the beams from the landing lights. Silhouetted in the scattered light was a lonely pilot, watching intently out the windows, alert for any sign of danger.

"Thomas, come here for a minute and watch." Red Vengeance glanced down at her radar display, then out at the distant globe of Eau hanging in the sky.

"Eau is getting pretty active," she said. Thomas squinted a bit at the large red globe hanging over the dark mountain of water in the sky, then framed the scene between his two hands.

"It's a great shot!" he said. "I think I'll go get my long-distance lens." With a bound he was across the bridge and swinging down the passway to the crew quarters. He was back in less than a minute.

Red heard an electronic whistle as the liquid-crystal shutter activated and then a chitter as the microprocessor loaded the bits into a mass memory. It cost Electropix an extra few dollars to bridge a piezoelectric disk across the data bus so the customer would *know* that the picture was taken and stored, but it was those little touches that kept Electropix at the top of the heap.

There was another chitter from the camera, then Thomas, still peering through the lens, made a questioning sound.

"What is it?" asked Red. She looked up at Eau, then saw for herself. Rising from the top of the water mountain was a huge fountain of water. Slowly it rose and rose and continued to rise, glowing redly in the sunrise light of Barnard.

"Wow!" said Thomas, then all Red heard was the whistle-chitter, whistle-chitter of the Electropix, cramming bits into its nearly inexhaustible memory.

"It looks like a volcanic eruption on Io," said Red. "It must be because of the tides from Barnard."

"You didn't see it up close like I did," said Thomas. "It didn't rise up from inside like a hot bubble, it just drew back and jumped! Too bad it was dark on Eau when it started. I would have liked to see what caused it."

"That fountain must be ten kilometers high," said Red.

"It's twelve and a half kilometers," said Jack. "That was its maximum. It is starting to fall now."

"But it's getting so big!" said Red.

"Yeah!" said Thomas, his camera whistling into action again as the fountain spray spread out into a huge white oval.

"And it moves so slowly," said Red.

"That's 'cause it's so big," said Thomas, finally putting aside his camera. The oval was getting splotchy and completely inadequate for artistic photography, and besides he was sure Jack was taking very good scientific pictures of the eruption.

"It's developing a mustache," he said.

"Whorls of some kind," said Red. "They're going north and south, then disappearing into the shadow.

"Wait forty-five minutes," said Thomas. "Then Barnard will be shining straight down between the inner poles. Wow! Look at those clouds spread out!"

"Those winds must be something ferocious near the inner point of Roche," said Red. "Perhaps that's what causes the linear rift valleys leading away from the point."

"Either that, or it's stretch marks from the tides," said Thomas. "Look, the mustache ends are starting to curl."

"It looks like the top of a tornado," said Red.

"A tornado two hundred kilometers high and still rising!" said Thomas, reaching again for his Electropix. "Is it moving?"

"No," said Red. "Its base seems to be fixed to the high-density region between the inner poles. Thomas . . . ?"

"Yeah, Red? (whistle-chitter, whistle-chitter) Something bothering you? (whistle-chitter)"

"We can't run the ascent module in that weather. Tell *Dragonfly* to wait until after periapsis."

"What's the matter, Red? You chicken?" said Thomas, instantly regretting the flip comment.

There was a dead silence for a minute.

"This chicken didn't live to be thirty-eight in the asteroid belt by jetting off on stupid missions!" said Red furiously. "Have Jack check the numbers if you want. With those winds, the ascent module has negative margin. Goodnight, Thomas."

A green streak with a red head launched itself angrily across the bridge and down the passway, leaving behind a trail of gently falling drops of water that settled slowly to the cling-carpeted floor.

Thomas was left alone on the bridge. A short conversation with Jack confirmed that Red's intuition was correct. Conditions had changed enough that the crew on *Dragonfly* could not be rescued. The ascent module was designed for fighting gravity, not an Oz-sized tornado.

Thomas called up Carmen from the galley below.

"I think you'd better raise *Dragonfly* through the commsats," he said. "There's a change in plans." To comfort his personal agony over his mishandling of Red during a crucial situation, he nervously unholstered his camera and started taking more pictures. Later he would admit they were the worst he had ever taken.

Carmen finally broke through the preoccupation and the whistle-chitter. "None of the commsats have had any contact with *Dragonfly* in over three hours."

Thomas suddenly felt old.

Shirley, whose sleep was as light as that of a nervous young mother with a newborn, opened her eyes in the darkness of her bunk, the blackness softened by the tiny flicker of lights from the imp in her hair. Something had changed on *Dragonfly* and her alarm system had wakened her. She lay there listening to the subtle throbbings of a ship at work keeping six humans safe while submerged deep under a poisonous sea. There was nothing really wrong or Jill would have awakened her, but something had changed. She listened more intently, then she suddenly realized what it was that was bothering her. She couldn't hear! She swallowed violently and her ears cleared.

"We've changed pressure, Jill. What's going on?"

"The tides are getting stronger," said Jill through her imp. "The water level above us has dropped over ten kilometers in the last hour, so I changed the internal pressure accordingly. There is no danger, go back to sleep."

"Are you sure that the decrease in pressure won't trigger anything, like a phase change in the ice that will cause the glacier to fissure and swallow us up?"

Jill paused a second as she ran the various possibilities through a detailed analysis.

"Positive," said Jill. "Go back to sleep."

As Shirley closed her eyes and started the ten-second process of putting her brain back on idle, the tide above them reached its minimum. Deep within the bowels of the planet, a chamber of magma that had been kept bottled up by the overburden of water was finally able to push its way up to the surface, rumbling as it came.

"Earthquake!!!" shouted Shirley, who was out in the aisle and halfway to the engineering console before she woke up. Another rumble threw her against the galley. Holding on to whatever she could grab, and wishing that her bare feet had corridor boots on, she made her way forward through the rocking ship and strapped herself into the chair in front of the engineering console and started to take Jill through a checkout.

"What'f going on?" said a sleepy Arielle, who had tumbled out of her bed in her bunny suit and was now trying to keep upright by holding on to one of the stools in the galley. "If it an earthquake?"

"I don't think so," said George from up front. "It's been going on too long, and is getting stronger. I'm afraid that this volcano we're sitting on is about to erupt. I don't know what we can do about it, but you'd better get up here."

Arielle let go of the stool and started forward, but was thrown back into Richard's arms. The nearly naked young man, dressed only in shorts but wearing corridor boots to hide his disfigured feet, took the bunny-suited pilot under one arm. Carrying her forward, he installed her in her seat in the cockpit. Once there, the alert pilot brain checked over her console and turned to George.

"I try to get free," she said. "If I make fan go with earthquake, maybe I get ice off."

"It's worth a try," said George. "Go to it!" His eye caught something high above them in the unlit darkness at the peak of the mountain.

"My God!!!" he cried, his voice choked with fear. He pointed.

"It's red hot lava!" shouted Shirley. "It's coming down the mountain right at us!"

"It's got to eat through a lot of glacier before it gets to us," said Richard. "Get us out of here, Arielle!"

Arielle, like every test pilot living, became even calmer and more deliberate in her motions as the danger grew.

"I think I'll try a yaw twift," she said, operating the fan levers in synchronism with the shaking of the ice beneath them. She kept it up for ten seconds, then stopped.

"Nope," she said. There was a second's pause in her

motions while her brain moved at high speed through her other options.

"Now I try fome pitch," she said, and tried raising and lowering the nose of the plane with the fans in an attempt to buck the ice off. After another ten seconds she stopped.

"Nope."

A hushed silence fell over the crew, and David took advantage of a lull in the shaking to rush from his bunk to his computer console seat. Everyone was looking at Arielle.

"I've got the lava flow on the science scanner cameras," said Katrina. "It's moving at a kilometer per minute through the glacier. Through the infrared imager you can see a wall of melted water flowing down just ahead of it and getting bigger as it comes."

George switched his console to the infrared scanner display. A white-hot tongue of fire flowed down from the top of the mountain to the middle of the screen, where it met the cool-blue ice of the glacier. At the intersection was a roiling mound of yellow with large blue chunks floating on the surface.

"What are those blue chunks?" he asked.

"They look like blocks of ice," said Katrina. "Yes, they must be. The glacier is pure water ice, which sinks in Eau's ocean because it is heavier than the ammonia solution. The mound of yellow is ice melted by the lava and is nearly pure water. The glacier ice will float on water, so it is breaking up into blocks and rising to the surface of the water mound as the lava burrows under the glacier and weakens its hold on the rock."

"Those blocks are as big as office buildings! Get us out of here, Arielle!"

"Let me fee now," said Arielle calmly. "Maybe a yaw twift with a pitch maneuver . . ." Tiny hands rapidly flickered over the controls, and *Dragonfly* bucked and pitched in an attempt to get free.

George stared at the infrared scanner image showing the yellow wall of warm water pouring down the slope at them at high speed. They only had a few seconds before it would be on them.

"Nope," said Arielle calmly. "Hmmm . . . Maybe . . ." and the plane lunged backward and stuck.

George looked up from the screen and gazed out the cockpit window. He turned the landing lights upward. He couldn't see the invisible wall of water sweeping down on them, but he could see, floating hundreds of meters above the surface of the glacier in seeming defiance of gravity, blocks of white ice tens and hundreds of meters in size, tumbling through the turbulent water.

"Nope," said Arielle. "Maybe . . ."

"Brace yourselves," commanded George.

The *Magic Dragonfly* surged upward as the tongue of warm heavy water swept under its wings and lifted it up.

"The ice blocks are floating off the wings!!!" shouted Shirley.

George noticed that he was no longer in control of the landing lights. He glanced quickly at Arielle and saw flickering eyes on a serious face alternating glances between console display and cockpit window. He turned his glance back out the window. They were rising rapidly up the steep slope of the flowing water. Ahead of them was a tumbling block of jagged ice over thirty meters in diameter.

"Twelve o'clock high!" he said.

"Got it," said Arielle. The nose dipped and *Dragonfly* dove deep into the water. George watched the undersurface of the iceberg pass overhead, not ten meters away. Now that they were deep in the water, they were relatively safe from the ice chunks floating above, but they were being carried downslope by the turbulent water. *Dragonfly* creaked as its wings were stressed near their limits.

"Can't ftay here," said Arielle. "Up we go. Help me find gap." She turned the giant plane on its tail and applied full thrust with the fans to accelerate the rise of the buoyant airplane in the dense water. George peered out, trying to see beyond the reach of the landing lights. There was a large white shadow far above them, then another.

"Bogey at twelve o'clock, another at two o'clock low . . . a little one at eleven . . ."

Arielle went into a spiral, then stopped with the wings

aligned with the flow of the water. The shaking and creaking abated a little as they drew closer to the ice-cluttered surface.

"Big one at twelve o'clock low," warned George.

"Fee anything on the high fide?" she asked, adding her eyes to his.

"Nope," he said.

"Then we go that way," said Arielle, pulling them upside down for a moment, then resuming the upward climb. George watched the iceberg pass beneath their nose as the plane broke through the surface of the dense water. The plane hesitated as it entered the lighter ocean water and lost much of its buoyancy, then continued its climb on the fans. Arielle set the controls for a steady climb, then changed her display to the sonar.

"How far to the top?" she asked.

"Twelve kilometers," said Jill. "At our present rate of ascent we should reach the surface in two hours, but the tide is coming back in and the surface level is increasing, so it will take longer than that."

There was a rumble through the water. Arielle tilted the plane back and they peered upside down at the volcano below them. A bright spot of yellow-white welled up from the crater and poured down the slopes in all directions, covering over the dull-red cooling flows that had preceded it.

"I'm really surprised that the flouwen put us there," said George. "They nearly killed us."

"Don't forget," reminded David. "They normally have better sense than to be in this part of the globe during periapsis. By the time they get back, the lava will have cooled off and been covered again by snow."

There was a rattle on the hull as they ran into a snow flurry of faceted hailstones. Arielle tilted the plane back, and they continued their climb. With the plane on autopilot, Arielle finally noticed the pink elastic cuffs on her wrists and looked down to see she was still in her bunny suit.

"I think I'll go get dreffed," she said to George, blushing slightly. She unbuckled her seatbelt and fluttered lightly down to the rear of the airplane. Richard climbed up to take her seat so he could look out of the window of the cockpit.

"That was close," he said.

"You just witnessed the most spectacular feat of underwater flying you'll ever see," said George.

"And with mismatched fans, too," added Richard. "That girl is *some* pilot!"

"Yeah," agreed George. "Pretty, too."

"Yeah!" agreed Richard.

"Men!" muttered Shirley.

"Ya!" agreed Katrina, as she kept the science scanners busy during their slow ascent.

After about half an hour Arielle climbed up to join them again. The neuskin bandage was off her lip and some carefully applied makeup made the fine line of scarless new skin almost invisible. She paused when she reached the cockpit, stuck her head up between the two men, and smiled. The mini-imp was still holding her tooth in place, and lights flashed between red lips.

"I have my seat back now?" she asked.

"Sure," said Richard. He unbuckled and climbed down, using various nooks in the scanner instrument racks as hand- and footholds. He paused to boost Arielle up to her seat, then stepped down to stand on the strut holding Shirley's console chair to the deck. She swiveled and looked up at him, her calves brushing against his.

"I'm making lunch down below," he said. "Any preferences?"

"Soup would taste good," she said.

"No soup," he said. "I just washed my hair, and with our attitude the way it is you'd be sure to spill some down on me. Finger foods only."

"Protocheese and an algae shake in a squeezer, then," she said.

Richard picked up some other orders in his climb down, and soon lunch was being passed up by a busy Christmas Branch as *Dragonfly* continued its vertical climb. Lunchbreak entertainment included a replay of the two-way snow show.

Through bites of a pseudosausage, George discussed the sonar display with Jill.

"What are those bars that move across the screen?" he asked.

"Those are wind waves," said Jill. "Although we have passed high tide and the ocean is falling again, the sun has heated up Eau's atmosphere, and the winds are now blowing up the mountain again. We're now so close to Barnard we get a lot of heating, and the winds are quite strong and make large waves."

"How large?" said George, not really sure he wanted to know.

"They are one hundred meters high, have a wavelength of fifty kilometers and are moving at two hundred kilometers an hour."

"That sounds dangerous," said Arielle in a worried tone. "Shall I slow ascent until waves die down?"

"Are the tops breaking?" George asked Jill.

"The sonar gives no indication of it," replied Jill. "Although I am sure they will as they approach the inner pole and grow larger."

"No, Arielle, keep her on the same heading," said George. "We've got to get to the surface and warn the crew in Rocheworld Base about the danger. Besides, I've got an idea for putting those waves to a good use."

SURFING

"Two kilometers to go!" said Shirley from the engineering console. She took another sip of her algae shake and grabbed the squeezer between her knees as her fingers tapped over the screen.

"Whoops!" cried Katrina. "What happened?"

The airplane heaved upwards, rotated slightly, then dropped again, in the process shaking something loose that clattered its way to the tail of the airplane.

"It was a wave going by overhead," said George. They continued their rise. The darkness above began to turn into a dark green, then grew lighter and redder.

"Good!" said George. "These waves are a little sportier than I'm used to, but at least it'll be daylight when we break the surface so I can see them coming."

"What are you going to do?" asked Richard, his head sticking up into the cockpit area.

"We're still a hundred kilometers from the ninety-five percentile confidence pickup footprint region," said George. "The waves are heading our way, so I'm going to surf them! This is going to be rough, so get into your bunk. In fact, I want David and Katrina to strap into your beds, too. Shirley! You stay at the engineering console. The minute we break the surface I want you to lock onto a commsat and send a message to Rocheworld Base to warn them of the interplanetary waterfall. The first one is only two hours away."

"Right!" said Shirley, and her hands became busy on the screen as she set up the automatic track, lock, and speedsend of the critical message. Richard climbed down past her, pausing to let David and Katrina descend ahead of him. As he passed by Shirley, he gave her a friendly pat on the shoulder.

"Go to it, Marconi."

George looked over at Arielle.

"I've got it, Arielle," he said. She lifted her hands from the controls, tightened her seatbelt and lay back, her hands folded across her stomach, but her eyes constantly flickered back and forth between console and cockpit window. George rolled the plane from its vertical climb into a steep bank, headed in the same direction as the wave motion.

Until now I've regretted that decadent summer I spent between college and flight school. Three whole months in Hawaii doing nothing but surfing. This is one crazy surfboard, but it's the best I've got. He ran the fans up until an overspeed indicator lit up. Watching a plan map on his screen that showed a line indicating a wave overtaking a tiny red dot, he pushed the speed control even higher, and the *Magic Dragonfly* shot upward. It broke through the surface of the water on the forward face of the speeding wave. For a few seconds the plane was airborne again, enough so that its tail broke free of the water. George dipped the nose and dove down the sloping front of the wave, gaining even more speed, then the airplane-turned-surfboard settled the bottom of its hull into the water. George kept the fans lifting, and that, together with the rush of air passing under the wings, kept the hull from sinking and dragging them under.

"Comin' down!!" hollered George, his hands constantly moving to keep the plane balanced on the blanket of air passing under its wings. Behind him he could hear Shirley talking with Carmen and Thomas. While the speedsend message was clattering over the link between Jack and Jill through *Walter*, carrying a complete description of the alien play and Jill's interpretation of it, Shirley talked directly with Thomas.

"At the next high tide, there is going to be the first of a number of transfers of the ocean from Eau to Roche," she said.

"That bad?" said Thomas. "We saw the tidal bore turn into a geyser at the last change of tides, but that one just blew a little spray into the zero-gee region. We never realized that it would go that far."

"What tidal bore?!?" asked Shirley.

"This one," said Thomas. For a second Shirley watched his face glancing down at the console screen in front of him, and then his face was replaced with a speeded-up time-lapse picture of a large ring wave starting at the base of the water mountain just after low tide and rising rapidly up the conical mountain of ocean as a single high-speed wave with a steep front.

"It covers six hundred kilometers in the hour and a half between low and high tide," said Thomas, "and it gets bigger and meaner as it's compressed into the smaller and smaller area around the peak. You'd better dive under again before it gets you."

"We can't," said George. "*Dragonfly* was never meant to be a submarine. Unless we have some rocks or heavy aliens for ballast, we always have positive buoyancy. We'll have to think of something else." His words sounded strained as the effort to maintain the delicate balance of lift, speed, and drag on the face of the moving wave began to take its toll.

"We're moving pretty fast," said Shirley. "Can we turn on the nuclear jet and take off?"

"I'm aquaplaning and the tail is dragging the surface," George said. "If I open the air scoops, all they'd scoop up would be water and the nuclear jet can't handle that."

"How about the monopropellant?" said Shirley. "I know it's meant for space use, but it could at least get us airborne enough so that we could switch to the nuclear jet."

"I'm afraid not," said George. "Don't forget that the exhaust port is underwater. If I introduced the monopropellant into the chamber it would be like trying to fire a shotgun plugged with dirt. We'd blow the tail off."

"There must be some way," said Shirley. "How about having Jill divert some of the crew air supply through the jet in place of the monopropellant? That would give us enough boost to get airborne, then we could open the scoops and turn on the nuclear jet. I'll get Jill to figure out whether it will work."

"Such diversion of crew air supply is not allowed," said Jill in a severe tone. "Calculations will not be done on disallowed options."

Shirley didn't argue, but turned to her console and spoke as she typed in a code word.

"SEM-1, this is Chief Engineer Shirley Everett. Suggested diversion of crew air supply is essential to save crew from certain death by tidal wave. Obtain authorization to consider diversion from Flight Commander and Mission Commander, then proceed with analysis."

In a few seconds Shirley heard Jill again through her imp. "I still object to the diversion, but my objections have been neutralized. The analysis shows that your plan is feasible, although it will take the Christmas Branch fifteen minutes to rearrange the plumbing in the tank section. The amount of stored gas available is still not enough to lift the plane from the water by itself. We will need more airspeed and a downhill run."

"I can get that," said George. "On the face of a wave—the bore wave. If it's big enough and we time things just right, we can be airborne before we get trapped by the curl at the top." As he talked, he adjusted the pitch of the nose, and the plane lifted a little and climbed up to the top of the wave.

"The wind is dying down, and this wave is going to peter out soon anyway," he said. "Might as well get off here and get ready for the big one." He dipped, then rose, and the wave slipped out from under them and the *Dragonfly* settled into the trough behind. The short day was almost over, and Barnard was setting in back of them over Eau. They watched the sunset through the long-distance lens of the scanner video, and as they watched, a frothy wave grew on the horizon and swallowed up the sun.

"We're going to have to do this in darkness," said George

to Shirley. "I want you to get me an infrared and low-light-level video picture of this region from the commsat, then go back and check out the crew." He turned to Arielle.

"Get your suit on, Arielle, then come back and relieve me. If the wave gets us, *Dragonfly* is going to get broken up. Not that the suits will keep us alive much longer," he said with a grim face as she made her way back through the heaving corridor.

"Richard, Katrina, David!" said George. "Suit up! Then David and Richard come forward and take up your console stations. Katrina, as soon as you have your suit on, you'd better get back in your bunk and strap in."

"I still have some chemical analyses to do on the water samples that we took on the way up," said Katrina. "I'll fasten my safety lines to the Christmas Branch's work wall. It is essential that the data be transmitted back to *Prometheus* before the wave hits."

George shrugged. It really didn't matter where she was. There was no "safe" place anywhere on the plane. She was probably right to keep on working, too. It sure kept you from brooding about the dangers ahead. He took the advice, and clearing his screen, pulled in the infrared image from the commsat overhead. *Dragonfly* was a tiny hot cross in the middle of a blue ocean. He zoomed the picture back until *Dragonfly* was a tiny white dot, then he saw the warm yellow whitecaps at the peak of the bore speeding toward them, leaving a roiling, blotchy sea of warm and cold patches behind it.

"How much time do we have?" he asked Jill.

"Twenty minutes," said Jill.

Arielle was standing at his shoulder, her pert face and curly hair distorted by the fishbowl helmet on her head.

"Your turn," she said, climbing into the pilot seat and copying his display.

"Not much to do except wait," said George. "See you soon." He made his way to the back where Shirley was waiting for him, holding his suit open for him to step in.

"How is the tank switchover going?" he asked.

"It was completed five minutes ago," she replied. "Fortunately we had never used the monopropellant line, so it didn't need to be purged. Here, let me get that zipper while you get your helmet on."

Fifteen minutes later everyone was suited up and at their stations. "I've got it on the scanner camera," said Shirley. David picked up her display on his console and watched the stars disappear one by one as the horizon in back of them rose up into the air. "It's a kilometer high!" he said.

"It is one point seven kilometers high and growing," said Jill. "It will be over two kilometers tall by the time it reaches us."

"The bigger the better," said George, increasing the speed of the fans into their danger region once again as *Dragonfly* swam away from the approaching wave. "There is no way we can build up enough speed to surf this one, but if it's tall enough, we can get airborne and away before the whitecaps at the top slap us down."

The view from the back through the scanner camera became blacker and blacker as the wave rose up to cover the sky. The crew felt the plane tip forward and rise as if they had hit an updraft. The horizon in front of them dipped, and the landing lights peered downward at the falling ocean surface. They were a half-kilometer up in the air.

"Now!" said George as he manipulated the controls that normally controlled the thrust level of the monopropellant rocket system. The plug of water was blasted from the jet exhaust by a burst of air, and *Dragonfly* leaped forward. The sea was briefly illuminated with a brilliant yellow-white blowtorch flame from behind as the oxygen combined with the ammonia and methane in the atmosphere.

"Wow!" said George. "I forgot about that effect." He turned to Arielle. "We're in the air."

"I've got her, George," she said. She dove down the surface of the wave until they had sufficient airspeed, then opened the atmosphere scoops and pushed forward on the throttle for the nuclear jet. There was a pale glow from the rear as the heated atmosphere rushed from the exhaust and the plane started to fly away from the face of the towering wall of water. A cheer arose inside the plane, echoed by cheers from the lander; then a noticeable fraction of a second later cheers could be heard from the remainder of the crew on *Prometheus*.

"We're airborne, Rocheworld Base. We'll meet you at L–4 where we can watch the show, then transfer for the trip out to *Prometheus*."

Suddenly there was a yellow-orange glare from behind and the ominous thuds of control rods being jammed into a reactor core at emergency speeds. The thrust stopped.

"Reactor overheated," reported Jill. "We have a major leak in our liquid-sodium heat-exchanger loop."

"It was corrosion from the ocean water," said Shirley. "I was afraid of that, but there was nothing we could do."

"Switch to monopropellant!" hollered George, beginning to panic. "We've got to get altitude!"

"The monopropellant tanks are no longer connected to the jet," reminded Jill.

"Fire the air jet again, then . . . Do something!"

"I will glide," said a quiet voice, and the silent cabin tilted as the tiny pilot traded altitude for speed and came into equilibrium with the wave above and behind them, gliding on the pocket of air pushed in front of the wall of water.

Using her glider experience, Arielle slid back and forth on the air in front of the bore, gaining a little altitude each cycle. The crest of the wave was still far above them, growing taller as they approached the inner pole. Arielle called up a commsat low-light-level video image of the ring wave converging to a central point. On one side of the ring was the dot of *Dragonfly*, its landing lights making it visible from space. For a long time Arielle stared at the screen, judging the motion of the aerospace plane and the converging ring-shaped bore wave moving up the water mountain to the peak, and trying to visualize the invisible ring of trapped air just inside the water ring. Suddenly she dipped the nose of the silently gliding airplane, and trading altitude for speed, streaked down the surface of the wave and out across the flat ocean, putting the wave temporarily behind.

"Just like the cliffs at La Jolla," she said as she streaked

straight at the opposite wall of the twenty-kilometer-high
ring wave. Now, trading kinetic energy for altitude, she
zoomed almost straight upward. Rolling out, she picked
up the top of the air geyser that was starting at the center
of the ring. They were thrown upward, and Arielle fought
her way out from the turbulent center to the strong outside winds.

George stared at his screen in fascination with the converging ring of white water as seen from the commsat. The
ring turned into a foaming circle.

"The water geyser has started," said Shirley. "You'd
better get us to one side. It has a lot more energy and
inertia and is going to blast its way up here at high
speed."

Arielle nodded and pulled out and upward.

"We're only ten kilometers from the zero-gee point,"
said David, watching a trajectory plot on his console screen.

Arielle allowed herself a little smile.

"We make that easy," she said. "Then she is all downhill
to Rocheworld Base. How many do we have to go?"

"Fifteen hundred kilometers," said David. Arielle was
silent for a minute.

"Well, I have forty kilometers altitude, too bad my
Dragonfly is not a real glider. I could make that easy.
Well, we shall see." They all hung loosely in their seats as
Dragonfly shot through the zero-gravity neck and started
downward for Roche.

"Look ahead," said Arielle, pointing to a thin line of red
light on the dark globe ahead of them. "We have come out
on the other side. It is dawning at Rocheworld Base."

"Here comes the geyser," said Shirley, who was watching toward their rear through the scanner instruments.

George copied her screen. It was too bad that the
sunlight wouldn't reach into the inner poles for another
hour. If it was this impressive on the infrared scanner, it
would have been spectacular on video.

"How thick would you say it is?" he asked.

"About ten kilometers," said Shirley. "The column is
starting to break partway up."

George watched as the top portion of the geyser pushed

its way through the narrow gravitational neck between the two planets, then started its slow fall toward the rocky lobe below. In the infrared scanner, every one of the volcanic craters below the falling, frothy blob had a bright red pseudocolor, while the pseudowhite ones could be correlated with the view out the cockpit window of the patches of dull red dotting the black peak of Roche ahead. On the Eau side of the blob, the geyser column thinned out as the base fell back under its gravitational pull, while the top portion continued to coast through the zero-gravity region.

"That's the first one," said George. "Get me Rocheworld Base, Shirley." Soon Red's concerned face was on his screen.

"The first batch of water has transferred over and is heading for the surface. We've still got fifteen hundred kilometers to go and no propulsion power. The only thing that's keeping us up is Arielle. You'd better leave without us. We'll try to crash-land on a high ridge when we run out of altitude, and if the next two transfers don't get us, you can come back again and pick us up."

"We're not leaving until we're in real danger," said Red determinedly. "How big is the water ball?"

"I would guess about ten kilometers in diameter," said George. "How about it, Jill? Will it get to them?"

"The amount of water transferred is sufficient to cover Roche to five centimeters deep."

"Hah!" said Red. "Just barely enough to get our feet wet."

"But you're in lowland country," said George, looking at the sunline moving rapidly across the surface of the rocky globe. "And right in line of one of those channels leading from the inner pole. It sure is obvious now what eroded those channels."

"What's the chances this first flow will get to Rocheworld Base, Jill?" he asked.

"Unknown," said Jill. "It depends on how much is absorbed as it flows."

"You just keep coming," said Red. "We'll stay here until we see the whites of their tides."

"The leading edge of the drop is hitting the surface," said Shirley. George switched his screen to her infrared scanner view. For a few seconds all he could see was a cold blue column seen from above, partially blocking a dull-red warm conical mountain with yellow and white hot spots. Then at the base of the column there exploded a boiling cloud of yellow as the icy water poured down on the red-hot lava of the erupting volcanoes and turned into steam. For twenty minutes the torrent continued to fall, and soon the base of the waterfall was hidden in an expanding cloud of steam. From the bottom of the cloud streaked rivers of water streaming down the channels, riding a layer of steam over the tops of the tongues of lava that had preceded them. Fingers of steam rose into the air, twirled by the strong Coriolis forces near the center of the rapidly spinning double-planet system. Large, lazy tornadoes were spawned and moved ahead of them across the sunlit planet.

"Just what I need," said Arielle, putting *Dragonfly* into a dive that was aimed at the base of the nearest tornado.

"What are you doing!" shouted George in alarm. Yet he knew better than to try to stop her.

"We still have thousand kilometers to go and I need altitude," said Arielle. She turned to grin at him, knowing full well what was bothering him. "You Western types are used to tight, nasty one-gee twisters that can rip apart airplanes," she said. "Just look at throat on that one, George. It over kilometer in diameter. Just pretend it's a thermal—with clouds in it."

George did relax a little at that image as Arielle dove the plane at the ground. Timing her approach carefully, she swooped in under the funnel at high speed as it lifted a few hundred meters from the surface. She slammed *Dragonfly* into a tight bank and started spiraling up.

"Are you *sure* you've never flown fighters?" asked George as the gee load pinned him to his seat.

It may have been a lazy tornado, but it was still more tornado than thermal. The first few turns were through rough air that had *Dragonfly* creaking. Something broke loose in the rear of the plane and banged around until the

Christmas Branch corralled it. It was dark gray inside the funnel, but they had plenty of light from the almost continuous flashes of lightning. *Dragonfly* was struck twice on the wing and had Shirley and Jill frantically reconfiguring circuits to work around burned-out cables. As they spiraled upward, the radius of the funnel widened and the turbulence dropped. They clattered through a small cloud of blue hailstones, then flew out the top just in time to witness the sun setting behind Roche. Arielle set the plane on a long shallow glide angle and reached up to take off her helmet.

"We have still a thousand kilometers to go, but now we have some altitude. It is not enough, though." She turned to look at Shirley. "Could I please have monopropellant tank reconnected?"

"Jill and I did that long ago," said Shirley. "But it isn't going to do us much good. It'll only give us fifteen minutes of thrust."

"That's enough to get us up out of here to L–4!" said George.

"If that were true, I'd have reminded you long ago," said Shirley. "Unfortunately we no longer have the nuclear reactor to augment the monopropellant exhaust velocity. By itself the monopropellant isn't strong enough to put us in orbit, even in this low-gee planet."

"But it can give me altitude," said Arielle. "And altitude means distance."

Arielle turned to George. "Keep glide angle shallow and let me know when we at one kilometer altitude. I'm going to get something to eat and take a nap." She hopped down from the flight deck and made her way back to the galley, where a still open-mouthed George heard her order a huge meal from the galley imp. He shook his head and turned back to his console. There was no way he could get himself to sleep at this point. He looked at the control settings, started to reach for them, then slapped the back of one hand with the other.

"No need to fiddle with them, George," he muttered to himself inside his helmet. "The lady's setting is perfect." To pass the time he watched the second of the interplanetary waterfalls as seen from *Clete* and *Walter* at L–4 and L–5, and discussed them with Shirley and Red.

"This one looks smaller," said George. "Of course, I was closer to the last one."

"It is smaller," said Red.

"How come?" said George. "We're closer to periapsis and the tides should be stronger."

"Thomas has been modeling the details of the system, including simulating the ocean with a collection of tiny mass points. There is some complicated interaction of the orbital dynamics with the rotary dynamics and the tidal dynamics that makes the periapsis high tide slightly smaller than the high tides just before and just after periapsis."

"Don't forget the atmosphere," said Shirley. "At periapsis Barnard is heating Roche and Eau is in shadow, so the atmospheric winds are blowing down the mountain. At the high tides on either side, Barnard is heating Eau, boiling off the ammonia and adding wind waves to the tidal bore."

"There doesn't seem to be as much steam this time either," said George, as they watched the blob of water fall on the volcanoes and drown them in a torrent of icy liquid. The sun was rising on the other side of Roche and although both airplane and lander were in darkness, *Clete* gave them a sunside view of the forming of the north and south polar vertical tornadoes, made visible by the steam boiling up from the point of Roche.

"Wow! Look at that!" said Red as a silvery form sprang out from the shadows of the inner pole and moved rapidly across the sandy valleys of Roche.

"That's why I think you'd better get ready to leave," said George. "The volcanoes are drowned and no longer boiling away the water. With the head and the velocity that the blob builds up dropping the forty kilometers from the zero-gee region, you get air entrapment, just like an avalanche. Those fronts must be moving at five hundred kilometers an hour."

"I've got an infrared image of the flow below us," said Shirley.

"Let's see it," said George, and his screen flickered to show the dull-red warm rock beneath them. Streaking out in fingers from the grooves worn in the rocky point of Roche were blue, cold streams of high-speed menace.

"Doesn't look good," said George. "Are you ready to go?"

"Yes," said Red. "But we've voted to stay."

George started to argue with her, then lapsed into silence as one by one the fingers of speeding cold water seemed to stumble and break into a warm yellow froth as the trapped air layer failed and dumped the tons of high-speed water into the salty sands, where it spread into a more slowly moving flood.

"See, George," said Red. "No problem."

"That one got within one hundred kilometers of you," said George. "You leave when the next one hits. That's an order!"

"You just get here before it does," said Red. She paused. "That's an order."

"Yes, ma'am!" he replied.

"We're at three kilometers altitude," reminded Jill.

"Wake Arielle up," he said. "We need altitude."

Ten minutes later Arielle strolled down the corridor, dressed in a freshly pressed tailored jumpsuit and nibbling on a large chunk of pseudocheese. She paused at Shirley's console.

"We are ready with a maximum altitude program?" she asked pleasantly.

"It will use all but ten percent of the monopropellant, but I can give you twenty-five kilometers," replied Shirley. Arielle wrinkled her nose, then had a short conversation with her imp.

"I take all one hundred percent," she said.

"Don't you need some in case there is a problem with the landing approach and you have to go around? Don't forget you don't have the VTOL fans."

"Don't forget," Arielle smiled. "There is no such thing as a go-round in a shuttle landing." She tossed her head back to get the curls out of her eyes, climbed up to the pilot seat on the flight deck, and strapped herself in.

"We are ready?" she asked. Then after a pause she dove the airplane at the invisible surface below.

"I do wish you had your radar, Jill," she said as she watched the blurred infrared image grow in her screen.

"Aren't we getting a little close?" said Jill.

"The monopropellant gives better thrust when used with high-density air," said Arielle confidently.

When the infrared image stopped looking blurred, Arielle pulled *Dragonfly* out of its dive, opened the atmosphere scoops slightly, and shoved the throttle all the way forward and held onto it as she turned the long-winged airplane into a vertical rocket. Only when the roaring at the rear of the plane had subsided into some empty coughs did the little hand pull the throttle back to its initial position. No other motion was made as the plane coasted upwards on its inertia, the crew floating lightly in their harnesses after the high-gee climb. At the very top of the climb, Arielle switched to the space attitude control system, and with the last bursts of monopropellant left in the lines to the nose jets, she tilted the plane forward and again started the long glide toward Rocheworld Base.

"Five hundred kilometers to go," she said. "How much time do we have?"

"The next waterfall comes in ten minutes," said David. "But it takes twenty-five minutes to fall, and then the flood has to travel from the inner pole to Rocheworld Base. It depends upon how fast the water travels, and that depends upon how long it stays in the air-entrapment state. It could be two hours, it could be four, it could be that it never even gets there and we have all the time in the world."

"I think I go faster," said Arielle, tilting the nose of the plane slightly. She then put her console into compute mode, and long fingernails tapped on the screen as she and Jill optimized a curved trajectory that would put them at Rocheworld Base at zero altitude in minimum time.

"This is going to be a big one," said Shirley, watching the ring bore build up on Eau through the infrared imager on the commsats. Richard was sitting next to her on the science console. His screen had two pictures: one just like Shirley's, and the other taken at a similar time in the first of the tidal transfers.

"There must be a partial resonance in the ocean basins of Eau," said Richard. "This one is bigger than the first one that had the wind helping it."

The entire crew except Arielle watched in fascination as the ring wave contracted and generated a thick climbing column of water. The deadly menace rose like the head of a cobra from its coiled base. The underportions of the column thinned while the top portion that had enough momentum to overcome the weakening gravity continued upward and squeezed its bulk through the zero-gravity neck, compressed to a ten-kilometer-wide throat by the strong gravity gradients pressing inward around the zero-gravity point. The blob grew into an ellipsoidal ball on the other side and started to stretch as the lower portions were pulled along faster than the upper regions. Richard's screen had an overlay that Jill had traced out around the infrared image of the elongating ball.

"It's thirty kilometers long by twenty in diameter," said Richard. "That's enough to cover Roche a half-meter deep in water."

"And the volcanoes aren't going to be much help in evaporating this one," said George.

As the ball fell, it pushed air ahead of it and flattened out on the bottom. When it reached the surface, the trapped air built up in pressure and squeezed out at high speeds from the edges, only to find itself trapped by an enlarging blob of water that moved rapidly over the nearly frictionless air, trading its gravitational head and inertia for speed.

"The bottom is moving like an express train, and the top is still falling!" said George.

"It's faster than an express train," said Richard. He generated a new "tagger" from the menu at the side of the screen and moved it with his finger to the front of one of the racing tongues of water. The green cross "tag" stuck at the change of illumination between the blue cold water and the disappearing warm red rocks of Roche. Richard's finger went back to the menu and picked out the second parameter—VELOCITY.

580 KM/HR was Jill's reply on the screen.

"It'll be at Rocheworld Base in less than three hours," said Richard. "Are we going to make it in time, Arielle?"

"We also arrive in less than three hours," she replied calmly, her eyes on the groundspeed indicator. She pulled back slightly on the controls to take advantage of the slight tailwind in the level they were presently passing through. She would later use the altitude she had saved to gain more speed.

"Can you get us a more accurate time prediction, Richard?" asked George.

"I'll work on it," said Richard. A flick of his finger at the parameter ACCELERATION produced a positive number. He flinched, then read POSITION. He set up another tag at the position of Rocheworld Base, then read the separation.

"It's at thirteen hundred kilometers from the base and still accelerating," said Richard. "The top of the drop is just feeling the back-pressure of the ground below, and the pressurehead wave is still pushing out around the boundary. I'll have to wait until the acceleration stops before I can predict an accurate arrival time, but it looks like two hours and fifteen minutes."

George glanced at Arielle. She was moving very slowly and deliberately, with only the rapid moving of her eyes giving any indication of the whirling thought processes going on under the curly hair. She was in her "test pilot in trouble" trance. A silence fell over the ship as everyone waited for her to speak.

"I would like rest of air, please. At any point below two kilometers altitude would be useful." She dropped out of her trance and turned away to tend to her flying.

"Everyone back in their suits," George said. "And give Shirley one of your suit tanks. One tank will last more than two hours, and that's more time than that bore will give us."

"Reconfigure the plumbing again, Jill," said Shirley to her imp. "I'll get the tanks hooked up to the supply lines and you drain them as fast as you can." She swung from the console seat and walked down the corridor in the twelve percent gravity. At least they would have some solid footing for their dash to the lander.

Richard was soon suited up and back at his console, his bloated silver fingers pulling information off the image on the screen. The bore was now out in the sunlight. From a distance it looked like a river of quicksilver in the lined palm of an old Indian soothsayer.

"The pressure head is decreasing, but the velocity is six hundred ten kilometers an hour, three times faster than we're flying. Estimated time of arrival at Rocheworld Base is one hour and twenty-four minutes."

George looked quickly over at Arielle, looking for the trance. There was a pause as the colloid computer integrated a lifetime of experience in the air with the present situation and the new numbers.

"I think I have some bite to eat before I suit up," she said, hopping down from the flight deck. "I'm hungry. You keep watch on my *Dragonfly* for me, George?"

George grinned through his visor and checked over his control panels. For some reason his shoulders felt like they were moving to a region of lower gravity.

"Don't dawdle," he said in a pseudogruff voice. "Shirley wants to have Jill suck up the last of the cabin air after we're all in our suits." Arielle strolled down the corridor in her trim jumpsuit, weaving her way around the armored forms of Richard, David, and Katrina. She stopped at the galley for a slab of pseudochicken, then ignoring a patient Shirley holding up her open suit at the end of the corridor, she disappeared into the head.

Ten minutes later a refreshed Arielle with a newly remade face exited the bathroom, where she was met by an exasperated Shirley, who unceremoniously stuffed her into her suit. As soon as the last seal was closed, the suit started to balloon as Jill pumped out the air in the cabin and added it to the tanks.

"Two kilometers altitude, Arielle!" hollered George through his suit-imp.

"And the bore is at five hundred kilometers and still levitated," said Richard.

Arielle made her way carefully back up the corridor and climbed into the pilot seat. She checked the display carefully, her hands still folded in her lap. Satisfied, she raised her hands and nodded at George. He nodded back, and she took control again with the flick of a few switches.

"I'd like a status report, Richard."

"Bore distance from Base is four hundred sixty kilometers, velocity five hundred fifty kilometers per hour, arrival time forty-eight minutes."

"Jill, we arrive in forty minutes?"

"Forty-one," replied Jill.

"Too close," said Arielle. "I use air." She pushed forward on the controls and dove *Dragonfly* at the ground. As she pulled up she triggered the valve and the last of the air supply shot out of the jet in a blue-yellow flame. Arielle stopped the climb and pushed *Dragonfly* into a fast glide at a still-invisible target eighty kilometers away.

"Jill?" she asked.

"Twenty-four minutes."

"Richard?"

"Thirty-four minutes."

Arielle made one tiny adjustment to the controls, tightened her seatbelt and shoulder harness, then put her hands into her lap. She turned to look at George out of her helmet.

"We have hard landing," she reminded him.

"And just ten minutes to get the six of us up the side of the lander," George said as he tightened his seat belt and held a conversation with Shirley.

"You four get into the lock and cycle it, but don't open the outer door until we've stopped moving. Put your backs to the front wall and take some bedding to protect your helmets. Jinjur will never forgive us if we add anyone to her butcher bill."

"Are you and Arielle going to have time to cycle through? We could cram in six."

"You forget someone has to land this thing, and I'm not leaving Arielle up here all alone. The minute we stop I'm blowing the front canopy and Arielle and I will go out over the nose. Carmen! Are you monitoring?"

"Yes," came the reply from Rocheworld Base.

"Is the winch down?"

"Yes," came Red's voice over the intercom. "Ready and waiting. Hurry up!"

"I see the bore on the scanner video, it's gaining on us," said Richard.

"Give us a last reading on time difference, then get in that airlock!" said George.

"Eleven minutes," interrupted Jill. "Get into the airlock, Richard," she bossed. Richard obeyed and trotted to the rear of the plane and the lock door closed behind him. George and Arielle were left with the hiss of air passing over the silent airplane and the distant throb of airlock pumps going through their motions on almost nonexistent air. George could now see the lander, sticking up into the air, its dark outline standing to just one side of the setting globe of Barnard.

"Bad luck," complained George. "We're flying right into the sun."

"No! It's good!" said Arielle. "I can now see rocks easy because of their big shadow." She banked the plane slightly to pick a path that was relatively clear of boulders and gave up the last of her altitude for speed.

"BRACE YOURSELF!" screamed Jill to everyone but Arielle through their suit-imps. Arielle pulled the plane up into a stall.

"Flaps!" she commanded, both her hands busy, one with the airplane controls and the other operating the fans at full reverse thrust. George pushed at the flap controls but found that they were already moving.

"Flaps, down," he and Jill said at the same time. The plane started to drop heavily to the surface, but Arielle dipped it just enough to bring it under control again, the forward speed almost gone, and slid the plane through the sand directly at the lander.

We're going to hit! thought George, his voice too tight to speak.

Arielle wrenched the rudder around at the same time as she twisted the fan controls. The *Magic Dragonfly* went into a broadside slide and came to a stop with its nose on one side of the lander and the left wing on the other, not ten meters from the legs of the lander.

"I made ringer, George!" shouted Arielle with delight.

"BLOW THE HATCH!" came a sharp command in George's ear. His thumb flipped the safety latch, but a waiting imp beat his gloved finger to the switch. There was a loud BANG! and the cockpit windows flew into the air. The ammonia-methane atmosphere rushed into the plane and there was a dull THUMP! as the inflowing gasses burned with the residual air in the plane. George clambered out on the nose and jumped to the surface, then turned to catch Arielle. Together they hurried toward the distant lander. Jill, her voice turned into that of a martinet, drove them with verbal whiplashes. Over the voice George could hear some leakage from the high-speed data link between Jack and Jill.

"SHIRLEY, RICHARD, KATRINA, DAVID—TO THE WINCH.

"GEORGE, ARIELLE—UP THE LADDER.

"RED, START THE WINCH AND GET THEM UP AND IN!

"MOVE IT, GEORGE!

"ARIELLE IS WAY AHEAD OF YOU!

"MOVE IT, YOU FAT OLD MAN!"

George found another source of adrenaline in his anger, and he sprinted harder for the ladder. Arielle ran lightly up the rungs on the landing legs without using her hands, then when she reached the main body of the lander, crouched and leaped up the side of the rocket in the low gravity, then continued on, hand-over-hand, her legs dangling. George knew he couldn't do that, and scrambled after her. He got up the landing leg and paused to look up at Arielle.

"NO SIGHTSEEING! MOVE IT! MOVE IT!!! MOVE IT!!!"

Jill's voice took on a harsh tone that sent George back to his first week in ROTC summer camp under the tender ministrations of a drill instructor. Fear and hatred drove him up the ladder. He could see the wall of water coming over the horizon to his left, its foaming top colored blood-red in the setting sunlight. The water was swallowing the kilometers-long shadow of the lander as George clambered into the airlock filled with Red and the five others.

"I've got the winch stored," said Red. "Shut the outer door."

George was nearest the door and started to close it. He stopped. With him in the lock, there was no room for the door to close, and no time left to cycle the lock. He stepped back out onto the top rung of the ladder, holding himself steady with his left hand on the vertical handhold next to the door.

"George!!!" shouted Red, as George started to pull the door shut with his right hand. "Nooooo . . ." she wailed as he pushed the door lever over and locked himself outside.

"Take off, Thomas!!! That's an order!" said George through his imp.

The ten-meter-high wall of water hit the base of the rocket, and it started to tip.

"Got to go!" said Thomas.

The atmosphere around George was ablaze with flame as the ascent module lifted from the toppling rocket and boosted into the sky. George's feet slipped from the rung and he was left hanging by the inadequate grasp of his sausage-fingered gloves. As the acceleration built up he found his left hand slipping from the vertical handhold. He grabbed for the horizontal ladder rung and got it, but that cost him his right handhold on the door lever. Dangling by one hand from the bottom of the accelerating spacecraft, he was blinded, deafened, and burned by the exhaust from the powerful rocket engine. He felt the suit cooling shift to maximum power to prevent his legs from frying in the intense heat. He tried to get his right hand up to the ladder rung, but couldn't do it. They hit max-Q and the supersonic blast was finally too much. His fingers slipped off the rung and he fell through the flaming exhaust toward the distant ground below. He was still moving upward, coasting on the momentum of the rocket that had left him behind. He came to the peak of his trajectory and started to fall.

Time seemed to stop. George found that he had auto-

matically assumed the spread-eagle position he'd learned
when skydiving, only this time he didn't have a parachute.
He felt a faint twinge of regret. Regret that he would
never again see Jinjur and Red and the others again.
George felt cheated. There was so much more he wanted
to do on this world. Then there were all the moons of
Gargantua to explore. Well . . . he had made it to Barnard
alive and had fun exploring at least one world.

We all have to go sometime, he said to himself. *Might
as well get this over with.* He pulled in his arms from the
spread-eagle position and dove headfirst for the ground.

"NO! GEORGE! NO!" screamed Red's voice over his
suit-imp.

George rapidly resumed the spread-eagle position and
looked around. The ascent module had turned, rocketed
back down, and was now rising up to meet him! As it came
closer he could see a grinning brown face peering up at
him through triangular windows. The entry port at the top
of the spacecraft was open. Reaching up from the lock was
a slender, space-suited figure. She had a long lanyard, but
it wasn't needed. Thomas swooped the rocket up underneath George and scooped him right into Red's arms.

"I always was the best one on the block at the ball-and-
cup game," Thomas bragged.

George felt the acceleration increase as Red dragged
him into the lock and the air cycle started.

"I nearly lost you!" said Red as she took off his helmet.
Tears were streaming down her face and into her suit.
George started to cry, too. He put his arms around her and
tried to give her a comforting hug, but the suits got in the
way. When Sam got the inner door open he found them
nuzzling each other's faces, both wet with tears.

With his suit off and holding Red by the hand, George
joined the rest of the crew in the view lounge as they
floated at L–4, waiting for *Prometheus* to arrive. Arielle
was at the telescope, tracking the fractured cross of duralloy
that used to be the *Magic Dragonfly* as it was being borne
off by the waves, the wing tips crumbling as they were
dashed against boulders and tumbling rocks.

"Good-bye, Jill," she cried, her voice breaking.

"Arielle, dear," said Jill's voice through her imp. "I'm still here. You must remember that these voices we computers use are just to aid you in identifying which computer is talking to you."

As it spoke, the voice changed slowly from the overtones of Jill to the overtones of Jack. It then switched to that of James, who in a most butlerish voice continued to drive in the lesson as its voice changed to that of a tinny robot. "It is very important that you realize that we are noth-ing but ro-bots."

"You right," agreed Arielle. "I am silly to cry over computers." Then she burst into tears again.

"What's the matter now, Arielle?" said George.

"My *Dragonfly* was such a pretty plane, and now she is all broke!"

"We've got three more dragonflies for you," said George reassuringly. "And you have all the rest of your life to fly in them."

"Here comes *Prometheus* to pick us up," said Sam, peering out the side of the viewport window.

"C'mon, Red," said Thomas. "Time to fly this ship back to its dock."

REPORTING

With the bulk of the lander left on Roche, it was an easy job for Thomas and Red to slide the ascent module in between the shrouds on *Prometheus* and attach it again to the docking port above the hydroponics deck. George opened the port and peered down. There was a stern, round black face peering back up at him.

"That's the last time I give you an airplane to play with," said Jinjur. "You're too rough on your toys. Just for that you'll have to stay home next time."

George grinned and jumped down to the hydroponics deck, where he was immediately grabbed around the waist in a bear hug. Jinjur didn't say anything else, but as George returned her hug, he could fell the front of his shirt getting wet. Soon the corridor was crowded with other bodies, as the crews combined into one large happy family again.

After a joyous dinner featuring some of the more special treats from Nels Larson's gardens and tissue cultures, George and Jinjur sat together on the control deck to make plans for the next phase of the mission.

"I know we have only three landers left, and more than three moons around Gargantua to study," said George. "But it's vitally important that we go back to Rocheworld. Those aliens are so far ahead of us in mathematics that we need to set up permanent communication with them."

"But what good is pure mathematics?" said Jinjur.

"It is the key to physics and technology," said George. "At first glance, it would seem that advanced mathematics is just a barren exercise in pure logic and should have no relationship at all to the real world. In fact, our mathematicians go out of their way to design the logic of mathematics so that it isn't contaminated by any rules based on human 'common sense.' But, for some reason, the behavior of the real world follows the logic of mathematics and no other logic. If we have a mathematical tool and can calculate something using it, we are sure nature will behave the way the mathematics predicts. But we don't have enough of those mathematical tools, and we know it.

"Astronomers can't calculate the exact motions of more than two gravitating bodies except under special conditions. Aerodynamicists can't calculate the exact flow of air over anything but very simple wing shapes. Weather forecasters can't predict more than a few days ahead. Atomic scientists can't exactly calculate anything more complicated than a hydrogen atom.

"The human race needs that math, and the beauty about math is that unlike being given the secrets to advanced technology, being given advanced mathematics will not stifle the technological creativity of the human race, since *we* will have to figure out how to apply the mathematics."

"OK," said Jinjur. "But how are we going to get the information out of them? This crew may be pretty smart, but none of us are theoretical mathematicians. We may be able to understand some of the simpler stuff, but after the second or third infinity I know *I* would be lost."

"What we should do is set up an interstellar laser communicator in the Hawaiian Islands on the Eau lobe where their older thinkers stay," said George. "That way the long-lived flouwen could communicate their advanced mathematical knowledge directly back to Earth—even long after you and I and the rest of the crew have fluttered out the last of our mayflylike lives."

"You're getting poetic, George," said Jinjur. "I never knew you had it in you."

George looked pensive for a long moment, eyes staring

past her out the control-room window. "Reaching terminal velocity at ten kilometers up with no parachute makes a person think a little more about the fundamentals—like living and dying," he said soberly. Jinjur leaned over from her seat and squeezed both of his hands.

"I don't know what I would have done if I had lost you," she said softly, tears rising once again in her eyes.

George grinned, squeezed her hands back, and rose from his seat.

"I'd better go talk to Carmen and Shirley to see what we can put together that the flouwen can use. The laser should be in a well-sheltered place on land with a reactor that will keep it going for a few decades until the follow-on expedition gets here. But the operating console will have to be underwater."

"Now, just a minute there, George," said Jinjur sternly, getting up from the seat in front of the commander's console and reassuming her command voice and command posture. She motioned for him to take her seat. George stopped, puzzled.

"Remember what they told you in officer's training? 'The program isn't complete until the documentation is done.' You just finished an important and exciting mission, and there are a few billion people back on Earth that are waiting to hear what happened. You've got a report to write."

"Aw, Jinjur, that'll wait," George said. "I've got to get the work started on the communicator."

"Nope," said Jinjur, pulling him over and pushing him down until the sticky patch on his coveralls stuck onto the seat. "You stay here and cram words into the console. *I'll* go find Carmen and Shirley and start planning the next landing."

She continued to talk as she bounced away in the low gravity. "This next mission will need more biologists and fewer geologists, so I'll definitely want to take John along . . ."

George rotated around in the still-warm seat and stared glumly at the waiting blank screen on the console. As Jinjur reached the lift shaft she turned for a last word.

"If you hurry, they will get your report just after New Year's Day in 2076. That should get the Tricentennial Celebration off to a good start."

ENDING

Red slowly drifted out of her apartment on *Prometheus* and palmed the door closed. She paused and looked across the lift-shaft to the two doors that opened into Thomas's and George's rooms. George was not in. He was probably down in the control room working with James on data reduction. Thomas had not been in his room for two years now. When they had floated him out the portal to take him down to the sick bay, Thomas had insisted that his door be left open.

"I'm not going to let a little heart attack keep me down," he had said. "I'm going to get well and come back to my studio. I've got a lot of pictures to work on."

They assured him he would soon return to work on computer enhancements of his world-famous shots of the ring waves on Eau mountain and the ten-thousand-kilometer atmospheric volcano on Gargantua. James, however, had been quite insistent that Thomas stay in the sick bay where there was better access to the medical equipment. Thomas had argued with the computer for a while, but after two more heart stoppages that would have been fatal if the Christmas Bush had not been there to apply shock treatment, Thomas finally stopped arguing and accepted the life of an invalid. The view-wall above his bed in the sick bay was identical to the one in his room, but it just never seemed the same. The real problem was that the complex photographic enhancement and display console that took up most of Thomas's private room could not be fitted into the sick bay, and Thomas was reduced to more modest processing of his picture pixels.

Red's eyes swept past the seven other doors ringing the lift shaft on this floor. They and all the doors on the floor above had been closed for a long time. Ten of them at once, some fifteen years ago, when *Slam* IV had been stranded on Zuni, third moon of Gargantua. The others had died of one cause or another over the years while *Prometheus* slowly wandered back and forth through the Barnard system, collecting data on the planets and moons as the seasons changed. There were only three of them left now—all old, but still busy. They were presently engaged in a two-year survey of the star itself, following it through one of its sunspot cycles. For that job they had used the light from the star to slow *Prometheus* in its orbit, so that the spinning parasol of their ship had fluttered down closer to the dim red sun. For the first time since they had come to Barnard they had to use filters over the viewing ports.

Red looked upwards at the gaping maw of the central shaft and hesitated. In the past she would have simply flung herself up into the empty hole and used an occasionally flick of hand or foot on the walls to propel herself through the shaft to her destination. She would still do that for a 'tween-decks jump—but now she wanted to go to the starside science dome nearly sixty meters away. They were getting close enough to the sun that the acceleration from the light pressure was becoming almost noticeable. Getting cautious in her old age, she called for the shaft elevator and took it to Starside.

Her arthritic joints creaking in protest, Red wormed her way past a large telescope swung out under the dome. There was very little room left for a human. Red looked up to see a minibush working the controls. It was very busy, scrambling back and forth between the various control knobs at a speed that no human hands could have duplicated. Red was slightly puzzled. "Why are you using such a little branch, James?" she asked. "You'll wear yourself out running back and forth like that."

She heard James chuckle, both in her hair-imp and from the minibush on the telescope. "I can handle the telescope fine this way," it replied. "It's a little more wasteful of energy than using a larger motile that can reach both knobs at once, but I felt that it was better to have most of the Christmas Bush elsewhere at this time."

Red's heart skipped a beat. "What's going on?" she asked in alarm, then instantly knew the answer. "There's something wrong with Thomas!" she cried, and started to wiggle her way past the slowly moving telescope.

"I didn't want to worry you," said her imp. "There's nothing bad happening to him, but I just thought it best to have more of my motile close to him since his vital signs are slowly worsening. Red! . . . Elizabeth!! . . . Wait for the elevator!!!" the imp screamed in her ear as she dove headlong down the shaft.

"I'll pay for that later," Red said to herself as her adrenaline-anesthetized joints ignored their arthritic signals and brought her to a violent stop at the living area deck. She made her way to the sick bay. Most of the Christmas Bush was there, monitoring the medical instruments. Red noticed that Thomas's upper torso was naked and covered with a lacelike net of motile threads. She looked at Thomas and understood why James had been concerned. Thomas's face, usually a handsome and healthy light-brown color, was now a muddy gray. He had aged well, and usually looked much younger than his sixty-eight years. He didn't look young now, more like George's eighty-seven.

Thomas looked up as she came in. He grinned weakly at her and winked their special wink. She blushed, then put an exasperated frown on her face.

"Thomas," she scolded, "you're incorrigible."

"But it's been over two years, Red," he said. "A guy could die if he goes without getting it for that long."

". . . and he'd die if he did," she replied.

"But what a way to go!"

Ignoring his remark, Red moved over to him and put one hand on his forehead and one on his cheek. He moved his head and nuzzled his nose in her hand, his lips kissing her palm softly. She tried to hold back her emotions, but finally gave up, fell sobbing across his chest, and hugged him. Through her anguish and tears she could feel the motiles moving between them, keeping out of the way as much as possible, but still maintaining their vigil on the body of the dying man. Thomas ran his fingers through the brilliant red hair that he had loved for so long, grinned inwardly at the slight trace of gray at the root of each hair, and closed his eyes to rest.

After a while, Red got control of herself. She sat up and twisted her body until the sticky patch on the back belt-line of her jumpsuit stuck to the holding pad of a work-station arm the Christmas Bush had swung out for her. Now she could stay beside the bed without drifting away. She looked at Thomas's closed eyes with concern, then turned to the Christmas Bush.

"He's just sleeping," said James. "But it won't be long now. In his weakened condition his usually benign sickle-cell anemia condition is flaring up and aggravating his other problems."

Red took Thomas's hand and waited, occasionally brushing him on the cheek with a wrinkled, freckled hand.

George was in his bed, staring up at the viewscreen in the ceiling and scanning through an old science fiction novel, *Dragon's Egg*. He'd read it many times before, but it was so full of scientific tidbits that he always enjoyed dipping into it before going to sleep. His favorite part was when the alien "cheela" came up from the surface of a neutron star to visit the humans in orbit above them, riding on miniature black holes.

George heard the rustle and the occasional odd noise of Elizabeth coming up the shaft. He looked out his open door to watch Red rise up out of the floor and bring herself to a halt at the railing. Instead of going to her door, however, she circled around the railing ringing the lift shaft and disappeared behind the edge of his door. He heard the splat of a human palm on the wall, the sibilant hiss of a compartment door sliding shut, and the deadly click of a bolt. He sat up under his tension sheet as his imp whispered in his ear.

"She wanted to tell you herself," it said.

Red appeared at his door, an inward strength glowing in the tall, green-suited body. Her red hair glistened in the bright corridor light as she said, "There's just the two of us now, George. Can I come in?"

"Sure," he said. "Just a second and I'll get dressed."

"Don't bother," she replied. "I just don't want to sleep alone tonight." She came over to the bed, and kicking off her corridor boots, climbed in under the tension sheet, her back to him.

"Just hold me," she pleaded, and George put the grizzled arm of an old man around the green-clad little girl and lay his head on the pillow next to hers, his imp scrambling around to his other shoulder as he did so. He closed his eyes and went to sleep, while James turned off the bedroom light and the scan book, and closed the corridor door.

Another year passed. George was now hanging loosely from a pylon on the control deck, monitoring the video feedback from the deep-space probes in the outreaches of Barnard. The screens showed little that was new, and James could have handled the data by itself, but George insisted on viewing all the scenes that differed in any significant aspect from those that had been seen before. A typical scene of frozen blackness on a distant moon nearly forty light-minutes away had changed to a scene of frozen grayness. The computer had asked the human element in its loop to evaluate the situation.

"Nothing here, James," George said. "Just another mound of dirty ice."

The screen flashed to a new scene, one that had been held up while the previous one had been evaluated. George scanned the picture, looking for anything that the well-trained senses of the computer might have missed. Suddenly, his eyes caught a flash of green out of the corner of his eye, and he turned to see a tumbled mass of green satin clothing converging on his face. He brushed away the intruding jumpsuit and underwear just in time to see two tantalizing white mounds swim out of sight behind the control room door, tiny pink feet propelling them on their way.

It didn't take long. Within ten seconds he was stripped to the uniform that the "Game" called for and was searching through the downs and outs of the corridors that had made their life a heaven in the stars. They had tried other hiding spots, but the best—yes, the very best—was the exercise room.

George found her behind the exercise mats. She thought she was stretched out enough to be as invisible as a pea under the many thick mattresses. He noticed the slight mound, however, and his body rising to the occasion, dove under the layers of mats and pulled a squealing, skinny, red-haired vixen into the open.

"STOP!" she cried. She twisted expertly in the air, trying to break his single handhold.

Her struggles to retreat were defeated by a single brushing kiss that he implanted on the tips of her hair. It was his turn to run now, and he bounded off the wall and entered the dim lounge that led to one of the video rooms. She smiled and stopped at the lift shaft, her lithe naked body relaxing for a moment. She waited, scanning the tumble of furniture and panels in the lounge, then dove full speed at a bulky gray form bouncing from one panel to another, and caught him in mid-flight as they tumbled through the door into one of the video rooms.

Their play had risen to ecstasy, the dim lights of the video room adding to their games. They were coupled. Her face flushed with pleasure until it was almost the color of her hair. Her body arched back . . .

"RED! GEORGE!! STOP!!!" imps shouted in their ears.

"Goddamnit, James!" George exploded with fury. "Can't you stay out . . . ." He grabbed the handful of brittle sticks from their perch on his naked shoulder and flung them at the far wall. The mangled twigs and wires hummed to a halt about a meter from his hand and buzzed back past him—heading toward Elizabeth.

George looked quickly around and watched his small

wisp of imp merge into the imp on the side of Red's face, a face gasping for breath and wide-eyed with agony. He turned at another sound, a deep thrumming in the air. A thicket of sticks and twigs hit the two of them amidships and thrust him aside.

The fuzzy hands of the Christmas Bush then attempted to press life into Red's naked curvaceous chest, while a dense cluster of cilia pumped a pulsating stream of air into her lax mouth. The Christmas Bush worked on Red for a number of minutes, then the automatic motion finally stopped. Not abruptly; not slowly; but like some automaton given both stop and start signals at the same time.

"She is dead," said James, finally stopping.

"NO!" shouted George. "Don't stop! Save her! *Do something!*" He reached out and started pulling the Bush off her. "She can't die! I won't let her die!!"

"There is nothing either you or I can do," replied James calmly. "She has suffered a massive cerebral aneurysm."

"Oh . . ." said George, his hands coming to a halt.

He let go of the Christmas Bush and ran his fingertips tenderly up over Red's face while he slowly calmed himself down.

"Thanks for trying," he finally said. He moved back and floated motionless, eyes staring longingly at her face.

"Are you OK?" said James, a large chunk of Christmas Bush breaking loose from the floating nude to hover at a distance from him.

"I'm fine, James," George said, finally recovering. "Just take care of her, will you?" He went off to cry in a quiet place, his imp reforming unobtrusively on his naked shoulder as he left.

James waited patiently. George's grief eventually shed itself in a floating stream of sparkling spheres. George's imp tenderly flicked each tear from around his red-rimmed eyes, launching them toward the nearby air intake ducts. There was still a deep emptiness in him, however. That void would only be filled by the wash of tears from the intermittent floods of emotional catharsis that would return again and again in the weeks, months, and years ahead. The deaths of the others had been hard, but there had always been someone to share the grief with. This loss he would bear alone.

The computer made no attempt to comfort the human in his grief. Its condolences could have been some temporary help, but psychologists long dead had decided that the last human would be better off if he or she were to regain control of their stricken emotions themselves. The humans were necessarily dependent upon James for their physical survival. It would not do to have them become psychologically dependent on their electronic companion and its bushy motile.

When George finished his crying, he found himself in the starside science dome, lying back in the control chair and looking outward at the distant yellow star studding the end of Orion's belt.

He had decided to get all the misery out of his system at one time, and had deliberately worked up a good case of homesickness to add to his loneliness. He now had cried himself out, and getting up calmly, he floated away from the chair as it folded itself into its niche in the wall. He called for the elevator to take him to the control deck.

"I'd like to read a few words before you put her in cold storage, James," he said quietly to his imp.

"Red left some last wishes with me, as a verbal will," said James. "She didn't want her body to stay on board *Prometheus* with the others—even if there was a chance that someday it could be returned to Earth. She has no family or friends there. She felt more at home around this strange red star and wants to be buried here."

"A sailor of the skies, her body cast into the deep," mused George. "OK. I'll look up a sea captain's farewell."

"It's going to be more complicated than that, George. She wants to be cremated in the star."

"We can't do that. If we put her out a port, she'll go into orbit," said George, puzzled. Suddenly, he looked up.

"Of course!" he said. "I forgot what kind of ship we're in."

"Shall I decelerate and assume a hovering orbit?" said James.

"Yes," said George. "How long will it take?"

"Two weeks. Less if you don't mind feeling a few percent of gee."

"SURE! I can take the gees!" grumbled George. "I may be old, but I'm not decrepit—you obsolete hunk of frayed wires and diffusing silicon. What'll we do with Red in the meantime? Put her in cold storage with the others?"

"Yes, we'll have to," replied James. "But before that, I'll have to make some preparations. She gave explicit instructions on what she was to wear and how her hair and makeup were to be done. The Christmas Bush is working on that now in the sick bay."

"I want to help," said George, pushing himself over to the lift shaft as the computer began to tilt the huge sail to slow its orbit about the star.

"Are you sure?" asked James, with a concerned overtone in its voice. "I am perfectly capable of handling the whole thing myself."

"Yes!" said George gruffly. He padded into the sick bay and approached the still-naked body strapped lightly to the table. The thick red hair that was Red's crowning glory was now full of twigs from the Christmas Bush. One small clump of the Bush was controlling a plastic squeezer full of a reddish liquid and spraying a mist into the air. Each tiny droplet was snatched individually by the cilia on the twigs, carried to the base of each hair stalk, applied to the root, then carefully wiped off as the few millimeters of gray hair became as red as the rest.

"I don't think she would have wanted you to see this," rumbled the Christmas Bush.

"She never fooled anyone," George replied. "We never talked about Red dyeing her hair, but we all knew that she did, and knew that everyone else knew, too."

James hesitated a little at that statement. It quickly sifted through sixty-eight years of conversation picked up and recorded by its imps. George was right. No one on the ship had ever talked with anyone else about Red's hair. They must have understood each other from facial expressions.

I still have a lot to learn about humans was the summary judgment it entered into its memory.

James let George brush, comb, and arrange Red's hair, but insisted on doing the makeup itself.

"She would come back and haunt me if I allowed you to mess up her lip line," James joked.

As they were finishing, one limb of the Christmas Bush appeared with a set of green satin clothing and a long pair of alligator-hide boots.

"Where'd those boots come from?" said George in surprise.

"She brought them on board as part of her personal baggage allotment," James replied. "She was planning to wear them for parties, but she forgot that her ankles swell in free-fall. After trying to get them on a few times, she gave up and shoved them in the back of her locker. Her last instructions about them were very explicit. I recorded them."

Red's voice emerged from the vibrating cilia at the tips of the Christmas Bush as the computer replayed the exact sequence of bits which it had recorded in that long-ago conversation. "I want those boots on when I go out the port. Even if you have to cut off my feet to get them on. But don't you *dare* stretch them."

George winced visibly as he heard Red's hauntingly beautiful contralto. "Please don't ever do that again," he finally said.

"I'm sorry," said James in a subdued whisper.

A few minutes of firm pressure on her lower legs by the massive paws of the Christmas Bush allowed the green leather to slide over the sheer green stockings. There was even plenty of room to tuck in the legs of the green satin slacks. As they were putting on Red's shirt, the Christmas Bush stopped, reached into a breast pocket and took out a small gold coin. It handed the coin to George.

"She didn't say what to do with this," James said. "I guess you should keep it."

"I'm sure I can think of a thousand ways to spend a sixty-billion-dollar gold coin in this thriving metropolis," remarked George sarcastically. He took the coin, folded it up carefully in one of Red's hands, and crossed her arms across her chest. He leaped up toward the ceiling, hung on to the light fixture, and stared down at her critically.

"She looks fine," he said. "Now take her away before I get all soppy and smear her makeup."

The Christmas Bush picked up the stiffening body and headed for the lift shaft as George, floating slowly downward from the ceiling, watched them go.

As the days passed, the huge sail tilted, then tilted back again. George noticed that the maneuver took almost two weeks, and that after the first day, the acceleration had subtly changed from its earlier high level. He couldn't blame James for trying to take care of an eighty-eight-year-old man and let the computer get away with trying to fool him. Finally, the ship was hovering over the star. The light from the red globe shot straight up through the bottom science dome and illuminated the ceiling of the control deck. The ship was slowly drifting downward, for the star's gravity was slightly stronger than the push of the light on the sail.

George had been looking through the library for a suitable eulogy for Red. He had skimmed through the Bible and the prayer books for three religions but hadn't found anything that really suited. Then he remembered a phrase. It was simple and short, and spoke of their last years together in this structure that was a combination of home and prison and tomb. He couldn't recall the exact words, however, and all of his reconstruction attempts seemed to lack the poignancy of the original.

The name of the author also persisted in eluding his searching thoughts, and it took George nearly four hours to track the phrase down with the help of James's library program. He finally found it, then realized why his brain had refused to come up with the source. He found the phrase in the humor section. The author was Mark Twain.

George followed the Christmas Bush in the two percent gravity as it put the frosty body of the beautiful red-haired woman into the airlock and closed the inner door. The Christmas Bush waited, its colored lights blinking, while

George read in a husky voice the words he had carefully copied onto a slip of paper.

"Wheresoever she was, *there* was Eden."

James, overriding the airlock controls, activated the outer door with the lock still pressurized. The rush of air twirled the body out the hatch, one elbow striking the side of the lock as it left. The last thing George saw before his eyes filled again with tears was a distant figure in frosted green, and between them, just outside the airlock door, flashes of red-gold light reflected from a spinning disk of metal. The coin was slowly dropping sunward as the sailcraft hovered above the all-consuming fire below.

Twenty-four hours and fifty-eight minutes later, the energy in a gold coin, a green-clad figure, and a misplaced alligator from Earth became a burst of photons bathing the farthest reaches of the universe with a minute flash of luminance.

Two years later George picked up the beacon signal from the incoming space vehicle. A large antimatter-powered rocket, it had left the solar system thirteen years ago, and accelerating at thirty percent of Earth gravity had reached its cruise speed of half the speed of light in only twenty months. After coasting for a decade it had turned around and started to brake. It was decelerating rapidly as it neared Barnard, but it still had a year of thrusting to go before it stopped.

This follow-on mission to Barnard contained a large crew of specialized exploration robots and a small contingent of humans. George's first communication sessions with them were brief, for a round-trip message time of one hundred days made it difficult to engage in brilliant discourse. Besides, both of them were busy collecting data.

George now had *Prometheus* in a slow spiral about the north pole of Barnard, mapping it from the polar regions outward. As the year passed and the rocket ship of the follow-on expedition drew closer, George visited the communicator more often. When they were a month of travel time away, the round-trip communication time became about twenty-four hours and he enjoyed a short one-way conversation each morning at breakfast. It was about this time that he was able to use the science telescope to pick up the faint speck of the blazing exhaust from the braking rocket as it entered the outskirts of the Barnard system. A few weeks later, when the time-delay was only an hour, and they were only a few days from zero relative speed, George suddenly realized that he was going to have visitors and the place was a mess. He cancelled the science plan, put the Christmas Bush to "cleaning up," and began to prepare for company.

The huge interstellar exploration ship dropped into an orbit about Barnard, not far from Rocheworld. A flitter would come to visit him, while the rest of the expedition started in on the exploration tasks that were ahead.

The small sleek flitter flew smoothly in under the giant sail of *Prometheus* on a nearly invisible jet of antimatter energized hydrogen. George watched them approach from the bottom science dome, then floated over to the EVA console and readied the airlock. The first to cycle through was one of the new general-purpose robots. Built along the same lines as a human, they could replace a human at any station. They, of course, did not need space-suits.

The robot exited the lock. It looked carefully around, then fixed its eyes on the human. George noticed a gold caduceus on the breastplate of the shiny black plasticoid. Probably a medic of some sort. There was a dramatic increase in the light display on the Christmas Bush, and George realized that James and the robot were trading information. The robot drifted toward him, propelled by a precision flick of its foot on the airlock hatchway. It spoke in a deep baritone voice.

"I have received a report on your state of health from the ship's computer, but I would like to calibrate my medical sensors if I may," it requested as it drifted to a halt just an arm-length away.

"Sure," said George. The robot placed its right hand on the side of his neck, its thumb resting on his jugular. As the hand approached, he could see each finger was a complex maze of tiny sensors. He was surprised to feel that the hand was warm, despite its cold-looking appearance.

"Nice bedside manner," thought George as he felt an ultrasonic hum pass through his body, while at the same time a tiny section of the robot's chest plate was emitting a multicolored display of lights that explored the front portion of his body. After a second, the robot moved both its hands to place them at opposite sides of George's head, then dropped them at its side.

"Thank you," it said, then backed away.

George cycled the lock to let the next visitor in, and a space-suited figure stepped through. The plasticoid was very efficient, and soon the suit was off the human. The Christmas Bush took it off to the locker and hung it up.

"Hello, there," said George with a twisted smile. "Welcome to Barnard."

The visitor looked at the ancient astronaut. George was dressed in a neatly pressed coverall, but that couldn't hide the angular structure of a computer-controlled motile exoskeleton activating his arm and leg on the left side. The visitor estimated it must have required about one-third of the Christmas Bush. As he looked, his computer implant fed him the background information that it had picked up from James and the recent examination by the medic. George had suffered a massive stroke just eighteen months ago and had only barely survived to greet them. He was getting better, though, and probably had a good many years left.

"Hello, George, said the young man. "I bear a proclamation from the President and Congress of the Greater United States, and a personal message from my great-grandfather."

"Your great-grandfather?" asked George in bewilderment.

"I am cursed with the jawbreaking name of Beauregard Darlington Winthrop the Sixth," the young man replied with a faint smile. "But just call me 'Win.' My great-grandfather was Senator Winthrop, formerly General Winthrop, one of your old friends in the Air Force."

George clouded up. "Winthrop?" he said. "What was his message?"

"I don't know," said Win. "It's here in this envelope. Since he was the person in Congress that knew you best, they asked him to write you a personal note to go along with their formal commendation."

He handed over a yellowing ancient envelope with the embossed imprint of Senator Beauregard Darlington Winthrop III in the upper left corner. George tore the envelope open and pulled out a folded sheet of Senate office stationary. There in fading black ink was a short note dated July 4, 2076.

Your goddamn friends in the goddamn Congress finally finagled you a goddamn star. May you be dead and frozen in Hell before it gets to you!

There was no signature.

George smiled quietly, folded the letter carefully, his motile-assisted left arm acting in near-perfect coordination with his good right one, and put the letter into his breast pocket. There was no need for this puppy-dog of a young man to know the contents of the message.

"What did it say?" asked Win, eager to know the family secret. As a child he had become fascinated with the time-spanning history of the piece of paper, and had worked until he was chosen for the follow-on mission to Barnard so he could deliver it personally.

"He mentioned a star," said George.

"Oh, yes!" said Win. He reached into another pocket, and pulled out a small box.

"In recognition of your services to the country," he parroted, "the President and Congress of the Greater United States hereby promote you to the rank of Brigadier General of the Air Force." He handed him the box and George opened it. He took out one of the silver stars inside, snapped the box shut and looked at it contemplatively.

He hobbled over to one of the viewing ports in the side of the command deck and stared out at the dull red sun off to one side. He turned to face the two robots and the human, and said, "James, send the Christmas Bush over here next to me."

The computer obeyed, and soon the scraggly-looking motile was floating in front of him. George reached up and stuck the shining silver star into the branches at the apex of the Christmas Bush, where the cilia automatically gripped it. He leaned back against the view port and looked at the greenly-glowing Christmas Bush, its colored lights blinking on and off in its never-ending communication with the main computer. The five-pointed silver star stuck in the top branches glittered brightly as it reflected the reddish rays streaming in through the viewport window from Barnard.

"I think you're the one that deserves a general's star, James, so why don't you keep this one." Stiffly, he turned his back on the group and looked out the window at the dull red globe that was six light-years away from the home to which he would never return.

"I already have my star."

HEARING

before the

SUBCOMMITTEE ON
SPACE, COMMUNICATION, POWER, AND
EXTRATERRESTRIAL MINING

of the

COMMITTEE ON
SCIENCE AND TECHNOLOGY
G.U.S. HOUSE OF REPRESENTATIVES

One-Hundred-Forty-Fourth Congress

second session

January 14, 15, 2076

BARNARD EXPEDITION

Tuesday, January 14, 2076

G.U.S. House of Representatives,
Committee on Science and Technology
    Subcommittee on Space, Communication,
      Power, and Extraterrestrial Mining
        Washington, D.C.

The subcommittee met, pursuant to notice, in room 2318, Rayburn House Office Building, 9:37 a.m., the Chairman of the subcommittee, the Hon. John Ootah, State of Saskatchewan, presiding.

Mr. Ootah. The subcommittee will be in order. Without objection, permission will be granted for radio, video, and holophotography during the course of the hearing.

During the next two days, the subcommittee will review the reports recently received from the brave crew of interstellar explorers visiting the Barnard system nearly six light-years distant—the first ambassadors of the Greater United States to the worlds across the great void of interstellar space.

Our first witness this morning is Dr. Morris Philipson, Professor of Astronomy at Cornell University, who will brief us about Barnard and its unusual planetary system. Then the Honorable Frederick Ross, Chief Administrator for the Greater National Aeronautics and Space Agency, will describe the mission and the vehicles used in carrying it out. Dr. Joel Winners, GNASA Associate Administrator for space sciences, will be our wrap-up witness for this morning, telling us about what the expedition found in the star system—another race of intelligent beings, creatures so alien in their life-forms and culture that they are almost beyond imagining.

We will ask the witnesses to present their testimony first. Then we will have questions after all of the testimony is completed. The House is going into session at eleven o'clock. There will be a series of votes, then a lengthy recess which will allow adequate time for more testimony.

We hope in this process the delays in the testimony will be held to a minimum.

Dr. Philipson, if you will proceed?

Dr. Philipson. Mr. Chairman and members of the Subcommittee on Space, Communication, Power, and Extraterrestrial Mining, I appreciate this opportunity to testify before you about the Barnard system. I have a few holoslides that I would like to project during my testimony.

Mr. Ootah. Would the Guardian of the Committee Room Door please ask the room robots to dim the lights? Thank you. You may proceed, Dr. Philipson.

Dr. Philipson. Thank you, Mr. Chairman. I will read from a personally proofed printout. With your permission, we can relieve the clerk from having to transcribe manually the robotic record and just insert the printout into the committee robotic reader.

Mr. Ootah. That will be fine, Dr. Philipson.

STATEMENT OF DR. PHILIPSON

Barnard

In 1916, the American astronomer Edward E. Barnard measured the proper motion of a dim red star catalogued as +4° 3561. He found it was moving through the sky at the amazing speed of 10.3 seconds of arc per year, or more than half the diameter of the Moon in a century. Barnard's Star (or Barnard as it is known now) is very close to the solar system, only 5.9 light-years away, but it is so small and dim that it takes a telescope to see it.

The statistics for Barnard are given in the table:

BARNARD STAR DATA

Distance: 5.9 ly
Right Ascension: 17 hr 55 min
Declination: 4 deg 33 min
Coordinates: X = −0.1 ly, Y = −5.9 ly, Z = +0.5 ly
Spectral type: M5
Effective Temperature: 58% solar (3330 K)

Luminosity: 0.05% solar (visual), 0.37% solar (thermal)
Mass: 15% solar mass
Radius: 12% solar radius
Proper motion: 10.31 arcsec/yr
Radial velocity: −108 kilometers/sec

Barnard Planetary System

The planetary system around Barnard is dominated by a gigantic planet, aptly named Gargantua. A huge gas giant like Jupiter, Gargantua is four times more massive than Jupiter. Since the parent star, Barnard, has a mass of only fifteen percent that of our Sun, this means that the planet Gargantua is one-fortieth the mass of its star. If Gargantua had been more massive, it would have turned into a star, and the Barnard system would have been a binary star system.

Gargantua seems to have swept up into itself most of the original stellar nebula that was not used in making the star, for there are no other large planets in the system. Gargantua has four satellites that would be planets in our solar system, plus a multitude of smaller moons. These planets will be the subject of further exploration by the Barnard mission. Today, however, we will be concentrating on the first world (or worlds) that they landed on—Rocheworld.

As seen in Figure 1, Rocheworld is in a highly elliptical orbit around Barnard. The period of Rocheworld about Barnard is forty days, while Gargantua's orbital period is exactly three times the Rocheworld orbital period. Thus, once every three orbits, Rocheworld passes within six million kilometers of the giant planet Gargantua, not too far from the orbit of Gargantua's outer moon, Zeus. It is believed that the present orbit was established many million years ago by the encounter of a stray planetoid with what was once an outer large moon of Gargantua.

Orbits such as that of Rocheworld are usually not stable. The three to one resonance condition usually results in an oscillation of the orbit of the smaller body that builds up in amplitude until the smaller planet is thrown into a differ-

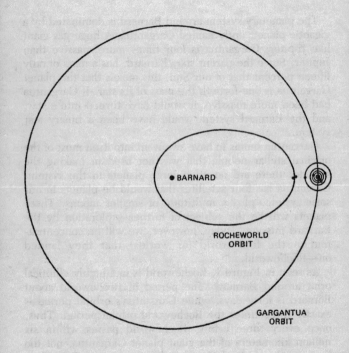

Figure 1—Barnard Planetary System

ent orbit, or a collision occurs. Due to Rocheworld's close approach to Barnard, however, the tides from Barnard cause a significant amount of dissipation, which stabilizes the orbit. This also supplies a great deal of heating which keeps Rocheworld warmer than it would normally be if the heating were due to radiation alone.

Rocheworld

Rocheworld is a dumbbell-shaped double planet. As shown in Figure 2, it consists of two moon-sized rocky bodies that whirl about each other with a rotation period of six hours. There are exactly 160 rotations of Rocheworld around its common center (a Rocheworld "day") to one rotation of Rocheworld in its elliptical orbit around Barnard (a Rocheworld "year"), while there are exactly three orbits of Rocheworld around Barnard to one rotation of Gargantua around Barnard. This locking of Rocheworld's rotation period and orbital period to the orbital period of Gargantua keeps the strange double planet in its highly elliptical orbit. The energy needed to drive the Rocheworld configuration and compensate for energy losses due to tidal dissipation comes from the gravitational tug of Gargantua on Rocheworld during their close passage every third orbit.

The two planetoids or lobes of Rocheworld are so close that they are almost touching, but their spin speed is high enough that they maintain a separation of about eighty kilometers. If each were not distorted by the other's gravity, the two planets would have been spheres about the size of our Moon. Since their gravitational tides act upon one another, the two bodies have been stretched out until they are elongated egg-shapes, 3,500 kilometers in the long dimension and 3,000 kilometers in cross section. Although the two planets do not touch each other, they do share a common atmosphere. The resulting figure-eight configuration is called a Roche-lobe pattern after E.A. Roche, a French mathematician of the later 1880s, who calculated the effects of gravity tides on stars, planets, and moons. The word "roche" also means "rock" in French, so the

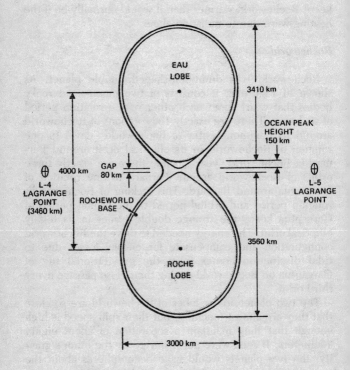

Figure 2—Rocheworld

rocky lobe of the pair of planetoids was given the name Roche, while the water-covered lobe was named Eau after the French word for "water."

The average gravity at the surface of these moonlets is about ten percent of Earth gravity, slightly less than that of Earth's Moon because of their lower density. This average value varies considerably depending upon your position on the surface of the elongated lobes. The gravity at one of the outward facing poles is eight percent of Earth gravity, rising to eleven percent in a belt that includes the north and south spin poles of each lobe, increases slightly to a maximum of eleven and a half percent at a region some thirty degrees inward, then drops precipitously to a half percent at the inner-pole surface. This low-gravity point is some forty kilometers below the zero gravity point between the two planetoids, where the gravity from the mass of the two lobes cancels out.

On each side of the double planet are the L–4 and L–5 points, where there is a minimum in the combined gravitational and centrifugal forces of the system. A satellite placed at either of these two points will stay there, rotating synchronously with the two planets, without consumption of fuel. For the Earth-Moon system, where the Earth is much more massive than the Moon, those stable points are in the orbit of the Moon at plus and minus sixty degrees from the Moon. In the Rocheworld system, where the two bodies are the same mass, the stable points are at plus and minus ninety degrees. The exploration crew established communication satellites at these two points to give continuous coverage of each side of both lobes.

The Roche lobe is slightly less dense than the Eau lobe, and thus is larger in diameter. It has a number of ancient craters upon its surface, especially in the outer-facing hemisphere. Although the Eau lobe masses almost as much as the Roche lobe, it has a core that is denser. Since its highest point is some twenty kilometers lower in the combined gravitational well, it is the "lowlands" while the Roche lobe is the "highlands." Eau gets most of the rain that falls from the common atmosphere and thus has captured nearly all of the liquids of the double planet to form one large ocean. The ocean is primarily ammonia water, with trace amounts of hydrogen sulfide and cyanide gas.

The Roche lobe is dry and rocky, with traces of quiescent volcano vents near its pointed pole. The Eau lobe has a pointed section like the Roche lobe, but the point is not made of rock. The peak is a mountain of ammonia water a hundred and fifty kilometers high with sixty-degree slopes! One would think that the water would 'seek its own level' and flow out until the surface of the ocean became spherical, but because of the unusual configuration of the gravity fields of the double planet, the basic mountain shape is stable—except at periapsis.

When Rocheworld is at its farthest distance from Barnard, everything is serene on the double-planet. The two lobes whirl about each other and the gravity from the star causes modest tides on the ocean on Eau. As Rocheworld moves around in its orbit, it experiences stronger tides as it approaches either Gargantua or Barnard. At these times, the variations in gravitational tides from one rotation to the next cause large surges in the seas. The low gravity accentuates these surges into large waves that reach kilometers in height, breaking at the low-gravity pole between the two planetoids.

As Rocheworld begins to approach Barnard in its elliptical orbit, the effect of the tides from the star begins to become very large. The peak of the water mountain now begins to rise and fall a number of kilometers, with the pattern repeated each half-rotation. As is shown in Figure 3, when Barnard is on one side of Rocheworld, the two lobes separate by thirty kilometers. This causes the mountain of water to drop one hundred kilometers. [Dr. Philipson interrupted his prepared text at this point to interject a comment.]

Dr. Philipson. By the way, this behavior is not what would be predicted by a naive model of the gravity forces. I myself would have thought that with Barnard off to the side, the gravity tidal forces from Barnard would have drawn the lobes closer together, not farther apart. I also would have expected the change in the height of the mountain of water to be about the same as the change in

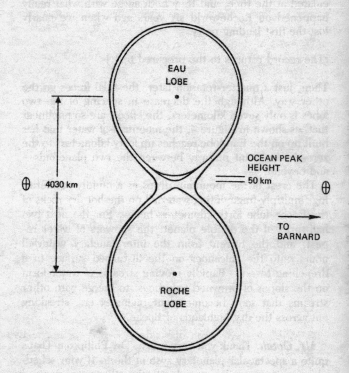

EAU
LOBE

OCEAN PEAK
HEIGHT

50 km

4030 km

TO
BARNARD

ROCHE
LOBE

Figure 3—Periapsis tides during first quarter-rotation

the separation. But recent detailed computer studies here on Earth, which take into account the coupling of the angular rotation and the orbital motion with the planetary dynamics, confirm what Captain Thomas St. Thomas calculated at the time, and they both agree with what really happened on Rocheworld six years ago when we nearly lost the first landing party.

[The record returns to the prepared text.]

Then, just a quarter-rotation later, the tidal forces go the other way. Although the decrease in spacing of the two lobes is only seven kilometers, the effects are so nonlinear that, as shown in Figure 4, the mountain of water that has built up on the Eau lobe reaches up forty kilometers to the zero-gravity point midway between the two planetoids—and beyond.

The crest of the mountain drops as a rapidly accelerating, multiply-fragmenting waterfall on the hot dry rocks of the Roche lobe forty kilometers below. For the next two half-turns of the double planet, the showers of water repeat, and the torrent from the interplanetary waterfall pours onto the volcanoes on the disturbed surface in a drenching torrent. Rapidly moving streams of water form on the slopes of drowned volcanoes, to merge with other streams that soon become giant raging rivers, streaking out across the dry highlands of Roche.

Mr. Ootah. Thank you very much, Dr. Philipson. That's quite a spectacular planetary system there. If your schedule permits, we will proceed with the other witnesses and then have the questions and answers.

The next witness will be the Honorable Frederick Ross, Chief Administrator for the Greater National Aeronautics and Space Administration. We want to welcome you here and congratulate you for one of GNASA's most successful missions.

Mr. Ross. Thank you very much, Mr. Chairman, and members of the committee. I hope you remember your

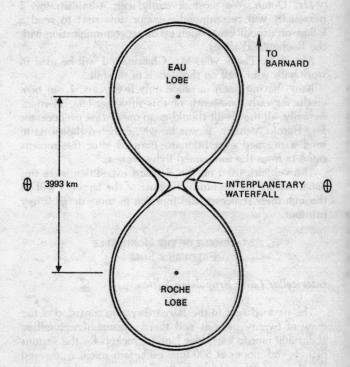

Figure 4—Periapsis tides during second quarter-rotation

congratulations when you are working on our budget for the coming year.

[Laughter.]

Mr. Ootah. We most certainly will, Administrator. I personally will recommend a major new start to send a follow-on expedition to open up direct communication with the Rocheworld aliens.

Mr. Ross. Thank you, Mr. Chairman. I will be glad to work with your staff on the details of the bill.

Now, having been in office only five years, I can take credit for only one-tenth of this fifty-year-long mission. Actually, all the credit should go to my distant predecessor Dr. Harold Mosher. It was he who initiated the plans to send a manned expedition to Barnard after the returns came in from the unmanned flyby probes.

The vehicles used on the Barnard expedition were unusual because of the unusual nature of the target. I will go through their structure and function in some detail in my printout.

STATEMENT OF THE HONORABLE FREDERICK ROSS

Interstellar Laser Propulsion System

The payload sent to the Barnard system consisted of the crew of twenty persons and their consumables, totalling about 300 metric tons; four landing rockets for the various planets and moons at 500 tons each; four nuclear-powered VTOL exploration airplanes at 80 tons each; and the interstellar habitat for the crew that made up the remainder of the 3,500 tons that needed to be transported to the star system.

This payload was carried by a large light-sail 300 kilometers in diameter. The sail was of very light construction, a thin film of finely perforated metal, stretched over a lightweight frame. Although the sail averaged only one-tenth of a gram per square meter of area, the total mass of the sail was over 7,000 tons. The payload sail was not only used to decelerate the payload at the Barnard system, but also for propulsion within the Barnard system.

The 300-kilometer payload sail was surrounded by a larger ring-sail, 1,000 kilometers in diameter, with a hole in the center where the payload sail was attached during launch from the solar system. The ring sail had a total mass of 71,500 tons, giving a total launch weight of the sails and the payload of over 82,000 tons.

The laser power needed to accelerate the 82,000-ton interstellar vehicle at one percent of earth gravity was just over 1,300 terawatts. As is shown in Figure 5, this was obtained from an array of 1,000 laser generators orbiting around Mercury. Each laser generator used a thirty-kilo-meter-diameter lightweight reflector that collected 6.5 terawatts of sunlight and reflected into its solar-pumped laser the 1.5 terawatts of sunlight that was at the right wavelength for the laser to use.

When fed the right pumping light, the lasers were very efficient and produced 1.3 terawatts of laser light at an infrared wavelength of 1.5 microns. The output aperture of the lasers was 100 meters in diameter, so the flux that the laser mirrors had to handle was only about 12 suns. The lasers and their collectors were in sun-synchronous orbit around Mercury to keep them from being moved about by the light pressure from the intercepted sunlight and the transmitted laser beam.

The 1,000 beams from the laser generators were trans-mitted out to the L–2 point of Mercury, where they were collected, phase shifted until they were all in phase, then combined into a single coherent beam about 3.5 kilome-ters across. This beam was deflected from a final mirror that was tilted at 4.5 degrees above the ecliptic to match Barnard's elevation, and rotated so as to always face the direction to Barnard.

The crew to construct and maintain the laser generators were housed in the Mercury Laser Propulsion Construc-tion, Command, and Control Center. The station was not in orbit about Mercury, but hung below the "sunhook," a

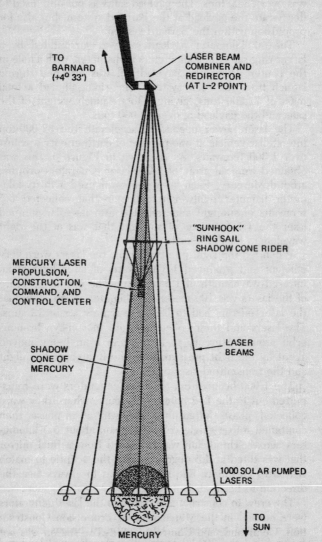

Figure 5—Mercury Laser System

large ring-sail that straddled the shadow cone of Mercury about halfway up the cone.

The final transmitter lens for the laser propulsion system was a thin film of plastic net, with alternating circular zones that either were empty or covered with a thin film of plastic that caused a half-wavelength phase delay in the 1.5-micron laser light. (During the deceleration phase, when the laser frequency was tripled to produce 0.5-micron green laser light, the phase delay was three half-wavelengths.) This huge Fresnel zone plate acted as a final lens for the beam coming from Mercury. Since the focal length of the Fresnel zone plate was very long, the changes in shape or position of the billowing plastic net lens had almost no effect on the transmitted beam. The zone plate was rotated slowly to keep it stretched, and an array of controllable mirrors around the periphery used the small amount of laser light that missed the lens to counteract the gravity pull of the distant Sun and keep the huge sail fixed in space along the Sun-Barnard axis. The configuration of the lasers, lens, and sail during the launch and deceleration phases can be seen in Figure 6.

The accelerating lasers were left on for eighteen years while the spacecraft continued to gain speed. The lasers were turned off, back in the solar system, in 2044. The last of the light from the lasers traveled for two more years before it finally reached the interstellar spacecraft. Thrust at the spacecraft stopped in 2046, just short of twenty years after launch. The spacecraft was now at two light-years distance from the Sun and four light-years from Barnard, and was traveling at twenty percent of the speed of light. The mission now entered the coast phase.

For the next 20 years the spacecraft and its drugged crew coasted through interstellar space, covering a light-year every five years. Back in the solar system, the laser array was used to launch another manned interstellar expedition. During this period, the Barnard lens was increased in diameter to 300 kilometers. Then, in 2060, the laser array was turned on again at a power level of 1,500 terawatts and a tripled frequency. The combined beams from the lasers filled the 300-kilometer-diameter Fresnel lens and

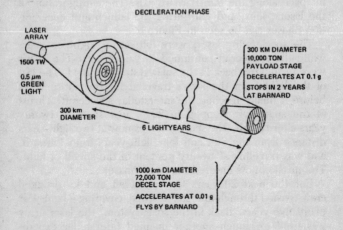

ACCELERATION PHASE

LASER ARRAY

1300 TW

1.5 μm IR LIGHT

PLASTIC FRESNEL LENS

100 km DIAMETER

2 LIGHTYEARS

LASER SAIL

ACCELERATES AT 0.01 g

VELOCITY AFTER 20 YEARS 0.2 C

1000 km DIAMETER 82,000 TONS

DECELERATION PHASE

LASER ARRAY

1500 TW

0.5 μm GREEN LIGHT

300 km DIAMETER

6 LIGHTYEARS

300 KM DIAMETER 10,000 TON PAYLOAD STAGE DECELERATES AT 0.1 g STOPS IN 2 YEARS AT BARNARD

1000 km DIAMETER 72,000 TON DECEL STAGE

ACCELERATES AT 0.01 g FLYS BY BARNARD

Figure 6—Laser-pushed light-sail
[*J. Spacecraft*, Vol. 21, No. 2, pp. 187–195 (1984)]

beamed out toward the distant star. After two years, the lasers were turned off, and used elsewhere. The two-light-year-long pulse of high-energy laser light traveled across the six light-years to the Barnard system, where it caught up with the spacecraft as it was 0.2 light-years away from its destination.

Before the pulse of laser light had reached the interstellar vehicle, the vehicle had separated into two pieces. The inner 300-kilometer payload sail detached itself and turned around to face the ring-shaped sail. The ring-sail had computer-controlled actuators to give it the proper optical curvature. When the laser beam from the distant solar system arrived at the spacecraft, the beam struck the large 1000 kilometer ring-sail, bounced off the mirrored surface, and was focused onto the smaller 300 kilometer payload sail as shown in the lower portion of Figure 6. The laser light accelerated the massive 71,500-ton ring-sail at 1.2 percent of Earth gravity, and during the two-year period the ring-sail increased its velocity slightly. The same laser power reflecting back on the much lighter payload sail, however, decelerated the smaller sail and the exploration crew at nearly ten percent of Earth gravity. In the two years that the laser beam was on, the payload sail slowed from its interstellar velocity of twenty percent of the speed of light to come to rest in the Barnard system. Meanwhile, the ring-sail sped on into deep space, its job done.

Prometheus

The interstellar spacecraft that took the exploration crew to the Barnard system was called *Prometheus*, the bringer of light. Its configuration is shown in Figure 7. Although quite large, from a distance it would be difficult to see *Prometheus* in the vast expanse of shining sail that carried it to the stars.

A major fraction of the spacecraft volume was taken up by four units. They consisted of a planetary lander called the Surface Landing and Ascent Module (SLAM), holding within itself a winged Surface Excursion Module (SEM).

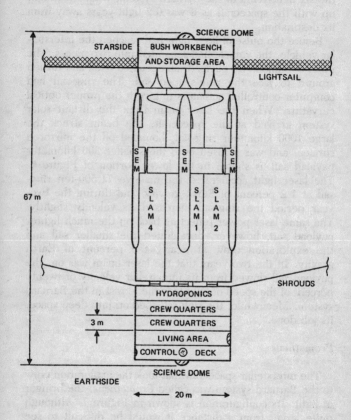

Figure 7—Prometheus

Each SLAM rocket is forty-six meters long and six meters in diameter, and masses 600 tons including the SEM.

Running all the way through the center of *Prometheus* is a four-meter-diameter, sixty-meter-long shaft with an elevator platform. Capping the top of *Prometheus* on the side toward the direction of travel is a huge double-decked compartmented area that holds the various consumables that will be used in the 50-year mission as well as the workshop for the spaceship's computer motile. At the very center of starside is a small port with a thick glass dome that is used by the star-science instruments to investigate the star system they are moving toward. There is enough room for one or two people under the dome, but the radiation level is high enough that the port is mostly used by machines, not people.

At the base of *Prometheus* were five decks. These are the home for the crew. Each deck is a flat cylinder twenty meters in diameter and three meters thick. The bottom control deck contains the consoles that run the lightcraft, with the earthside science dome at the center. The living area deck is next. This contains the communal dining room, lounge, and recreational facilities. The next two decks are the crew quarters decks that are fitted out with individual living quarters for each of the twenty crew members. Above that is the hydroponics deck with four air locks that allow access to the four SLAM spacecraft. The water in the hydroponics tanks added to the radiation shielding for the crew quarters below.

The Christmas Bush

The hands and eyes of the near-human computers that run the various vehicles on the expedition are embodied in a repair and maintenance motile used by the computer, popularly called the "Christmas Bush" because of the twinkling laser lights on the bushy multibranched structure. The bushlike shape for the robot has a parallel in the development of life-forms on Earth. The first form of life on Earth was a worm. The stick-like shape was poorly adapted for manipulation or even locomotion. Then these stick-like animals grew smaller sticks, called legs, and the animals could walk, although they were still poor at manipulation. Then the smaller sticks grew yet smaller sticks, and hands with manipulating fingers evolved.

The Christmas Bush is a manifold extension of this idea. The motile has a six-"armed" main body that repeatedly hexfurcates into copies one-third the size of itself, finally ending up with millions of near-microscopic cilia. Each subsegment has a small amount of intelligence, but is mostly motor and communication system. The segments communicate with each other and transmit power down through the structure by means of light-emitting and light-collecting semiconductor diodes. It is the colored lasers sparkling from the various branches of the Christmas Bush that give the motile the appearance of a Christmas tree. The main computer in the spacecraft is the primary controller of the motile, communicating with the various portions of the Christmas Bush through color-coded laser beams. It takes a great deal of computational power to operate the many limbs of the Christmas Bush, but the built-in "reflex" intelligence in the various levels of segmentation lessens the load on the main computer.

The Christmas Bush shown in Figure 8 is in its "one gee" form. Three of the "trunks" form "legs," one the "head," and two the "arms." The head portions are "bushed" out to give the detector diodes in the subbranches a three-dimensional view of the space around it. One arm ends with six "hands," demonstrating the manipulating capability of the Christmas Bush and its subportions. The other arm is in its maximally collapsed form. The six "limbs," being one-third the diameter of the trunk, can fit into a circle with the same diameter as the trunk, while the thirty-six "branches," being one-ninth the diameter of the trunk, also fit into the same circle. This is true all the way down to the sixty million cilia at the lowest level.

An interesting property of the Christmas Bush is its ability to change size. Just as a human can go from a crouch to an arms outstretched position and change in height from less than one meter to almost three meters, the Christmas Bush can shrink or stretch by almost a

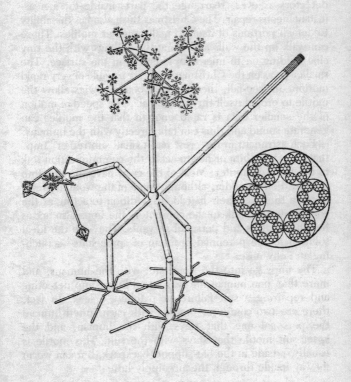

Figure 8—The Christmas Bush

factor of five, from a short, squat bush to a tall, slender tree.

The "hands" of the Christmas Bush have capabilities that go way beyond that of the human hand. The Christmas Bush can stick a "hand" inside a delicate piece of equipment, and using its lasers as a light source and its detectors as eyes, rearrange the parts inside for a near-instantaneous repair. The Christmas Bush also has the ability to detach portions of itself to make smaller motiles. These can walk up the walls and along the ceilings with the tiny cilia holding on to microscopic cracks in the surface. The smaller twigs on the Christmas Bush are capable of very rapid motion. In free-fall, these rapidly beating twigs allow the motile to propel itself through the air. The speed of motion of the smaller cilia is rapid enough that the motiles can generate sound and thus can talk directly with the humans.

Each astronaut in the crew has a small subtree or "imp" that stays with him or her to act as the communication link to the main computer. Most of the crew have the tiny imp ride on their shoulder, although some of the women prefer to keep theirs in their hairdo. In addition to acting as the communication link to the computer, the imps also act as health monitors and personal servants. They are the ideal solution to the perennial problem of space-suits—scratching an itchy nose.

The imps go into the space-suit with the humans, and more than one human life was saved by an imp detecting and repairing a suit failure or patching a leak. In fact, there are two computer motiles with each suited human: the personal one that stays with the human, and the space-suit motile that stays with the suit. This motile is usually outside in the life-support backpack, but can worm its way inside through the air-supply hose.

[Dr. Ross interrupted his prepared testimony at this point.]

We think that life would be strange with a semi-living creature always attached to us. Yet think how bereft you would feel if you had forgotten your eyeglasses, pen, or wristcomputer.

[Dr. Ross returned to his prepared testimony.]

The crew exploring Rocheworld and the moons of Gargantua used some unique vehicles that were designed especially for those worlds on the basis of the flyby probe data obtained some decades before. In the following figures we will outline the construction details of the vehicles, since GNASA is proud of their outstanding performance.

Surface Lander and Ascent Module

The Surface Lander and Ascent Module (SLAM) is a brute-force chemical rocket that was designed to get the planetary science crew and the Surface Exploration Module (SEM) down to the surface of the planetary bodies so they could explore. The upper portion is designed to take the crew off the world again and back to *Prometheus* at the end of the expedition. As is shown in Figure 9, the basic shape of the SLAM is a tall cylinder with four descent engines and two main tanks.

The SLAM has a great deal of similarity to the Lunar Excursion Module (LEM) used in the Apollo lunar landings, except that instead of being optimized for a specific airless body, the SLAM has to be general-purpose enough to land on planetoids larger than the Moon that also have significant atmospheres. The three legs are the minimum for stability, and the weight penalties for any more are prohibitive.

The SLAM has an unusual problem (in addition to its unfortunate acronym). It had to carry the Surface Excursion Module (SEM), an airplane that is almost as large as it is. Embedded in the side of the SLAM is a long, slim crease that just fits the outer contours of the SEM. The seals on the upper portions were designed to have low gas leakage so that the SLAM crew could transfer to the SEM with minor loss of air.

The upper portion of the SLAM consists of the Crew Living Quarters plus the ascent module. The upper deck is a three-meter-high cylinder eight meters in diameter. On its top is a forest of electromagnetic antennas for

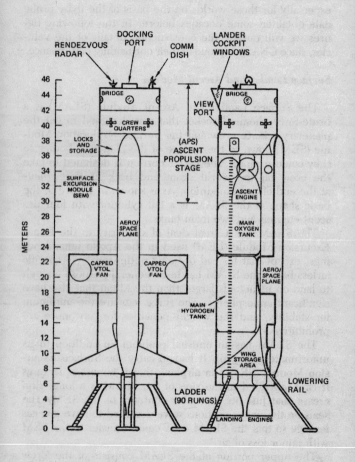

Figure 9—Surface Lander and Ascent Module (SLAM)

everything from laser communication directly to Earth (almost six light-years away) to omniantenna that merely broadcast the present position of the ship to the relay satellites in orbit around the planetoids.

The upper deck contains the main docking port at the center. Its exit is upward, into the hydroponics deck of *Prometheus*. Around the upper lock are the control consoles for the landing and docking maneuvers and the electronics for the surface science that can be carried out at the SLAM landing site.

The middle deck contains the personal quarters for the crew with all the comforts of home. Individual sleeping cubicles, a good shower that works as well in zero gee as in gravity, and two toilets. After the SEM crew has left the main lander, the partitions between the sleeping cubicles can be rearranged to provide a more horizontal orientation for the four crew members left in the SLAM.

The galley and lounge are the favorite spots for the crew. The lounge has a video center facing inward where the crew can watch six-year-old programs from Earth, and a long sofa facing a large viewport window that looks out on the alien scenery from a height of about forty meters. The lower deck of the SLAM is all work. Most of the space is given to suit or equipment storage and a complex airlock. One of the airlock exits lead to the upper end of the Jacob's Ladder. The other leads to the boarding port for the SEM.

Since the primary purpose of the SLAM is to put the SEM on the surface of the double-planet, some of the other characteristics of the lander are not optimized for crew convenience. The best instance is the "Jacob's Ladder," a long, widely-spaced set of rungs that start on one landing leg of the SLAM and work their way up the side of the cylindrical structure to the lower exit lock door. The "Jacob's Ladder" was never meant to be used, since the crew expected to be able to use the powered hoist from the top of the ship. However, it is a sure, though slow, route up into the ship if everything else fails.

One leg of the SLAM is part of the "Jacob's Ladder," while another leg acts as the lowering rail for the SEM.

The wings of the Surface Excursion Module are chopped off in mid-span just after the VTOL fans. The remainder of each wing is stacked as interleaved sections on either side of the tail section of the SEM. Once it has its wings attached, the SEM is a completely independent vehicle with its own propulsion and life support system.

Surface Excursion Module

The Surface Excursion Module (SEM) is a specially designed spacecraft capable of flying as a plane in a planetary atmosphere or as a rocket for short hops through empty space. An exterior view of the aerospace plane is shown in Figure 10. The exploration crew christened the aerospace plane the *Magic Dragonfly* because of its long wings, eye-like scanner ports at the front, and its ability to hover. The *Dragonfly* was ideal for the conditions on Rocheworld. For flying long distances in the rarefied non-oxidizing atmosphere, the propulsion comes from heating of the atmosphere with a nuclear reactor operating a jet-bypass turbine.

For short hops outside the atmosphere, the engine draws upon a tank of monopropellant that not only provides reaction mass for the nuclear reactor to work on, but also makes its own contribution to the rocket plenum pressure and temperature.

Dragonfly uses a nuclear power plant for its primary propulsion. Rocheworld has two large lobes to explore that are equivalent in land area to the North American continent. Although the humans used the excellent mapping and exploration instruments on-board the plane to supplement their own limited senses, even these have distance limitations, and a long criss-cross journey over both lobes was needed to determine the true nature of the double-planet.

A naked nuclear reactor is a significant radiation hazard, but the one in the aerospace plane is well designed. Its outer core is covered with a thick layer of thermoelectric generators that turn the heat coming through the casing into the electrical power needed to operate the computers

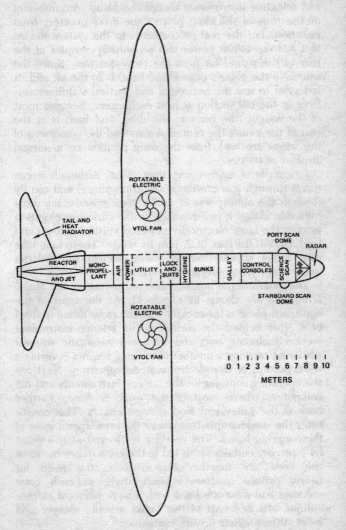

Figure 10—Exterior view of Surface Excursion Module (SEM)

and scientific instruments aboard the plane. A number of metric tons of shielding protect the crew quarters from radiation, but the real protection is in the system design that has the entire power and propulsion complex at the rear of the plane, far from the crew quarters. Since the source of the plane's power (and heat) is in the aft end, it is logical to use the horizontal and vertical stabilizer surfaces in the tail section as heat exchangers. Because most of the weight (the reactor, shielding, and fuel) is at the rear of the plane, the center of mass and the placement of the wings are back from the wing position on a normal airplane of its size.

Dragonfly is more insect than plane. Although it can travel through space without any atmosphere, and can fly through the atmosphere at nearly sonic speeds, the attribute that makes it indispensable in the surface exploration work is the large electrically powered vertical take-off and landing (VTOL) fans built into its wings. These fans take over at low speeds from the more efficient jet, and can safely lower *Dragonfly* to the surface.

The details of the human-inhabited portion of the *Magic Dragonfly* are shown in Figure 11. At the front of the aerospace plane is the cockpit with the radar dome in front of it. Just behind the cockpit is the science instrument section including port and starboard automatic scanner platforms carrying a number of imaging sensors covering a wide portion of the electromagnetic spectrum. Next are the operating consoles for the science instruments and the computer, where most of the work is done. Farther back is the galley and food storage lockers. This constitutes the working quarters where the crew spend most of their waking hours. The corridor is blocked at this point by a privacy curtain which led to the crew quarters. Since the crew are together for so long, the need for nearly private quarters is imperative, so each crew member had a private bunk with a large personal storage volume attached. Aft of the bunks are the shower and toilet, then another privacy curtain.

At the rear of the aerospace plane are the airlock, suit storage, air conditioning equipment, and a "work wall"

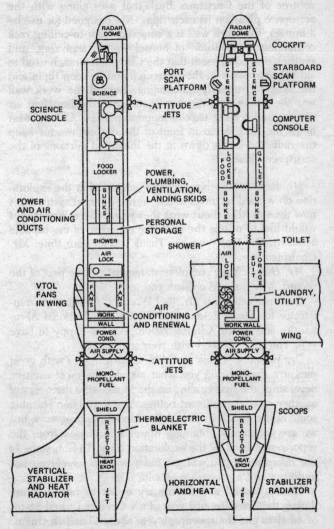

Figure 11—Interior of Surface Excursion Module (SEM)

that is the province of the Christmas "Branch," a major subtree of the Christmas Bush that goes along with the aerospace plane on its excursions. Not designed for use by a human, the work wall is a compact, floor-to-ceiling rack containing a multitude of housekeeping, analyzing, and synthesizing equipment that the Christmas Branch used to aid the astronauts in their research and to keep them and the *Magic Dragonfly* functioning. Behind the work wall was the power conditioning equipment, the liquefied air supply, and a large tank of monopropellant. All this mass helps the lead shield in front of the nuclear reactor keep the radiation levels down in the inhabited portions of the aerospace plane.

Mr. Ross. Well, those are the vehicles that the exploration crew used to travel to and in the Barnard system. It's now time to hear about what they found there. For that, I would like to utilize the scientific expertise of my capable assistant, Dr. Joel Winners. Thank you for your time, Mr. Chairman.

Mr. Ootah. Your complete statement will be part of the record, Mr. Ross. We thank you.

Our next witness is Dr. Joel Winners, Associate Administrator for Space Sciences of the Greater National Aeronautics and Space Administration. We are happy to have you. You may proceed with your statement.

Dr. Winners. Thank you, Mr. Chairman. It's with great pleasure that I bring you what may be the most exciting news since the first landing on the Moon—the discovery of another race of intelligent beings. You have been learning some of the details in your daily video-news programs, but we are constantly obtaining newer information from the reports sent back by the exploration crew. In fact, some of the information you will get today was only received last night.

This is *indeed* a extraordinary event to be occurring during the Tricentennial year of the Greater United States of America and the seventieth year of the Canadian Union.

I, too, have a printout statement for the record.

STATEMENT OF DR. JOEL WINNERS

Rocheworld Ocean

There is an ocean covering one of the two lobes of Rocheworld. The liquid is a cold mixture of ammonia and water similar to what was found inside Jupiter's moon Europa. There are no land areas of any size, so the climate is determined by the heating patterns from Barnard as modified by the shadowing effects of the Roche lobe. There is a warm "crescent" that is centered on the outer pole and reaches around the equator. This crescent receives the most sunlight, and the surface temperature reaches minus twenty degrees centigrade. The cold crescent is centered about the inner pole and reaches out to include the north and south polar regions. The temperature of the ocean surface here is minus forty degrees or colder. Because of these two regions covering Eau like the two halves of the cover of a baseball, we have quite unusual weather patterns. The ammonia boils from the surface in the hot crescents, leaving behind the heavier water, and falls on the cold crescent. We then get strong currents, with the warm heavy water flowing under the cold lighter ammonia-rich mixture. At the bottom of the ocean underneath these surface currents, it is very cold, reaching minus 100 degrees centigrade.

There are a number of mixtures of water and ammonia possible in the ocean. This is seen in Figure 12, which is a phase diagram for ammonia and water at 0.2 atmospheres. At this pressure level, pure water boils at plus 64 degrees centigrade, while pure ammonia boils at minus 61 degrees. The ocean composition varies from twenty to eighty percent ammonia, so a good portion of the phase diagram is covered.

There are four kinds of ice possible, one pure water, one pure ammonia, and two with varying ratios of water molecules to ammonia molecules. Ice floats on water, but sinks when the ammonia content of the ocean exceeds 23 percent. Since the cold inner poles are generally ammonia-rich from the ammonia rain falling on the cold crescent,

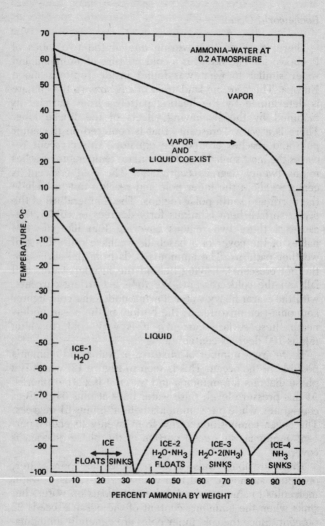

Figure 12—Phase diagram for ammonia-water mixture

the water ice that forms drops to the bottom and accumulates into glaciers. Ice-2 floats and Ice-3 sinks, leading to situations where you can have underwater snowstorms with one type of snow falling down and the other type falling up.

Rocheworld Aliens

The aliens on Rocheworld live in the ocean. In genetic makeup and complexity level they have a number of similarities to slime-mold amoebas here on Earth, as well as analogies to a colony of ants. Each of their units can survive for a while on its own, but is not intelligent. A small collection of cells can survive as a coherent cloud with enough intelligence to hunt smaller prey and look for plants to eat. Larger collections of cells form into more complex structures. When the collection becomes large enough, it becomes an intelligent being. Yet if that being is torn into millions of pieces, each piece can survive. If the pieces can get together again, the individual is restored, only a little worse for its experience.

The aliens are large, weighing many tons. They normally stay in a formless, cloudlike shape, moving with and through the water. When they are in their mobile, cloudlike form, the clouds in the water range from ten to thirty meters in diameter and many meters thick. They often concentrate the material in their cloud into a dense rock formation a few meters in diameter. They seem to do this when they are thinking, and it is supposed that the denser form allows for faster and more concentrated cogitation.

The aliens are very intelligent, but nontechnological—like dolphins and whales here on Earth. They have a highly developed system of philosophy, and extremely advanced abstract mathematical capability. There is no question that they are centuries ahead of us in mathematics, and further communication with them could lead to great strides in human capabilities in this area. However, because of their physical makeup and their environment, the aliens are not yet aware of the potential of technology—again, the similarity to the cetaceans is striking.

The aliens use chemical senses for short-range information and sonar for long range. They have some sensitivity to light, but cannot see like humans. In general, sight is a secondary sense, about as important to them as taste is to humans. One of the aliens is known, however, to have deliberately formed an imaging lens that it used to study the stars and planets in their stellar system. Called White Whistler by the humans, this individual was one of the more technologically knowledgeable of the aliens.

There are fauna on Rocheworld, all in the ocean and similar in chemistry, genetics, and structure to the intelligent aliens. One type are huge gray rocks that stay quiescent for long periods of time, only to suddenly explode, stunning all within a hundred meters and capturing them in their sticky thread nets. After absorbing their prey, they reform into multiple rocks that slowly convert the captured food into copies of themselves.

Another type are bird-like creatures that don't do much except float around, perfume the water, and make twittering sonic vibrations. The aliens seem to tolerate them as pets.

The major flora are gray and brown plants that look like sedentary rocks with controlled thick clouds about them. They send out streamers and form new bud rocks at the ends. The plants do not use photosynthesis, since the red light from Barnard is too weak. Instead, the whole food chain is based on the energy and minerals emitted by volcanic vents. We have similar isolated colonies of plants and animals around underwater vents in our own ocean depths. All life on the planet is concentrated at these few oases, and the rest of the ocean is barren, without significant numbers of bacteria or other microscopic life-forms. Because of this, the exploration crew was unaware there was anything living on the planet until one of the aliens made contact with them.

Reproduction for the aliens is a multiple-individual experience. The aliens do not seem to have sexes, and it seems that any number from two aliens on up can produce a new individual. The usual grouping for reproduction is thought to be three or four. The creating of a new alien seems to be more of a lark or a creative exercise like music or theater than a physically driven emotional experience. The explorers witnessed one such coupling put on for their benefit. In this case it involved four aliens, Loud Red, White Whistler, Green Fizzer, and Yellow Hummer. They each extended a long tendril that contained a substantial portion of their mass, estimated to be one-tenth of the mass of each parent. These tendrils, each a different color, met at the middle and intertwined with a swirling motion like colored paints being stirred together. There was a long pause as each tendril began to lose its distinctive color. We don't know exactly what happened, but obviously some chemical change was taking place that removed the strong host-origin identity from the units in the tendrils. Then finally the tendrils were snapped off, leaving the pale cloud floating in the center by itself, about forty percent of the size of the adults that created it. After a few minutes, the mass of cells formed themselves into a new individual, who took on a color that was different than any of its progenitors. The humans called the new baby Blue Warbler, because of its color and the distinctive acoustic note that it used for sonar sensing. The adults then take it upon themselves to train the new youngster. The adults and youngsters stay together for hunting and protection, the group again being very much like a pod of whales or porpoises.

The aliens have a complex art-form similar to acting, which involves carrying out simulations of real or imaginary happenings by forming a replica of the scene with their bodies. You can see this activity on a short segment of videotape that was transmitted back by the crew. I apologize that we have only a flatview version of the scene. The technology to produce holoprojection tapes had not yet been developed when the crew left the solar system.

[The prepared testimony was interrupted by the showing of a flatview projection tape. Copies may be viewed in the holoprojection rooms at the Library of Congress or purchased from the G.U.S. Government Printing Office, Washington, DC 20402.]

More than one actor takes part. The alien Yellow Hummer seemed to be most proficient in this art-form, and used it as one method of communicating with the humans. The aliens warned the explorers of the danger of the ocean transfer by simulating the Rocheworld with its seas. Two of the aliens, lighter in color, formed the rocky worlds. Another, blue in color, acted out the part of the seas. They showed how the rocky worlds whirled about each other, and as the year passes, and the elliptical orbit of the dual planet approaches periapsis, the tidal forces become stronger, and the sea on the smaller Eau lobe sloshes back and forth, gaining momentum. Then the aliens showed the humans how, as the tidal forces become great enough, the seas cross the gap between the planets in a huge interplanetary waterfall that nearly engulfs the larger Roche lobe. Warned by the aliens, the humans made their dramatic escape off the Eau lobe by riding a huge wave, then gliding back through tornadoes to their rocket, which took them off the planet before the tidal wave struck.

Dr. Winners. That's all the information that we have at the present time on the aliens, since the crew had to leave the planet. However, they have informed us that they will go back on a prolonged visit, this time landing their rocket in a safe place in one of the larger craters of the dry lobe, Roche, so they can stay there through a number of tidal cycles while they get to know the aliens better. They plan to leave some interstellar laser communicators behind and teach the aliens how to use them to communicate directly with Earth, while the exploration crew goes off to visit the other worlds and moons about Barnard.

Of course, since it takes six years for messages to reach us from Barnard, that next visit has already taken place, and the radio message to us is somewhere in transit in the empty space between there and here. But in a few years, we will be back with more news and information about what the aliens can teach us in the way of abstract thought and mathematics. We also expect that the crew will have a much better idea of the chemical and genetic makeup of this new race of beings after a year or so of study. This could have a profound effect on our understanding of the life process itself, and will produce great advances in medicine, perhaps even a life-prolonging drug without the side effects of No-Die.

Mr. Ootah. Thank you very much for your fascinating testimony, Dr. Winners. We also would like to commend the brave exploration crew who are out there gathering this information for us. They certainly will deserve a heroic welcome when they return.

Dr. Winners. The Chairman forgets. This is an interstellar mission. They will not return—ever.

Mr. Ootah. Oh . . . Yes. I forgot. There was a great outcry prior to the start of this mission that we were sending these brave people on a one-way "suicide mission." Yet, as one of them said, "We all are on a one-way mission through life." These people are fortunate enough to be doing something really significant for mankind with their lives, and probably having fun doing it.

Dr. Winners. If it were possible, I would trade positions with any one of them instantly.

Mr. Ootah. I think I understand, Dr. Winners. Well, the bells are ringing on our pagers. There is a roll-call vote in progress. If you gentlemen will excuse the committee, we will make the journey through the tunnel. After lunch, we will continue with the question and answer session. The subcommittee will recess until one-thirty.

[Whereupon, at 11:15 a.m., the hearing was recessed.]

CASTING

Humans

Major General Virginia "Jinjur" Jones—Commander of *Prometheus* and entire mission. 158.5 cm (don't neglect that half-centimeter!) (5′2″), 61 kg (135 lbs), 42 years old at start of mission. Short and solid with dark-black skin and a no-nonsense black pixie Afro haircut. Graduated high in her class at the U.S. Naval Academy, chose the Marines. Distinguished herself in the Greater San Diego tourist riots in 2009 during her first tour of duty with the Marine Recruit Training Command. Became commander of a fleet of lightweight solar sailcraft that kept the spacelanes swept of debris, inspected new foreign spacecraft for compliance with the Space Treaty, and resupplied and protected the Laser Forts. Jinjur's nickname comes from the spicy female general that conquered the Emerald City in one of the lesser-known Oz books. Virginia does not mind reference, feels it is a sign that the troops have accepted her (which it is).

Colonel George G. Gudunov—Second-in-Command on mission, Commander of surface exploration mission on Rocheworld, and Copilot of *Magic Dragonfly*. 185 cm (6′1″), 100 kg (220 lbs), 51 years old, he is the oldest person on the mission. He has a Ph.D. in physics and is a writer of science fiction and popular science articles. Air Force ROTC commission from University of Maryland and first in class in flight school. Worked on the Air Force Space Command Laser Forts project. In 1998, when a twenty-three-year-old captain, he suggested testing the laser fort system by using it to send interstellar probes to the nearest star systems. When a number of space laser forts suffered catastrophic failures under this two-day test, he was commended by Congress for exposing the problems, but the military brass never forgave him. They shunted him off to be a permanent flight instructor, and he was promoted as slowly as they could legally do it without raising the ire of Congress. When the positive reports from the Barnard probe came in twenty-four years later, he had just made lieutenant colonel. He was promoted to colonel and sent on the expedition.

Dr. William Wang—Surgeon and Leviponist. 175 cm (5'9"), 60 kg (132 lbs), 41 years old. Chinese-American with thin black hair, friendly face, and large ears that make him look harmless. By the age of twenty-eight, he had obtained Ph.D.'s in both leviponics and organic chemistry. Spent four years at Goddard station doing levibiology research in the huge free-fall hydroponics tanks at the Leviponics Research Facility, then went back to Earth to obtain an M.D. in aerospace medicine in order to qualify for the interstellar expeditions.

Colonel Alan Armstrong—Astroplanetologist and Optoelectronic Physicist. 187 cm (6'2"), 85 kilograms (185 pounds), 33 years. Very handsome, well built hero type with the face of a movie idol, charming blue eyes, welcoming smile, and curly blonde hair. Football hero, most popular boy, and valedictorian in Hollywood High School, he broke two dozen hearts when he left for the Air Force Academy. First in his class and first string on almost all the Academy sports teams in his plebe year, he remained preeminent during his entire stay and was naturally first in his class standing upon graduation. He won a Rhodes scholarship and studied mathematics and astrophysics at Cambridge. While there, he developed new signal-processing techniques that were used to build a large optical interferometer antenna array that could obtain detailed images of planets in other nearby star systems.

Richard Redwing—Planetary Geoscientist. 195 cm (6'4"), 110 kg (225 lbs), 34 years old at start of mission. Very large, very strong outdoorsman of American Indian heritage. College champion weight lifter and black-belt karate expert, won a gold medal in the 2012 Olympics. Got his B.S. in geophysics in 2014 and started work for a mining company in the Alps, where he was also a part-time mountain-climbing guide. Distinguished himself in a mountain rescue that cost him his two little toes. He grew tired of the lack of mental challenge and returned to school to get his Ph.D. in planetary physics and geophysics. Did his post-doctoral field training on the Moon and Mars, then joined the Ceres and Vesta expeditions. Was part of Callisto field crew when he was accepted for the Barnard mission.

Sam Houston—Planetary Geoscientist. 200 cm (6'7"), 80 kg (176 lbs), 45 years. Very tall, very thin, with pale face and skin, long bones with knobby joints, gray-blue eyes, and long graying hair. Does not have a doctorate, but has years of field experience. He started field exploration in 2003 on the Canadian shield with Exxon. By the next decade, he had worked on all the continents, both poles, and the continental shelves of five of the seven seas. One of the first full-time geologists on the Moon, he spent 2015 making a preliminary geological map of the backside, then spent two years on Mars with the first Mars colony. His experience made him the lead geologist on the 2018 "Big-Four" asteroid mapping expedition. His experiences on Ceres, Vesta, Pallas, Juno, followed by the two moons of Jupiter, Ganymede and Callisto, made him an obvious choice for the Barnard expedition.

Elizabeth "Red" Vengeance—Asteroidologist and Lander Pilot. 178 cm (5'10"), 70 kg (154 lbs), 38 years. Tall, thin, with an aristocratic nose, a short, straight cap of red hair, green eyes, and the typical redhead complexion with freckles from an Irish heritage. She has over 150 hours of credits in mineralogy from University of Arizona but no degree. Elizabeth was one of the first independent prospectors in the asteroid belt. She struck it rich, became a billionaire, and then realized that there were more interesting things to do than loafing for the rest of her life. Her extensive space experience as an asteroid prospector and heavy-lift asteroid-tug operator got her onto the Barnard expedition.

Arielle Trudeau—Aerodynamicist and Chief Pilot of *Magic Dragonfly*. 165 cm (5'5"), 50 kg (110 lbs), 35 years old at start of mission. Thin, delicate, beautiful, shy, fair-skinned, with short, curly light-brown hair and deep-brown eyes. She was born and raised in Quebec, Canada, before secession of Quebec from Canada. She emigrated to the United States and became an American citizen after the absorption of the rest of the Canadian provinces into the Greater United States of America in 2006. Her father taught her how to fly at an early age and she has hundreds of hours experience in a glider. She obtained a Ph.D. in aerodynamics at Cal-Tech and entered the space program as a non-pilot Mission Specialist. On her first flight into space, there was an explosion that killed both Super-Shuttle pilots. Single-handed, encumbered by a space-suit, she brought the crippled Super-Shuttle safely down in the smoothest landing ever recorded on the shuttle program. Arielle was given special dispensation to take Super-Shuttle pilot training after public acclaim, later became one of the best Shuttle pilots. She was training for Lunar Pilot status when the Barnard expedition let her travel to the stars.

Shirley Everett—Chief Engineer and Astronaut Aerospace Pilot. 190 cm (6'3"), 85 kg (185 lbs), 33 years old at start of mission. A tall, strong, tanned, blue-eyed, blonde-haired "California Surfer Girl." Obtained B.S. in electrical engineering with minors in nuclear engineering and mechanical engineering from USC. Played on both women's and men's basketball teams in college, and was top scorer in women's collegiate basketball. She became the third woman to play on a men's professional basketball team, but gave up her pro basketball career as a second-string forward for the Los Angeles Lakers to return to USC to get an engineering doctorate. After learning to fly, she went to work for the company that designed and built the *Magic Dragonfly* aerospace plane. With her eidetic memory, Shirley knows everything about the spacecraft she flies, except details of the computer software programs, where David Greystoke takes over. She can fix anything, not with the proverbial kick and a hairpin—she is too well trained and equipped for that—but could if she had to.

Captain Thomas St. Thomas—Astrodynamicist and Lander Pilot. 188 cm (6'2"), 85 kg (187 lbs), 33 years. Good looking, clean-shaven, with Air Force trim short black hair, and a light-brown skin from a Jamaican heritage. Graduate of the U.S. Air Force Academy, he became a Rhodes scholar in 2014 and obtained his Ph.D. in astrodynamics at Oxford in England. Went into Air Force pilot training and became a heavy-lift rocket pilot in 2019. He had over five years of experience raising and lowering the heavy, cumbersome rockets in Earth's gravity before joining the Barnard expedition. He is also an amateur photographer who takes strikingly artistic photographs of the terrain.

David Greystoke—Electronics and Computer Engineer. 158 cm (5'2"), 50 kg (110 lbs), 35 years old at start of mission. Short, thin, red-haired, quiet young man. He has perfect pitch and perfect color sense and can see color differences in the flouwen that others cannot see. An undergraduate at the prestigious liberal arts college at Grinnell, Iowa, he went on to Carnegie-Mellon University for a Ph.D. in robotics and computer programming with a minor in music. He wrote most of the programs used on the computers operating the various vehicles. David's hobby is computer-generated animated art-music forms, somewhat similar to, but much more sophisticated than, Walt Disney's *Fantasia*.

Katrina Kauffmann—Nurse and Biochemist. 150 cm (4'11"), 45 kg (99 lbs), 40 years. Small, compact, efficient no-nonsense scientist with short eap of straight brown hair. Trained in Europe, she had started out in a nursing school, but after getting her R.N. she found she liked working more on scientific problems than working with sick people, so switched professions. Received a Diploma in Biophysics at the University of Frankfurt A.M., Germany, in 2010, went on to get a Ph.D. in Biochemistry.

Came to the Greater United States on a post-doctoral fellowship and stayed.

Captain Anthony Roma—Lightsail Pilot. 168 cm (5'6"), 70 kg (155 lb), 30 years. Small, very handsome, with a dark complexion, dark eyes, dark wavy hair, and a neat mustache. Was a cadet in the first class at the Space Academy and went directly into lightsail pilot training. Was assigned to the Space Marines Interceptor Fleet, where he invented a number of new lightsail maneuvers.

Nels Larson—Leviponics Specialist (Height and weight not relevant), 33 years old at launch. Very muscular arms and barrel torso, large head with a strong jaw, light-blue eyes, and long yellow-white hair that he combs straight back. When Nels was born without legs, his parent quit their jobs on Earth and moved to Goddard Station, where Nels grew up. He took college courses by video and apprenticed in levibotany and levihusbandry at the Leviponics Research Facility on Goddard. He initiated the famous Larson chicken-breast tissue culture ("Chicken Little" to most astronauts) and many new strains of algae with various exotic flavors.

John Kennedy—Mechanical Engineer and Nurse. 183 cm (6'0"), 80 kg (176 lb), 32 years old at launch. Bears a striking resemblance to his distant relative. Tried the pre-med curriculum at USC, but gave it up in the sophomore year and went on to get a Ph.D in mechanical engineering. Didn't feel satisfied working solely on machines and went back to get his R.N. His strange mix of talents just fit a slot on the Barnard expedition.

Caroline Tanaka—Fiber-optics Engineer and Astronomer. 165 cm (5'5"), 60 kg (132 lb), 33 years old at launch. Long dark hair, brown eyes, and light-brown skin from a mixed Hawaiian heritage. Intense, hard-working engineer who pays no attention to her looks.

Linda Regan—Solar Astrophysicist. 155 cm (5'1"), 55 kg (121 lb), 31 years. Short, stocky, bouncy "cheerleader" type, with sparkly green eyes, curly brown hair, and lots of energy. Took physics at USC, went on to get a Ph.D. in astronomy at Cal Tech, and earned her way to a position at the solar observatory around Mercury.

Carmen Cortez—Communications Engineer. 165 cm (5'5"), 80 kg (176 lbs), 28 years. Youngest person on expedition. Chunky, very feminine Spanish señorita, with black nearly-afro curly hair. Always wears makeup and tightly tailored uniform. She went to University of Guadalajara in 2015, and became president of the College Radio Amateur Club. She was in charge of the generator-powered base station during a moto-cross radio transmitter hunt, when the 9.1 magnitude earthquake struck Salamanca, Mexico, in 2018. For 48 hours she ran the only operational emergency communication services in West Central Mexico. Obtained her B.S. in Engineering from the University of Guadalajara in 2019, then a Doctor of Electrical Engineering *magna cum laude* from University of California, San Diego, in 2022. Applied for the Barnard mission upon graduation and placed third. Was in training for the Alpha Centauri mission on Titan when called to replace a primary crew member who had to resign for health reasons.

Beauregard Darlington Winthrop III—Eldest son of ex-General and ex-Air Force Chief of Staff Beauregard Darlington Winthrop, Jr., and cherished grandson of Governor Beauregard Darlington Winthrop of South Carolina. Sent by his father to the Air Force Academy, he graduated near the top of his class. He used his father's influence to get assigned to a post in the Pentagon bureaucracy, and then rose rapidly to Air Force Chief of Staff. After a four-year tour, he resigned and easily won a seat as senator from South Carolina.

Aliens

The aliens, called "flouwen" by the humans, are formless, eyeless flowing blobs of jelly weighing many tons, that swim in the ocean on the Eau lobe of Rocheworld. Like whales or dolphins, the flouwen group into social "pods," and use sound to "see." Although they have no eyes, they are sensitive to light, and can "look" at things with that sense, although poorly. Their IQ is many times that of humans, but their only developed science is mathematics. In the following list of individuals mentioned in the story, the human version of their name is in parentheses.

Clear ◇ White ◇ Whistle (White Whistler)—A white, mature elder who is one of the three dominant adults in the pod. Clear ◇ White ◇ Whistle is a scientist who is trying to "invent" physics and astronomy. Unlike most of the others, who would rather cogitate than experiment, it has explored the physical world, developed an artificial "eye," discovered the stars, and is starting to develop a theory of gravity. It understands the technologically oriented humans better than any of the other members of the pod, but their way of thinking is still quite foreign to it.

Roaring☆Hot☆Vermilion(Loud Red)—A middle-aged, mature elder with an iridescent red color that looks like flame. Very deep roaring voice, boisterous nature, and eager to ☆Get on with it!☆ He is nominal leader of the pod, although Warm✳Amber✳Resonance and Clear ◇ White ◇ Whistle are co-equal and Strong☐Lavender☐Crackle is the elder of the pod. One can see that Roaring☆Hot☆ Vermilion will become more and more like Strong☐ Lavender☐Crackle as the seasons pass.

Strong☐Lavender☐Crackle (Deep Purple)—A large, massive purple elder, with thousands of seasons of experience. Has participated in the formation of many younglings including Sweet○Green○Fizz and Roaring☆Hot☆ Vermilion. Spends much of its time as a deep purple boulder—thinking. Sometimes, however, it dissolves and joins in group play as enthusiastically as if it were a youngling. The oldest one of the pod, it is looked upon for advice and wisdom.

Sweet○Green○Fizz (Green Fizzer)—A bright-green young virgin who has never participated in making a youngling. From an emotional and experience viewpoint is equivalent to a bright, young, nubile, unisex college junior. Has developed considerable mass, and is an innovative thinker, but has not learned how to settle down to concentrated thinking. It would rather laze around, doing nothing and watching its collection of flitters.

Warm✳Amber✳Resonance (Yellow Hummer)—A mature, clear yellow-brown elder. Stable in personality and given to poetry, song, and theater rather than hard logic, although a better abstract mathematician than any human. Warm✳Amber✳Resonance is the one who organizes and directs the complex plays that the flouwen perform using their own bodies as stage, backdrops, and actors. It also acts as primary parent for Dainty△Blue△Warble.

Dainty△Blue△Warble (Little Blue)—The youngling of the pod, a light, clear blue in color. The human exploration crew witness its forming by the combined mingling of Warm✳Amber✳Resonance, Roaring☆Hot☆Vermilion, Clear◇White◇Whistle, and the virgin, Sweet○Green○Fizz. The four are surprised and pleased by the transparent blue color, the beautiful warbling acoustic sonar note it emits, and the delicate wisps of feeler tendrils. Dainty△Blue△ Warble is a very precocious and reasonably massive youngling since it had four progenitors, is very inquisitive, and is always asking questions. In fact, it is a real pest, and the others often give Dainty△Blue△Warble tough logic questions to solve so it will rock up to think and stop bothering them.

Sour#Sapphire#Coo (Old Bluey)—A very old, very massive, deep-blue elder who has spent the last hundred seasons rocked up as a thinking boulder trying to derive an example of the fifth cardinal infinity. The others sometimes pester it, but mostly they leave it alone with its thoughts. It is perched near the eddy point for the seasonal flow, so it doesn't even have to move with the seasons. There are many other colored boulders around, each one some elder thinking through some complex problem. Some have not shifted since anyone can remember. They are probably still thinking, but they could be dead for all anyone could tell. They slowly waste away due to energy expenditure, surface losses, and nibblings of rogues and fauna.

Bitter†Orange†Chirr (O.J.)—A greenish-orange member of a neighboring pod. It is torn to pieces by a tornado and restored again by Roaring☆Hot☆Vermilion.

Ranks of Bronze
Alien traders were looking to buy primitive soldier-slaves—they needed troops who could win battles without high-tech weaponry. But when they bought Roman legionaries, they bought *trouble* . . .

Vettius and His Friends
A Roman Centurion and his merchant friend fight and connive to stave off the fall of Rome.

Lacey and His Friends
Jed Lacey is a 21st-century cop who plays by the rules. His rules.

Men Hunting Things
Things Hunting Men
Volumes One and Two of the *Starhunters* series. Exactly what the titles indicate, selected and with in-depth introductions by the creator of Hammer's Slammers.